BOTTOM OF THE WORLD

A Max Strong Thriller

MIKE DONOHUE

ALSO BY MIKE DONOHUE

MAX STRONG/MICHAEL SULLIVAN PREQUELS

Sleeping Dogs

The Devil's Angel

MAX STRONG THRILLERS

Shaking the Tree

Bottom of the World

Hollow City

SHORT STORIES

October Days

For Ce & Ally –
Welcome distractions.

RIGHT AFTER

Garbage saved him. Twice.

Alexei Yushkin knew his mistake as it was happening but knowing something and stopping it are two very different things.

He was past stopping. His left heel came down and the weak, rotten wood of the abandoned mill's third floor gave way like wet tissue paper. He threw his arms out sideways but caught only air. He fell fast, crashed through two more rotted floors, and didn't stop until he landed on the bags of old garbage in the sub-basement.

Five stories below where he'd started to take that step.

Five stories below the suitcase that would spare his life.

He saw a flash of black, then white. He opened his mouth but couldn't draw a breath. His lungs were locked, his chest frozen tight. He could feel nothing below his neck. For a terrifying moment, he thought the fall might have done something to his spinal cord. He bit back a flooding sense of panic and willed his body to listen to his brain. After five more heart-pounding seconds, his chest loosened and he took in a wracking, shuddering breath of dusty air.

It was heaven and hell.

Once he'd flipped his brain back on and was able to breathe, he knew the bags of garbage hadn't saved him completely—there was collateral damage.

A searing pain was radiating out in hot waves from his shoulder. He turned his head and tried to assess the damage, but only saw a gauzy curtain of soft shapes. He tried again. He concentrated on breathing. In. Out. The shapes locked into focus, and he saw a shaft of metal pushing through his collarbone like a waxy, red candle.

Blood, dirt, and flecks of rust coated the length of the pole. God knew what else was on it. He shifted his eyes down. He could see bits of jagged bone sticking out from his skin. Around the edges of the wound, more blood oozed out in time to the beating of his heart. He'd live. For now. But he'd need to get it taken care of fast. The oxidized metal was sure to give him an infection or blood poisoning. It would kill him faster than any open wound or broken bone. He'd seen more soldiers die in hospital beds from unseen infection than on the battlefield from open wounds.

He moved past the shoulder wound and was surveying the rest of his body for additional injuries when a shadow filled the hole fifty feet above him. He could hear whispered consonants like soft rain on glass. The pounding bass drumbeat of his own blood in his ears blotted out all other sounds. Max, no doubt, was standing up there with a parting message that Alexei would never hear.

He laid still and watched Max move around the crooked opening of the hole. What was he doing up there? Why was he still here? He saw a glint of metal in Max's hand as he stopped pacing, then the white-orange muzzle flash of a gun. Once, twice, three times. He flinched. He didn't think the odds were good of being hit with a handgun at this distance, but as soon as the thought passed through his mind a stinging bite on his thigh trumped the pain from his shoulder.

Goddammit. He bit down on his tongue until warm blood pooled around his teeth. Another wound, but he didn't want to give away the fact that he was even still alive. Lying amid the garbage in the bottom of the shadowy pit, he didn't think Max could see him clearly.

A moment later, the shadow disappeared. Max was gone. Alexei was alone, left behind to rot with the rest of the garbage.

He cursed his bad luck in four languages. Ten minutes ago, he'd been less than ten feet from the money. Ten feet from saving his hide. Ten feet from getting Drobhov's whole operation back on track.

Now, he was badly wounded in at least two places in the basement of a deserted mill on some backcountry road miles from anywhere or anyone who might be of use.

He took a slow, shallow breath. Hurt, bleeding, wounded, but not dead.

Prematurely buried.

Underestimated again.

He needed to stay awake. If he shut his eyes, he knew he might never open them again. He sat up. His head buzzed and the world became momentarily unhinged, sloshing left, then right before it settled. In the gloom and shadows, he couldn't see any stairs or doors or another obvious way out.

He'd deal with finding a way out next.

First, he had to deal with the pipe sticking out of his shoulder.

THE PIZZA MAN

Later, as his sweat mixed with blood and soaked his gym shorts before dripping into a dark puddle on the warped and gray hardwood floor, he realized he should have felt the noose on his neck when they used not just his usual pie place, but the right *toppings*.

Maybe if he hadn't been sampling again that morning as he weighed and measured, he would've seen all that for what it was: a tell. A big screaming siren that they knew. All of it.

The instant the smell of that pie drifted under the door, he should have been slipping out the bedroom window onto the old fire escape. Maybe they already had someone back there. Maybe Slim Jim was grinning and waiting to catch his legs when he dropped the last few feet. Carter was always thorough which made the sideshow shit Danny was trying to pull all the more stupid.

It had somehow all begun to feel like part of the job: get the product, step on it, divide it up, sell it, skim it, send the envelope up the chain, pocket or snort the rest. Junkie logic was irrefutable in the heat of the moment.

Of course, Carter knew exactly what he was putting up

his nose and exactly what was going into his pocket. Maybe, based on his name and his personal history, they'd given him time to come to his senses and make amends, but the sand had run out of that hourglass.

Now, the pizza man was at the door, and it was time to pay the freight.

He stood in front of the apartment's cheap door.

"I didn't order any pizza."

He heard a Velcro strip being pulled. "Extra cheese, double meat, Danny. This is your usual pie, man. You sure you didn't order it?"

Shit, had he ordered it? He tried to think past the last ten minutes, but it was a wall of white static. He'd been bagging and buzzing all day. He couldn't remember calling. Then again, he couldn't remember not calling, either.

"C'mon Danny, open up man. Pie's getting cold and I got other deliveries."

He looked through the peephole again at a young guy with greasy hair spilling over his ears below a mesh hat. A stained, red Mr. Pizza vest sat on his skinny frame. He held a black and white checkered box in his hand, the insulated warmer sleeve now tucked under his arm. He looked vaguely familiar. The smell of sausage and cheese leaked under the door and Danny's stomach got into the argument. Maybe he *had* called.

"All right, hold on. Let me get some dough." He smiled to himself. Dough for the pizza. That was good.

Danny went back and shut the door to the second bedroom, which held his workshop. No need for Mr. Pizza to get a peek in there. He left the gun on the card table next to the scales, drugs, and little glassine baggies. Walking through the living room, he picked up his wallet from the peeling Formica kitchen table. Other than a long black leather couch in front of a 60-inch flat screen TV, it was the only furniture in the house. He'd scavenged the table and an old rusted lawn chair out of the alley last month when he got tired of eating all his meals on the couch hunched over his knees.

At the door, he checked the peephole again. The delivery guy shifted from foot to foot. A sheen of sweat slicked his forehead. The kid looked like he was up on something himself. Danny started popping the locks open. He had four on the door and a security chain plus a skid-proof door bar that he put up when he wanted to crash on the couch. In his clearer moments, he knew all the locks were overkill, but other times it felt like way too few.

"Nine seventy-five, right, buddy?" Danny said as he swung open the door. He dug through the bills in his wallet and tried to figure out how much to tip. It was a lot of coordination for his brain in its current state. He gave up on the math and decided to give the guy a fiver regardless.

When he looked back up, Mr. Pizza was gone. Frankie and Little John filled the door.

"Oh, I'd say the total is a little more than that, huh, Danny boy," Frankie said, showing his teeth but not smiling.

Frankie held the pizza. Little John held the gun. It was down loose at his sides. They all knew he wouldn't need it. It was just for show, but it was effective. Danny felt something low in his gut rumble and threaten to cut loose.

"You gonna invite us in or what?" Frankie asked after a few more beats of silence. "Haven't been to your new place. You give up the other place?"

"Hey, guys. Um, yeah, sure, c'mon on in. Wasn't expecting you. I was just working. No, I still have the house. This is just for working. For business. Keep it separated, right?"

"Business must be good then with you fronting two rents."

"It's been all right. Can't complain. Maybe a little soft. The economy, you know. But, all in all, it's paying the bills."

"Right, I hear you. But soft? Our business? It's ... shit. What's it called, Little John?"

"Recession proof."

"Right, recession proof. I mean, a serious habit doesn't know shit about the economy. Am I right, Danny?"

Frankie dropped the pizza box on the kitchen counter and took a seat on the couch. Little John stayed by the door, his small black eyes cataloging the room, the gun now gone, lost somewhere in his giant leather coat.

"You're right, Frank. Recession proof. I like that. The serious junkies will always pay. I just meant I'm not seeing many of the kids. You know, the ones that drive in from Braintree or Newton or wherever. That's all."

"I hear ya. Still not a bad line of work to be in right now, huh?" He ran a hand over the soft leather. "Damn, this is nice, Danny boy. This feels like the genuine article, right here. Whaddaya think, Little John? This the real deal?"

Little John finished his survey of the room and swung his eyes back to Danny. "Looks like it, Frank."

"It sure does. Feels like it, too. Little John, you get a chance you should try this out."

"Maybe I'll do that." Little John stayed rooted by the door.

"How much you think this would set me back, Little John?"

"Leather. Sectional, reclining ends. Gotta be at least a thousand, minimum. Maybe two."

Frankie whistled. "Pretty steep. Not sure I can afford that. Tell you the truth, nice as it is, I don't think my ass knows the difference between this fine leather and some repro Naugahyde. Gotta admit, though, sitting here, this is nice. Smells nice, too."

"Sophisticated."

"Rich."

Both men stared at Danny.

Silence of any kind made Danny edgy. He liked noise. He liked crowds. He liked action. This silence felt dangerous, like the quiet inside a coffin. He clenched his hands into fists inside his baggy shorts and pressed them to his thighs to keep them still. Pinpricks of sweat made his head itch. His left foot started to tap. He started talking.

"Frank, listen, you're a couple days early. I haven't sold it all yet. I was actually weighing the second half now. Pass it on to my boys. Start getting it on the streets tonight." He started moving toward the closed bedroom door. "Here, have a look."

"That's not necessary, Danny. I don't need to see it to believe it. You've always been good with the distribution and logistics. When you're involved, it's always as smooth and slippery as a stripper's snatch. Ain't that right, LJ?"

"That's right, Frank. Danny's slick." The big man brought his two cinderblock-sized fists together, cracking his knuckles in a rippling string of pops.

Frankie pushed himself up and paced into the kitchen. He leaned on the sill and looked out the grimy window. The only view was the faded bricks of the tenement next door. It seemed to engross Frankie.

"Which makes it all the more strange why you suck so bad at cheating us. Why is that, Danny?"

"Whoa. Hold up. Cheating? Frank, what are you talking about? I'm not cheating you guys."

"That's right, Danny. You're not cheating *us*, you're cheating Mr. Carter. And trust me, he's smart enough to know when he's being cheated. You've seen his spreadsheets."

Frankie flipped open the lid on the pizza box, looked at the congealing pie, then thought better of it.

Danny felt like his tongue had swelled up as he tried to stammer out an answer. "No, no, no. You guys got it all wrong, Frank."

Frankie dropped the lid on the pizza box. "Are you calling Mr. Carter a liar, Danny?"

"No, not all! I—"

"You callin' us liars, then?"

"No, of, of, of course not. It's just, well, r-r-recession proof or not, the economy is in the toilet, Frank. You know that. Sure, the hopheads still come around like clockwork, but like I said, I'm not getting the drive-bys. The, whaddaya call it, the leisure shoppers. Sometimes I can't move it all in a week. It takes a week and a half, sometimes two, before I'm ready to re-up. That's why the envelopes might be light. I'm not cheating Mr. Carter. I swear!"

Frankie stepped across the room and got close enough for Danny to smell the artificial mint on his breath. He tried to hold the man's eyes, but his foot kept tapping, his hands were sweating, and he kept finding his eyes drawn to a crack in the plaster just over Frankie's shoulder. He could hear his lies breaking apart like cheap scaffolding.

"You know, Danny, I've known you a long time and, if you weren't as jittery as a virgin in a whorehouse, I might be inclined to believe you, but I got only a few ironclad rules in life, and you are definitely in violation of one right now. You wanna know which one?"

"Um, sure, Frank, which one?"

Frankie grabbed one of Danny's wrists and pushed up the hoodie's sleeve. "Junkies. Always. Lie. Ain't that right, Little John?"

Danny hadn't even heard the big man move from his spot by the door. Fat bastard was light on his feet. He felt the hulking presence at his back just before one of those cinderblocks slammed into his kidney.

He crumpled to his knees. Little John hauled him back up.

"Putting that much up your nose is just as bad as shorting

the envelope. You can't wheel *and* deal. Either way, you're taking bills out of Mr. Carter's wallet. That makes you just another worthless, pickpocket junkie."

Another fist slammed into him. Then again. And again. He could hear Little John grunting with effort. Finally, as if through a fog, he heard Frankie call it off. Little John let him go and Danny watched as the scuffed, dirty wood floor came up fast. He still smelled the cooling pizza, but tasted his own blood as he blacked out.

A MODEST PROPOSAL

She heard her father's voice in her head chastising her for carelessness.

Always be aware of your surroundings.

This isn't a case, Dad, she hissed back.

There's always a case. You just don't know it yet.

She slowed her pace a bit and started window shopping the Macy's display on Washington Street. In the reflection, she watched the man in the gray fedora and matching topcoat ten yards back. He slowed to match her pace without looking up and ducked his head while reading the headlines of the tabloid in the yellow honor box. It looked very natural and fluid. People pushed by her on the sidewalk and she lost sight of him in the shuffle.

What was this guy up to? Was it an old case? She'd only caught his profile, but it didn't ring any bells. Men who wore hats these days did it out of habit or affectation, and she'd never had a fedora-wearing client. It couldn't be a current case. They'd wrapped the Milano thing yesterday and, other than a couple skip traces Jaimie was running down for peanuts on the Internet, they were dry, bone dry, which was really why she'd missed the tail in the first place.

Her father was right, she was distracted, but with good reason. The bills were piling up faster than the work. They needed cases. This morning's meeting wasn't going to work out. She could tell by the woman's eyes when she'd mentioned the fees. It wasn't a huge loss. She'd rather dumpster dive than take marriage work. Still, it was lean times, and if they didn't pick up a few paying clients soon, something was going to have to give.

While she walked back to the office, she'd been running the debits and credits through her head, mentally calculating which bills to let slide this month and which ones had to be paid. Over the last year, it had become a familiar juggling act, and it was really starting to wear on her.

Should have spotted him sooner, Katie.

Always know the situation, Katie. Especially in public.

Always stay alert, Katie.

Well, Christ, Dad, you shouldn't have left me a business on a respirator then.

She moved down a few windows and paused again. He matched her, this time pausing in front of a jeweler's shop to study the watches on display. That clinched it. Once could be a coincidence of timing. Twice, no dice. Mister Topcoat and Fedora had walked right up her back, and now she had to deal with it.

From his reflection, she could tell he was about her height, a small man. Slim, almost bony. His elbows and shoulders poked out from the charcoal fabric like metal coat hangers. The fedora and jacket didn't look ironic; maybe a little anachronistic, but what they really looked like was expensive and tailored. Her mystery man wore them with assurance, despite his awkward frame. He looked like a man comfortable and accustomed to finer things. Who was this guy?

She stared blankly into the shoe store's window and thought about the lower end of Washington Street. Straight for another two hundred feet or so, then a slight bend to the left before dead-ending in a T intersection with Chestnut. She'd have to do something before the intersection. The park and plaza were on the opposite side, and it was too open out there to be of any use.

Think, Kate. She walked this strip to and from the gym almost every day. She traced the route in her head. Down Washington. A couple more jeweler's shops. No good. Then a sporting goods store, then a Borders, then a coffee shop before the apartment building on the corner that fronted the park. Would the coffee shop work? She thought it might. She couldn't remember for sure. If it didn't, she'd have to hope this guy was as delicate and sophisticated as he looked, because she'd be trapped in that alley.

She took a breath, turned away from the window and started walking down Washington again at her normal pace.

Her father piped up again. Jesus, he was chatty today.

This guy might look like an accountant but never underestimate an opponent.

She didn't argue with that one. She learned that lesson more than once. Still, a fedora?

As she walked, she reached into her handbag and felt the grip of the small .25 Beretta Bobcat. She unclasped the snap on the leather holster and used her thumb to flip the safety to off at the top of the grip. Bring it on, buddy.

She didn't look back. She didn't need to. Now that she knew he was there, she could feel his eyes between her shoulder blades as she walked.

She saw the gourmet tea and coffee shop in the distance and then the dark space of the alley between the end of the shop and the apartment building next to it. So far, so good.

As she neared the shop, she slid the gun out of her bag

and into her jacket pocket. She also picked up her pace, weaving in and around the people on the sidewalk, to give her a few extra seconds. She came to the end of the brick building, pivoted left, took two steps, then started running full tilt.

Four seconds later and twenty yards into the alley, she hit the door.

As she'd hoped, it was propped open. It was easier, during business hours, to let employees go out and drop the trash or meet deliveries without needing an additional person to hold the door open. She swung it open, kicked the wedge aside, stepped in, and let the door close behind her. She walked briskly around the counter, ignored the stares of the employees, zigzagged through the short queue of customers, and pushed out the front door.

She threw a quick glance back up Washington Street to see if the man had balked at her turn into a dead-end alley. Her eyes flashed up the street, looking for the fedora. Nothing.

She snapped her head around. It was clear all the way to the intersection and the park. There was only one other place he could be.

She walked quickly to the mouth of the alley and found the man slowly stepping down the alley, unsure and out of his element. He walked with a careful hesitation as if he knew something was wrong, he just didn't know where the trap was yet.

Kate pulled her gun and followed him into the shadows. The passing traffic from the street covered her approach. She was only five feet behind him when he finally heard her and started to turn. She moved forward quickly and jabbed the barrel of the Beretta into his kidney, hard.

The man stopped, but Kate noticed he didn't flinch or buckle. Not the first time he'd been introduced to a gun. Maybe he wasn't so far out of his element.

"Hands out of your pockets," Kate said. "Take it slow."

The man complied and dropped his hands to his sides. Up close, he was even bonier than his reflection in the window, all pointy edges and sharp angles. Kate thought she might get cut if she got too close. She pushed him forward, deeper into the alley. They were in the lee of the dumpster now and couldn't be seen from the street. She ran a hand up under his arms and down his legs, found nothing.

She stepped back but kept the gun up. "Turn around."

He did but didn't say anything. He didn't look at the gun either; just kept his eyes on her and waited. Kate fought an itch to step further back. They stood in silence. It was clear the man wasn't going to speak first. Kate didn't have time for this.

"What's the deal, Pennybags? Why are you following me?"

"Excuse me?"

"Really? You going to play it like this. You're what? An alley inspector? Look, I have a business to run. I don't have time to be playing spy versus spy out here on the street with you. Either tell me what you want or leave me the hell alone."

He took another moment, studying her face. "Fine. Point taken. First, Ms. Willis, allow me to compliment you on that maneuver. It was quite unexpected. We were told many things. You were recommended for a variety of attributes, but few people mentioned your ..." He paused and pursed his lips like he was considering a violin concerto, not staring at a gun in a back alley. "What would someone in your line of work call them? Field skills? Regardless, it was an apt demonstration."

"Jesus, what is this? Some hidden camera show?" Kate didn't dare take her eyes off this guy, but now she was the one that felt wrong-footed. Her dad was right. Whatever she'd been expecting, cowering accountant, mealy personal injury lawyer, or something else, she had not been expecting this.

Not a suave, well-spoken man unruffled by the barrel of a gun.

"Who have you been talking to?" She didn't like the nervous edge in her voice. She tried to put a little more confidence into it. "What do you want?"

"I spoke with some of your colleagues. Some of your former clients." He made a small motion with his hand while tipping his head. "A few other people. I was surprised. You're quite well-connected in this city. First your father, now you. But all of that is rather beside the point. I like to be careful. Judicious, you might say. Some find it tiresome, but I like to check people out thoroughly before I enter into any business arrangement. Or even propose any sort of arrangement."

"What are you talking about?" Kate felt like she'd followed the white rabbit down the hole. "Jesus, man, talk some sense."

For the first time, he seemed to notice his surroundings. "Yes, I agree, let's talk business, but perhaps not in this alley. And not," he nodded at her hand, "with the gun." He peered over the dumpster back toward the light and activity of the street. "I believe that's a tea or coffee shop next door. Care to join me for a cup?"

Kate looked at him, then at the gun in her hand. She thumbed the safety and dropped the gun into her pocket. "Fine. Tea it is, but you're buying." She gestured for him to go first.

She was curious despite herself.

I don't like ... She cut her dad off before he even got started.

HAM AND EGGS

"Fry two and let the sun shine. Side of Jack Benny."

"Got it. We're eighty-sixed on the Zeppelins."

"Okay. Next?"

"Ready."

"Flop two, wreck 'em, with a heart attack on a rack. Everything on wheels."

"Got it."

Max Strong was hip deep in the weeds and loving every minute of it. Bob's Riverside Diner did a brisk breakfast and lunch trade every day, but Sunday morning was in another league. It was all hands on deck, with orders flying in left and right from 5 a.m. when the hunters and hikers came through until noon when the late churchgoers and the hangover crowd capped off the day. Bob Jr. liked to call the last seating "the sinners and the saints."

Max didn't have to glance up at the clock to know it was close to 11 a.m. The light from the small casement window was creeping onto the grill like a sundial, and he knew when it hit the backsplash that the orders would start to slack off.

He broke two eggs but flubbed a yolk. Those two would be the scramble, he decided. He grabbed two more and this time kept the yolks intact. He gave the gravy pot a quick stir and slid two more pieces of bacon onto the flattop.

"Ramon, more biscuits," he yelled out.

"You got it, hermano."

He wiped at the sweat dripping into his eyes with his sleeve and studied the order chits hanging in front of him. He looked down and compared it to the grill. It was busy, but he was on top of it. Only three months ago, he would have been struggling, his eyes as big as saucers, fumbling around the kitchen, drowning in orders, and needing Junior to jump in and steady the ship. Now, he had the patter down, knew what to get going first and what to wait on. He didn't need to think about what items he could keep warming on the grill and what he needed to do fresh each time. He just did it. The rhythm was like a wire in his blood, a pulse he had come to crave and thrive on. The rush kept you busy, the threat of the weeds kept you on your toes. There wasn't room for any other thoughts, any other memories, beyond the next order.

Junior pushed through the swinging door, paused to check the scene, gave Max a quick nod, then kept going into the walk-in freezer.

On the way back out he couldn't help himself. "Staying on top of it?"

"You know it, boss."

"Good. Watch those eggs."

"Got it." Max took the spatula off the rack and scrambled up the two eggs. He grabbed a to-go container and put the eggs in, piled in the biscuits, and topped it all with gravy before popping the top shut.

"Sue. Wheels up."

"Thanks, Matt." Sue gave him a quick smile, grabbed the

order, and kept going, leaving a faint trail of double-mint gum and menthol in her wake.

In this town, his name was Matt Diver. He felt the familiar gut-level pain of lying to these people he now thought of as his friends. The heat from all the events in Essex had died down, but he doubted it would ever go out completely. He might get six months, a year, more if he was lucky, but Max Strong would always be on the move. His life depended on it.

"Sinners are outnumbering the saints this morning," Junior said, looking out through the kitchen's pass through.

"Just the way I like it."

"Better tippers." Junior smiled, clapped him on the back, and went back to his high-back stool next to the register, the same stool his father had sat on before him and his grandfather before that.

Forty-five minutes later, the rush was over, the sun covered the grill, and Max was scraping down the flattop and soaking pots. The diner was open until 3 p.m., but Junior shut down half the big grill by noon and let Ramon handle any of the stragglers.

"You polish up my baby for me?" Ramon asked, sliding a half-sheet onto a rolling rack and walking over to the grill. He was twenty-three and the world hadn't knocked him on his ass yet.

"Just keeping it warm for you."

"Nice. You catch those two honeys sitting at the two-top by the window?"

"Missed 'em. Too busy doing your job."

"Aww, man. Don't even go there. Those two were fine. They come in again, maybe we see if they want to do something."

Max had at least ten years on Ramon and started laughing.

"What's so funny?"

"Nothing, just the idea of double dating with you."

"Hey man, you might look like the grill of my pop's Chevy, but I can carry you for a night. Maybe some of my game rubs off on you. Maybe you get lucky."

The whole idea was so farfetched that Max ended up laughing even harder, which got Ramon going.

Sue stuck her head through the pass through. "What's so funny back here?"

"Nothing." They both answered. She shook her head and disappeared. Max heard her say something to Junior about a gas leak in the kitchen.

He finished wiping down his prep area and threw the dirty towel at Ramon. "You working this week?"

The kid caught it one-handed and flipped it into the linen bin. "Nah. Got midterms. Junior wants me to keep the grades up. I'm back on Saturday."

"All right. Good luck on the exams." They slapped hands. "See you next weekend."

Max pushed out the swinging kitchen doors and waved goodbye to Sue and Cherie, Bob's other regular waitress. Sue held up a hand, and he waited as she weaved around the tables and banquets and met him by the door.

"I noticed in the City Paper that the Broadmoor is running *The Man with No Name* this week. Interested?"

"Oh yeah? Never seen it on the big screen. You working tomorrow?"

"'Til six."

"Ok. Me, too. Let's see how tomorrow goes."

It wasn't a yes and it wasn't a no. He'd become very good at deflecting and non-answers. Sue didn't push, but she was persistent. She would ask again tomorrow. Who knows? Maybe he'd go. He took his coat from the rack by the diner's front door. "See you tomorrow, Junior."

"All right Matt. Have a good one."

———

The blissful nothingness of the hot grill and filling orders lasted four blocks. The pulse in his blood ticked away to nothing and the world started pushing in again. Sights, sounds, and smells filled his head. He did his best to hold it back and thought about a shower and watching the late afternoon game or a movie on his small television. Why think about your problems when someone else's are beamed right into your living room? But Max knew it wouldn't be enough, for him anyway. It was too passive. There were too many breaks, too many commercials, too many opportunities to let his mind wander. Maybe he needed a second job? Something part-time. The extra dough wouldn't hurt either. Or maybe he just needed to move on again, find somewhere new. Traveling had a way of making a man too weary to think.

He could just see the pitched roof of the old red and white motel poking up above the fast-food joints and strip mall signs when he remembered his money. Damn. Junior had handed him the envelope at the start of his shift, and he'd left it pinned to the board by the clock. He thought about using the roll under his bed, but he hated to let that dip much lower, even for just a day. The small color television had been a splurge and put a serious dent in his savings.

It was also Sunday, which meant two things. First, Michelle was working the counter at Gary's Cash N Carry. She was the least likely to hassle him over ID. If he waited until tomorrow, he'd be into Jean's shift. She'd given him the stink eye the first time he'd gone in to cash his check and he hadn't been back to give her a second chance. Second, rent was due tomorrow and the best way to keep a low profile was to pay on time. It had to be today.

He turned around and started walking the half-mile back to the diner.

———

Bob's Riverside Diner was raised two feet off the ground on a cinder block foundation. A set of three concrete stairs ran parallel to the diner and led to a railed landing. You turned left and passed through two sets of glass doors before hitting the hostess stand.

Max didn't see the guy until he was through the diner's first set of glass doors and aiming for the second. The guy's back was to the door. Max clocked him for a beat—thin, jittery, a black ski mask pulled down over his face, the heavy Sunday take in a bulging plastic Shop Rite bag. He was saying something, the gun waving around. He saw Cherie's eyes widen a fraction at the sight of him in the little glass vestibule. He stepped back out onto the steps and waited. He would be below the guy, and his gun, on the lower steps. It should give him an opening. He hoped.

Someone started leaning on their horn. He was aware of a door opening and motion to his right. Max kept his eyes on the door. The timing would be key.

The guy exited with his head turned backward, tracking the customers in the diner, making sure no one was going for a cell phone or trying to follow him. Max waited for him to clear the second set of doors and step onto the small landing. The guy brought his gun arm around first. His head followed a little more slowly. Max used that fraction of a second to his advantage. He brought his own arm arcing up from his side, clipping the guy hard on the wrist, sending his arm up and back, the gun now pointed at the sky. Next, he reached out with his other hand, grabbed the guy's ankle, and sent him sprawling to the parking lot pavement. The man threw both arms out to break his fall, losing both the money bag and the gun.

Max caught the guy's collar and bounced him off the cement once. His head made solid contact and the guy groaned once before going limp. Max dropped him and stood up. An old silver Camry pulled quickly out of the lot. Mud was slicked over most of the Oregon plate, and Max only caught sight of long blonde hair on the driver before the car pulled out onto Central, narrowly missing a pickup and disappeared into traffic. Max kicked the gun further out of reach.

The whole exchange took five seconds. No one else had made it through the door by the time the guy was disarmed and unconscious on the sidewalk. Junior was first out, carrying his scarred Louisville Slugger. He stopped and his mouth dropped open at the sight of Max standing over the would-be stick-up artist.

"Never seen you so speechless, Junior."

"Matt, Christ, are you okay?"

"I'm good."

Junior walked over, nudged the guy's shoulder with the barrel of the bat before he leaned down and pulled the ski mask off.

"Just a kid," Max said.

No more than twenty, the kid's dirty brown hair was sweaty and stuck to his forehead. Acne dotted his nose and chin, while his cheeks had the sunken, sallow look of a user.

Max watched Junior's knuckles tighten on the bat; Max reached over and took it. "Why don't you go call the police."

He thought Junior might argue, but after a moment he let go of the bat and took a deep breath. "Right. Yes, of course, you're right. Hey, where's the gun?"

Max nodded toward the cement gutter below the landing. "He dropped it when I tripped him."

"Christ, look at that thing. Looks like a toy my grandson might play with."

Max looked down at the scraped up black gun and couldn't disagree.

Junior shook his head and turned to go back inside to report the attempted robbery.

"Here, don't forget this," Max said, holding up the plastic bag stuffed with the morning's cash.

HELLIONS

S tan watched the elementary school bus roll by, brake
at the corner, and let a gaggle of students off at the
corner. A gaggle? A group? What do you call a bunch
of kids, Stan wondered. Never married, never even came
close, Stan hadn't ever felt the itch to be a father. Sometimes
he had a hard time understanding those who did. Wife and
kids? Spills? Tantrums? Constant worry? No thanks. He liked
his routines. He liked his space. And he liked his doughnut
shop. He'd long made peace with all those feelings, along with
the lingering stares and whispers from the women in town. If
he hadn't already balled half of them, he was sure they'd be
convinced he was gay.

Hellions, he decided. That would be an apt name for a
bunch of kids just let out of the cell blocks that passed for
schools these days. He listened to their screams and taunts
die away as they broke up into ones and twos and headed
home into a setting sun.

The school bus signaled the unofficial end to the day for
Stan. Technically, the shop was open until 4 p.m., but once
the bus went past, Stan knew parents would now be more

concerned with picking their kids up from various practices and getting dinner on the table, not with stopping by for a cup of joe, a pastry, and some gossip.

He turned away from the big plate glass windows that fronted his shop and went to the register. He cut the tape and looked at the number. "Not bad for a Thursday."

Pete looked up from the pile of dust he was pushing across the floor. "What was that, Mr. Tucinni?"

"Nothing, Pete. Just saying I can afford to pay your wages."

"Oh, okay. That's good, right, Mr. Tucinni?"

Stan had given up trying to get Pete to call him by his first name. After exchanges like this, Stan longed for Max's company.

Almost two years had passed since that bloody and mysterious night, but Stan still couldn't get up the energy to hire another assistant and made do with high school kids like Pete to get the scut work done around the shop.

"Yeah, that's good, Pete."

He wrote the day's number in a green ledger book he kept underneath the counter, then took a bank deposit bag and filled it with cash from the register. He left about forty bucks in ones, fives, and tens, plus the coins in the drawer, to make change for tomorrow's early customers. He took the bag and walked through the swinging doors into the back kitchen. He took an envelope of cash from the refrigerator and added it to the bag. He didn't like the register getting too full of cash and often took some out after the morning commuter rush.

He brought the full bag back out front, put it next to the register, and started wiping down the long front counter.

"I can get that, Mr. Tucinni."

"I know, Pete. Just feel like helping out today, that's all. In fact, if you're done with the sweeping, why don't you knock off early and enjoy the rest of the day. Not many like this left before the weather turns."

"You sure? I can stick around. I don't mind."

"I'm sure. I'll pay you the full time. Not much left to do anyway, nothing an old man can't handle. Just do me a favor and drop the trash in the dumpster on your way out."

Pete didn't argue after that. He was at least old enough to know the value of a fine fall day. He picked up the dust pile he'd made and dumped it in the can, tied the bag off, and carried it out the back. Stan heard him pause to put on his jacket.

"See you tomorrow, Mr. Tucinni."

"All right, Pete."

A bit of a strange boy, Stan thought, and not for the first time. He chalked it up to age. You weren't normal if you weren't a bit strange as a teenager, or at least appeared a bit strange to an adult. The kid had a good work ethic, though, Stan would admit that. Kid took some pride in keeping the shop clean. That was hard to teach.

———

Much later, after he woke up and bits and pieces came back like a jumbled up jigsaw puzzle, Stan would realize the back door never shut. An early warning alarm that his brain never caught until it was far too late. The pneumatic catch at the top of the rear door, the one that helped ease it closed, had broken two weeks ago and he'd yet to get around to fixing it. Anytime someone went out the back, the door had been slamming shut and rattling the pans and supplies on the back shelves.

After Pete left with the garbage, the door never slammed. The pots never shook. Stan should have noticed it. He should have bolted out the front or gone for his crowbar sitting on the little shelf under the register. It probably wouldn't have made any difference, not in the long run, but it might have made it easier to live with the aftermath if he'd been doing something, anything other than staring out the front window again.

The two men came through the door wearing dark suits and leather gloves. Stan remembered the gloves, with almost microscopic precision. The damn gloves seemed to be the only thing he could remember at first. When he shut his eyes in the hospital, he could see the handsewn stitching stretch and yield as the men flexed their fists in preparation.

Neither of them spoke. It was like watching a well-choreographed dance. One went left around the register to the front doors, flicked the lock closed, then began to lower the shades. The other went right, came at Stan, and backed him into a corner at the end of the counter.

"Take the money. It's right there in the bag by the register. Just take it and leave. I don't want any trouble." Stan said it even though he knew these guys weren't here for the money. They weren't some two-bit thugs or junkies looking for some quick cash. They were pros, and they were here for information or blood or both.

Stan glanced around, but his crowbar was out of reach. The only thing close was a metal napkin dispenser. He picked it up and threw it at the man closest to him but the throw was wild, and it sailed past the guy's head and skidded over the linoleum tiles into the corner.

Next, he tried for an empty coffee pot sitting on an idle burner, but the man caught his wrist and twisted. Hard. Stan heard, more than felt, something in his elbow give like an old cracked rubber band. He might have cried out then, but the man slammed a gloved fist into his gut and cut off the air.

Stan was old but tough. You didn't survive the tunnels and Ho Chi Minh City without a little steel in your spine. He was gristle and bone with a survivor's mentality and a brawler's mean streak buried under his affable smile. The blow to Stan's stomach had sent him to his knees, but it only knocked the wind out of him, not his senses.

He watched his assailant's shoes come forward and, when he felt a hand grab his collar, he lunged forward, leading with his head, right into the guy's groin. The top of the head is the hardest part of the human body, and Stan felt his skull connect hard with the guy's pelvic bone. The guy grunted and went to one knee. But the other guy was a tough, mean bastard, too. He was also younger and, before Stan could press his small advantage of surprise, the man retaliated with a fist into the side of Stan's head that sent it bouncing off the edge of the counter. Stan saw the world shimmer and slip out of focus. Before he could pass out, two hands gripped his collar and hauled him up and over the counter.

Now it was the other's guy turn.

Shit.

This time, Stan saw the fist coming. It was hard to miss seeing as it pulled back and pistoned forward into his nose. He heard the cartilage crunch and slide to the left.

The man paused. Stan saw his lips moving, but he couldn't hear him. It was as if his body was shutting down its functions to save power. Another punch, again to his nose. Or what used to be his nose. More soundless lip moving from the guy. Stan still couldn't hear, but he didn't have to. If they didn't want the money, there was only one other thing of value Stan knew they wanted.

Max.

Only he didn't know where Max was for this very reason.

He tasted blood as it ran down the back of his throat and he sprayed it onto the man's white shirt with a grim smile. He knew it would cost him.

Two more blows and Stan lost consciousness.

NAMES

"Yes, Mrs. Beasley, I got it." A pause.

"No really, I got it. I wrote it down." Another pause.

"Sure, if that will make you feel better." He cleared his throat. "'The Essex Gardening Club will have its monthly meeting at 7 p.m. on Wednesday the 19th in the town library's lower function room. Ms. Christine Baker of East Brunswick will be the guest speaker.' That sound about right to you, Mrs. Beasley?"

He held the phone away from his ear. He didn't have to listen. He knew what the next question was because they went through the same dance every month when Mrs. Beasley called to run the Garden Club's announcement.

After an appropriate amount of time had gone by, he put the phone back to his ear. "Yes, Mrs. Beasley, the announcement will run in this week's Friday edition."

"Okay, you too. Bye now."

"I was nominated for a Pulitzer, you know. I'm capable of dictating your announcement." The dial tone was a better listener than Mrs. Beasley, but hardly sympathetic. He dropped the phone back on the cradle and rubbed his arm.

The phone was a Ma Bell original, leased from the company in 1939, and was a genuine antique now. Most days, Porter loved the heft and solidity of it. If he was honest, curling the three pounds of hard molded plastic was his most consistent form of exercise. It made him feel like Sam Spade or Walter Winchell. All he was missing was the rakish hat and unfiltered cigarettes. On days when the likes of Mrs. Beasley called, however, the handset quickly turned into an anchor he had to struggle to keep to his ear.

He typed up the announcement and sent it to the print basket. At least he'd managed to get the print workflow set up electronically. He looked around the office. The computer and slim monitor in front of him were anachronisms in the room. Everything else belonged in a sepia-toned photo. The Bakelite phone, the wooden desk the size of a ship's prow, an actual maple coatrack, a balky steam radiator, and a tartan sofa that had probably picked up its stains in a speakeasy. It was all *Essex Standard-Times* original office décor that his uncle, and his uncle's father before him, had picked up at yard sales or at the curb on trash day. Hell, the old man would still be using the manual press in the basement if he hadn't keeled over and died on top of it.

He dropped his reading glasses on the blotter and marveled again at how he had ended up behind this desk. It had been the perfect storm, really. His collapsing marriage, the Pulitzer nomination (which looked like a boon at the time), his steady drinking, a particularly relentless Chicago winter, and, the cherry on top, his uncle's death had led Porter Gaffigan to sole ownership and editor-in-chief of the *Essex Standard-Times*. The very smallness of it, the perceived serenity, had seemed like the lifeline he needed at the time.

Now, he wasn't so sure. Most of the time it just felt like a tightening noose, maybe a slower death than his old life in Chicago, but the same inevitable conclusion.

The path to the Pulitzer nomination started innocuously enough with a vanilla story on returning Iraq and Afghanistan vets. Porter had little skin in the story; it was his editor who pushed him to finish the piece. And it was all shaping up to be a very light and puffy twelve to fourteen inches in the City section when one interview subject made an offhand comment about his buddy getting a job with City Hall while he was still over in Iraq.

The piece did run, to little fanfare, but that comment stuck in Porter's head and he started sniffing. It quickly spiraled into a wide-ranging investigation into the hiring practices of City Hall and its powerful mayor. It took over Porter's life. He was never home. He worked all the time and at odd hours. And it all paid off with the Pulitzer nomination and the fleeting gratitude of his bosses.

Only somehow, a sure homerun hooked foul. He lost the Pulitzer. He supposed the perception was that Chicago was so crooked these stories wrote themselves. Even more galling to Porter was, despite the solid evidence he unearthed and what the federal prosecutors would eventually describe in court as 'pervasive fraud' in hiring and contracts at City Hall, only three of the thirty people indicted saw any significant jail time. Most even kept their jobs! For eighteen months, he ran himself ragged, sacrificed his marriage, his sobriety, his physical and certainly his mental health and for what? So three lower-level bureaucrats could do some country club jail time and community service. It was disgusting and just sent him further into a spiral. He pushed everything and everybody away unless it was happy hour. It had been a devil's bargain. He had his profession's highest prize in his grasp, professional credibility, leverage with his bosses, and the jealousy of his peers. But the damage was done.

Two weeks after his wife walked, a month after the Pulitzer announcement, Porter's mother told him about his uncle's death. He knew she was only duly reporting the family news during his all-too-infrequent calls home, but something struck a nerve that day. It could have been the Jameson in his morning coffee or the nights he'd spent wallowing in self-pity, also alongside his triple-distilled friend; hell, maybe it was just the cold wind of Chicago in January scrambling his brain, but as he listened to her, he found wild utopian fantasies of small-town life and old-time newspapermen jumping into his head. He had a vision of writing novels in his downtime and making a tangible, even positive, impact on a community.

He knew his small-town fantasy was just that, a fantasy, but he couldn't keep it tamped down. He couldn't dismiss it. He found himself doing just the opposite. He nursed it. Before the week was out, he'd resigned, to everyone's astonishment, packed a few boxes, rented a small apartment in Essex, and vowed to rebuild his life and keep the presses running in his uncle's memory. He hadn't meant it literally, of course, but those first two weeks he had actually set and rolled the presses himself. Ernie, the deliveryman, waited patiently and helped where he could. The bootstrapping mentality, fly-by-night, ink-under-the-fingernails operation rejuvenated him. He was too busy and too exhausted to think or to drink. It was perfect.

———

Mrs. Beasley had sapped the last of his energy. He pushed back from the desk and was about to call it a day, already thinking about what he had in his fridge and how he'd spend the evening, maybe pull out the file again, when Mike Duffy walked in.

Duffy was a young stringer Porter used to fill the pages of the paper when he couldn't stomach another school board meeting or high school football game. That perfect halcyon glow of those first weeks had dissipated fast when Porter looked around and saw he really *was* in a small town. Not a cute, quirky town from a Capra script, just a small town on the outskirts of a medium-sized city in a flat flyover state. News didn't go much beyond homecoming, lost cats, and water main flushing.

He stayed because inertia was a powerful force. And he stayed because he couldn't go back. Big award nomination or not, he'd burned his bridges down to the piles on his way out. He stayed because a resting body tended to stay at rest and just because news didn't come around much, didn't mean it never came around.

Two years ago, when he'd still been in Chicago chasing down city hall corruption, it had come through Essex like a cyclone. Dead cops. Dead townies. Ex-cons. Rumors about organized crime. Drugs. Conspiracies. And, most important for a reporter, unanswered questions.

"Hey, Duff. Whaddaya got?" Porter said as he fell back into the old rolling desk chair.

"Couple stories. One on the high school soccer game from Tuesday and one on the selectman debate."

"There was a selectman debate?"

"Sure. Last night down at the library."

"Turnout?"

Duffy was young enough to still harbor ideals, and Porter held back a smile as the young man's cheeks colored.

"Including the librarians and the candidates' families, there were probably fifteen or twenty people in the room."

"That including the candidates and yourself?"

Duffy shrugged. "Not going to make much of a difference for the story, is it?"

"We'll see. Hand 'em over."

"I also sent them to your email."

Duffy handed Porter a couple typed sheets and sat down in the traditional wooden rocking chair that served as visitor accommodations in the office. Ernie had told Porter that his uncle liked to keep his visitors off balance. Ernie said everything with a straight face, and Porter could never tell when he might be pulling his leg. He'd kept the chair mainly because he was a sucker for a good story.

Duffy rocked slowly back and forth and stared up at the pockmarked ceiling. The kid was nineteen and taking what he kept referring to as a 'gap' year to see the world and find out what he wanted to do before he headed off to college. From what Porter had witnessed, he wasn't seeing much of the world and he doubted Duffy would get much of a worldly education hanging around Essex. Still, he was a decent writer, and the more he wrote the less Porter had to write. Even though he drew no salary and was technically a stringer, paid by the story, Porter considered him, along with Maureen Kelly, the paper's employees. Maureen came in three times a week to empty the 'Speak Up' voicemail (residents could call in and leave a message, some of which were transcribed for the print column), compile the police blotter, answer phones, and take care of the general administrative things that Porter always let slide. He was pretty sure this little adventure would have crashed into the side of a mountain a long time ago without either of them.

Porter grabbed a red pen from the blotter and looked down at the sheets. He scanned them both quickly, then went back and read them more slowly, marking the papers here and there with small notations.

"The soccer one is pretty good. Maybe lead with the third

'graph. Don't make them wait so long for the score; otherwise, I like it. I can use this. Lots of names."

"What about the other one?"

Porter knew Duffy thought of this one as the serious piece. He'd probably spent twice as long on it as the soccer one, but all the effort showed. It didn't flow. It was full of fancy vocabulary and long unbroken paragraphs about complex issues—as complex as issues got in Essex, at least.

"Duff, the *Essex Standard-Times* is not *The Economist*."

"The readers can take a little heavy lifting once in a while."

"Sure. Just not from their hometown weekly."

Duffy's face fell and, even though Porter knew it was the truth, he still felt like a jerk. "Look, tighten it up a bit. Lose the SAT words and cut down on the background. Get it back to me by tomorrow and I can find a spot for it."

"All right, I'll give it a shot."

Porter put the soccer piece aside and handed the marked-up debate story back to Duffy. "You get names on this one?"

Duffy nodded.

"Well, throw them in there, too. Can't hurt."

This was the ultimate irony for Porter. The less he tried, the better the paper did.

Six months after he'd moved, when the reality of the situation crashed down on him, Porter went on a three-day bender. When he woke up on Tuesday, he was facedown in the grass next to his driveway. There was an ant crawling along the ridge line of his nose and no paper to send to the printer. He'd written nothing that week and had less than twenty-four hours to get something, anything resembling an edition to the printer. Some perverse sense of duty compelled him to try despite his four-alarm hangover.

It was Duffy who came up with the idea that saved his bacon. He suggested they do a twenty-four hours in Essex edition and use the local journalism class from the community college two towns over to help. It worked like a charm. Yes, Porter had to do a lot of red line editing, but he could do it from the office with the blinds closed, with aspirin within reach.

They sprinkled people's names liberally throughout the paper to pad out the inches. You attended an event, your name went in the paper. You were outside walking by an event, your name went in the paper. You even thought about going to an event, your name might be in the paper. In many places, it read more like a phonebook than prose, but it went to press. And promptly sold out the entire run. People really liked to read their name in the paper.

In a time when most large papers were laying off staff and slashing budgets, the *Essex Standard-Times* was bucking the trend. He kept up the partnership with the community college, even expanded it by using the computer science kids to make the paper a website which was updated daily, or near daily, by Duffy or the college interns, in-between the twice-weekly print run. He'd inadvertently turned the *Times* into a successful hyper-local news source and he had the web traffic, increasing ad sales and subscriptions to prove it. It didn't exactly translate into riches, but he didn't need it to, living in a small town had the distinct advantage of being cheap.

"Got any more inches?"

"No, just those two for today."

"All right. Good work," Porter said. "We still on for the press tomorrow morning?"

"Sure," Duffy said.

After Duffy left, Porter pulled up the electronic versions from his email, made a few minor edits to the soccer story, filed it, and shut down the computer.

He leaned back in his chair and rolled his neck until it cracked. Suddenly, even reheating dinner felt like a lot of effort. Maybe he'd hit the diner. Too bad the strongest thing it served was beer. He pulled out his bottle from the bottom desk drawer. He thought about taking a pull right from the neck, but that felt like a slippery slope. He'd been having a pretty good patch lately. Not too much, not too little. He grabbed a coffee mug, wiped it out with his sleeve, and poured a couple of inches as an appetizer.

RIGHT AFTER II

Alexei fought to keep his eyes open and concentrated on his wounds. Taken right to the edge, he knew the pain could keep him awake. Blood was still running freely from both his shoulder and his leg and neither showed signs of clotting. If he didn't deal with them now, he wouldn't get fifty yards before he passed out.

He unbuckled his belt and used his good arm to strip it off his waist, then he carefully fed it under his leg and buckled it above the bullet wound as tight as it would go. If he had time, he would have chewed a new hole in the leather to make it even tighter, but this would have to do for now. Tourniquet in place, he probed around the edges of the leg wound with his fingers and could feel the hard mass of the bullet lodged in his muscle, but, with only one good arm and no knife, there was little else he could do. He ripped a strip of fabric from his shirt and tied it over the wound to try to slow the blood, then he moved on to his shoulder.

The pipe must have been sticking out of one of the garbage bags. It had pushed straight through his shoulder. In that respect, he was lucky. The shoulder was full of tendons and muscles, but little of vital interest. A couple inches lower and it would have hit a major artery, or punctured his aorta, or collapsed a lung and he'd already be starting to rot.

Looking more closely at the pipe, his first thought still held true. The rust on the pipe promised to kill him faster than the bullet in his leg. He needed to get it out. He could feel at least two inches of pipe sticking out the back of his shoulder. There would be no easy or painless way to do it. He moved as quickly as he could. He used the tail of his shirt to wipe off as much of the blood as he could so he could get a decent grip. He didn't want to have to try this twice. He grabbed a scrap of wood off the floor and clamped it between his teeth to keep from biting his tongue in half, then he took a breath, counted to three, and pulled.

———

When he woke up, the pipe was still there. It took two more slow, agonizing pulls before the pipe slid out with a slippery, sucking pop. Alexei gasped and passed out again.

———

He was surprised the next time he woke up. He knew his body was quickly approaching its limits. Something brushed against his foot, and he watched a rat crawl over his ankle and disappear back into the dark. Maybe the vermin knew it too.

His head was fuzzy and his limbs oddly light. He felt little pain, and this alarmed him the most. His body was pumping him full of something, some feel-good endorphins, to override the maxed-out pain circuits his field surgery had tripped. His body was prepping to let him down easy.

The pipe had rolled a few feet away. Alexei looked up and saw light still filtering through the hole above him, though it had shifted across the floor. He guessed he'd been out for maybe an hour, no more than two. The edges of the wound had begun to clot and dry, but the center was still gooey and leaking. Alexei counted that as progress.

He untied a shoe, slid off a sock and jammed it into the hole in his shoulder.

Did the wound smell sweet? Or was he imagining that?

He slid his shoe back on without tying the laces and managed to use the garbage and debris to climb to his feet. He felt lightheaded and unsteady. He wanted to sit back down and close his eyes, just sink into that soft blackness, but he didn't dare. After all he'd suffered through in his life, he wasn't going to let death catch him napping. The bullet wound in his leg throbbed. Each step was torture, but he was able to limp around and deal with the pain.

Alexei made a slow circuit, feeling with his hands along the wall when he was too far away from the ambient light of the hole. He found a large empty rectangle on the far side that he guessed was the freight elevator at one time. He felt around in the shaft for anything useful but only came up with spiderwebs and old congealed grease.

He took a handful of the grease and smeared it over his shoulder wound. The sock was saturated and useless. Maybe the grease had a better chance of staunching the wound. If he didn't stop the bleeding, there'd be no infection to worry about.

Outside of the area directly under the hole, the sub-basement was remarkably clean. No debris, little dust, just clean cold concrete. A crypt. The demo and salvage must have started at the bottom and worked its way up. If only they'd started at the top.

Next to the abandoned shaft, he found bolts and holes on both the floor and wall where stairs had once been attached. Any egress there was long gone. He finished his circumnavigation of the room and kicked the bloody pipe away into the dark. He was trapped, entombed in this old mill for however long he had left.

A wave of dizziness swept over him, the floor and ceiling switching places. He sank to his hands and knees amid the black garbage bags. Lying there, waiting for the dizziness to pass, he heard it: a tiny trickling hymn of hope. He struggled back to his feet, waited for the dizziness to ebb away, and then started shoving aside the bags with his good arm.

There were more bags in the pile than he thought. He was covered in sweat and had to pause twice to avoid passing out. Finally, he pulled the last bag away and uncovered a small stream of dirty water running down into the floor's storm drain. His fall must have burst a bag or overturned a container.

He cleared a larger path around the square grate, then bent down and pulled. It was held fast with rusted screws. Nothing would come easy today.

He went back to the piles of garbage and started ripping open bags. He found nothing in the bags themselves but did find a slim metal file in the loose debris around them. It was far from a perfect fit for the old screws, but it was the best he was going to get.

It cost him the skin on all his knuckles and two torn nails before he worked the last screw loose and threw it aside. He put the file in his pocket, then grasped the old grate and pulled. It was heavy and solid and probably hadn't been lifted since the day it was laid. It clung to its spot like a stubborn ox. Light and dark rings striped his vision, and his shoulder felt like it was about to dislocate when the grate gave a rasping sigh and came loose.

Alexei stumbled back and stared into a hole that was three feet by three feet, perfectly square and perfectly dark. He couldn't see the bottom even with the light from the hole above him. He picked up a can and dropped it in. It disappeared into the shadows and a moment later made a small thwack and splash as it hit the bottom. The bottom of what though? If it was just a dirt-bottomed floor that leeched excess runoff into the soil, then he was no better off down there than he was up here. Far worse off, in fact. The alternative, though, was that it was a drain that led to a pipe that maybe led outside.

He considered his two choices. The bags scattered around told him that someone still came out here. But was it a one-time thing or once a week? The makeshift campfires he'd seen on the first floor when he entered told him other visitors also came around. But, again, time was the constant in this equation, and he didn't have long. He would go into septic shock soon without first aid. The smell from his shoulder wasn't his imagination. It was getting stronger, and the dizzy spells were coming more often. He was dehydrated. He'd lost a dangerous amount of blood. Staying still was certain death. Jumping in the hole was likely death, but not certain.

He stepped into the empty space over the hole.

MR. SMITH

"I'd like to hire you."

"You've got a funny way of asking. I have an office. Even a phone."

"As I mentioned, I'm a careful man. I don't like to rush into things. If possible, I like to get to know the people I plan to do business with. Collecting references and observing you seemed like the best way to do it in this situation."

"Observing? That's one way to put it. Stalking might be another."

He gave a small flip of his hand, as if it was all just semantics, before returning his hand to the brim of the fedora in his lap. "Now we both know something about the other."

Be careful with this one. The rich like to play by different rules.

"All right, Mr.—?"

"Smith."

"Smith? Right."

He shrugged. "Sorry to disappoint you Ms. Willis, but my name really is Timothy Smith."

"At least you didn't go for John."

"I can't help that my people were not imaginative."

"Okay, Mr. Smith, as much as I enjoy an afternoon cup of tea, could you please tell me what you want?"

The man looked at her, seemed to look inside her, with his preternatural stillness. She fought the urge to fidget in her seat and stared back. He had clear blue eyes that looked almost gray in the afternoon light that slanted through the coffee shop's front window. Up close, he smelled like warm leather, shaving cream, talc, and lavender soap. Kate noticed his manicured nails wrapped around his paper cup. Collectively, it all spoke of money and, despite Kate's annoyance at being followed, she desperately needed clients, the more well-heeled the better.

"I'd like you to find someone for me," Smith finally said.

"Okay, now we're getting somewhere. I do missing persons."

She pulled a small notebook and pen out of her purse. If they were back at the office, she would have had him fill out a standard form and sign a contract, but she had the feeling Mr. Smith didn't want to come back to the office. Or put his signature on anything.

Flipping to a blank page in her notebook, she decided to get the money conversation over up front. No sense in wasting any more time if he didn't want to foot the bill. She knew just from those perfect half-moon fingernails that it wouldn't be a matter of if he could pay but, rather, would he be willing to pay. In her experience, the richest ones were often the most miserly. She did a quick calculation in her head, then remembered the stack of bills waiting in the office and upped the number by twenty percent.

"I get twelve hundred a week, plus expenses. Two weeks up front."

He stared at her with those eyes again.

"Eight hundred plus expenses."

"Twelve hundred. My standard rate. You're the one asking

for help. You've checked me out. I'm good at what I do, and I'm very good at finding people."

"You're also broke and running your firm on a shoestring. And that's not your standard rate."

"All the more reason that your case will get my undivided attention. And that's my new standard rate as of three minutes ago. One of the perks of being the boss." She gave him a smile.

Don't get too cute with this guy.

He took a long business size envelope from his inner jacket pocket and put it on the small table, giving it a little push so it slid to the center of the table. "This is a cashier's check for five thousand dollars. That should meet your retainer and initial expenses. If you complete the job sooner, consider the rest a bonus."

Shit, she thought, as her smile faded. She'd low-balled him. His bartering had all been for show. He'd probably been ready to go higher. Maybe fifteen hundred. She glanced inside the envelope. It squared up with what he said. She cursed herself again and tried to keep her face composed.

"That will work. I'll provide receipts, daily activity logs, and status reports on request."

"I don't think daily reports will be necessary." He looked at her, hands folded, tea untouched on the table. That stillness again. She took a searing sip of her own tea just to do something. "Just keep me informed. I trust you."

Thoughts flitted around in her brain like flies trapped in a jar. Little warning bells were going off in her head. What was it about this guy that made her uncomfortable? Was it just his Zen-like calm, so opposite her own personality? She thought that was part of it, but not all of it. It was the clothes, the hooded eyes, the confidence that bordered on arrogance, the sense that he knew more than he was telling. Just who was her new client?

Don't dismiss your intuition.

But she tried. She tried to swat the thoughts away. More important than any of those questions was the fact that she actually *had* a client. An apparently rich one, too. And a check. She could keep the howling wolves at bay for another couple months. She tucked the envelope far down into her bag.

"Fine. No dailies. Whatever works for you." She picked up her notebook. "Okay, what can you tell me about this missing person?"

The blue-gray eyes darted around the room. The two of them sat at the first table inside the door. The rest of the place was empty except for the employees. It was that peculiar late afternoon dead time in the downtown business district, post lunch, after the afternoon coffee breaks, but before the start of the evening commuter rush.

"His name is Max Strong."

"Name sounds familiar." Kate started jotting down notes.

"His last known address was 42 Central Avenue, Essex, Minnesota. He worked at a doughnut shop, Stan's, also in Essex." A pause.

Kate looked up. "That it?"

Smith reached into his pocket again and pulled out a four-by-six snapshot. He held it out to her, Kate took it. It was a black-and-white, head-and-shoulders shot. Definitely not an original, and even the original probably hadn't been that sharp to start with. It looked like a file photo, the type taken for yearbooks or corporate directories. It was pixelated and jagged. Most of the fine details were soft or distorted. The original was probably only a couple inches, maybe two-by-three. This one had been blown up to a more standard size.

The guy in the photo could be working behind the counter in this very shop and Kate would have to look hard to match up the resemblance. It was better than nothing, but not by much. "This is him?"

"Yes."

"I take it this is the best you got?"

"Yes."

"Okay, it's a start. What else? Friends? Family? Associates?"

"None that I know of. He worked at the doughnut shop and lived with a roommate, now deceased."

"Does this guy have a record?"

"Not that I know of."

"Outstanding warrants?"

"Not that I know of."

"Did you check?"

"We checked as far as we could."

"Anything else you can tell me? Favorite ice cream flavor? Tattoos? A proclivity for strip clubs? Gay? Straight? Any tidbit could help. You never know."

"He had a girlfriend."

"That's not much."

"If I could find him on my own, I wouldn't have to hire you."

"Okay, let me get started and see what I can find out. What would you like me to do when I find him?"

He took out a slim case of burnished silver, slid his thumb over a small latch, and took out a business card. "Call me at one of those numbers. Either one. Day or night."

Kate took it. The card was thick with crisp printing. Like the rest of Mr. Timothy Smith, it spoke discreetly of wealth. Two phone numbers were printed and thermographed on the front. She ran her fingers over the raised print. Nothing else. No company name. No address. She didn't recognize either area code. Cell phones had made area codes almost meaningless anyway. Still, phone numbers themselves could lead to information.

"Okay." She stuck the card in her notebook and flipped it closed. "It's a start. Let's see where it leads."

Smith stood up and extended his hand. "I look forwarding to hearing from you, Ms. Willis."

Kate shook his hand. His grip was firm, but not overbearing. His fingers were smooth and cool. He pulled his leather gloves on, placed the fedora on his head, and left. Kate watched him walk back up Washington, away from the park. Kate considered following him, then remembered her bills. She finished her tea, then hustled to the bank to deposit the check.

THE MESSAGE

While Junior called the police, Max sat on the kid's legs in case he came to and tried to make a run for it. The kid was still out when Junior came back outside a short time later. Max handed him back the Louisville Slugger.

The kid finally started stirring as two patrol cars pulled to the curb in front of the diner, lights flashing, no wailers.

He craned his neck around. "Why are you sitting on me, dude?"

"You just tried to rob my friend here, *dude*." Max nodded toward Junior, even though the kid couldn't see him in his current position. If he could have, one look at Junior and his chipped bat and he would have realized the safest place for him right now was underneath Max.

"Where's Janee?"

"She the blonde at the wheel of that Camry? She peeled out and left your ass before you even hit the pavement," Max said.

"Bullshit," he replied. "Janee!"

"Sorry, no bullshit. She's long gone."

The kid's brain must have started to unscramble itself then because he shut up. His head slumped forward onto the concrete, and he didn't say another word until the cops walked up. That prompted him to start up again.

"Assault! I'm being assaulted, Officer. I want to file a complaint. Bodily harm. Get this asshole off me."

The cop just smirked. "Save it for the judge."

Max stood up, and the cop snapped a pair of cuffs on the kid's wrists and hauled him up by an arm. The cop noticed the blood and scrapes.

"Either of you do that?" He asked Max and Junior.

"Concrete did that. He slipped and fell," Max responded.

"That's what I thought," the cop said. He walked the kid down the diner steps and stuffed him in the back of the patrol car.

————

The reporter showed up as the second cop car was pulling out of the lot. Coincidence, or was he watching? Max figured the latter. With his dog-eared notebook held up like a dowsing rod, he came in and started firing questions like he, too, had a badge and a right to answers. He didn't. His notebook zeroed in on Max, but Max ignored him. After a few false starts and some dead-eyed stares, he gave up and worked the rest of the room.

Max roused himself from the counter stool and headed for the door, his paycheck now firmly tucked into his pants pocket. Junior saw him heading for the door and held up one finger. Max nodded and leaned against the door, waiting for his boss.

The adrenaline that had shot through him like quick-silver when he first saw the mask and gun was gone. It had used him up and hollowed him out. He felt shell-shocked.

His ten-hour shift had now stretched to fourteen, going on fifteen. The early morning, pre-dawn, wake-up call had sunk its hooks in deep. His whole body felt like brittle rusted metal. He was the tin man. His shoulders were sore, and the arches in his feet ached from standing on the line. Max was thoroughly whipped and just wanted to go home, stand under a scalding shower, and collapse on his crappy motel mattress.

It had taken more than three hours to take everyone's statements. Junior served coffee and handed out the remaining pastries from the revolving case. Max had to repeat his version to four officers, the last in a suit and tie, probably a detective, doubling and tripling back over certain details. They all seemed to think it was pretty convenient that he walked in and practically tripped over the guy. But Max stuck to his story, and Junior and the others corroborated the details and acted as his character witnesses. The police seemed reluctant to believe him, the efficiency motel address didn't help, and they wrinkled their noses like they could smell something off about him, but eventually they departed with only one guy in cuffs.

Junior finished talking to the reporter and walked over to Max. The reporter kept scribbling on his pad, following in Junior's wake. Max eyed the digital camera slung over the reporter's shoulder.

"How about a quick picture of the two heroes?"

"We're not—," Max started.

"Sure, sure," Junior said, smelling the free advertising. "But, like I was telling you, this guy here is the real hero." He draped a meaty arm over Max's shoulder.

The reporter swung the camera up to his eye. "Great, great. These stories are always better with some art. Okay, smile now."

Max tried to turn his head at the last moment. The sound

of the shutter snapping closed sounded like a warning bell in his head.

"What paper you work for?" He asked the reporter.

The guy was looking at the LCD display, frowned slightly, then dropped the camera back to his hip. "None. I'm freelance." Having collected what he needed, the reporter headed for the door, ready to chase the next story. He called over his shoulder as he went. "Don't worry. It's been slow today. It will probably run in one of the two dailies tomorrow or the next day. Check Metro."

Sue and Cheryl were in the back booth sipping coffee and dividing the day's tips. Ramon had skipped out earlier to get ready for a date. There was no one else left. Junior walked over and flipped the sign on the door to closed, then turned to face Max.

"Couldn't buy publicity like that. Here." He held out a new envelope. Max knew what was inside without looking.

"No, Junior. Just pay me for the hours I work. I'm really not a hero. Just in the right place at the right time."

"Nonsense. I'm getting off cheap. I'd be out a lot more than this if you hadn't been around. Another guy, most guys, would have stood out of the way. Let him go. I saw you through that door," he pointed out to the walk. "That guy didn't stand a chance. You took him out quick and easy. You learn that in the Army?"

"Something like that, yeah."

"Right, right." Junior held up his hands in front of him. "I'm not prying. You're a private guy. I get that. But I've known you long enough now to know that you're a good man. Whatever else has happened to you, you got a good heart. Take it." He closed Max's hand around the envelope. "And take the next three days off. I insist. I can still handle the grill on light days."

"Junior, that's too much. I can come in and work."

"No." Junior shook his head. The man was stubborn in the best and worst ways. Max knew it would be impossible to leave without the money or the days off. Junior would see it as an insult. Best to keep the boss happy. He'd made enough waves in the world today.

"Okay, Junior, if that's what you want."

"It is." He put out his hand again, this time to shake. Max took it, then left and made the walk back to his apartment a second time. After a shower and a bowl of soup made on the hot plate in his room, he laid on the bed and watched the small television. Slow news day or not, there was nothing about the attempted robbery on the news. He switched off the set and laid in the dark, but didn't sleep.

———

By lunch on the second day, he was going out of his mind. He'd gotten through the first day by hitting the gym on Second Street and working himself into an exhaustion before coming home and reading through one of the paperbacks he kept stacked by his bed and starting another.

This morning, he'd already been back at the gym when it opened and finished the book while he ate breakfast at a different diner after his workout.

He couldn't stand anything on television for more than five minutes, and now he was wearing a groove in the already thin carpet pacing back and forth.

Junior might think he knew him, but he was wrong. He was not a good man, far from it, and he was haunted by those deeds. It was why he had gotten the job at the diner in the first place. It was why he was happy to work doubles or take holidays. He didn't have anywhere to go and couldn't call anyone. He needed to work, keep busy. Too much idle time left too much room in his head for the past. It was not a place he liked to revisit.

He looked at his watch. Almost noon. He picked up the remote and flipped on the TV again. He switched channels to a local broadcast. He could stand the news. He sat on the bed and made it through ten minutes before the itching in his legs and arms got to be too much. He started pacing again. Five minutes later, he turned the television off and left his apartment.

He decided to walk down to the town library and use its Internet connection on the free terminals, maybe look through the quarter books they had on sale. See if they had any westerns he hadn't read yet. He didn't own a library card.

He took the long way around. He walked past the diner. He could see Sue chatting up a couple of the lawyers who came in regularly. She laughed. He smiled from the sidewalk and watched her for a moment. In a different world, he thought. She didn't look up, and he moved on. He walked through town until he hit the water, then walked the length of the retaining wall to the docks before circling back and finally ending up at the brick library building.

Midday on a Tuesday the library was quiet, almost empty. Two guys sat reading newspapers on long sticks at a wooden table near the windows. An older librarian was stacking books on a rolling cart to re-shelf. Max walked the stacks until he hit the back wall but didn't see anyone else. The librarian smiled and nodded as he walked past and sat at one of the computers.

He pulled up a browser window. He didn't have an email account, so there was no time to waste there. First, he went to ESPN.com to check the scores and stories. Nothing new. He browsed over to *The New York Times* website. He scanned a few world and national news stories, poked around in the local section and saw nothing of interest.

Next, he went to the homepage for one of the two area newspapers to check again if the reporter had sold his copy on the thwarted diner robbery. He'd checked both papers yesterday when someone left them laying around the locker room at the gym. Nothing. Max could imagine Junior's disappointment. He almost felt a pang of sympathy.

There was nothing on the first newspaper site he checked, but he found the clip in the Metro section of the second smaller paper. His stomach tightened. The story was short. How much was there to tell really? Still, the reporter did his best to punch up the drama and details. Worse yet, he managed to get the photo included. It was small and looked grainy even onscreen. But it was there.

He walked over and took one of the print editions off the rack. The photo was in the print edition as well. The story was tucked in the lower corner on an inside page, with the photo on the left. No more than four inches. Max had turned his head, but not quick enough. His face was clearly visible. A little blurry, but recognizable if you were looking.

Before closing out the browser and taking another wandering route back to his motel, Max pulled up the *Essex Standard-Times* website. Despite, or maybe because of, the events that happened, he felt a deep connection to the place. He could never go back, but that didn't mean he couldn't keep tabs.

Thinking about the robbery and the photo had him distracted as he clicked around the surprisingly robust local news site and he almost missed the story on Stan. It was a short follow-up, telling readers that the beloved local doughnut maker was still in a coma at St. Vincent's after the attack last week. Max gripped the table. Stomach churning, he navigated to the archives and found the original story.

Local Shopkeeper Assaulted

Stanley Tucinni, known to most in Essex as Stan, was

found late Thursday, beaten and unconscious behind the counter of his eponymous doughnut shop on Western Avenue.

He was found by his part-time employee, Essex High School student, Pete Kendall. Kendall dialed 911. No money was stolen or property damaged in the incident.

Chief Ken Logins had no comment. "We can't comment on an active investigation. We're looking into all possible leads."

Logins went on to say that they are still seeking suspects and asked that anyone with information come forward and help them solve this senseless crime.

The rest of the article was filled out by the history of the shop and comments from well-wishers. It alluded to a recent uptick in violent crimes in the area but did not mention the bloody events of two years ago directly.

Max realized he was holding his breath and let it out it slowly. His knuckles were white on the mouse. He forced himself to let it go. He printed out a copy of the story. The newspaper and Chief Logins might not have any ideas, but Max was pretty sure he could guess the motive.

It was a message. A very clear message.

I'm still here. I haven't forgotten.

A message taken out on Stan, but meant for just one person.

HOOKED UP

When Danny regained consciousness, his shoulders screamed the loudest, but the rest of his body was a close second. There was a twisting pain in his gut, a tight band around his chest that made it hard to breathe, and hot spikes in both ankles.

He opened one eye and stopped trying to open the other when he realized it was swollen shut. He turned his head and threw up. The vomit ran down the side of his bloody sweatshirt and pooled at his feet.

His wrists were bound, and his arms were stretched up over his head, looped over a big steel hook. His legs felt okay, other than his ankles, maybe bruised, but not broken. He got his feet under him and, standing on his tiptoes, he could just take the pressure off his shoulders. When his ankles screamed in protest after taking the weight for a few minutes, he sunk back down on his arms. He alternated the pain this way until he heard a click and a scrape behind him.

"He's awake."

Danny used his toes to pirouette around and face them. Little John sat in a folding chair by the door watching him and picking his nails with a pocketknife. Frankie stood in the doorway and shook his head. He took out a cell phone.

"He's awake." He repeated into the phone.

Danny's calves started burning. He gave in and slumped down onto his arms. Pain stabbed into his shoulder joints. The hook slowly spun him around, so his back was to the door again.

"Comfy?" Frankie asked.

Danny bit down on his tongue to keep quiet and found he was missing a few teeth.

"Don't worry, Danny boy, it's almost over."

He started shivering. Frankie spun him back around and Danny noticed Frankie's winter coat. Little John looked comfortable in his short sleeves. He didn't tend to notice things like the temperature or the weather.

Danny pushed past the pain and looked around. Some sort of meat locker. Steel hooks hung on lines from the ceiling and a large refrigeration unit hummed in the corner. Shelves lined three of the walls. Packages wrapped in brown butcher paper or wrinkled cellophane sat neatly on the shelves. The other wall was empty except for faded red butchering stains splattered on the wall.

It was cold enough to see tiny stalactites of spit and perspiration hanging from Frankie's mustache. With Danny's nervous system overloaded with all the other injuries, cold must have seemed a low priority. Until now. He started shaking uncontrollably.

"He's not gonna die yet, is he?" Frankie asked.

"Probably just having a seizure."

The room telescoped down to a point of white, then winked out.

————

He woke up to Frankie waving a packet of pungent smelling salts under his nose.

"These babies come in handy for a situation like this. Now, don't you die on us yet, Danny boy. Mr. Carter would like a word first."

Carter walked in ten minutes later. He was dressed in black slacks and a cream-colored shirt that shimmered as he moved under the fluorescent lights. He didn't wear a jacket, and he didn't look cold. Maybe Frankie was just a wuss.

Carter had a dime for racketeering on his resume. A neighborhood menace and hardened criminal by the time he was ten years old, he'd been on the payroll of the local outfit by thirteen. He'd risen up the ranks with that rare and terrifying combination of intelligence and viciousness.

Danny knew he also considered himself a businessman first and hated to think his empire was stained in any way. The truth was that none of it was legit, not the city apartments won on a rigged bid, the padded construction contracts, or even the liquor license over his bar, but self-delusion can go a long way.

Danny knew all this and more. Anyone who grew up in or around the neighborhood did. It was impossible not to. Everyone also knew the thing that pissed Carter off the most, other than insinuating that he was nothing more than a two-bit petty criminal, was cheats. Carter took it as a personal insult. Yet Danny had done it anyway. He was double the fool, and it looked like he was going to be paying double the price.

"So, Daniel, Frank here tells me business is a bit slow."

He didn't wait for an answer. He lashed out with a vicious right to Danny's chin that Danny never saw coming.

The punch sent Danny rocking back on the hook, his eyes rolling up into his head. Frankie stepped forward to settle the chain and wave the salts under Danny's nose again.

"That's a funny state of affairs, Daniel, since we've been

delivering the same product to you, but the return envelope keeps getting lighter and lighter."

Another punch, this time a quick rabbit jab to the kidney that somehow hurt worse.

"Why is that, Daniel?"

Another, an uppercut to the stomach that made Danny cough up blood and mucus on his sweatshirt.

"Could it be you're putting it up your nose? Huh? You stupid little shit? Maybe pocketing a little cash? You really think we're that stupid? You think you can cheat me? You think you can steal from me?"

Each question was punctuated with a shot to his body. Left, right, left, right. He spun on the hook like a blood-soaked piñata. He could hear Carter breathing harder, exerting himself, throwing his weight into each shot.

He couldn't feel the punches land. Not anymore. Danny's body reached a precipice. It shut down. His mind detached. He floated. He felt next to nothing, just a gentle slap and a light breeze as he swung on the chain. It was as if he was already dead and just waiting for the conductor to come down the line and punch his ticket. And that thought made him decide he wanted to live. Desperately. And he did the only thing he could. It hurt worse than the beating, but he did it.

"Sthulvn."

Carter was too busy tenderizing his internal organs to hear, but Frankie did.

"I think he's trying to say something, Boss."

"What the fuck do I care," Carter said, but he stopped to catch his breath. "Go ahead, you little fuck, you got three seconds. Whaddaya got to say for yourself before we put you through the grinder?"

Danny concentrated. He spit up some blood. Even his tongue was trying to betray him. "Sshullivan."

Little John looked up. Everyone got real still. Little clouds of breath burst and evaporated in the air. No one said that name lightly anymore. No one definitely ever said that name to Carter.

"What about him?" Carter said.

"I know where he is."

"Bullshit," Frankie said. "Bullshit. Bullshit. Bullshit. C'mon, Boss, let's end this. He's just trying to save his own skin. It's the only chip he's got."

"That right, Danny? You just trying for a few extra breaths?"

Danny's head fell to his chest. So tired. He didn't want to betray his brother. But bruised and alone up on that precipice, the will to live, even for only a few more minutes, was too strong to resist. He'd cracked, and Carter knew it. The man could smell it.

"You know, Frankie, I think this cheatin' shit heel might actually be telling the truth."

"I know where he is," Danny repeated.

"Where?"

"I'll get him and bring him back."

Frankie barked out a laugh. "That's a good one, Danny boy. Nice try."

"It's the only way I'm telling." He looked away from Frankie and stared at Carter. "I'm more than half dead now. If you want, go ahead and kill me. But you'll never find him."

Frankie stopped laughing. He looked at Carter. "You really considering this?"

"How do you know?" Carter asked Danny.

"He called me."

"Why? Why now?"

Danny tried to shrug. "I don't know. Everyone wants to come home at some point."

"What did you tell him?

Danny laughed and blood dribbled down his chin. He

hadn't actually talked to his long-lost brother, but Carter didn't need to know that. "I told him to stay the fuck away. Forever."

"Get him down," Carter said.

"What?" Frankie said. "Boss, c'mon, the guy's just saying whatever you want to hear. He has no idea where Michael Sullivan is. No one does except the Feds. We'll get him eventually. Pete's working on it, but it's gonna take more time."

Carter held up a hand. "I know. Can't hurt to listen, though right? If that rat was going to call anyone, it would be this shit heel here. If he's lying, we can always bring him back and kill him after dinner."

SHOT OF RYE

Porter walked into the little diner and saw the sheriff sitting by himself in one of the two booths. A half-empty glass of beer sat in front of him. Porter ordered at the counter, then carried his beer over and slid into the opposite seat.

"Sheriff."

"Gaff."

"Anything on Stan?"

Like most locals, Porter's routine was to stop by the doughnut shop and grab a coffee and bear claw on his way to work. It was out of his way, but no one made a better doughnut in a fifty-mile radius, and one of the perks of running your own shop was that no one complained when you rolled in well past nine. With Stan still in a coma and the shop closed, he'd felt off-kilter in the mornings. He was a creature of habit, many bad, including caffeine and saturated fats. Out of some sense of loyalty, he'd resuscitated the old drip percolator he'd found in the office closet rather than go someplace new for his fix. It didn't make much sense, but it made him feel better.

"No, nothing."

"Off the record?"

"Doesn't make a difference."

"Damn."

"I'll drink to that."

Porter liked Logins, but it was an uneasy relationship. Both of them were always aware of the other's occupation and it stunted any true friendship that might have formed. From what Porter heard around town, Logins was a vast improvement over the last man to hold the office. Porter had arrived only six weeks after Sheriff Heaney and his brother were killed. At the time, Porter knew it was a big story, way bigger than was currently being told to the public, he could feel it, but he'd been too busy just trying to keep the paper operational to give it a good look. By the time the paper was steady enough for him to think of other things, the story had gone cold, completely and utterly cold. Too cold. Someone had buried it. Deep.

He'd started his file a few days later.

Both men were quiet for a bit, sipping their drinks and thinking their own thoughts before Porter spoke up again. "Monument still going up next week?"

"Far as I know." The sheriff's lips twisted down. Porter knew there was no love lost between Logins and the former sheriff, but they'd already had that conversation over other drinks in another place and Porter didn't want to rehash it now. He was pretty sure the sheriff didn't either.

"DEA still around?"

"Nope. Not really. They call once a month, but I think it's more a formality at this point. Marking a checkbox on some cover-your-ass form. Michaels is still in the wind and even his own agency doesn't seem too invested in finding him."

"What do you think?"

Logins gave a short laugh. "You know what? All those calls

and visits from the staties, DEA, and FBI, I don't think anyone's ever asked me that."

"I've run into that arrogance. No way a beat reporter could ever know something they didn't."

"Right. I learned that quick. Small town equals small mind. You'd think that stereotype would have faded by now. I guess ego is timeless."

Porter waited. In his experience, the government was often right in the larger sense, but not in the smaller one. Small town cops may not have the latest training, seminars, or equipment, but they knew their turf, knew their people, and had a certain insight into the quirks and behaviors that made their towns tick. Too often outside agencies wanted to apply the textbook theories and were unwilling to take a breath and just listen to the little guys.

"To answer your question," the sheriff said, "I think he's dead. And I think he pissed off enough people or knew enough secrets that no one is complaining now that he's off the board."

"That could be. What about his car? Out at the airport?"

"Misdirection. I think Strong or someone else drove it out there to slow us down. Muddy up the trail. It did the job. By the time we pinpointed the car, the case had been flagged as radioactive. No one wanted to push too hard and it will likely remain that way."

"What makes you think Michaels is dead and not just running?"

"From what the Feds deem to tell me, Michaels wasn't the type. He had no reason. Came up to Essex on a spur-of-the-moment thing. Chasing that first body. His ex-partner. The one we found in the tree. Nothing pointed to him running. The internal DEA investigation into him was done. He had survived with his badge. He was in the clear and back on the job. Just doesn't add up that he would bolt."

Porter could think of another reason. One he might share with the missing DEA agent. "Maybe he was just tired of his life. Sure, he survived with his badge, but what else? The idea of just dropping out and starting over has its appeals." He slid out of the booth. "You want another?"

"Nah, gotta get home."

Porter ordered a second, drank off the head of foam—Walt never could learn how to properly pour a beer—then went back to the table. Despite what he'd said, Logins hadn't moved and sat in front of his empty pint glass.

"So, you think Strong, or someone else, killed Michaels and disposed of the body?" Porter asked.

"Why not? Makes as much sense as the rest of it. Look around, there are plenty of places to hide a body out there, Gaff. Wouldn't be too hard to put it where someone would never find it."

"But why?"

They were each playing a part, like actors running lines. They had done this scene before, many times, but this is how cases were broken. You kept asking questions, even the same questions, and if at the end you still had nothing? You went back to the beginning and started again.

"Why? I have no idea. Just like half the questions in this case. Body up in a tree. Three dead civilians. Two dead cops. A missing DEA agent. A truly nasty biker bleeding out in the ferns next to some trailers full of meth. It's a jigsaw puzzle without any corner pieces. Hell, I'd like to find out, but you know I'm boxed in. I even look sideways at it, I get the mayor, state senators, staties, feds, anyone who's supposed to care stonewalling me. Telling me to drop it."

"They say that? To drop it?"

Logins sighed. "No, of course not. You're from the big city, you know how they talk. They're slippery about it."

"Getting cynical on us already, Sheriff? You haven't had the top job more than a year yet."

Logins sighed. "You're right. Maybe I am getting cynical." He picked up the pint glass and rolled it between his hands. "You know, when I was a kid, I loved the Cubs. Didn't matter that they were terrible, I loved them anyway. But you want to know the funny thing? Even at ten, I knew I was terrible at baseball. Just awful. I'd never make the high school team, never mind the majors. But I figured I could be the manager. Was there a better job than getting to fly around the country and watch baseball all day? You couldn't convince me there wasn't. I bet now I could name a hundred jobs better than being the Cubs' manager. Can you imagine? Dealing with the press, the GM, the talk radio, the Internet yahoos, the players, the egos, the constant travel, the second-guessing. No thank you."

"I'm sensing some parallels here."

"It just pisses me off sometimes that I can't actually do my job, you know? You're hired for something, but then cut off at the knees at every turn."

"Anyone in particular?"

Logins waved the question away. "Sorry to unload on you there. Just wish I could dig up some answers. Town might look like it's back to normal, but it's not."

"I've seen worse."

The sheriff raised his eyes. "Yeah, big city reporter, I guess you have."

Porter shook his head. "Not what I meant, Sheriff. I meant I've seen worse, much worse, things that would turn your stomach and people still somehow manage to move on. You're right. It's the ones with no answers that have a way of festering and shriveling up the soul."

The sheriff nodded and finally stood up. "What happened in those cases?"

"I saw good people waste away. You have to either push 'til you get answers or pull 'til you convince yourself there are no answers to be found."

"And if you can't do either?"

"I don't know, but you can't stand in the middle and survive."

———

The diner was good for a happy hour drink, but once Reggie left, it was better to find food somewhere else. Porter settled up his tab and moved next door to Casabellas. He picked up a couple slices to go and started walking home.

The morning bear claws and late-night pizzas weren't doing his waistline any favors. The twenty-minute walk would at least make him feel marginally better about his dinner choice. The smell of the grease and melted cheese made his stomach roll over. He folded one of the slices and started eating as he walked. It was still exercise.

He took the rutted brick path that led past the town green. When the Heaney brothers had been killed, there had been some question about what to do. The town had never had an officer, police or fire, die in the line of duty. Eventually, a small memorial in the town center was decided on. Next week, a small granite plaque and black obelisk would be placed next to the monuments commemorating the town's sons killed in the country's various wars. He paused at the two long columns from World War II. It was hard to wrap his mind around that many killed from such a small town. It must have left a gaping hole.

He walked on. Porter's mind drifted back to the Heaney case. In the town's collective consciousness, it was spelled with a capital T and C. The Case. It would likely be a long time before anything qualified to take its place. Maybe after exacting such a toll in bodies during the wars, the devil had considered Essex paid up for a while.

He found the case was never far from his mind. Sometimes he wondered if he obsessed on the events because he was an outsider now living in Essex or because he was a reporter. The case was like a kernel of corn stuck between his molars, to be picked and probed at in his idle moments.

Over the last year, he had quietly rebuilt his uncle's local network of gossip hounds, lonely housewives, and barflies. At first, he didn't even realize he was doing it. Cultivating sources and pulling information out of people was almost second nature to him. He quickly discovered everyone had an opinion, a theory, or some tenuous connection to the case they were happy to share. If even half of the stories he heard were true, it was no wonder the powers-that-be were happy to let it rot away without answers.

He might have lacked his uncle's vast network of local contacts that would have allowed him to trounce the bigger dailies on the story at the time, but he was still here long after everyone else had left. He had homefield advantage, an advantage he planned on exploiting for his book, whether it was true crime or fiction, he didn't know yet, and he wasn't sure it mattered. It was a hell of a story.

He now had a file six inches thick of notes, documents, theories, and outlines. Well-thumbed and smudged, they represented the running total of his informal inquiry. And so far, the only thing it was good for was filling his idle time.

He turned onto his street, the pizza already making the acid in his stomach bubble and protest. He rented the first floor of a double-decker in an older part of Essex. It was a mile outside of the town center in the shadows of the old grain mills that had once spurred the town's creation before the owners moved farther south in search of cheap land and eventually overseas in search of cheap labor.

To his eye, the houses in his adopted neighborhood looked comfortably aged. A few probably needed new roofs or a fresh coat of trim, but they had solid bones and would still be standing upright long after Porter was laid out. His upstairs neighbor was a divorced lawyer who commuted to St. Paul and worked long hours. He rarely heard, let alone saw, the man. The landlord hired a local kid to mow the lawn once a week and Porter had a number to call if something inside broke. The whole arrangement worked out fine for everyone.

After two years, the hiss of the radiators in the winter and the sounds of settling in the summer were familiar. It was home, even if sometimes he was loath to concede it. Right now, he was looking forward to nothing more than his second slice, a hot shower, and a final glass, or two, of whiskey. Maybe make a few notes from his conversation with Logins, while it was fresh in his mind, and then add it to the file in the morning. Keep pushing that rock as his dad used to say.

Porter walked up the cracked driveway to the rear of the house. He took out the last slice and threw the takeout container in the garbage. As he fit the dented metal lid back on the can, he noticed his back door was open. Had he left it open this morning? Maybe. He'd had that interview at nine and was running late. It wasn't like him to forget, but it was possible. He pushed the lid of the can down tight and stepped inside. He nearly tripped over the small table he kept by the door for his wallet and keys. The kitchen was ransacked. Nothing appeared broken, but everything was strewn over the floor and counters.

"Shit," Porter sighed. He put the slice of pizza down on an overturned plate. He shut the door and turned the latch lock.

He was too tired to muster up any other reaction over being robbed. The lawyer's car was gone. No use trudging upstairs to ask him if he heard anything. To the left of the rented house was a tall fence that blocked any view of the back door or driveway. To the right lived Mrs. Baldwin, an older shut-in in her eighties. Judging by the typical volume of her television, it would take an act of God for her to hear something going on outside her field of vision.

He picked his way through the kitchen to the hall. The back door opened into an eat-in kitchen before leading to a central hallway that branched off into a living room and bathroom on the left and two bedrooms on the right. Porter used the second bedroom as an office and general storage.

It wasn't so much the robbery itself—his insurance would cover anything of value—it was the thought of cleaning it all up that made him want to sink to the floor and take a nap. Who knew a divorced bachelor had so much crap?

He walked through the living room. He was surprised to see the television still sitting on the milk crates. It wasn't the newest or most expensive model, but it wasn't cheap either. Lyla had kept the television from their Chicago apartment, and he'd bought this one after he moved to Essex. They'd also left his guitar, a '66 Les Paul, propped in the corner. His classic western movie posters were pulled off the walls and scattered. He picked up *Stagecoach* and leaned it against the wall. The frame was cracked, but the print looked untouched.

Even the books still sitting in the leftover moving boxes, he hadn't yet gotten around to buying shelves, were tossed out and emptied. The sofa cushions had been cut open, and he stared at the white synthetic tufts bursting from the slits in the fabric as he tried to make sense of what looked like a very odd robbery.

He turned and walked across the hall to the bedroom.

Clothes were tossed on the floor. He absently picked up a couple shirts. The mattress had obviously been moved, but a couple twenties still sat pinned under a paperweight on his bureau. Why break in and not take the easy money?

A slippery coil of nerves tightened around his stomach.

He dropped the shirts and walked back down the hall to the office.

The same chaos greeted him in here too, only this time they'd taken a big-ticket item. His personal laptop was missing. He had bought one for the paper but still had his older model at home for personal projects. It was gone. Digital camera, printer, and fax machine still sat on the desk, but a square, dust-free spot was empty in the middle of the desk. He picked up the camera. The memory card was missing.

Porter slammed a hand down on the desk. "Dammit."

Kurt Russell and Val Kilmer stared down at him from a sepia-toned *Tombstone* print but offered no help.

He tried to think about the last backup he'd done and what he might have lost. A small metallic rattling sound interrupted his thoughts. He knew that sound. The loose inner knob. Someone was trying to open the door.

He grasped in his pocket for his cell phone, then realized it was pointless. Any response would be far too late. It wouldn't take long to get past the simple latch on the door.

Porter looked around the room. Had someone been waiting for him to come back? He didn't keep a gun in the house and his only weapon options were a dull letter opener from the desk or a can of compressed air he used to keep the laptop keyboard clean. He picked them both up.

He listened again and heard the small creak of the floorboards under the linoleum in the kitchen.

They were inside.

"Go away, go away, go away," Porter whispered.

The footsteps turned and started coming down the hall. Porter stood still and listened to their approach, a slow scuffling of soles on wood. They weren't trying to hide. They knew he was home.

Porter's hand felt slick on the metal can. His whole body was rigid, staring at the open space of the doorway.

The footsteps hesitated by the bathroom door, then kept coming.

Porter's heart pounded hard against his ribs. His vision narrowed to just the doorway. His breathing sounded like a hurricane in his ears.

A silhouette filled the doorway.

"Mr. Gaffigan?" The voice was bland, calm, and neutral. It matched the man.

"Who are you?"

"Not important."

Porter would never know if Mrs. Baldwin heard the shots.

A PAPER GHOST

Kate walked into the office and dropped her bag on the table, then fell onto the couch under the windows.

"Where've you been? You said you were leaving the courts an hour ago." Jaimie said.

"I did."

"And?"

Jaimie must have caught something in her face. She started to stand. "Are you okay? Did something happen?"

Kate waved her back down. She wasn't in the mood to be mothered. She was still pissed at herself for missing the tail.

"Yeah, I'm okay. It's a long story, but the bottom line is we have a new client and a fat retainer."

"But?"

Kate recounted the story. It took almost a half-hour and she left out nothing. Embarrassing or not, Jaimie needed to know their client was the type of guy to stalk potential business partners and do it well enough that a seasoned PI like Kate missed him until he was almost close enough to tap her on the shoulder.

When she was done talking, Kate got up and went over to her bag. She pulled out the short page of notes she'd taken, along with the blurry photo, and handed them to Jaimie. "Let's start by seeing what we can dig up online. Smith said he'd been looking already, but it can't hurt to make sure. I'm going to grab a shower and wash this slimy feeling off. If we didn't need the money ..."

"Not every client is a saint, Kate."

"Not even half of them are saints, but this one makes the hairs on my neck stand up. And not in a sexy kind of way."

She let Jaimie get started and walked across the hall. She opened the door and immediately felt a little better. Her apartment had the same big windows as the office next door, but they faced west instead of north and caught the full afternoon sun.

On days like today, the late light streamed in over the top of the Chicago skyline and cast everything in a golden summertime haze no matter the season. Walking in that warm light, Kate always felt like she was living in the old family photo albums her dad used to keep in his bedroom closet.

The apartment was a large modified loft. The kitchen, living and dining rooms were in the big open room off the front door. Her father had carved out two bedrooms and a full bath off the living room to the left. It was much more than she would normally be able to afford in this neighborhood. Say what you want about George Willis, and Kate could say plenty, but the man had a knack for seeing potential in real estate.

Renting the office across the hall had been a stretch back in '72, but her father had been right about the type of clients an uptown address would attract. By the time the accountants across the hall had gone bankrupt in '77, Kate's mother was gone and her father had enough scratch and savvy to jump on the open lease. The economy was in the tank across the country, and her father had negotiated an ironclad rent-controlled lease. He'd converted the old office to a living space himself, and he had saved on childcare by just keeping the two doors open as he built up his business next door.

She stood looking out at the green edges of the nearby park and the sliver of river beyond. She stayed there for five minutes, letting the light wash over her and relax the knots in her shoulders. She was grateful her dad seemed to be talked out for the day.

She felt better still, more focused and optimistic, after a hot shower. Looking at the big picture, she had a client, a retainer, and money to spare in the till. Yes, the client raised her hackles, but she would just have to be careful.

She and Jaimie were good at missing person cases, and they typically weren't as tawdry as the marital stuff. After any marriage work, Kate felt like standing in a carwash to get the stink off. For long nights in a car, with an even longer lens, the money was bad, and each time she delivered a report she felt a little chip flake off her soul. In flush times, she would always turn such cases down, but flush times had been pretty thin lately. She'd had five maritals in the last three months. This case should keep any honeypots and nooners off her docket for at least a couple months, maybe longer if they were careful about expenses.

She cut up an apple, then grabbed a seltzer from the fridge before heading back across the hall.

When she walked in, Jaimie's long, vibrant nails were clicking over the keys and the printer was humming with activity. The two desks they used were pushed together and sat bumper to bumper like cars in opposite parking spaces. At a glance, you'd think Kate worked at her desk every day while Jaimie was the one out doing the legwork.

Kate's desk was awash in newspapers, files, copies, old

receipts, takeout menus, and loose-leaf pages of notes. Jaimie's desk looked like an Ikea catalog spread: neat piles of correspondence in wire baskets, color-coded folders, a jar of pens, two monitors, a fax machine, a computer, and a large desk calendar.

Kate sat down in her dad's old swivel chair. It was one of the few pieces she'd kept around when she'd redecorated the office. His sweat and aftershave were baked into the cracked leather. She would keep it until it disintegrated.

"Solve it already?" she asked.

"Well, you were right to think that the name Max Strong sounded familiar. He was the primary suspect in that big dustup a few years ago over in Minnesota. Essex, Minnesota, to be exact. Small town northwest of Minneapolis. Remember that?"

Kate drew a blank. "Remind me again."

"You remember. Happened over a weekend down there. Looking back at all the clippings, I'm not sure they ever sorted it all out. Seems like the whole mess just fizzled out. Or was covered up. Regardless, whatever *did* go down, no one seems to question that our missing man Strong was smack in the middle of it. His landlady and girlfriend were killed. A biker on the most wanted list was also killed, though perhaps mourned less. His roommate and a federal agent disappeared into thin air. Not to mention two of the town's three full-time cops were also killed in the line of duty. All in one day."

"Jesus, that's right. Drugs, wasn't it?"

"Yup. Part of it, at least. Meth cook trailers out in the woods. The banger bled out on his Harley's handlebars. Here," Jaimie pulled sheets off the printer and handed them across the desk, "these will refresh your memory."

"Weren't we—"

"Yeah. We thought about dipping our toe in that pond when Strong up and vanished. There was a hefty reward at the time. I'm sure most of the PIs between Detroit and Denver thought about it. But then Joe threw the Gonzales thing our way and, well, you remember that one. After all *that* shit went down, the moment had passed. Strong was in the wind, any trail was ice cold, and it looks like it stayed that way, too."

Kate rubbed at the scar through her shirt. She had no trouble recalling the Gonzales case. She woke up at least once a week back in that house, his rancid breath on her neck and the pressing cut of his blade on her chest. She could feel the wound throb as if it knew she was thinking about it. She was in the hospital for six weeks recuperating. Maxed out her insurance and probably ended up on a naughty list, do not ever insure this woman again, but they'd paid in the end. It's bad PR to nickel-and-dime a hero. The mental recovery was taking a bit longer. She pretended not to notice, but her fingers still shook when she stripped her Bobcat down to clean and check the rounds. Mr. Smith was lucky this afternoon that she hadn't shot first and asked questions later.

"They never caught up with Strong?"

"Nope. Not a sniff. Not that I can find."

"Takes some real effort to stay hidden these days."

Kate skimmed through the printouts. There were stories from CNN, the AP, the two big Twin Cities dailies, her own *Chicago Tribune,* plus it was juicy enough for spreads in *People* and *Time.* She was only through the first quarter of the pile. They ran the gamut from investigative to more salacious, but they all ended the same way: dead bodies, Max Strong vanished, and lots of unanswered questions.

As expected, the two big locals had the most coverage. The *Pioneer Press* had stayed on the beat and had a follow-up piece on the one-year anniversary. But the passage of time hadn't unearthed any new clues. The reporter had gone down to Essex and hit a lot of brick walls. Reading between the lines, Kate got the idea that he received a pretty hostile reception when he even tried to ask.

"This is just the public stuff. I'll start digging a little deeper next, but it's odd, huh? It's like only half the story was ever written."

"Yeah. Funny the way that works sometimes." Kate gave her a thin smile.

"You think someone with juice was involved?"

They were both thinking about a recent past case where a city councilman and the public safety commissioner had steered an abuse case into indefinite limbo. She'd pocketed the favors because she had few other choices, but it hadn't sat well with either of them. It still didn't. She'd promised herself that she would balance those scales one day.

"Maybe. Fireworks like that? Must have drawn a crowd. All those agencies? Still unsolved? Have to be some major leverage to make it go away."

"Maybe everyone involved was just happy to let it go."

"What I'm reading here," Kate waved the sheaf of printouts, "shit hit the proverbial fan hard down there. Wide debris field. Someone knows something. They're just not talking. Keep digging. Anything on Strong himself? Background? Record?"

"So far, he's squeaky clean. A square citizen. Not even a speeding ticket."

Kate ate her apple slices and let Jaimie work. She'd decided a long time ago that she would rather forgo a salary and be on the brink of bankruptcy before she let Jaimie go. Kate knew she didn't have half the computer skills Jaimie did, and increasingly the majority of PI work was done jockeying a keyboard or phone from behind a desk. She was invaluable to Kate's business.

Not that the job was all bits and bytes and Googling. There was still a human element, and Kate had a few tricks of her own. She shuffled the papers until she had the one she wanted, then picked up the phone. Richard Daniels picked up on the third ring.

"Daniels."

"Hey, Rich, it's your favorite PI."

"Hi, Kate."

"What, no friendly sexual banter?"

"Sorry dear, I'm working on forty-eight hours without sleep and a deadline staring me down. Couldn't get it up if I tried."

"Not even for me? You hurt my feelings. Do it again next time and I'll think I'm losing my looks."

"Did Jaimie get her license yet?"

"No."

"Then don't worry, you're still the hottest PI with a concealed weapon in Chicago."

"Very funny. Listen, do you know a colleague of yours there, uh," Kate picked up the printout and looked at the byline again, "Charles Zamora."

"Sure, Charlie Crimetime. I remember him. A shame what happened."

"A shame?"

"Oh. I thought that's why you were calling. He had some chops. Wouldn't let a story go. Wasn't long for the crime desk. Got hit and killed while he was jogging, I don't know, uh, probably six months ago now. I was out of town at the time, helping cover the local delegation at the convention in Boston. Way I heard it, he was jogging down by the lake. Early. Not unusual for him. One of those foggy mornings and someone came around a curve and clipped him. Pronounced DOA at Mercy. Hit and run, ironically, given his beat. Never caught the perp, as far as I know. Why are you asking?"

"Damn. I was hoping to talk to him about a case I'm working. You remember anything about a big meth bust in

Minnesota a couple years ago? Bikers, ATF involved. Bunch of citizens ended up as collateral damage. Suspect in the wind. Made the national news for a bit."

"Minnesota?" He laughed. "Kate, unless it had something to do with the caucuses or they caught a congressman smoking that meth himself, I wouldn't know."

"Okay, thought I'd ask. Thanks, Rich."

"Anytime."

Jaimie raised an eyebrow at her.

"Daniels. Shot in the dark. Figured I'd see if I could talk to the guy who wrote the original *Trib* story, get his feel on the whole thing."

"And?"

"And he's dead."

"No shit. How?"

"Hit and run while he was jogging by the lake."

"Anything funky?"

"Daniels didn't think so. Bad shit happens. Anything on Strong yet?"

"The only significant thing is that I've got nothing."

"Nothing? Driver's license?"

"Nothing. He's a ghost. According to the usual sources, he didn't exist until he popped up in Minnesota three years ago, and he doesn't exist since he left."

"Ex-con? Coming off a long stretch?"

"My first thought, too, but it doesn't look like it. Not unless he went in straight from juvie. Cons usually have large gaps in their history, but there usually *is* a history—a prison sheet, something. Strong literally has no paper on him before Essex. Then everything's normal. Worked at a doughnut shop. Paid his taxes. Used an ATM card regularly. Made and paid his credit card charges. Had a cell phone plan."

"And nothing since? Not a peep?"

"Nothing."

"Changed his name?"

"Not officially. We'll never be able to tell if he just purchased or created a new ID, but that's hard to pull off for your average citizen."

Kate stood up and started tossing darts at the paper target on the back of the office door. "You are not describing an average citizen."

"True. Might not be a con. Might be law enforcement. Undercover thing. But either one would likely know their way around creating a new ID and how to avoid the traps that would show up in searches like the ones I'm doing."

"A cop that just pops up without a history than disappears again. Not likely," Kate countered.

"I could see it. Undercover thing goes seriously wrong. All those innocents dead. No one would want the spotlight for that. Could explain everyone's sudden lack of interest, too."

"If that's the case, then we have little shot unless we happen to run into the guy on the street. Let's table that one for now and go with the possibility that he's out there. That we can find him. Too early to get cynical." She retrieved the darts from the door. "Maybe he's just lucky. Slipped the manhunt. Just wandered off the grid completely, working menial jobs, cash for everything. Lots of folks are living in the margins like that."

"Sure, but for Joe Six Pack that takes an enormous amount of self-discipline and effort, living unplugged, unconnected to anyone, unable to trust anyone."

"Tough, but not impossible."

"Next to impossible. And, certainly impossible for me to track from here."

"Keep at it. If he's out there, he's leaving tracks of some kind."

"I'm going to hit my ceiling soon. We got room for expenses?"

"We've got some money to burn." Kate tossed the last dart, hitting the target right between the eyes, then headed across the hall.

"Where you headed?" Jaimie called.

"Only one place I can go—Essex. Start at the beginning."

"Everyone leaves a trail."

Kate smiled. "Exactly. You just have to know where to look."

RIGHT AFTER III

Alexei landed hard, stumbled forward in the dark, and rolled the ankle on his good leg. Pain screamed up his wounded leg when he tried to shift his weight to compensate. He went to his knees and remained there, head bent, sucking air through his teeth until his vision cleared and the pain receded enough for him think about what to do next.

First, he tightened the tourniquet on his leg. The fall had ruptured any clotting that had started, and Alexei could feel a thin line of blood running down his shin into his shoe. He'd also scraped the side of his head on the way down and could feel more blood matting the hair over his right ear. He probed with his fingertips but found only superficial scrapes. He dismissed it.

It was dark at the bottom of the narrow shaft, but not quite pitch-black. He looked up. He'd fallen twelve to fifteen feet. The daylight slanting in from the hole in the mill's floor was enough to make out shadows and depressions.

The grate had emptied into a tunnel of some sort. He moved in a slow circle to get his bearings. The tunnel extended to the right and left, angled to run under the mill. Alexei could only see a few feet in each direction before darkness swallowed the rest. The walls were smooth, solid, and moist. He scratched with his fingernail: hard-packed earth, fieldstone—manmade, but definitely dirt, not concrete. Water dripped slowly down the sides, pooling in the concave center before trickling off into the dark.

It was old, but it had been made for some purpose. Alexei looked up again to orient himself, then faced east toward what he judged was the shorter end of the mill and started to make his way slowly into the dark, hunched over and dragging his bloody leg.

After forty yards of slow progress along the slick, muddy floor, Alexei couldn't ignore it, the tunnel was narrowing. Each exhale of his sour breath echoed back closer than the last. He felt like a mouse being slowly swallowed by a hungry snake.

He kept going.

Another two hundred yards and he guessed he was close to the outer wall of the mill. Yet, the tunnel extended onward. No light and no end in sight.

He kept moving.

Another twenty yards and he was forced to crawl on his elbows, shifting his hips and dragging his legs behind him. It was a familiar rhythm from his soldier days, but not comforting. His wounded left side pulsed as he dragged it through the dirt. Still no light ahead. And now nothing behind, either. He was blind. The blackness surrounded him like a shroud.

He let his mind go blank and crawled farther. Three hundred yards? Four hundred? He lost track. His back scraped against the top of the tunnel. Each foot gained was a struggle. He could feel the earth above pressing down on his back. He couldn't turn around. He didn't think he could get any traction to move backward with the bullet in his thigh anyway. It was either go forward and make it out, or die here, wedged in the rocks and dirt, a curious fossil to be found and debated in later millennia.

He inched forward.

He was pressed flat on his belly now. His head was wrenched to the left, pebbles and sand scratching his face. His shirt was shredded. Just breathing was difficult. His head felt fuzzy. The tunnel pressed down harder. He closed his eyes. It was no longer dirt and rocks, but the rough, nail-chewed hands of Vladimir Polstin pushing him down. St. Kristof's fiercest bully was a plague on Alexei for seven long years in the orphanage. Vlad cornering him, throwing him down, pressing his face into the rough fabric of the bedspread, taking his air, making him cry. But the fear only sticks until it's bested. Alexei beat Vladimir. Alexei still sometimes dreams about Vlad's screams as the janitor's old trap snapped over his leg. The memory still makes him smile.

Alexei opened his eyes.

He pulled in another shallow breath.

He inched his hips up and lurched forward.

And met solid earth.

Pebbles cascaded down into his hair. He reached out to either side. More dirt. The tunnel had caved in.

It was a dead end and he was a dead man.

He tried to move backward, but only wedged himself in tighter. This had been a one-way ticket.

He pushed his arm forward again, feeling more carefully. Nothing but clods of earth and debris from top to bottom.

He tried to remember to breathe. His thoughts were loose and wandering. Moscow. Leningrad. Natasha. An alley in Prague. Afghanistan. Vladimir crying and holding his bloody stump. He pushed against the tide of memories.

He scooped up a handful of dirt and pushed it behind

him. What choice did he have? He would move forward, one
handful at a time.

He resisted the impulse to claw at the dirt and throw it
behind him. He had to go slow, conserve oxygen, and
preserve the already weak tunnel. Another cave-in would be
the final coffin nail.

He scooped out the sand and gravel and pushed it down
the sides of his body as far as he could reach. He fell into a
steady rhythm but could feel time working against him. The
air felt thin and dry. It stuck to his throat and wouldn't fill his
lungs. He took shallow sips and forced his hands to keep
digging.

He contorted himself in the cramped space, forcing his
arms and shoulders to keep moving. Move forward, grab
some dirt, slide his arm back, release. His fingertips were raw
and bleeding after the first hour. The pain became an ally. It
focused his mind on the present. It built to a burning
crescendo, then crested and became part of him. He felt
nothing but the rough kiss of the dirt on his cheeks and the
cool earth packed in his palms. He kept digging.

Sometime later, long after time had become taffy in his
mind, he pushed his arm forward to grab another handful and
it came back empty. Alexei tilted his head forward and
squinted against the harsh square of light. Alexei moved his
arm to the side to widen the hole. He blinked his eyes to clear
the dirt. Opened them again. The light was still there. A star-
ling watched him from the scaly branch of a birch tree.

A light breeze eddied in and filled his cramped tomb with
fresh air. It was a jolt of pure electricity. He sloughed off the
wounded, dying creature that had existed in the tunnel. He
became himself again. A man you crossed the street to avoid.
A man you quickly cut your eyes away from. A dangerous
man. A predator.

Even as his mind rebounded, he couldn't deny the toll on his body. He was very weak, too weak to walk. He was dehydrated and he'd lost a lot of blood. He didn't care. He hadn't dragged himself through hell to now die in the woods like a wounded animal. Wasn't a wounded animal the most dangerous? He grit his teeth and bit down on that thought.

The sun was almost down, its last light slanted over the roof of the abandoned mill. He crawled back to the parking lot and saw that Max hadn't bothered with the car. Only now did he let his thoughts off their leash. With his car, he was going to survive. He was going to get his revenge. He put his head down and kept moving.

He crawled across the cracked pavement, leaving drops of blood and clods of dirt in his wake. He pulled open the driver's side door. The keys hung in the ignition where he'd left them hours before. Or was it days? Time still felt soft. Had it really only been hours? He pulled himself up and sat in the driver's seat. He watched his hand shake as he reached for the door handle. He couldn't make it stop.

His cell phone sat in the car's cup holder. He dialed Drobhov's number, waited ten rings, then hung up. He laid his head back against the soft headrest. Two minutes later he tried again. Still no answer. It told him all he needed to know. He had failed. His boss was dead. He was on his own.

Alexei pulled some leftover napkins out of one of the fast-food bags that sat in the passenger footwell, did his best to wipe the mud off his face and smooth his hair down flat. He didn't need some bored townie cop pulling him over just to hear the story of how he found himself driving a Town Car perforated with open wounds and slathered in foul-smelling mud. Not to mention the shredded fingertips that would hand over a fake license and registration. He used all the napkins, and, when he looked at himself in the car's rearview mirror, he figured he would pass inspection from a distance.

He pulled a folded state map out of the glovebox. His fingertip left a faint pink line as he traced the thin blue and black lines outward until he found the small town of Hannaford. It was the one thing he always insisted on when they set up a long-term operation. If they couldn't bring along their own, they needed to buy some doctors.

Drobhov had once needled him about it all the time, calling Alexei their wet nurse and telling him he would look pretty good in a white uniform. That all stopped when Drobhov caught a bullet that collapsed a lung during a botched deal back in Kosovo. Alexei had a doctor on the payroll within five miles that saved Drobhov's life. He never mentioned Alexei's little quirk again. He just gave a curt nod when Alexei mentioned it during a job's prep.

When they made the move across the ocean to America, it was no different. Drobhov set about navigating the political and competitive landscape of their new home, while Alexei focused on the tactical: guns, cops, foot soldiers, and doctors.

Alexei didn't know if it was because they spent so many thankless hours saving other people or the easy access to so many narcotics, but Alexei always found a ready supply of corruptible doctors. The ones who had already lost their license were simple to turn; the others only needed a bump or nudge to put them in a precarious enough position that taking Alexei's offer was their best worst choice.

———

After ninety minutes of careful driving, never above the speed limit, Alexei passed the quaint wooden sign announcing his arrival in Hannaford. Three more turns and he came to the gray weathered placard hanging askew from a rusting post.

The letters "Michael Hobbes, DVM" in small black letters were faded and hard to read. Alexei turned and winced as the car bumped down the rutted and unpaved drive.

The small parking lot that wrapped around the tidy white house was empty at this hour. Not that it would be any different during the day. The good doctor had drunk himself out of a license before turning to pills.

Alexei pulled around back and drove onto the grass. He left the car close to the back door so it wouldn't be seen from the road. It had taken everything he had left to keep his eyes open and the car on the road. Now, he opened the door, slid sideways, and fell out.

———

He woke up with a gasp as a jet of cold water hit him in the face before moving to his chest. He opened his eyes and saw a pair of mud-stained green boots.

"Used to wash the pigs and horses in here. Never thought I'd be spraying down a human being."

Alexei was naked and shivering too violently to respond.

"Gotta get that mud off and see what we're dealing with. Don't worry, I can see those two big ones. I won't spray 'em."

Alexei looked up from the oversized shower stall and saw a man in faded blue jeans and a red chambray shirt over the boots. Hobbes. A year older but the same man Alexei had visited. He was holding the nozzle of the hose in one hand and sipping from a chipped coffee mug in the other.

"Don't worry, I remember who you are. Or at least what you are. I don't need a name." He kept spraying. "Try to roll over a bit. Let me get your back." More cold water. "That's it. Good." Alexei couldn't feel his leg, but didn't know if that was an effect from the wound or just the numbing water.

After another minute of soaking, the water stopped.

"That should do it." Hobbes hung the hose from a hook on the wall and tossed an old threadbare quilt at Alexei. It smelled faintly of hay and manure. "Like I said, I know what you are. You remember what I am?"

Alexei nodded, still too cold to talk.

"Must be hard up then, huh?"

Another nod.

"Course you are. Not so hard up that you didn't have a plan if you needed one. Anyone coming after you? Cops?"

Alexei shook his head. Some feeling was starting to come back into his toes and hands.

Hobbes held out a hand. "Right. No more peanut gallery." He took a sip from the mug and looked at the blood pooling around Alexei's bare feet. I assume you'll be paying?"

Alexei nodded. "T-t-trunk."

"Okay. Long as we got that settled. Let's get you inside and take a look." Hobbes got an arm under him and helped him to his feet. Alexei left the wet stable blanket on the floor.

Hobbes led him to a steel table then pushed a bright overhead lamp back so it wasn't directly in Alexei's eyes and looked over his wounds.

"Now, I can't promise you anything, but I should be able to patch you up and give you something for the pain until you can get to a real doctor."

Alexei gripped the man's arm. Hard. "You do it."

The man lost the joking, put-upon tone for a moment and looked Alexei in the eye. "Look, buddy, you're pretty shredded up here. The shoulder at least is infected. I'm just a vet, but even I can tell that much." Alexei could smell the whiskey on the man's breath. "I treated horses, cows, dogs, the occasional rabbit. Not humans. Even before the drink got its hooks into me, I couldn't do this. You're going to need some real help. From a real doctor."

It was dark outside the circle of the bright halogen. Alexei couldn't see much. He could smell the dust and disuse. Alexei took the cup from Hobbes' hand and threw it into the dark. "Get sober, dig out the bullet, dress these wounds, and stitch me up. That's why we pay you."

"Buddy, you need more—"

"I heard you the first time, but it's not an option. It's you. Just do it. No excuses."

Alexei lay back on the oversized examining table, the stainless steel cold against his skin. He couldn't expose himself more or complicate matters by driving to another off-the-book doctor that might specialize in rebuilding shot up shoulders. They didn't exist. You made your choice and you stuck with it. For better or worse, Michael Hobbes, failed vet and whiskey hound, had to fix him up.

Alexei closed his eyes and passed out.

———

He woke up to the buzz of the rest of the overhead fluorescent lights humming to life in the operating room. Hobbes, dressed in frayed light blue scrubs, walked past. There were no windows, and the clock on the wall was fixed at 9:28. His internal clock wasn't any better. He closed his eyes again and listened to the high-pitched thrumming of the lights and Hobbes opening and closing drawers. When he opened them again, Hobbes was standing over him.

"Here, take these." He held out some pills.

The doctor's hand didn't shake. Much.

Alexei looked at the pills.

Hobbes put them on the table. "It would have been easier to kill you while you were passed out. Pills are iffy. I wouldn't leave it to chance like that. Trust me or don't. The white ones are antibiotics to slow down that infection that is eating you from the inside out. The blue ones are for pain. I don't care how tough you are. I haven't done this in a while. You're gonna want to take those even if they are expired."

Alexei picked the pills up and dry swallowed them.

"Good, let's get this over with. I'm dying for a drink."

Hobbes wheeled over a stand with an IV attached. The bag was filled with a clear liquid. "I'm not an anesthesiologist. Even when I was practicing, I had someone for that. It's too easy to screw up and kill someone. Even a drunk knows that. Didn't figure you wanted me calling anyone, so," he flicked a finger against Alexei's elbow to raise a vein, "best I can do is dope you up. This is morphine. Also past its due date, but it should still have some kick. Let's hope so, at least." He stuck the needle in.

Alexei knew it would also be easy to overdose someone with morphine, make them nice and comfortable and sure to never wake up again. He had a moment of panic and resisted the urge to yank the needle from his arm and roll off the table. Like the man said, trust him or don't. He put his head back on the table and took a deep breath.

"Count down from a hundred for me, will ya?"

———

He woke up with his head floating in a cloud of cotton. His tongue, rough and dry, was pasted to the roof of his mouth. He was in a narrow bed pushed up against a window. The moon was scraping the top of a cloudless sky. He guessed it was close to or just past midnight, what day he didn't know. He was still lost in time.

Next to his bed was a small table with a glass of water on a knitted coaster. A small, child-sized dresser was on the opposite wall. A door was closed at the foot of the bed. Another door to the left was open and showed a patch of hardwood floor and hallway.

Alexei started to reach out his arm for the water glass and a hot current of pain ran through him from the tips of his fingers to the bottom of his feet. He gasped and unexpected tears pricked the corners of his eyes. He slowly let his injured arm fall back to the bed. He rolled on his side and reached out with his other arm. He noticed he was still tethered to a slow dripping IV.

When he replaced the water glass, he noticed Hobbes in the doorway. In the yellow hall light, he looked even more tired and haggard. Dark circles pushed his eyes back in his head. Christ, Alexei thought, if the doctor looks like that what does the patient look like?

"I thought I heard some movement up here." The mug was back in the doctor's hand.

"How ..." Alexei's voice came out whispery and cracked. It clawed at his throat. The doctor held up a hand.

"It went fine. That's not to say good, but as well as could be expected, given the circumstances, I think. Then, again, that's a vet's opinion." He gave Alexei a small smile. The smile stretched the skin on his head and made him look even more skeletal and ghoulish.

Alexei had the sense that he was luckier than he first realized. Yes, he'd escaped the mill, but if he came back here in six months or a year, would Michael Hobbes still be here? Alexei had seen that hollow smile before. He'd seen it in the faces at St. Kristof's as the children aged; later, he'd seen it on entire families in the bomb-ravaged villages of Afghanistan and Bosnia. It was a smile of acceptance. A smile to welcome death. A smile because they could see it approaching now in the distance and they were waiting with open arms, not afraid but ready.

Hobbes flipped a wall switch and the overhead light filled his face and broke the illusion. He stepped to the bed and pulled the blanket down before he peeled back the dressing on Alexei's shoulder.

"This one was by far the worst of the two. A lot of infection and some internal ligament damage. I cleaned it out and stitched you up. You will not have full range of motion again. A good bit should come back in time, but not all." He prodded at the edges of the wound with his fingers. "The antibiotics should eventually take care of the infection."

He picked up a thermometer from the bedside table. "Which reminds me." He stuck it in Alexei's mouth. "Your color looks better, but let's confirm that your fever broke."

They waited in silence. After two short beeps, he put the thermometer back on the table next to the water glass. "Ninety-nine point eight. Not totally back to normal, but much better. After the surgery, you were up to almost a hundred and five. Close to the boiling point."

Next, Hobbes pulled the blanket all the way down. Alexei saw that he was wearing a pair of mesh gym shorts. Probably from Hobbes' own closet, though Alexei couldn't picture the doctor ever exercising.

"I guess it's all relative, but this one was better," Hobbes said. "The bullet lodged in your thigh. Missed all the bones and arteries, but tore up the quadriceps pretty good. It was in there deep, but nothing life-threatening. I dug it out and stitched you up. You'll have a wicked limp, but with some therapy you should be able to walk. Eventually."

He pulled the blankets back up. "I'll leave a couple pills here for the pain if you need them." He placed two oblong pills on the table next to the water glass. "Get some more rest. That's the best thing right now. Let your body heal. I'll bring breakfast up in the morning." Hobbes turned to leave.

"Wait."

Hobbes turned and looked at him.

"News?"

"You've been out for almost a day and a half. A lot of crazy stuff a few towns over in Essex. A bunch of bodies. Lots of rumors. No names I recognize. I'll bring the paper up in the morning." He pulled the door shut behind him.

Alexei waited ten minutes and then threw the blankets off and got slowly to his feet. He could stand, but if he tried to shift any weight to his leg, it threatened to buckle. He hopped over to the door on his good leg and turned the knob. It was locked. He pressed an ear to the door. The house was silent. The eight-foot journey had left him sweating and light-headed. Pathetic.

"I crawl through half a mile of muck, practically dig myself out of the grave, and now I can't even break out of a child's room. You are getting weak, Alexei. Soft."

He started to lean over and look at the lock, but suddenly felt like he was falling into a dark pit. He was back in the mill, jumping into the hole, only this time it wasn't his choice. Someone had pushed him. He straightened back up and grasped the knob for balance and waited, but the feeling of spiraling vertigo never left. If anything, it increased. He could feel bile rising in his throat. He turned around and hopped back to the bed.

He hesitated, then took the two pills and waited for sleep to steady him.

STRANGERS

Max's first instinct was always to run. He'd learned it early, and it had served him well. His darker impulses to turn and fight and keep on fighting until someone's blood had been spilled had never led him anywhere good. Based on recent events in Essex, that hadn't changed.

No, if someone's looking for a fight, the best thing you can do is take off. Man's survival instinct is stronger than the pull of gravity. Max felt that pull now from the pit of his stomach. He wanted to listen. He did. He wanted to run, hard and fast. Go to ground in a place that wasn't on any map. Take his meager cash, check out of his room, get on a bus and ride it to the end, then just keep on walking. Chase the sun until he was too exhausted to go any farther. Start over. Again.

He looked at the blotchy stains on the room's thin rug and the yellowed, smoke-stained walls. But would it ever be far enough? No. He could hide under a rock at the bottom of the world. Distance didn't matter. They would go on hurting Stan or the few others they could tie to him in some way.

They hadn't found him here. They didn't know where he was, but they had reached out and touched him anyway. That was the whole point of the message. Come to us or live with the consequences as we burn down your former life.

He read through the library printout again, not really seeing the words as much as feeling them. He decided to call the hospital. The motel room didn't have a phone. It had a jack, but it was five extra dollars a week for a phone, plus call charges. Max didn't make enough calls to justify the five bucks or the cost of a burner phone. He picked up his key and walked down the street to the Kwik Mart convenience store on the corner. It's where he bought most of his food and other sundry items. It also had a working payphone bolted to the side of the building.

Eugene nodded in recognition and changed Max's five without making Max purchase a pack of gum or anything else. Max thanked him and walked outside. He dialed information to find out the number of the hospital and then plugged a handful of quarters into the slot when prompted.

"St. Vincent's Hospital. How can I help you?"

"Stan Tucinni's room, please."

"Please hold," the switchboard voice said.

"Intensive care."

"Stan Tucinni's room, please."

"Are you family, sir?"

"Uh—"

"I'm sorry, sir, we can only connect family members at this time. Thank—"

"How's he doing? Just in general, could you at least tell me that?"

"I'm sorry, sir, we can't give out patient information. His condition designation is listed as critical, stable. That's all I can tell you over the phone. Thank you for calling. Have a good day." She hung up.

Critical. Stable. What did that mean? He stared at the graffiti scratched into the plastic phone enclosure. Was it critical: stable? Or critical, but stable? Critical, yet stable? More questions swarmed into his mind like mayflies. Was it good or bad? Improving or declining?

He did one of the old breathing exercises Dr. Fox had taught them in group. Half of the cons spent those sessions laughing and joking. The other half paid attention, maybe out of boredom, maybe out of desperation, but getting a little something out of the sessions either way. Stuck in a six-by-nine foot concrete box for twenty hours a day, Max thought Dr. Fox had probably saved his life. He focused on his breathing and felt the anxiousness and guilt recede a little bit.

There was no one else he could call. Other than the money for the invoices, that tiny filament of contact he maintained with Stan, he'd cut himself off from everyone else in Essex. He'd thought it was safer that way.

He replaced the receiver and collected a few coins in change from the slot. He went back into the Kwik Mart and bought a large coffee. He would try again later during a new shift. He'd be better prepared now for the questions; maybe he could finesse a little more information out of the next nurse. Max had always been a good liar.

———

He killed the last of his forced vacation days taking another long, wandering walk and trying to think about what he could do next without putting anyone else in intensive care.

He'd tried the hospital again but got no further with the next nurse. At least he knew Stan was still at the hospital. Would they try again? Probably not while he was in there. There was too much unnecessary risk. What would be the point? An exclamation point on their message? Would they try when he was released? *If* he was released? Maybe. Probably, if Max waited too long. And next time, Max knew, they probably wouldn't stop at a hospital.

He could feel the pressure in his gut increasing as he walked. Tick. One second gone. Tock. There goes another. Tick. Now a minute. He was on the clock and had to make a decision.

He went back to work the next day. He needed more cash and, short of robbing someplace, working was the easiest way to get it. He'd get paid on Friday and go from there. If Stan was in intensive care now, it was likely he'd still be in the hospital at the end of the week. He hoped that gave him some time.

At the diner, his coworkers welcomed him back like a conquering hero. It was embarrassing. Junior was telling the tale of the foiled robbery to any customer that would listen.

"... and he laid him out with one punch. Punk was out cold 'til the cops finally arrived ..."

Max smiled and took his place behind the grill. It was good to be back. He would miss the camaraderie. The sense of being missed when he was gone. It wasn't something he'd felt since the early days of running his crew and pulling jobs for Carter.

"Sorry I missed all the fun, bro," Ramon said when he walked in later that afternoon after classes.

Max had his arms in the hot water getting a jump on the dishes after the lunch rush.

"Don't believe everything Junior says. Trust me, it wasn't all sunshine and roses. It was dumb luck I didn't get shot."

"I don't know, man, the way Junior tells it, bullets would have bounced off your chest anyway."

"It was stupid and impulsive. I wouldn't suggest trying it."

"I'll tell ya, I wouldn't mind trading places with you now. Imagine the ladies I'd be bedding. You gotta get out there and market yourself. I look at your face, all tense and shit, and I'm positive you're not capitalizing on this situation. Not the right way, at least."

"A gentleman never tells."

Ramon shook his head. "Uh-huh. Goddamn monk."

"Stupid punk."

They both smiled. Max left him to the dishes and went to prep the vegetables for the next day.

———

Passing the Burger Barn on his way home, he spotted Spoon coming up the sidewalk, the worn-out, unstitched soles of his loafers slapping the pavement with each stride like large clown feet.

"Hey, friend."

"Sorry, Spoon. I didn't get paid today," Max interrupted, going past. "I got no money. End of the week, we'll get some burgers."

"Nah, nah, man. Hold up a sec. I don't want no money. I gotta ask you a question."

Max stopped. It was an awkward distance. They looked like two people waiting for the bus, not having a conversation. Max knew Spoon was oddly self-conscious of his body odor, though, and gave him his space.

Max had no idea why they called him Spoon, but everyone down here seemed to know his name and his game. Winter, summer, anytime in-between, you could find Spoon around Crosby Park, a concrete space that sat next to the Kwik Mart and the Esso gas station. He was bright and articulate. He constantly had a newspaper folded under his arm. Max knew a few folks had tried to help him out, get him in a shelter or offer him a job, but Spoon always refused.

"Go on and ask."

"I seen you around a bit now. What's your name again?"

"Matthew. Matt."

"Matt. Right, right. You living up in the efficiencies? Working at Junior's?"

"That's right." Max was a little disturbed at how easily Spoon had his life pegged.

Spoon looked at him and scratched his patchy beard with a dirty fingernail. Despite the mild fall weather, he was wearing a closet. A couple pairs of khakis, dress shirt, argyle sweater, red fleece and navy sports coat. "You sure, man?"

"About what? Where I live? Yeah, I'm sure."

"No man, the name. Matt. You sure?"

The question caught him off guard. Max's stomach dropped. It felt like Spoon had reached out and snipped his guidewires, left him untethered. Christ, was he sure? His life increasingly felt like a prism of different personas refracting and reflecting back on itself. So, no, Matt/Max/Mike wasn't actually sure. He pushed down the doubt.

"Yeah, Spoon, I'm sure. It's Matt."

The Kwik Mart payphone across the street started ringing, a tinny jangling sound that carried across the concrete.

"Goddammit. Stop, stop, stop." Spoon bent at the waist and started pulling at his greasy hair. "Make it stop, make it stop, make it stop."

Max stepped forward and put a hand on the man's shoulder. Spoon jumped away. "Hey, take it easy. It's just the phone."

They both turned and looked at the phone. After ten jangling rings, it went silent.

"See, no problem."

Spoon's breathing was still labored. He was obviously agitated. He took another step back to increase the space between the two of them. "No, it *is* a problem. Goddamn phone has been ringing all day. Can't sleep, can't eat, can't read, can't concentrate. It's driving me crazy." He paused and looked at Max out of the corner of his eye. "Well, more crazy." And flashed a smile full of rotting teeth.

"You answer it?"

"Sure, a bunch of times."

"And?"

"Guy asks for Sully. I say, 'Ain't no Sully here, there, or anywhere,' and then the guy hangs up. Half-hour later, phone rings again."

"Wait. Who does he ask for?"

"Sully. No first name, no last name. Just Sully." Spoon picked at something in his hair and flicked it off his fingernail. "You're kinda new. Seen you using that phone time to time. Thought maybe it was you. That's why I asked. But you're Matt, not Sully.

"I tell ya, I'd rip the damn thing off the wall if Eugene wouldn't have me arrested for vandalism. I need his bathroom for my morning constitutional. Still, I might do it if that damn ringing keeps up much longer. It just gets in your head, you know? Bounces around like a loose marble until you can't think of nothing else. Ring, ring, ring all the damn day. I'll sully that caller's ass he ever comes 'round here."

Max wasn't listening. He was still trying to process Danny calling him back. It couldn't be anyone else; it was too big a coincidence. It was Danny, and Max knew it wasn't good news. It was never good news with Danny. Christ, why now? He had too much other shit going on to deal with Danny's problems. But Danny had a special talent for calling at bad times and making it worse. The worst part was that Max knew this time it was mostly his fault. Most of his headaches and all his hangovers could, one way or another, be traced back to Danny. Except for this one. This one was all of his own making.

A couple weeks prior, after work, a double shift for him, they'd all gone out to a bar for Sue's birthday. He'd let them pull him along. In truth, he was lonely. One drink turned to two, then a couple more, then some shots. He liked a beer now and then, but he hadn't drunk like that since they'd actually pulled off the Suffolk job clean. The infamous last job for Carter. He stopped short of getting fall-down drunk, but not by much. He'd been careless. He remembered a sloppy kiss on the sidewalk, then groping in the building lobby before he awkwardly avoided going upstairs to Sue's apartment. It felt selfish, and he could see the hurt in her eyes and things had never been quite the same since, but he wasn't going to drag her into what little there was left of his life. And now he knew it had been the right choice.

He'd made the solitary walk home, each block passing with lit apartment windows and people being together. He took one look at his empty daily-rate apartment with its thin walls and cheap sheets and walked back out. He considered walking back to Sue's, it wasn't far, but he figured he'd burned that bridge and going back would just screw up any chance of rebuilding it. Instead, he crossed the street and called Danny from the Kwik Mart payphone.

"Hello? Who is this? Paddy? That you?"

As soon as he heard Danny's sleepy voice—or was he stoned?—everything came rushing back.

A car horn honked. The bell jingled over the Kwik Mart door as a guy came out carrying a carton of Marlboro Reds. There was a long pause. Maybe Danny felt the connection, too.

"Sully?" he whispered.

Max hung up.

It had been a mistake.

Too bad his mistakes always had the bad habit of boomeranging back on him.

"Hey, you all right man?" Spoon asked. "You look like you gonna hurl."

He shook off the memory and looked back at Spoon. "I'm good. Don't worry about the phone. I'll take care of it." Despite his earlier remark, he handed Spoon a five he couldn't afford from his share of the tips. "Get warm. Get some food."

He walked back to his room and changed out of his grease-spackled work whites. He was waiting by the payphone twenty minutes later. The streetlights clicked on. He stood in the shadows outside of the yellow circle of lamp-light and watched the patrons go in and out of the convenience store. Spoon hustled change from cars stopped at the intersection. Max scanned the park and the storefronts opposite. Seven minutes later, the phone started ringing again. He looked around and saw no one paying attention.

He walked over, picked up the receiver, and held it to his ear. He didn't say anything. He could hear someone breathing on the other end.

"I'm in trouble, Sully."

Max sighed.

It was hard to say no to family.

STRINGER

The following day, Mike Duffy was still smarting from Porter's criticism of his town meeting story. He knew the man was probably right. Hell, he had almost won a Pulitzer, he was definitely right, but it still stung. He'd rewritten it four times before he showed it to him. He kicked a small stone down the sidewalk as he walked toward town.

He'd spent two hours last night going over the story yet again, cutting anything he felt was superfluous. It was tough. He liked a lot of the lines he ultimately trashed. He thought it gave the story some personality. Still, by the end, he could see where Porter might have had a point. The revised version was lean and to the point.

Gotta toughen up, he thought. This is just a tiny hometown paper, a first baby step. Listen to him. Take his advice. No matter how bitter it tastes. Keep your mouth shut and just keep writing.

It was a familiar pep talk. He'd seen a Tony Robbins infomercial once and, while he hadn't actually ordered the tapes, some it of it sort of stuck. He'd developed a habit of repeating certain affirmations when he felt down.

He kicked the stone again and watched it skitter and jump toward the storm drain. It came to rest on the grate but didn't fall through. Duffy left it like that and kept walking. He waved to Mr. O'Neill and his standard poodle as the old man walked past on the opposite side of the street. At the corner, he ducked into Bleeker's Drug Store to get a cup of coffee.

"Howdy, Mike." Mr. Bleeker said from behind the old-fashioned lunch counter that ran across the back of the five and dime.

"Morning, Mr. Bleeker."

"What'll it be this morning?"

"Just a cup of coffee." Same as I've ordered every morning for the past year, Duffy thought. "To go." He wasn't sure if the old man was going senile or just never wanted to make any assumptions.

Bleeker filled the cup from a dented metal percolator that sat on the back counter. "Here you go, son."

Most folks went to Stan's or the diner for their java fix, but Duffy had always favored Bleeker's. He was convinced that years of grinds had flavored the percolator to provide a distinctive tang to the coffee. It couldn't be replicated at home or in a shiny new chain.

"Thanks, Mr. Bleeker. See you tomorrow."

Duffy paid him and left, pausing to study Essex High's sports schedule taped to the front window. The football team was awful, but both soccer teams were winning. Neither team was playing today. The boys' team had a home game tomorrow. Mike juggled his coffee in the crook of his arm and wrote the date in his notebook before walking on.

The *Essex Standard-Times* occupied two floors of the old brick general store. An office and meager staff space took up the second floor. The massive old printing press and the paper's archives were in the basement. The third floor had been vacant for the last year, after Jim Knox had a heart attack at his desk and his wife made him give up his accounting practice and move to Naples. Viva, a small women's boutique, took up the first floor of the building. Duffy could see Mrs. Olsen inside folding shirts. She looked up and smiled as he went past the window. He waved and blushed.

Upstairs, the door was locked. Duffy frowned. He was naturally an early riser, but, after a few false starts, had started coming in well after nine because Porter was most definitely not an early riser. Duffy had a key. Porter had had one made up after the third time he'd found Duffy waiting at the door like a stray cat. Duffy was still reluctant to use it. It felt like a violation, like walking into a stranger's bedroom. He preferred it when Porter was already inside.

He checked his watch. Porter had set the time. He had some idea about commemorating the paper's upcoming seventy-fifth anniversary with some antique issues and thought they could use the, now defunct, press in the basement to add some authenticity to the venture.

Duffy was beginning to think that maybe Porter was a touch manic-depressive. He'd have these fallow stretches where nothing seemed to matter: the paper, grammar, basic hygiene. Then, turning on a dime, he'd be freshly pressed and shaved with an idea and it was all hands on deck, guns blazing, until the idea came to fruition. The mood swings kept Duffy and Maureen on their toes. You never knew which Porter might show up.

After fifteen minutes, he had finished his coffee and could feel his bladder filling. Still no Porter. Where was he? Last year, back when Duffy was still in high school and filing the occasional movie or music review, Porter had gone on a ripping three-day bender, eventually surfacing just in time to get an issue out, with lots of help from Duffy. It had been long hours, but Duffy had had a blast. It was what gave him the idea, despite his parents' objections, to defer college and work at the paper for a year.

Duffy stood. Mrs. Olsen waved again and gave him a look through the window. He returned the look with a loose shrug that he hoped said, "Porter, what can you do?" He knew where Porter lived. Better to walk down and check on him than risk getting tongue-tied and embarrassed with Mrs. Olsen. He dropped his cup in the garbage and started walking.

———

Porter's little-used Nissan Sentra was in the driveway. Despite living in Essex for almost two years now, Porter still maintained his city habit of rarely driving. No one answered the bell or Duffy's repeated knocks on the front door. He walked around back. The door was shut, but not latched tight. He opened the screen and nudged it open further.

"Mr. Gaffigan!" No response. He called again out again. "Porter?" Like the office key, Duffy was still getting comfortable using Porter's first name. He had to force himself. "It's Mike." No answer. "Mike Duffy."

He'd dropped Porter off a few times, but he'd never been inside his house. He pushed the door open wider. The kitchen was a mess. No, he thought as he stepped inside and had a closer look, it's been ransacked. He felt his pulse kick up and his stomach drop.

"Porter?" It came out as a whisper.

He stepped carefully through the kitchen and started down the hall. Four framed western posters that had once hung in the hallway were now laying on the carpet like steppingstones. Duffy leaned them up against the wall to make a path.

The house was quiet. It felt empty. And there was something else. A smell.

The first room was the bathroom. The medicine cabinet was open, and the lid was off the toilet. Bottles of cleaning supplies from under the sink were scattered on the floor.

He moved on and looked in the next room to the right. It was an office. This room was in worse shape than the kitchen or the bathroom. Someone had taken their time. Everything was upended. Books tossed off the shelves. The old heating grates were unscrewed. Drawers were upended.

He almost tripped over Porter's body amid the books, folders, and old newspapers that littered the floor.

The two holes in his forehead were small. The circles ringed with dried, dark blood. Three fat flies had already found the body. Duffy felt the coffee rise and burn the back of his throat. He tripped, got back up, made it outside, and threw up in the empty flower pot next to the door.

DIGITS

After taking the cloverleaf exit off the highway, Kate followed the GPS prompts into the little strip mall on the right and killed the engine. The silence was nice, and she let her head tilt back against the seat. It was a few minutes past seven in the morning. The lot was almost empty, even as a flurry of commuter traffic buzzed past on the way to the interstate. The low-slung strip was filled with commuter-friendly stores: barber, coffee shop, mini-mart, pizza shop and video rental outfit. A retirement home sat across the street. Everything built for easy in, easy out access. Grab a coffee, get a trim, pick up the starched shirts, see grandma, be on your way.

One other car was in the lot, parked in front of a dry cleaner in the middle of the lot. Kate had parked on the end, in front of the coffee shop. She looked at the looping red script on the window that spelled 'Stan's.' It was dark and empty inside. It didn't look like it had gone out of business, with pots on the burners and sugar canisters on the counter, just closed. Shouldn't a coffee and doughnut shop be open at seven in the morning? Wasn't that primetime? Closed or not, she was getting out of the car. She had a desperate need to stretch her legs after driving most of the night.

The cool morning air was a tonic after the stale, recirculated stuff that had been blowing from the Acura's vents for the last nine hours. She arched her back, then reached over and touched her toes. Her spine cracked and popped like an old accordion. Her dad would always squirm and grimace at the sound. She felt a momentary thickness in her throat at the memory.

Stop getting sappy on me, Katie, and keep your eyes open. You're here to work, not reminisce.

She walked up to Stan's double doors and cupped her hands against the glass. She couldn't see anyone inside. She pulled on the door handles. Locked.

You're quite the detective.

"Can it, Dad. I just drove through the night. I'm thinking of breaking in just to make some coffee and use the bathroom."

"Who are you talking to, hon?"

Kate looked to her left and saw a gray-haired woman poking her head out of the dry cleaner's door. A pair of pink reading glasses hung from a thin silver chain around her neck.

"Oh, no one. Myself. Sorry, bad habit."

"Don't worry, I understand, dear. I'm my only audience most of the time too since my Don died. I have the best conversations nowadays." She nodded at a dead bouquet of supermarket flowers propped next to a support beam by the door. "Isn't it just a shame what happened?"

"Excuse me?" Kate said.

"Stan. You know about what happened to Stan, dontcha?"

"Um, no. Not really."

None of the printouts Jaimie had given her about the events in Essex that led to Max Strong's disappearance mentioned anything other than Stan being Strong's one-time boss. Given that the rest of the people mentioned in the stories were either dead or missing, Kate figured Stan was the best place to start.

Kate waved an arm at her car. "I just pulled off the highway. Saw the sign for 'Gas, Food, Lodging,' and my stomach spoke up."

"Oh dear. Well, Stan would have taken care of that." She smiled. "Probably talked your ear off, too." The old bird looked Kate up and down. "Or made a pass at you. Or all three." She laughed. Kate could hear a smoker's cough and a pack-a-day habit lurking in the woman's lungs. "That was Stan," the woman continued. Kate smiled along. "Stan was getting on in years, but boy he was a charmer. Your pants would start sliding off and you wouldn't even notice."

Despite the earlier mention of a husband, Kate thought she could hear the personal experience in the woman's voice. "I'm sure he was a nice man," she said. "What happened? Heart attack?" Given the woman's tone, Kate assumed Stan was dead. She mentally started flipping through the files trying to think of the next best person to approach. She hoped the long drive didn't turn out to be a complete waste of time. She didn't relish the thought of turning around and driving all the way back to Chicago.

"Oh no, dear Lord. Stan's still alive. At least last I heard." Her hand pulled at a loose thread from her cuff. "He was attacked. Right in there. Beaten very badly." The woman clutched her sweater closer. "I was right next door. Never heard a thing. Can't hear nothing over the steam cleaners when they're going. Not that I would have been able to do much other than call the police, and even then I'm not sure it would have made a difference in the end. But I still think about it."

"Attacked? Do the police know who did it?"

"No. I don't think the sheriff knows *why* they did it, let alone *who* did it."

"Where is Stan now?"

"I believe he's still in St. Vincent's. That's where I sent my flowers."

Kate started to ask another question, then realized she wasn't asking things that a typical highway drop-off would ask. She didn't want rumors spreading around town about a blonde woman asking a lot of questions. "That's so sad. I hope Stan makes a full recovery. Anywhere else you'd recommend for coffee around here?" Kate asked.

————

The woman's name had ended up being Lydia, and her suggestion to skip the mini mart on the corner and drive a mile further into town to the diner had been worth the extra ten minutes of small talk.

It was close to 8:30 a.m. by the time Kate had slurped down three cups of black coffee and a stack of buttermilk pancakes with a side of crispy bacon. She was feeling full and a little sleepy.

You can always tell the quality of a breakfast place by their bacon or home fries.

"No argument there, Dad." She murmured into her coffee cup.

There were a number of older men chatting about sports and weather at the counter, but the booths around Kate had emptied out while she ate. She paid the check and walked outside to call the office. Jaimie preferred to come in early and beat the rush hour traffic. She picked up on the third ring.

"It's me."

"How was the drive?"

"Straight, flat, and dark."

"I'd say that's how I like my women, but that's not exactly true."

"No, definitely not."

The last girlfriend of Jaimie's that Kate had met was a six-foot towering blonde with plenty of curves. "Dig up anything new?"

"No, nothing exciting. More articles and background. I'll start doing the real digging today. If I run into too many walls, should I try Miguel?"

Miguel was Jaimie's slightly disreputable hacker cousin. They had used him in the past when Jaimie had been unable or unwilling to jump behind some firewalls or security systems. He was good and he knew it; therefore, he was expensive, even with a family discount. It always made Kate slightly squeamish to deal with him, but she usually got over it when she looked at his results.

"Let's see how we do today on our own. I certainly don't think Mr. Smith would mind paying for it, though, if it came to that."

"All right." Kate heard keys clatter in the background. "I'll send you a message if I find anything."

"Okay. Oh, hey, wait. I almost forgot. The pancakes must be dulling my brain. Can you do a quick local search on the newspapers in this area? My coverage down here isn't great."

"Sure. What am I looking for?"

"Turns out Max Strong's old boss Stan Tucinni got himself battered last week. Pretty badly, too, according to the busy-body who runs the dry cleaners next door. He's still in the hospital."

"Okay. You just wanna hold? Shouldn't take long."

"Sure." Kate started walking down Essex's version of Main Street as Jaimie's nails clicked over the keys back in Chicago. She passed an older man walking a poodle and a young man looking pale and dazed, maybe hungover, maybe a touch of the flu. She gave him a wide berth. She didn't need anyone throwing up on her shoes. She paused to window shop at a cute little boutique before Jaimie found what she was looking for.

"Okay, I got a story in the local paper. And two inches in one of the larger Twin Cities dailies. Says here—"

An ambulance swung around the corner in front of Kate, and the wail of the siren cut Jaimie off. They both waited a minute until the sound dissipated enough to talk again, but as it did a sheriff's car flew past, also lit up with flashers and siren.

"Jesus, sounds like you never left the South Side."

"Probably just some poor guy down at the nursing home I passed on the way into town. What were you saying?"

"Not a lot here. Sounds like that woman had it right. He was assaulted and beaten in his shop. In a coma. Or he was at the time of printing. No apparent robbery or vandalism."

"Coincidence?"

"Maybe, but you know what your dad used to say about coincidences."

Coincidence is the devil's fingerprint, Kate.

"Oh yeah, I know. So, what's the motive then?"

"If you rule out money and hate crime, I don't know. Maybe fun?"

"Fun?"

"You know, thrills. Small town. Small opportunities. A certain kind of teenager gets a little restless."

"Jesus. I don't know. That's pretty extreme. I can see throwing rocks through the window, but beat a guy into a coma *and* leave the money? That doesn't sound like teenagers, unless they are budding psychopaths."

"Okay. Probably not. You think it was Smith?"

"Maybe. But then why involve us?"

"Shotgun approach? Spray around enough bullets you're bound to hit something."

"I don't know. Maybe something more personal. The dry cleaning woman implied he was a bit of a player, liked the ladies. Maybe a cuckolded husband?"

"This story puts him at sixty-eight."

"In the age of Viagra, still possible, I'm not writing it off. How about a grudge? Or a message, maybe?" Kate said, warming to the topic.

"A message? For Stan? What are you thinking? A protection racket?"

"No. I didn't get that sense from the dry cleaning woman and she owned the shop next door."

"Maybe it wasn't a message *for* Stan. Maybe Stan *was* the message."

Kate could hear the trace of excitement in Jaimie's voice.

"Now you're talking. I like that. He was one of the only remaining links to Strong. Hell, it's why I'm down here. It's the logical place to start in the field. I can't be the only one to think of it. Okay, so we might not be the only ones looking for Max Strong. Can you email me links to the stories?"

"Done."

"I'm going to hit the hospital, see what I can find. Call me if you get anything else."

"Will do. In the meantime, watch your back for killer teenagers."

"Very funny."

"Seriously, Kate, be safe."

"I will," she said and slipped her phone back in her pocket.

The sirens had silenced the birds. The two men she'd passed were gone and the street was quiet and still. The brick storefronts and old-fashioned streetlamps made the little strip look like a damn Rockwell painting. She found it very hard to imagine any evil setting foot on this street. Meth labs? Bikers? Murder? Now a vicious beating that put a man in a coma?

The brighter the sunshine, the deeper the shadows.

"You're full of wit and wisdom today, old man."

———

St. Vincent's Hospital was a large new complex that looked more like a college campus than a hospital. Kate wound her way through the manicured lawns and brick buildings until she found the visitor parking lot near the ER entrance. Inside, she followed a twisting maze of color-coded signs until she made it to the main hospital. A woman with a big blue and yellow "Ask Me" button on her sweater pointed her up two flights of stairs to the intensive care unit.

A security guard stood inside the doors, but only glanced at her and nodded slightly as she passed. She felt his eyes on her backside as she walked to the nurses' station. That could be useful, she thought.

A large black woman in pink patterned scrubs was on the phone behind the desk. She smiled at Kate, held up a finger, finished her call, and hung up.

"What can I do for you, honey?"

"I'm looking for Stanley Tucinni's room."

"Well, child, visiting hours aren't until two this afternoon. You'll have to come back then. You friend or family?"

"Family. Niece. Step-niece? I'm not sure what you call it actually. Families get so mixed up these days. He's my mom's step-brother-in-law from her second marriage. I don't know. I'm just concerned for Uncle Stanley. That's what I've always called him. I was at a dig site in Utah. I'm an archaeology student. And my mother finally got around to telling me what happened only yesterday. Can you believe that? She might not get along with him anymore, but he was always so nice to me. Jeez, I'm sorry. I talk a lot when I'm nervous. I'll come back at two. Can you tell me how he is at least?"

"Well, honey," she looked down and to the right at some folders on the desk and Kate knew the woman was prepping a lie. It must be bad. "He's been pretty stable the last couple days, but whoever did this beat him but good. The superficial stuff has started healing but he hasn't woken up, so the doctors don't know much. They did get the swelling in his brain down. That's positive. And his vitals are steady, but they just won't know 'til he wakes up."

"When will that be?"

The woman shrugged. "If only it were that easy. This isn't an induced coma. Could be today. Could be tomorrow. Could be ..." She didn't finish, just trailed off, but then rallied. "But listen, child. I'm so glad you're here. He hasn't had many visitors. Hardly any calls asking after him. Lots of town folk sent flowers and cards, but not many stopped by in person. Even those who did, at first, they couldn't go in, only look through the glass. The swelling was still bad, but it's been a few weeks now and people are moving on. No one likes to think about the bad stuff. You come on back at two. It will do your uncle good to have someone sit with him and talk. It will help. I believe that. I really do."

She reached out and squeezed Kate's hand. Kate felt her cheeks get hot with shame for deceiving this kind woman.

"Thanks. I'll do that," she managed before backing away and going out the doors. As she walked, the cell phone in her pocket buzzed. She pulled it out. The caller ID said it was Jaimie, but the signal was flipping between roaming and a single bar so she let it ring to voicemail.

Back at the ER entrance, she watched a tall man in a brown and tan sheriff's uniform talking to a nurse and gesturing down the hall. She paused in front of a crowded bulletin board. Just like lying, she had a natural proclivity for eavesdropping. But she couldn't quite hear what was being said and decided to keep moving the second time the uniformed man glanced up at her.

Outside, near the parking garage, she found a clear signal and called Jaimie back.

"Got something for me?"

"You're going to need to give me a raise."

"This sounds good."

"It is."

"Lay it on me."

"Okay, after reading through the stories on Tucinni, it hit me that they never mentioned any family. Beloved by the community. Sponsored Little League teams. Pillar of the community, but nothing on the family. No quotes from the wife or kids."

"Right. I just got the same thing from the nurse at the hospital. Said it's been a ghost town up in his room since he arrived."

"Want to know the one person other than Tucinni mentioned in the clips?"

"Strong?"

"Exactly. Max Strong, former employee, accused murderer, now fugitive, seems to be one of the few real friends this guy had. Lots of admirers and acquaintances, but few friends."

"I don't know. Friend might be stretching it a bit. The guy worked for Tucinni, so it's natural the guy with that history might come up in any background story. Doesn't necessarily make them bosom buddies."

"Fair enough, but I went back to the original stories on the incident involving Strong. The quotes in the papers and magazine from Tucinni back when Strong first went missing have a real vehemence to them. This guy felt enough to seek out every reporter sniffing around and deny that Strong was the guy responsible for the body count. He was like a politician hammering home the talking points. That says something. I'm not sure what, but it says something. These guys had a connection."

"Okay, I'll buy that. You work shoulder-to-shoulder every day you develop a rapport, but so what?"

"I don't know. Might be nothing, but it got me thinking. Both of these guys were loners. Not exactly swimming in friends. Maybe they *still* have a connection. Remember the Burnett case?"

"Sure, the insurance fraud one we worked on with Dillon."

"Right. And the state court ruled that hospitals have to maintain call records for audits and insurance purposes."

"Yes. In Illinois."

"You don't think other states pay attention to that?"

"Okay, what're you thinking?"

"Despite the fines and SJC ruling, most hospitals just aren't all that up-to-date with their technology, but we got lucky this time. St. Vincent's was renovated less than three years ago. Complete overhaul."

"Believe me, it shows. It still smells new here. I'm ready to check in and get a room. It probably beats the motel I'm going to end up at."

"Plus, you could get room service. Now listen, I dug a little more. That's what you pay me for, right? It has a cutting-edge phone system. IP telephony. Not only do the calls get logged, but the system also creates transcripts. Luckily, they do not have cutting-edge security. I took a peek. It's been a light couple weeks in intensive care. I guess if you've got someone in intensive care, you're going to go in person, not call. Good for me, fewer calls to search. I started the week after the assault. Crossed it with Tucinni's name and room number."

"I'm with you."

"The nurse wasn't lying. This guy doesn't have any family, at least not anymore. Or none who call anyway. There are a couple incoming calls with local prefixes, but nothing else."

"Okay, but we already confirmed the guy is a lifelong bachelor with no family."

"I wasn't finished. I expanded the search criteria. There were two more calls. Both short. I almost missed them. They didn't go directly to the room, but to the nurses' station. A caller asking to speak to Tucinni. But the nurse denied putting it through or giving further information. Both were made from a payphone in a small town in Oregon."

Kate was silent thinking it through. "You think it's Strong."

"Yup."

"Possibly. Could also be word finally reached a long-lost relative."

"Could be, but the caller doesn't say he was family. It's why the call dead ended at the nurse."

"Good work. It's a solid lead. Keep on it. I'm going to poke around here a bit more. You get a confirmation, or anything close, call me ASAP and I'll get a flight out there."

She felt the hairs rise on the back of her neck. It was faint, but she knew they had the scent. Max Strong could run, but he couldn't disappear. Not completely.

RIGHT AFTER IV

Alexei stood in the shadows. The night was cold and dark, the moon tucked behind stacks of clouds that had brought showers earlier in the day. It was a good night for surveillance. The house at the end of the cul-de-sac was large, three brick stories, and mostly dark. It was late for this neighborhood. One window on the top floor, left corner, was still illuminated.

He glanced at his watch. He expected the light to go out soon. People were creatures of habit. The neighborhood was full of overly large, overly ornate homes, but the one at the end was the biggest. A wrought iron fence with a gate surrounded the property, with bars close enough to stop anyone but a small child from slipping through. The fence was electrified in certain areas. A discreet guardhouse partially concealed by sculpted shrubbery stood at the end of the curving drive. Cameras were perched high on the cornice posts of the fence. Every hour, armed guards in black windbreakers walked the property in roving patrols. It all spoke of money, power, and privilege.

Alexei just needed to find a way in and kill the owner.

He had circled the property when the two guards on duty had gone inside, either to use the bathroom or warm up. Alexei ignored the cold. He had made the entire circuit in just under twenty-five minutes. He took it slow and careful, diverting into the woods that flanked one side and the back of the house when necessary. The guards had yet to reappear by the time he was back behind his tree. A good sign for him but not for the owner. They had become lazy and indulgent. Instead of expecting trouble, they expected none.

His reconnaissance had shown that the perimeter itself was solid and well maintained. There were no breaks, and the fence extended from the manicured backyard two hundred yards right into the woods before an almost impenetrable thicket of brambles and underbrush cascaded down a steep hill that eventually leveled out and gave way to middle-class neighborhoods and shopping centers far below. A castle looking down on the peasants.

Initially, Alexei had thought the rear of the house would make the best access point but soon found that the shrubs and trees had been cut back to make climbing over the fence using an overhanging limb almost impossible, certainly out of the question for someone with a crippled leg and wounded shoulder. He didn't check but guessed that all the posts had been sunk at least five feet into the ground to discourage any thoughts of tunneling under. He wasn't in the mood for any more digging.

Even if the guards were sloppy, Alexei had to admit the fence and boundary precautions were very good. Perhaps he'd only have to make a few changes.

He continued to watch. He massaged his leg and tried to lean his weight against the tree to take some of the weight off. This was the third night he'd stood out here and the long sentries were taking their toll on his still healing body.

Hobbes had done a decent job. Better than Alexei had

expected or hoped. There had been a staph infection in his shoulder that left him weak and bedridden for almost three weeks, but the antibiotics eventually overcame it. He couldn't lift his arm over his shoulder, but otherwise he felt nothing more than a dull ache from that wound. His leg was giving actually giving him more trouble, despite what Hobbes initially thought. It hadn't hit any major arteries, but the bullet had bounced around and chewed up the muscles and tendons and, almost three months later, it was still difficult to stand for more than twenty minutes without throbbing pain.

He took a pill from the small metal case in his pocket and ground it between his teeth as he watched the guards finally reemerge from the house. They paused and spoke to each other near the garage, then separated and started walking the property line. Alexei knew they'd meet up in the back for a smoke. Everyone was a creature of habit. After they both cleared the front, he stepped out, watched as the fence cameras methodically swiveled outward to sweep the side yards, and limped up the street to study the gate.

It wasn't the first time he'd done it, but he wanted one last look. It wasn't electrified here. Zapping the mailman or the neighborhood kids led to attention and questions the owner didn't need. It wasn't hot, but it was just as solid. No gap where the two swinging ends met in the middle. Reinforced supports were anchored into the driveway at an angle inside the fence. A tank would need a couple of passes before taking that gate down.

Alexei looked up and noted that the gothic scrollwork along the top was discreetly sharpened. He doubted it was a standard design. A call box and security keypad were attached to a post to the left of the driveway. The keypad was recessed and difficult to see. He'd never get close enough to see anyone punch in the code without being noticed. He shined the small light he carried at the box. All the keys were metal and new with no signs of wear that might aid in guessing the code. He'd seen two deliveries during his other visits. Two guards came down to the gate. One inspected the driver and paperwork while the other inspected the vehicle. Not on the list, you don't get inside.

Satisfied that he hadn't missed anything, he limped back into the shadows. He watched the guards make one more pass, then, cursing this new weakness in himself, retreated down the hill to his parked car.

Back in his hotel room, he poured vodka into a plastic cup and drank it in two swallows. He added ice and poured a second drink and carried it over to the bed. He stripped and laid down on the cheap mattress, trying to ignore the sounds in the next room. Alexei stared into the dark and sipped the vodka. He rubbed the hard mass of scar tissue and thought about another pill, but pushed past it. Instead, he thought about the house some more. He made a plan.

———

The guy sat alone in the booth, his hands guarding a whiskey. An empty pint glass sat at his elbow. Alexei dropped into the opposite side and leaned his wooden cane against the edge of the table. The guy was about to say something when the waitress came by.

"A vodka, double with a separate glass of ice. And another round for my friend here."

The waitress nodded and retreated to get the drinks.

"Americans never serve vodka cold enough."

The man looked at him with deep-set, hooded eyes. "I'm not your friend."

"Not yet."

"Not ever."

"Maybe. Maybe not. You're getting a drink out of it. Don't be so quick to judge."

"It's a talent."

They kept quiet after that and eyeballed each other. The man was big, his forearms threaded with veins and biceps that stretched his shirt. He was thicker through the chest and at least a few inches taller than Alexei. But Alexei could also see the years catching up to the man. The burst capillaries in his nose and the weight hanging over this belt.

The waitress returned with their drinks. Alexei poured the liquor over the ice in the glass and held it up. The man didn't reciprocate. Alexei shrugged and took a sip. The man finished his own and left the fresh ones on the table untouched.

"I'm not looking for company, *friend*."

"Fair enough. I'll say my piece and leave you to it." Alexei took another swallow and held up the empty to the waitress.

Drobhov usually handled this type of situation. Alexei was the tactician. Drobhov was the talker. They'd made a good team for a long time. Drobhov was able to sweet talk street vendors into giving them pieces of old fruit to stay alive another couple of days. Alexei led their ragtag army of orphans into the street to swarm and steal. As young men in the Soviet Army, their roles stayed much the same and they were equally successful. Now, it was just Alexei. He was a hard man who prided himself on always moving forward, but some days even he acknowledged the dull ache of a missing friend. A feeling that he was now at a disadvantage. A soldier being forced to fight with only one hand.

Alexei had spent two more fruitless nights casing the house, trying to peel back its defense and find the Achilles heel. He'd come up empty. The place was locked down. An impregnable fortress. It took another night of drinking, pulling straight from the bottle, to think of trying Drobhov's way.

"You're going to die," Alexei said.

The man smirked. Below his drinker's nose his face was wrinkled and grooved in the way one gets from spending long periods outside. He'd been a guard or something similar for a long time. Trusted enough to watch the gate, but not trusted enough for anything else.

"We're all going to die."

"True enough, but you are going to die tomorrow."

"That right?"

"Yes."

"You a psychic?"

"Nope."

"What then?"

"I'm the executioner."

"Very funny. You going to beat me to death with your walking stick there?"

"No. Either a knife or I'll break your neck. I haven't decided. You have a preference?"

The man gave a short bark of a laugh that lacked any humor. "That's a good one, *friend*. I don't know what your game is, but why don't you get the fuck out of my booth and take it elsewhere?"

"I don't think you should raise your voice like that."

"I'll talk however the fuck I want."

"I doubt your boss would like that."

He gave Alexei a look. "How do you know I got a boss?"

"Everyone's got a boss, just like everyone's going to die, right? And bosses don't usually drink in shitholes with dollar tap specials. So, you've got a boss. Am I right?"

"Whatever you say."

"On the other hand, not everyone's boss lives in a big

house in a swanky, secluded neighborhood with bodyguards and electrified gates."

The man dropped his hands below the table "I'm tired of this shit. Who the fuck are you, huh? You don't look like a cop."

"I'm not."

"Then what?"

"Just a soldier. Like you."

"For who?"

This was the delicate part. If the man was more in the know than Alexei thought, he could easily call Alexei's bluff. "No one you've heard of. Not yet. Just someone a couple links up the chain from your boss. Everyone answers to someone, right? Things have changed. Maybe you haven't heard. New people in charge."

"And what? My branch is being closed?"

It was Alexei's turn to laugh and slap a palm on the table. "I like that! I never thought of it that way, but yes, you could say that. No severance for you guys though, right?"

"What do you want?"

"The alarm code for the front gate."

The man looked at him and then down at his drink before he drained it in one swallow. "What do I get?"

Alexei took out an envelope. He was getting near the end of his cash reserves, those that were close at hand, at least. He had others, but he'd have to travel out of the country, and he didn't want to do that. Not right now. If things stayed on track and he finished his business soon, he wouldn't need them. He could let them sit for another day.

He slid the envelope across the table. It held five grand. He had another in his right pocket with the identical amount. If he had judged right, five was enough. This guy was old. He'd been around the block. The flame of ambition he had when he was younger was thoroughly doused. He just wanted to keep on keepin' on. Have his dollar specials, walk his beat. Die in his sleep.

The man lifted the envelope's edge and riffled the bills with his thumb, then looked up. "Tell me why I shouldn't just take the cash and let them know you're coming?"

"Because then I'll be sure to make you suffer. You'll die screaming. At least until I cut your tongue out."

The man looked across the table and must have finally seen the hard truth in Alexei's gray eyes.

"I stay on the payroll?"

"We'll need local people. People with experience. With localized knowledge."

He picked up the fresh sidecar of whiskey and swallowed it. He looked around the dive bar as if expecting someone to stop him. No one looked their way. No one cared. He slid the envelope off the table and into his pocket. "Nine, seven, nine, nine, two, three, five."

"How many guards?"

"Six."

"Including you?"

"Yeah. Two outside. Two in the control room by the garage and two inside."

"You work tomorrow night, right?

"Yeah."

"Your two o'clock rounds. Double back and meet me by the driveway gate."

———

The storm front that had stalled over the city for the past week was gone. The moon was nearly full. Its pale, bluish spotlight lit up the open expanse of grass around the big house. It was too bright for what he had planned, but Alexei shrugged it off. He was committed. If the moon was his biggest complaint, he would take it. Things were in motion and he had to stay ahead of the breaking wave. He wouldn't get a second chance at this.

Earlier, just after dusk, Alexei had moved through the shrubs and dug up the bundle of cables that ran to the security cameras that looked down at the front gate. The electrical power was a one-off that hooked into the house's main electrical box sitting just twenty yards away behind the screen of a boxwood hedge. No need to run cable all the way to the house or build redundancies. It was a flaw—one he would exploit.

Alexei clipped the bundle with a pair of bolt cutters, quickly covered the severed ends with dirt, and smoothed the mulch before retreating.

As predicted, he watched two guards from the house come to check it out. They looked up at the camera, then stood arguing before one man left. The other guy continued to stare up at the disabled camera as if he could divine an answer. The first guy returned with a ladder. He placed it against the fence and climbed up for a closer look. Two minutes later, he was back down, shaking his head. Together, they walked back down the driveway toward the house. He could imagine their conversation. They'd call the company that installed it. No, it was just one camera, not the whole system. The gate was still locked. They'd get someone to come out first thing in the morning to take a look.

Good for Alexei. Much too late for the rest of them.

The night passed quietly. He took out an orange he'd brought and peeled it. He ate the segments slowly, as he thought about the operation to come. He did his best to avoid thinking about the past. Any emotion would only get in the way.

At a quarter 'til two, he stood up and stretched his stiff muscles. He massaged his thigh until the numbness faded and he could move his toes. He slipped a pill under his tongue. He needed the pain in the background. He buried the remains of the orange peel out of habit then checked his pockets, found what he wanted, and started walking toward the gate. It was time.

At three minutes after the hour, Alexei watched his guard hustle up to the gate. Alexei stepped out from the shadow of the guard post. The man flinched, then hurried over. He lifted the anchors behind the gate.

Alexei stepped to the security pad and keyed in the code. There was a pause, and then the two gates began swinging smoothly inward. The guard had to skip back out of the way to avoid being hit.

"Was that you with the camera?" the guard asked. Alexei didn't respond. "Well, if it was you, you got them stirred up inside. Not sure that was the best plan." A radio was clipped to his belt. He fingered one of the dials on top like a worry stone. "What is the plan, by the way? Maybe I should have waited inside. More surprise that way."

Alexei moved toward him. The man looked over Alexei's shoulder. "Where are the rest? I thought you said ..."

Alexei put the blade between the man's third and fourth ribs and angled it upward. The man gasped once before his eyes opened wide, then rolled upward. It was a practiced move, almost muscle memory for Alexei at this point. Quick and painless, relatively speaking.

Alexei wrapped an arm around the dead man's back and eased him to the ground. He laid him on the grass behind the open gates. He was now out of sight if someone came up the drive from the house.

He tugged off the guard's black windbreaker and put it on. He took the 9mm Glock from the guard's shoulder holster. He ejected the magazine and found it full. He then reinserted it, thumbed the safety off, and racked the slide to put a round in the chamber. As satisfied as he could be with a strange gun he hadn't cleaned and fired himself, he put it in his jacket pocket. Alexei's own gun was somewhere in the mill, lost during the fall. Hobbes had only had an old .22 hunting rifle in the house that was of no use. He could have bought a gun, but felt comfortable with his knife and had wanted to save his cash for emergencies.

A thought came to him and he went through the rest of the guard's pockets but didn't find the money. He shrugged it off. Five thousand was a fair price to get inside. He looked down at the body and wondered briefly if the man had actually thought he was going to live. Probably, he decided. A man can talk himself into anything if he wanted to believe it badly enough.

Finally, he took the guard's radio, then covered the body with his own coat to further conceal it in the shadows.

Alexei moved off to the left, continuing the guard's circuit along the fence line. He found the second guard in back, smoking a cigarette, looking off into the woods, waiting for his partner. His blue shirttails were untucked and hung out below his jacket in the back.

"Took you long enough."

The guy was younger than the snitch who had given up the code, naïve and easily distracted. Clearly, he was confident in the fence itself to do his job for him.

"Check it out." He gestured with his cigarette. "Something's out there. I don't know, a fox maybe, and it's got something on the run. I heard it—"

The guy never even turned. Alexei stepped close and pulled the blade across the guy's throat. The body fell, twitching and gurgling in the dark. Messier than the first one, but the guy was facing away from him and something about him, his lack of pride in his job maybe, or maybe his general sloppiness, rubbed Alexei the wrong way.

Alexei took the radio and gun off his belt and threw them over the fence. He looked at the drowning man squirming on the ground. There were a lot of easy ways to kill, but not a lot of easy ways to die. He turned and walked toward the house, wiping his blade on the sleeve of the black jacket. Two down.

THE WINDY CITY

Max gripped the plastic handset tighter and leaned his head against the cinderblock side of the convenience store. "What kind of trouble, Danny?"

"The Carter kind."

Shit. He watched a prostitute named Rae exit the store with a super-sized cherry slushy. She'd add the vodka later. She waved and he nodded.

"Hey, you still there?" Danny asked.

"I'm here. What did you do?"

"Skimmed some." He didn't even try to bob and weave. He must be in real bad shape, Max thought. It's a bad sign when a born liar comes right out with the truth.

Danny wasn't actually his brother, not directly. He was his cousin. Max, or Michael Sullivan, as he was known three lives ago, lost his parents in a car accident when he was five years old. Back then, the neighborhood didn't let their own go into the system, the regulations were looser, and his mother's sister had taken him in. He moved one street over, and the memory of his parents slowly faded away until he had to look at photos to remember their faces. Danny was two years younger and happy to have an older brother. A sister, Mary, would come later.

"That it?" Max had a feeling there was more.

"Might have used some."

"Shit, Danny, c'mon. What happened to your cut from that last thing?"

"Gone. Long gone."

"Christ. All of it? How? On what?"

"Gambling, coke, girls. Shit, does it matter?"

"I guess not."

"Look, I know, I'm a loser. I realize it now. Should have never started back up. I knew it then, too, for what it's worth. I just couldn't ... after all the shit ... and you were gone. I went a little crazy. I know it was weak, but there it is. I did it. I'm not denying it."

"So, you're skimming and using, coming up short on your payments. I gotta say, Danny, I'm surprised Carter didn't have Little John throw you in the river."

"Me, too. I think maybe it's 'cause of our history. You know, you, Dad, and all that."

Max doubted that. Carter may have worked with Danny's old man coming up in the '70s, but Max had never heard of Carter letting sentiment get in the way of business. You didn't last in Boston if you did. Carter certainly hadn't let it get in the way of what he did to Max and his family. There was only one reason Max could figure that would make Carter so generous.

"How long you got?"

"'Til Monday."

"How much?"

"Fifty."

Max turned and put his back to the wall. He watched the caramel-colored sunset make the low-rent surroundings look almost pretty for a moment. Then the sun dropped behind a high-rise and everything turned gray and gritty again. Where the hell was he gonna come up with fifty large by Monday to save his little brother's neck? Again? He was living hand to mouth out of a fleabag motel while he pulled double shifts as a short-order cook. Fifty grand was a lifetime ago. It might as well be fifty million. He didn't have any scratch saved beyond the bills he was carrying now and the small roll in a coffee can back in his room. If it was five grand, he might have gone to Junior and begged for a favor. After the robbery thing, he had some goodwill to trade on. But not fifty grand worth.

He thought about Stan. Never mind seriously needing to deal with all of his own problems.

"Can you travel? You know I can't come back."

"I think so. I'll have to tell him I'm leaving though. They think I tried to do a runner on my own, it'll only make it worse."

"Okay, tell 'em you got a job lined up that'll cover your losses. Give 'em whatever collateral they need. Can you get to Chicago by Friday?"

"Chicago? That where you are these days?"

"No, but that's where I'll be on Friday."

"Oh. Okay, yeah, I guess I can be there."

"You got any money?"

"A little. Not much."

"Good, bring it. We'll need supplies."

"We getting the band back together?"

"No. Let's call this a charity show unless I think up a better way to bail out your ass." He'd once promised Cindy he'd never go back to stealing. Another broken promise to put on the pile. It was a growing stack. "All right. Meet me at that place Joyce took us on that vacation to see Aunt Dehlia. You remember that?"

"Sure, I remember."

"One o'clock on Friday."

————

Frankie took the phone away from his ear and hung up. "I can't believe it."

Danny just looked at him. He felt like he was going to throw up. And not from the beating. The one good thing he had left in the world was his brother. Sure, a lot of shit had happened, but deep down in a place he'd never let these people see, Danny always felt a little spark of pride knowing that Mikey was still out there in the world. That he had gotten away. And what did Danny do? How did he repay Mikey for all the times he'd gotten him out of tight spots, stepped in and took the punch? Traded places so Danny was out of harm's way? He gave him up after a couple of punches. He wished he could have swallowed his tongue.

"I gotta tell you, Danny boy. I really thought you were pulling our chains. Trying to catch a couple of extra breaths with the living. I honestly didn't see this coming."

Danny stared at him. Frankie just shrugged and looked back at Little John sitting on his folding chair. "You believe this shit, Little John? Michael Sullivan alive and kicking?"

"I wouldn't have believed it if I wasn't sitting right here, Frankie."

"Damn right. Okay, Danny boy. Sit tight. I gotta go talk to Mr. Carter. See if I can't get our little field trip approved."

A PRESSING MATTER

Duffy sat on the bench outside the paper's office and rubbed the key Porter had given him. He was in a daze. It felt like his world was wrapped in cotton. After he found Porter's body, his parents wanted to send him to a therapist, the sheriff had even suggested it might be a good idea, but he refused. I'm fine, he said. And he was. Sort of. He'd just disconnected. It just felt like everything was playing out in front of him while he watched an old *Law and Order* re-run. Maybe he wasn't okay.

The next edition hadn't been printed. The news of Porter's death had spread through the town's gossip wire, but an official ID and statement had yet to be released. Duffy had told the sheriff that Porter's mother had passed last year. The sheriff, in turn, said Porter's ex-wife was somewhere in China on assignment for *Vanity Fair* magazine. They were still trying to reach her or any other next of kin. Porter hadn't gotten around to making out a will. Everything was in limbo. There appeared to be few clues and fewer suspects.

The sheriff had said the newspaper's office had also been ransacked like the house, but that they had finished processing it, in his words, and Duffy was free to go inside if he liked.

Duffy looked up and saw Mrs. Olsen watching him through her shop's window. He had an idea she was about to come out and be sympathetic. He couldn't face that. He'd received enough plastic smiles in the last couple days from his parents. Duffy stood, put the key in the lock, and went inside.

Processing the scene didn't apparently include cleanup. The small office still looked ransacked. A few haphazard piles had been made so people could presumably walk around without stepping on things. Black fingerprint dust from the state police techs (he'd learned Essex didn't have their own) covered most of the surfaces. The desk chair was on its side, and all the drawers from the desk were pulled out and laid on the floor.

Porter wasn't neat, he always said no self-respectable newspaperman had time to be, but he had been organized in his own way. Duffy started straightening up and tried to get used to using the past tense when thinking of Porter.

After two hours, the room looked better. He still had the fingerprint dust to take care of and a couple piles of trash he'd accumulated, but once those were gone the office would look close to normal.

Duffy knew a cleaning crew came in every other week to vacuum, dust, and keep the place semi-habitable, but he had no idea if Porter had any cleaning supplies on hand. He looked in the two upstairs closets but found nothing useful. He headed down to check the basement before he went out and bought anything himself.

He nearly decapitated himself at the bottom of the stairs on a low-hanging water pipe before he found a string that connected with two rows of overhead tube fluorescents. He pulled the string and, after a moment, the bulbs flickered to life with a quiet hum.

Duffy looked around. Even with the lights on, the big room was still mostly shadows. The hulking printing press ran the entire length of the back wall. Covered by a green tarp, its spiny ridge scraped the ceiling and looked like a natural history exhibit undergoing renovation. The rest of the room was taken up with the paper's unofficial archives, haphazard rows of file boxes, some on makeshift shelves, others just stacked up to the ceiling. He was thankful that whoever had messed up the office upstairs didn't know about the basement. Cleaning up and reorganizing all the boxes of yellowing papers would have taken a week, if not more.

Duffy knew the cold dank interior wasn't the best place for the old papers. You could smell the rotting pulp as soon as you opened the basement door. Porter had mentioned hiring someone to digitize it, but had yet to get around to it. Each of the boxes was marked with dates and other notations, strings of numbers and letters. Duffy couldn't make heads or tails of it. Porter's uncle had been a true and meticulous packrat at heart and the moldy, cluttered basement stood as his masterpiece.

Duffy pulled a box down off one wobbly shelf and popped the lid. He ran his hands through the dusty sheets and brittle negatives, then carried it closer to the lights. Pictures and stories from the fall of 1951 filled the box. Duffy suddenly felt like he could spend all day down here. Someone should save this stuff. It shouldn't just rot away. Maybe he could call the historical society or library. He put the lid back on and gently placed the box back in its assigned spot.

He found a dustpan, broom, and ancient vacuum cleaner in an alcove in the far corner of the basement. He was dubious the vacuum would run, but it was the best he was going to get today. He'd give it a try. He pulled it all out and started back up the stairs, then stopped. He looked at the draped press. He'd only been down in the basement once before when Porter gave him the key and a brief tour, but they'd just stopped at the bottom of the steps when Porter had been overcome with a sneezing fit. Duffy had never seen the press up close.

He leaned the cleaning supplies against the stairs and walked back over to the press. It was a good twenty feet long and ten feet wide. He reached up and pulled the tarp off one end. Dust and spider webs clouded the air. Duffy fought off a sneeze himself and waved his hand until it settled.

Disrobed and up close, it looked, to Duffy, like one of the machines pictured in history books from the Inquisition, a terrifying piece of machinery that priests would have used to elicit confessions of heresy in the 1500s. It loomed over him in the dim space, a tangle of bent metal, bars, rollers, gears, and grease. Duffy was both awestruck and dumbfounded. He wondered how it all worked. He walked the length of it and pulled the tarp off the other end. He thought it ran from left to right. The paper and press would be loaded from the left and then fed through the ink and cutters on the right. It was fascinating. It reminded him of the game Mousetrap that he had loved to play as a child. The press was one big Goldberg device.

Standing at the end, Duffy saw that the press didn't sit flush against the wall. There was a narrow space to allow access to the other side, probably for troubleshooting or repairs. He walked behind it to get a look from the other side and almost tripped, grabbing a metal arm of the press to stay on his feet.

He looked down. It was a manuscript box. And it looked new. Or, at least, newer than the rest of the boxes scattered around the room.

"What the hell?"

Duffy bent down and picked it up. Maybe Porter was writing a novel. But why keep it down here in the basement?

He lifted the top off. A small USB drive sat on top of a stack of printouts and loose pages torn from a notebook. All together they filled half the box. Duffy tried to read them, but there wasn't enough light. He put the top back on and carried the box back upstairs with the cleaning supplies.

Having lost interest in further cleanup for the moment, he dumped the dustpan, broom, and vacuum inside the office door and took the box over to Porter's desk. He sat and took out the stack of pages. It wasn't a novel. It was notes of some kind. Some handwritten, some typed, all in a sort of shorthand. Notes for a story Porter was planning to write? He hadn't mentioned anything to Duffy, and this looked much too big for the paper. Maybe a novel after all? But why write that in shorthand?

He continued to flip through the pages. This must be a backup of sorts. Maybe he had the rest on his laptop at home. He read through the first couple pages. The names were all initials or codes and a lot of it didn't make sense, but Duffy was able to get a whiff of the story and, more importantly, he saw the potential. This was no work of fiction. He'd read some of it in the paper before, but not like this. He kept reading, picking up what he could, then flipping the pages facedown on the blotter.

"Holy shit." He whispered.

This was something worth killing for.

THE LAW

His desk phone rang. Logins glanced at the caller ID. He grimaced and picked up the phone; better to deal with it now. He'd only keep calling.

"Logins."

"Afternoon, Sheriff. It's Carl."

"No, there's nothing new, Carl."

"Nothing? No leads? Suspects?"

"If the place hadn't been tossed and valuables left, I'd say it was a random act of violence. A home invasion gone wrong or a burglary interrupted."

"Nothing in Porter's past?"

"No. Nothing that throws up any flags for this kind of thing. He was a reporter, he drank too much, got divorced, survived Chicago and somehow died here."

"How about the other thing? Tucinni. Anything there?"

"The same. Nothing."

"Isn't that something right there? Two out-of-the-blue attacks?"

"Maybe. Might also just be an outlier, a fluke of the statistics. I try not to draw causality between two incidents without evidence." Of course, he was looking at it, but Logins would be damned if he told this man any more than necessary.

"All right, Sheriff, keep on it. I don't have to say the mayor has the utmost confidence in you, Ken. You're going to be at the dedication, right?" Logins didn't miss the switch to his first name.

"Carl, I just finished telling you I've got squat on two violent crimes in the past two weeks, and you want to know if I'm coming to your meet and greet?" Logins couldn't keep the frustration out of his voice.

"That's right. A meet and greet for two of your fellow fallen officers. Your job extends beyond just investigating. You are the sheriff. You have to be out in the community. Visible."

Logins frowned at the thought of being thrown in the same boat as the Heaney brothers. "You mean there's going to be press there."

"Yes, if you want to be gauche about it. Image is important in these times."

"What times are those? The coming campaign season?"

"No. I meant in these times of new media and twenty-four-seven coverage. If you don't feed the beast, it feeds on you. Better to get out and be seen dedicating a memorial to your fallen brethren than show up in an op-ed about how you can't seem to make any headway in the increasing amount of violent crime in our little burg."

Logins rolled his eyes. He'd listened to some variation of this from Carl Hagel for the last two years: political horse-trading as subtle as a sledgehammer. "I get it, Carl. I don't suppose you thought any more about my request to hire a detective. It could free me up for more photo ops."

"I've spoken to him about it, but really, Ken, you yourself

just said it was likely a random act of violence. I'm not sure we can afford the extra expenditure right now."

"Can I get that on the record for when those op-ed pieces start?"

"You know we have your back. You're our guy. You don't have to sweat that."

"How about authorizing that request for some assistance from the state barracks?"

"I'm not sure what kind of message that would send, do you? The newly elected sheriff calling for outside help at the first drop of blood?"

"It says I'm understaffed, know how to ask for help, and I'm doing everything possible to keep this town safe."

"Maybe. Maybe not. I guess it all depends on how the press sees it." Logins felt the sledgehammer right between his shoulder blades. "So, we can count on seeing you there?"

"Yeah, Carl, I'll be there to smile for your cameras."

"Good. I'm glad we can count on your support."

Logins dropped the receiver back in its cradle. Hagel had shown up shortly after that bloody night. He was nominally Sanderson's chief of staff, though why the man needed a chief of staff for a town that barely needed a mayor was beyond Logins. Sanderson had moved on, but Hagel had almost inexplicably remained in town and taken a similar post with the new mayor. Logins wasn't sure what Hagel's job was except to be a pain in his ass.

"Lulu!" He called.

"What is it, Sheriff?" The dispatcher hollered from the front room. The intercom was redundant with Lulu.

"Be sure to remind me that I need to get my uniform cleaned and pressed for the Heaney dedication."

"Dry clean uniform. Ten-four, boss."

The whole thing was a sham. The Heaney brothers weren't

saints and shouldn't come within fifty yards of any memorial. Two years ago, Logins had started gathering evidence that Chris, and possibly Tom, were mixed up in a burgeoning rural meth trade based in Essex. How far and how deep they'd crossed the line never became exactly clear. Hagel had shown up and Logins had quickly found himself stonewalled at every turn, any investigation withering on the vine.

Back then, the economy was booming, and Essex was suddenly a real estate hot spot, an idyllic small town with open space and still within driving distance of civilization. Developers, young people, retirees, suddenly everyone wanted a piece. Murder, drugs, and unsolved mysteries were not good for the town's burgeoning reputation. Logins, the lone full-time officer left after the Heaneys were killed, was too new and too overwhelmed to put up much of a fight. He'd folded in the face of Hagel's pressure and was given the sheriff's star for his cooperation. The memory of that complicity still turned his stomach, but it also motivated him to stick around and look for an opportunity to fix his mistake.

In the years since, the economy went in the toilet and Essex's star had faded, it's time in the spotlight fleeting and gone. One part of him wanted to let it all go, good riddance, another part wanted to dredge up that bloody night and throw the whole stinking thing at Hagel's feet in the hopes that it would submarine whatever plans had been cooked up. And Logins was certain something was keeping a man like Hagel in Essex. Logins would go down, Hagel would make damn sure of that, but at least he'd go down shooting.

The only problem was he didn't have anything to really throw in their faces. What did he know? He had a paddy wagon full of dead bodies, two missing suspects, and enough unanswerable questions to fill the town's reservoir. It all added up to a lot of smoke, but no fire.

Would he have cracked it, if given the chance? He'd like to

think so, but he'd never know for sure. He'd been frozen out. The state police showed up, made a cursory investigation, and wrote up a report that was almost laughable. Logins was sure markers were cashed in, favors granted, promises handed out. The press sniffed at it, but without an easy villain or neat ending, the story died. Just like he was sure Hagel knew it would. But why? Was it worth all the capital that it must have taken to bury the thing?

Logins sat up. He realized he was brooding over it again. He got up, put on his hat, and left.

He drove around for ten minutes trying to find something to take his mind off it. Driving down Main Street for the second time, he saw Mike Duffy pass in front of the window of the *Times* building. He pulled the cruiser to the curb and got out.

He smiled at Mrs. Olsen in her boutique, then went up the stairs to the second floor. He turned the knob and was surprised to find the door locked. He knocked on the frosted glass. Duffy opened it a crack and peered out at him.

"Hi, Mike," Logins said.

"Oh, uh, hi, Sheriff."

"Mind if I come in?"

"Sure. Sorry. Wasn't expecting anyone." He stepped back and opened the door wider.

Logins walked in and heard the click of the lock again as Duffy closed the door after him. The kid had cleaned the place up a bit. "Sorry, the techs left a mess. I tell 'em to clean up, but they don't answer to me and rarely listen."

"It was no problem. Someone would have had to go through it all eventually."

"You gonna try to keep the paper running?"

The kid shrugged. "Don't know what I'm gonna do now. I guess Porter's ex owns the place now, huh?"

"Not sure myself. There was no will. The courts will probably have to sort it out." Logins started to walk around the room. "Door was locked."

"Yeah. With everything that's happened, you know, I just felt better with the door locked. I'm still a bit jumpy."

Taking a seat in the old rocking chair, Logins saw a kid who suddenly looked his age, big hands and feet still waiting for his body to catch up, smooth cheeks that only needed to feel a razor twice a week. The past few days had definitely left a mark on Duffy, but Logins envied that innocence even if he knew the eventual loss of it would be painful.

"Thought of anything else you want to tell me?"

"What do you mean?" Duffy started shuffling papers around on the desk, placing them in a white box on the blotter.

"Just what I said. It's been a few days. Maybe something came back to you. Maybe some detail. Some story you guys were working on. Something that might have gotten Porter in trouble, caused someone to come looking for him. Anything. Doesn't matter how small. Any of it might be important."

Duffy looked back down at the desk, picked up a few more sheets, put them in the box. "Sorry, Sheriff, nothing like that comes to mind."

REST IN PEACE

B ack in her car in the hospital parking garage, the sun had warmed up the interior and that, combined with the pancake breakfast and night of driving, was making her very drowsy. She put the key in the ignition but then let her head fall back against the headrest. Her eyes started to slip closed before she caught herself. She shook her head, then cracked both windows to let in some cooler air and grabbed the file Jaimie had put together.

This is why she would live on Ramen noodles and spare change before she ever let Jaimie go. She flipped open the manila folder and found a list of names written on the inside cover. Next to the names, in the same neat hand, were addresses, both home and work, and all the phone numbers Jaimie could find on them. Left to her own devices, Kate would have scribbled various bits of info on old envelopes, gum wrappers, or gas station receipts and shoved it all in her purse or the black knapsack that often doubled as her briefcase.

She ran her finger down the page until she came to Stanley Tucinni. She already knew his work address. She found his home address and plugged it into her phone. It was less than two miles from the hospital. She hopped out of her car and went to the trunk. She rooted around until she found what she needed.

The advantages of a small-town case: everything was nearby, friends and enemies alike.

———

She made two lefts and a right before a final turn onto Cedar Street. She braked and let a woman cross with a golden retriever. Kate rolled the window down, took the yellow cherry light off the passenger seat and popped it on the roof of her car.

Cedar was a quiet cross street in a largely residential section about a mile from the Essex town center. Kate wondered if Tucinni walked to his shop each morning. At this time of the morning, the neighborhood felt deserted. Kids off to school, commuters off at work, everything was still and quiet. Kate drove slowly down the street, K-turned at the dead end, drove back and parked two houses down from Tucinni's brown-on-brown raised ranch.

Most people might be away, but Kate was sure a few people were still home. A strange car in a nice neighborhood was going to draw attention. She stepped out of the car. She wore an orange reflective vest and held a clipboard heavy with random paper. Her shoulder length hair was tucked into a Cubs baseball cap.

That's right. This never failed me. Carry a clipboard and carry some confidence and people will open their doors right up. Even let you inside if you ask the right way.

"Yeah, and they also would have let in a Girl Scout or a student selling magazine subscriptions."

Don't rewrite history. You loved it. Always thinking up those elaborate backstories.

"Maybe. But it wasn't normal for a 14-year-old kid."

She made a show of staring up at the telephone pole and making various notations on the clipboard. She moved up the street and walked up the driveway of Tucinni's neighbor. This house was sunny yellow with black trim and a nicely land-scaped yard. More doodles on the clipboard. She walked around the side of the house and found the meter and squatted in front of it. If you were going to use a charade, you had to sell it. She folded a blank piece of paper, went to the front door, and tucked it into the black tin mailbox by the doorbell.

She walked back to the street, up the cracked sidewalk, then turned into Tucinni's driveway. She felt the muscles tighten in her shoulders, but no alarms or sirens went off. The street remained quiet. She repeated the process from the prior house, checking the meter on the side before walking up to the front door.

A small veranda ran the length of the front of the house, from the far side to the garage. Tucinni's yard was the oppo-site of his neighbor's. A line of shaggy evergreens and other shrubs ran along the decorative rail and, once on the veranda, Kate found herself hidden from the street. Tucinni must take care of the yard work himself, but now he can't.

There was a simple black mailbox mounted next to the door. Kate lifted the top and pulled out the bundle inside. There was a lot of mail, but it wasn't overflowing. Someone was checking the box. She flipped through the stack. Water and electric bills, six credit card offers, a number of card envelopes, an electronics catalog, a glossy housewares catalog, and a coupon advertisement for an online flower shop. Nothing helpful like a get-well postcard from Max Strong with an Oregon return address or postmark. She put the mail back and tried the front door. Locked up tight with a modern deadbolt. She could get through it, but didn't think it was worth the risk. Not yet. She walked back to the curb. She did two more houses to keep her cover, then walked back to her car.

She didn't have any other immediate next steps in mind. She could pay the sheriff a call, wait for visiting hours at the hospital and take a chance on Stan waking up, or find a place to stay and take a nap. The last option was the most appealing. Maybe Jaimie would come through with more on the hospital phone call records while she napped.

Driving out of the tangle of side streets, she saw a discreet sign nailed to a telephone pole for Mount St. Mary's Cemetery. She paused, then turned left and followed the arrow on the sign.

Stick to the facts, dear. It's a case. It pays the bills. No more, no less. No need to go visiting gravesites.

"You know I work better when it's personal. Your best tools were your old cop buddies and keeping everything at arm's length. That's not me, Dad. Instincts and emotions are the best tools I've got."

She could almost see him roll his eyes, but she tuned out anything else he had to say. She already knew the rest. The only conversations she had with him these days were ones she'd had a thousand times.

She followed three more signs and parked in a deserted lot next to a small caretaker's cottage. The cottage was empty inside, but the interment book and the plot map were open on the desk. Kate thought it was unlikely that a town the size of Essex had more than two or three cemeteries, maybe divided by religion. Kate flipped through the book, cross-checking the names from the case against those listed in the book. She found two: Strong's one-time landlady, Esther Langdon, and his girlfriend, Sheila Thomas. She took a slip of paper from a small wooden box next to the book and jotted down the grid locations. She grabbed a photocopy of the map, oriented herself, and started walking.

Esther Langdon's plot was between her husband and her son near the edge of the cemetery under a mature elm. It was a pretty spot. Looking at the dates and insignia, Kate guessed her son had died in combat. The husband had passed eight years before Esther. A small flower arrangement in a white plastic pot leaned against her headstone. Kate brushed some grass from the polished stone. She wasn't particularly religious and didn't know any prayers, but bowed her head and hoped the three of them were together again somewhere.

She expected her dad to speak up with some snide comment about the afterlife, but he kept quiet, too. She continued on down the path toward Sheila Thomas's plot.

Thomas's plot was in the newer section of the cemetery on a grassy hillock overlooking a small manmade lake. Fledgling birch trees mixed with ash saplings and a couple of stone benches ringed the newly cleared landscape. Kate thought it would probably be a nice place to spend eternity when it filled up, but right now it just felt desolate and lonely, an empty lot waiting for more souls.

Thomas's headstone was a small, simple lacquered gray slab flecked with white and gold, laid flush with the ground. A small lamb and cross decorated the surface, along with an inscription in flowing script, "Sadly missed, she sleeps with angels now." Another flower arrangement sat next to the stone. Kate frowned. It looked almost identical to the one on Langdon's grave, except the dying tea roses in the center were red instead of yellow. Kate knelt in the damp grass for a closer look. There was no card, but there was small a purple stick among the stems. She pulled it out: '*Compliments of ProFlowers.com,*' on top of a white logo.

What are you thinking?

Kate walked back to Esther Langdon's grave. The florist's stick wasn't in the arrangement, but she'd been right, the arrangement was almost identical. It had to have come from the same florist.

"Damn."

She stood up and brushed grass clippings from her knees. Then she saw it: a flash of purple. The stick had fallen out or had been jostled free by the landscaper, perhaps, or the wind, and was lying behind the stone in the short grass. She picked it up.

Same company from ol' Stan's mailbox, right?

"Yes, but why is he buying these arrangements? Kindness? Guilt?"

Death affects people in different ways, Katie. You of all people should know that.

"Very funny. I can understand empathy, but guilt? Stan had no reason to feel guilty that I can see. The flowers are old, but not more than a couple weeks. If he was feeling empathy or guilt for either woman's death, would those feelings extend for almost two years?"

True. That would be some extraordinary dedication.

She tapped the purple sticks against her leg.

"Maybe Stan was just the messenger, then?"

Maybe he was delivering the flowers for someone else.

"A friend."

Or a former employee.

BAKER CITY

The number Jaimie pulled from the St. Vincent's hospital log was a payphone outside of a Baker City, Oregon, convenience store. It wasn't Times Square, but it wasn't a residential address either. They had narrowed it down, but not far enough. She was actually surprised at the call volume in this cell phone era. Payphones weren't quite dead yet.

Depending on how careful Strong was, he could live next door or in the next town. Don't get ahead of yourself, she chastised herself, it might not be Strong at all, but she would be surprised if it wasn't. She had an instinct for these things. It was honed razor-sharp during many long hours of database queries and sifting through Google results. It was what she did. Narrow the gap, and track people down. It was Strong. She could feel it.

She scrolled through the online editions of the local papers in the Baker City area, looking for a local PI who might be able to sit on the phone and help them out when she suddenly sat up straight in her chair. Max Strong staring back at her.

It was the eyes. You can change a lot of things about yourself easily and superficially. Most people aren't all that observant. Add some glasses, change your hairstyle, grow a beard and you could walk by anyone other than maybe your own mother and they wouldn't recognize you, but the one thing you can't change is your eyes.

The prison ID photo of Max Strong showed a man with a square face, thick neck, and a close, almost military brush cut. Even in the harsh flat prison photo, the gray eyes were bright and striking. Those same eyes now peered out from the *Baker City Press* website. This man was identified as Matt Diver in the caption, a short-order cook at Bob's Riverside Diner. He was leaner in the jawline and had long hair that came down over the tops of his ears, but he still looked back at the camera with a mix of hostility and resignation, eyes bright and striking.

Jaimie tapped a fingernail against the screen.

"You knew this would happen. You knew any photo, any mark you made on the world, was trouble."

Jaimie read through the story and stared at the photo some more. She clicked on the next story, then went back. She felt an unexpected pang of sympathy. It would be easy to keep going and tell Kate she'd come up empty on the phone number. Let those tired eyes rest. Then she remembered he was running for a reason. He was the prime suspect in multiple homicides.

She printed out the story with the photo of Diver and laid it side by side with the blown-up snapshot of Strong that Smith had provided. He was a little older, with less bulk and more hair, but she was sure it was the same man.

She punched Kate's cell number into her office phone. It rang six times before going to voicemail. "Shit." She hung up before the beep.

They had a policy of never leaving case info on voicemail.

You never knew who might be listening or who might end up with the phone. Kate would see a missed call from her and call back when she could. Should she leave a message anyway? No. Kate would call back and want to hear it from her directly. Nothing gained by leaving a message. The info would keep. The newspaper photo was from the prior week and Strong had been hiding for two years. One more night wouldn't change anything.

She shut down her computer, leaned back and cracked her neck. It was after six. She had been in early. She should be getting home before Lupe got to worrying. Before she lucked onto the website photo, it had been a long, exhausting, frustrating day. Now, it was all forgotten. She smiled and gathered her things. This is why she loved the job. There was nothing like the feeling of that wire in your blood when you start cracking a case, especially one that was ice cold.

Damn, she felt good.

RIGHT AFTER V

The bright sodium floodlights clicked on when Alexei was halfway across the wide swath of grass that ran from the back patio to the edge of the woods. Light pooled and overlapped the grounds, leaving little in shadow.

He froze for a beat. With guards doing roving patrols outside, it was unlikely the lights would be motion activated. Something was off. Had they seen him? The guard's radio on his hip was silent. The back doors to the house remained closed. He resumed walking, moving at a steady pace, veering left to try to stay on the edge of the light.

During his week's reconnaissance, he had noted the cameras mounted high under the eaves on all four corners of the house. Each would provide a wide-angle shot with good perimeter coverage, but there would be holes the closer you came to the house. The cameras were a redundancy, the third line of defense. They had placed their primary trust in the guards and the fence to keep people out.

But Alexei was already inside.

He kept moving forward, aiming for the glassed-in

breezeway that connected the large garage with the rest of the house. Stacks of firewood and the other miscellaneous tarp-covered objects nearby would provide camouflage if any guards came outside.

He was ten yards away from the house when a door on the side of the garage opened and a guard stepped out. Alexei stopped. He was inside the arc of floodlights now, standing in the softer shadows cast by the house lights near the back door. He knelt behind the pruned shrubbery that dotted the landscape near the patio. He was too far away for a quiet knife strike. He slipped the knife back in his pocket and took out the gun he'd taken off the first guard.

"I'm telling you, I saw something."

A muffled voice replied from inside. The door must lead to the control room the guard had told him about.

"Carl might turn his off, but Gene always has that thing on. Taking a crap, sitting by the monitors, eating in the kitchen. I'm telling you, something is queer out there. First, the camera going on the fritz, and now Gene and Carl not responding."

More muffled responses from inside.

"I've tried, and why would they be on the other channel?"

A pause. "Fine."

Alexei went to one knee and checked the radio on his belt. There were two bands. There was a small switch on top. He was on the wrong channel. It must have gotten bumped when the guy fell. He twisted the volume knob to zero.

"Gene? Carl? Someone respond, dammit. What's going on out there? Over."

Alexei turned away from the house, pressed the transmit button down, and brought the radio to his lips. "Uhhhh. Help. Front gate."

"Gene? That you? Repeat that. Where are you? Over."

"Help. Please. Ohhhh. Front gate."

"Holy shit. Pete, we got trouble. Gene's down." The man was turning back inside. "Gary, meet me at the front door. Hans, stay inside. Something—"

The rest was lost as the man went back inside and closed the door.

Alexei stood and walked to the door. He counted to thirty, then turned the knob and stepped inside. The guard hadn't locked it in his hurry. More sloppiness.

He stood at the far end of the windowed breezeway. To the right was a glass hallway and the door to the house proper. To the left were two doors set at right angles to each other: one for the garage and one for the control room, presumably.

Alexei went left.

The doors were standard double-hung wood core hardware, available at any home improvement store. Alexei made a note to swap them out for something more solid. He put his ear to the first door and could hear the creaking sounds of movement and fingers clicking over a keyboard. Control room. He moved to the next door and opened it. A long dark garage filled with the boxy shape of a dark sedan and the low sleek shapes of three expensive sports cars. He closed it and went back to the first door.

He went in quick and stayed low. A young kid, maybe twenty years old, sat in an office chair facing Alexei with a stunned expression. He was alone. The kid wore a black Megadeth T-shirt over blue jeans and vintage Air Jordan sneakers. A bank of computer monitors, controls, and blinking lights were set up behind him.

Alexei held the gun on him. "Stand up."

The kid didn't move. Alexei watched a dark stain grow across the front of the kid's jeans.

"Stand up." The kid's legs were shaking. "Turn around." Alexei had to nudge him to get him moving, then he brought the butt of the gun down hard on the base of the kid's skull. He fell onto the chair, moaning. Alexei hit him again. He crumpled and lay still.

Alexei looked at the monitors. They all held outside views except one, which showed a carpeted hallway. One monitor was black; the one he'd disabled. He didn't see anyone moving on the active monitors. Had they found Gene's body? Were they on their way back?

Alexei stuck the gun in his waistband and grabbed two computer mice off the desk. He used them to bind the kid's hands and ankles. He'd be out for a while, but he didn't want him going anywhere or alerting anyone if he woke up.

Alexei moved back through the breezeway toward the main house. The outside door was locked. He bent and studied the lock. It had no deadbolt, just a simple latch. He might have lost the element of surprise, but they still didn't know where he was. That was still a valuable asset. Rather than smash the pane of glass, he pulled a tension bar and pick from his wallet. He was inside in twenty seconds.

The door opened into a mudroom with a coatrack, closet, and a big upright washer-dryer unit. More glass doors at the opposite end led back outside to the patio. To the left, an open doorway led into the house. Alexei eased around the corner, gun up.

The guy standing in the middle of the kitchen drinking a glass of orange juice sensed the movement at his back and turned. To his credit, he didn't hesitate, he came hard and fast. There was no time for Alexei to pull his knife. He hesitated to fire the gun and give away his position in the house. The man was big and wide, but approached loose, on the balls of his feet, his black nylon jacket stretched tight across his frame.

Alexei had time to register the flattened nose and cauliflower ears that said his opponent was familiar and comfortable with hand-to-hand combat an instant before the man ducked low and hit Alexei with his shoulder right under the solar plexus. Alexei's breath whooshed out as he was lifted up and pinned to the wall. He lost his grip on the gun and heard it hit the floor. The man's arms tightened around his chest, squeezing out the air. With his bad arm and weak leg, Alexei was no match for this man's size and strength. He couldn't let it go on too long.

Dark spots appeared in his vision as the guard grunted and kept up the pressure. Alexei could see the outline of a shoulder holster through the guard's jacket and reached for it, but the man countered and brought his elbow down on Alexei's wrist. He didn't get the gun, but the movement did ease the vice-like pressure for a moment and allowed him to draw half a breath.

Alexei arched his back and kicked out his legs hard, but the guard didn't flinch; he just absorbed the blow as he tried to lock his hands and regain his grip. It was like fighting a concrete pillar. After a brief struggle, the man locked Alexei up again and the crushing pressure in his ribs resumed.

The guard appeared to sense his advantage and actually smiled. Alexei smiled back. The guard frowned, confusion clouding his eye. Alexei brought his forehead down once, twice, three times, hearing the cartilage of the guy's nose crunch and pop before the guard finally broke his grip and stumbled back. Blood poured from the guard's nose and a gash at his hairline. It ran into his eyes and down the front of his shirt before dripping onto the floor and pooling around his feet.

The guard swiped at the blood. Alexei now pushed *his* advantage. He stepped to the man and stomped down hard on the inside of his foot. The guard howled and tried to step back, slipped on his own blood, lost his balance, and swung wildly. Alexei lashed out with his good leg at the inside of the man's knee. There was an audible pop. He dropped his hands to grab his crippled joint and Alexei came in fast. He hit him three times quick, right behind the ear. The guard wobbled, then slumped to the ground. Alexei grabbed him from behind, locked him up in a triangle choke and squeezed. After thirty seconds, the man's legs spasmed once and then went still.

Alexei held on for a full minute, then stood up, retrieved the gun and stuck it in his waistband at his back. He checked the guy's pulse. Nothing. The whole thing had lasted three minutes. It had been quick, brutal, and mostly silent. He leaned against a butcher block island in the center of the kitchen to catch his breath. It felt like he'd gone fifteen rounds. Both his shoulder and knee throbbed from the effort of putting the man down. He pulled the small case from his jacket and chewed the two white pills to dust as he tried to listen for voices or footsteps over his own ragged breathing. Nothing. He continued further into the house.

The kitchen opened onto a large family room divided into three different seating areas by various couches and sofas. There were two fireplaces. Alexei limped over to the one closest to the kitchen and took an iron poker from a set of tools next to a neat stack of wood. He gave it a quick one-handed swing. Heavy enough to do some damage, especially on the joints, but light enough to swing with one hand.

He liked quiet weapons.

He continued on through the family room and found himself in the foyer. Two great oak doors led out to the front yard. A large, ornate chandelier hung over his head and, to his right, a curving wooden staircase led to the second floor.

He saw movement outside to his left and saw two guards jogging back up to the house. Tired and bruised from the last fight, he knew he wouldn't be able to take both guards at once. He needed them to separate. He ducked down a short hallway and into a room that turned out to be a study. He moved to the right of the door and waited.

The men didn't enter directly through the front door; they went around and through the garage, likely their usual route. He'd hoped they'd come through the front where he might catch them while they were still confused and reacting to a developing situation. He would wait. He took a deep breath, held it, let it out slowly.

He heard a shout from the back of the house. They had probably found the kid in the control room. A few seconds later came another shout as they discovered the dead man in the kitchen. The smart play would be to stay together and clear each floor, take the strength in numbers. But based on what he'd witnessed so far, he expected them to split up. Each man was amped up and ready to confront the danger, eager to take the spotlight and be the hero in the boss's eye.

He heard them coming through the family room, then their feet moving across the wooden parquet tiles of the foyer. He gripped the poker tighter, then took out the knife and held it in his left hand. If they came together he'd look to take one out quickly with the knife.

"Motherfuckers killed Anton, man."

"I know. I heard you the first time. I saw the body."

"Goddamn motherfuckers. He didn't deserve that. What about Carl? He's gotta be toast too. He wouldn't be sitting this out if he knew. I'm gonna kill 'em. Kill 'em with my hands. You hear me?"

"Yeah, I hear you. Now calm down and shut the fuck up. Whoever's in here is going to hear you, too. You're gonna walk right into them and end up just as dead as Anton."

"No fuckin' way. I'm gonna gut these guys and feed 'em their own intestines. Piece by piece."

"Fine. Do that. But first, go check upstairs on the boss.

Then clear each floor, starting at the top. I'll check down here and meet you in the middle."

"Fine. You find them, you'll call me, right?"

"Right. I'll ask the guy to take five until my backup shows. Just get up there and take care of it before she wakes up and shoots us herself. It's gonna be bad enough as it is."

Alexei stood in the dark and listened to the angry one move away up the stairs. He put the knife back in his pocket. The one on the ground floor, the calmer one, would be the tougher of the two. Rage was always easy to beat.

Whether through fear or ignorance, the guy left the foyer light on and his approach was easily visible in the half shadow that slowly crept into the room. Alexei brought the iron poker up and swung it two-handed in a fast arc where the man's head was about to be.

But shadows worked both ways.

The guard brought up his forearm to block the blow and Alexei heard bone snap. The guard grunted and dropped his gun, but didn't panic or make a move for it. He pivoted low and kicked out a foot that clipped Alexei's heel and sent him sprawling. Alexei rolled with the fall and came up on one knee.

The man was quick. He'd jumped back and was crouched by the corner of the large mahogany desk. His arm hung at his side. Alexei could see a bulge of bone pressing out at an odd angle near the guard's wrist. The man picked up a large Lucite cube that sat on the desk and threw it. Alexei turned slightly, and the cube dug into his shoulder. It wasn't meant to damage, only distract. His opponent lunged across the room.

Alexei brought the poker up. The guard was too close to stop his momentum. The point speared him in the gut before pushing through his back. He stumbled to the side, hit the wall, and slid down. His hands grasped the poker. He coughed up blood. Alexei stood, checked the hallway to see if the man's partner had heard the commotion. It was empty and quiet.

He felt the pills dialing down the pain as they worked their way into his blood.

He took out his knife. One more to go.

CHICAGO

The trip from Oregon to Chicago took two days. By the time the bus pulled into the city terminus, Max's knees were stiff to the point of pain and he was tired of staring at crabgrass and litter on the side of two-lane interstates.

He'd left right away, the morning after talking to Danny. He'd called Junior and drained any goodwill he had left by leaving him in the lurch for a cook.

"Family emergency. I hope to be back in a week or so."

"I hope I have a job for you when you get back."

"I understand, Junior. I hope so, too."

And he did. He liked working the grill at the diner and part of him really did want to make it back, but the other part of him knew it was a long shot. He knew he was saying goodbye. He could feel the storm gathering, could feel the knife's edge on his neck. Things were going to get messy, and he was sure his time manning the grill in Baker City was going to be a casualty. He hoped it would be the only one, but doubted it.

"I'm sorry to put you in this spot."

"I'm sorry, too." Junior softened a bit. "Take care of your-self, Matt."

"I'll try."

Outside the terminal, Max decided to walk to the Field Museum rather than take a cab. The city air was sharp and refreshing after being cooped up on the bus. It had been a long time since he'd been in Chicago. After that visit as a kid with Danny and his aunt, he had been only once more: a business trip for Carter that he'd rather forget.

He checked the free city map he'd picked up inside the bus station. The museum was three miles into the teeth of the wind, toward the lake, but he couldn't stand the thought of getting into another moving tin can. He could definitely use the exercise after the bus ride, and he had a few other things to look into on the way.

He walked east, then south, zigzagging his way toward the water, enjoying the flare of horns, and shoulder-to-shoulder bustle of pedestrians. After the solitude of Baker City, the impatient eagerness and energy of a big city put a little charge in his step. It wasn't Boston, but it wasn't bad.

It took almost an hour to walk to the museum, but he was still early. He walked to a spot that offered good sight lines to the main entrance but kept him partially hidden behind a small fountain. He sat on a stone bench on the edge of the museum's grounds and thought about that childhood trip. It was the summer between fifth and sixth grade. On those rare occasions when he let himself think of his childhood, that summer stuck out in his mind. A golden summer balanced right between childhood and adolescence. A perfect summer of long, carefree days. He was sure every kid had one. If you were lucky, maybe you had more than one, but he wasn't greedy.

From the bench, he watched Danny cut across the trimmed grass and up the path to the museum's entrance.

Here he was, risking his life again for his brother.

He waited ten minutes. He didn't expect Carter to send Danny alone. Danny didn't exactly inspire trust. He'd put a marker on his investment. Max walked around the block. He found Frankie sitting in a rented La Crosse on the east side of the museum. He was watching the front door, a cup of coffee in one hand and a Marlboro between fingers that hung out the window. Good ol', Frankie. So predictable.

Max remembered sitting next to Frankie in similar vehicles back in Charlestown late at night, waiting for some poor schmuck to show so they could twist his arm until they got the money the loser owed Carter. Frankie would drink gas station coffee and bitch about the pain in his lower back from sitting on his wallet.

Should he take care of it now? Was that an option? No. It was too open, with too much potential for complications. Carter would find them without breaking a sweat. Danny couldn't live a life on the run. He was a social animal. He'd never make it.

Max turned on his heel and walked back the way he came in a light flow of pedestrian sidewalk traffic. He kept his head tucked low into his collar. Frankie didn't move. Max looped around and went in the museum's back entrance.

He needed the money to save Danny's neck first, and then an exit plan. One step at a time.

He spotted Danny outside the gift shop. It was an old joke. Joyce had been upset that of all the things at the museum, Danny and Max had loved the gift shop and the cafeteria the best. Old bones and dusty plaques or plastic dinosaurs and mummy putty? It was no contest for 12-year-old boys.

Even from a distance, Max could see the yellowing bruises and delicate way Danny moved. He had a knit hat pulled low and a nylon jacket zipped up high, but it didn't hide the

mouse under his left eye or the split and swollen lip. They'd
worked him over pretty good.

Danny didn't immediately see him. Max watched him pick
up a large, peach-colored candlestone filled with agate. Max
wondered vaguely who bought these things.

"Hey, little brother."

Danny turned and smiled. "Whoa. Look at you. You look
like the Sully I remember from Pop Warner before Coach
Fitz and his weight room got a hold of ya. All slim and trim."

Max patted his middle. "Yeah, lost some weight. Being a
fugitive will do that to you."

Danny's smile slipped for a second before snapping back.
"It's good to see you, man." They hugged, Max being careful
with Danny's injuries, then stepped back.

Despite everything that had happened between them,
including the current circumstances, Max realized it was
good, really good, to see a friendly face, someone he didn't
need to hide from or lie to, someone with whom he didn't
have to remind himself of his own name or current backstory.
"You, too," he said.

Danny turned the candlestone over in his hands before
putting it back on the glass shelf. "I really did like this place
in spite of what Mom thought. Always liked history. It was
just so unreal to me back then, you know? Genghis Khan
and mummies and that T-Rex. It was all we talked about for
the next six months. Being explorers, bandits, finding
hidden treasure. You remember that? That Indiana Jones
shit."

"I remember you stole that man's hat at church. His old
fedora, and you tried to convince me it was the same type
Harrison Ford wore."

Danny laughed. "God, we were stupid, huh?"

"We were kids. C'mon, let's get out of here. I could use a
drink."

"Sounds like a plan." Danny turned and started back toward the front exit.

"Nah, over here. The neighborhood joints are this way."

———

They walked west until they were clear of the tourist traps and chain restaurants around the museum campus and settled on a place called O'Reilly's. It was early afternoon, and the place was mostly empty. The lone bartender was stocking glasses and a couple dedicated drinkers were scattered around sipping their beverage of choice, but the back booths were free. Afternoon drinkers rarely wanted company, and no one gave the brothers a second look. Max slipped into the corner banquette and kept his back to the wall and his eyes to the door. No one was sitting within twenty feet. Danny went to the rail and ordered two drafts and carried them back.

"Place couldn't hold a candle to The Arms."

Max glanced around. "I guess. It's not bad. I'd take this over the plastic places we'd find downtown crammed full of ties and fake smiles."

"Hate to be the one to tell ya, bro, but even The Arms has its share of yuppies nowadays. Not during the week, thank God, but on the weekends. Weird times on the home front, Mikey. It's all the rage now to live near the Hill. It's hip to buy up the double-deckers on L Street and renovate 'em. Fill them up with shiny floors and stainless steel. You believe that?" He took a long swallow of beer. "If we'd hung onto Mom's place, we'd be rolling in it. Half a mil easy with that view."

Max looked at him, not really hearing his patter. His brother had gotten older, but after two minutes across the table, Max knew little else had changed. Danny's maturity had leveled off at age sixteen, and nothing was going to change now except qualifying for his senior citizen's discount at the movies, if he made it that long.

Right or wrong, Max partly blamed himself. Should he have married Cindy? Should he have just turned his back and left right off? Should he have tried to straddle both worlds? Should he have made that last phone call? Or, why stop there? Should he have stepped in and intervened all those times for Danny? Maybe if he'd let Danny take a fall himself once or twice things would have turned out different. Maybe some time in juvie could have shaken him up, given him some perspective. Then again, maybe it would have made it worse, maybe instilled a mean streak, rotted out his core, and turned Danny more violent.

These weren't new thoughts and they ricocheted around his head in worn grooves.

He sipped his beer and listened to his brother chatter on.

"I tell you, though, Mikey, some of those yuppies are goddamn crazy in the sack, you know?"

He felt a sudden stab of pain in his heart. Max knew. He never told Danny this, but he'd first laid eyes on Cindy in the Purple Shamrock. Even today, Danny would probably still give him shit for ever stepping foot in that place if he found out.

Before more memories of Cindy bubbled up, Max decided to bring the conversation around to the point. "Must be good for business though, right? All them well-heeled types looking for some action. A little taste."

"Yeah, I guess. Can't deny that. Still, I'd rather sell to townies or junkies that I know than some dude in a Banana Republic shirt. More cash, sure, but lots more risk, too."

"Price of doing business."

Danny drained his beer. He waved a hand at the old photos, pennants, and street signs hanging off the walls. "I bet they bought this shit out of a catalog." He got up and went for two more beers. Max still had more than half a glass in front of him.

Sitting back down, Danny immediately knocked back half his new pint.

"Jesus, Danny, slow down. We're just having a drink, not going to a Pogues show. We gotta figure this out."

Danny gave him a crooked smile, and Max got a look at the pinpricks of his pupils and realized Danny's head was already up on something stronger than beer.

He reached across and grabbed his brother's wrist. "What are you on? Goddammit, Danny, I'm sticking my neck way out on this and you're high."

"Relax, bro. I just needed a little something for the pain. Frankie and his little sidekick really went to town on me. He says to say hello, by the way."

"I'm sure he does."

"C'mon, it's just a little something to take the edge off. You know I can carry my own water." He shrugged Max's hand off and took another sip but then nudged the glass away. "Speaking of water, let me hit the head and then we can talk shop."

Danny eased out of the booth and headed toward the back of the bar. Max watched him put an arm out and almost knock a framed picture of Bobby Hull off the wall. He wondered if maybe it would be easier to just do this himself rather than rely on Danny having his back.

That was also another familiar thought.

————

Danny went in the first stall and latched the door. He pulled out his cell phone and punched the first speed dial. It was the only number in the phone.

"Where the fuck are you? My ass is getting numb."

"Relax, we're down the street at some bar called O'Reilly's."

"You better not be trying to fuck me, Danny. You wouldn't last on the run, you know."

"I'm calling, aren't I? Mikey wanted to go out the side door. What am I supposed to tell him? No, let's go out the front so Frankie Winters can eyeball your ass?"

Danny could hear Frankie's heavy breathing on the other end.

"Fine. I hear ya. Where'd you say you were? O'Callahan's?"

"O'Reilly's. Go a couple blocks west and take a right, away from the water. You'll see the sign. It's on the left side. About halfway down."

"Hey, Danny?"

"Yeah?"

"It really him?"

For a second, Danny could feel it. He knew Frankie was feeling it, too. The crackle and snap of memory, back to a time when Mikey was a young comer: smart, tough, and utterly fearless. Carter's favorite. His go-to boyo. Everyone thought Mikey Sullivan would one day rule the world, at least the parts that mattered. It was a good memory, a time when they were all younger and all still friends.

"Yeah, it's really him."

CIPHER

Duffy looked down at the tangle of letters, squiggles, and lines that dotted the pages of Porter's handwritten notes. At first glance, it was a mess of indecipherable hieroglyphics, but he was slowly piecing it together. The notes were a mix of standard shorthand, some personal symbols, numbers, and initials. The clutch of typed pages was better. There were some full sentences and sometimes whole paragraphs. Duffy knew this was the way Porter liked to work. He would jot down scraps of sentences or strings of words whenever they occurred to him, then, as a deadline loomed, he would stitch it all together into a story.

The typewritten pages provided at least a partial skeleton of what Porter had found. It had the potential to be front-page news, and not just the front page in Essex. Porter's notes made it clear that a significant cover-up had taken place two years ago. The bloody events weren't just a drug deal gone wrong. It involved more people, in higher places, than just Max Strong. In fact, what little there was about Max Strong pointed to him being the fall guy, the convenient patsy.

The volume of notes in the box told Duffy that Porter

planned a long, in-depth piece. Was this meant for the paper or something larger? A book? Was this Porter's ticket out of whatever self-imposed exile brought him to Essex in the first place?

Could it be Duffy's ticket out as well?

What had Porter always ranted about after a few nips from the scotch he kept in his drawer? *The story was king. Nothing beat the story, kid.* The line sounded lifted from an old Bogart movie or maybe a bad late-night TV drama. Duffy smiled at the memory now. He pulled open the bottom drawer. The scotch bottle rolled forward and clunked against the wood. Duffy felt a sudden determination, selfish, foolish, or both, to finish what Porter started. He knew Porter wouldn't want the story to just wither on the vine because he was no longer around to write it.

The story was king after all.

He pushed the drawer closed with his foot.

The story could also get you killed.

Alone in the office, with the shadows getting longer, he felt an itch on the back of his neck and decided he didn't want to be in the building after dark. He printed off a list of standard shorthand symbols from the Internet and placed it back in the box with the rest of the notes. He put the box in his bag along with his laptop. He locked the office door and went down to the street. He paused outside; the feeling of eyes on his neck lingered. Mrs. Olsen was gone, her shop dark and locked. He looked up and down the street. No one was out or moving. Should he go home? Would he be putting his parents in danger by bringing this home? Maybe. He remembered the dark hole in Porter's forehead. Probably.

He decided to go to the public library. There were carrels in the basement he could work in, he'd have Wi-Fi access to the Internet, and he had his cell phone if he needed to call anyone. More importantly, it was a well-lit, public place with other people.

———

Three hours later, an announcement crackled over the library's PA system: closing time. Duffy had worked through all the handwritten notes at least once. With repetition, the translation was coming faster, the dips and whorls rearranging themselves in front of his eyes into words and sentences. He referred to the shorthand printout less and less. It looked like Porter had already done most of the legwork. Duffy knew he would have to reconfirm all of it, but the rails had been set down. The story was out there waiting for someone to follow the tracks.

One set of initials popped up again and again: WE. The letters were peppered throughout the notes. Whoever the initials referred to was the key source. WE didn't have all the answers. But they did provide a lot of the convincing details in Porter's narrative. WE was the first domino. If Duffy could figure out who WE was and talk to him or her on the record, get WE to trust him as Porter had been trusted, he could push the story forward until more dominoes fell and finish what Porter had started.

WE. WE. It circled in Duffy's head like a merry-go-round, but he couldn't come up with anyone Porter had mentioned, nor did the initials fit with a town official or prominent resident.

He marked his place and packed up the notes. He said goodbye to Mrs. Hartigan, the librarian (first name Emma, initials EH), and walked outside.

It was full dark with little moonlight. The old, balky streetlights hardly made a dent in the blackness. As he turned the corner onto Locust Street, Duffy began to have second thoughts about his decision to work at the library rather than back at home. The paranoia that seemed silly and far away under the bright lights of the library was creeping up on him again. He set off at a brisk pace for home.

WE. WE. WE. It blinked on and off in front of his eyes like a neon sign. WE. WE. WE. Nothing bounced back, just an empty echo.

As he passed the elementary school playground, he heard the squeak of metal on metal. He stopped and looked into the dark and saw nothing. He convinced himself it was just the chains on the swings moving in the wind.

He kept walking.

Something rustled in the thick hedges that backed onto the parking lot. Probably just a chipmunk or a squirrel.

Behind him, came the soft scrape of leather on gravel.

Duffy put his head down and walked faster.

SHORTCUTS

Walking across the park from their office, Jaimie decided, screw it, Lupe could wait twenty minutes for dinner. She wanted a drink. Check that. She deserved a drink. That newspaper photo of Strong was a find, pure gold. You could call it dumb luck. Or, you could call it being in the right place at the right time. Either way, it took work, damn hard work, to be in the right position, ready and waiting to take advantage of it. And that called for a celebratory drink.

She altered her course and exited the park through a side gate, coming out halfway down Windsor Avenue. Vintage, a new wine bar she'd been eyeing during her lunch breaks, was just two blocks over. She looked across the street. By cutting down Spring Street, she could save herself ten minutes and a long, chilly walk via the main avenues.

She crossed, but then paused at the top of the street. It was dark and narrow, with no overhead streetlights. It wasn't an alley exactly, but it wasn't a main strip either. The only light came from a couple of meager security lamps mounted over storefronts. By day, it was a funky bohemian side street that housed alternative bookstores, bead shops, vintage furniture and herbal stores, a place she wouldn't think twice about walking through. But, by night, it looked a lot different.

She looked up toward Windsor again. Cabs, Town Cars, and metro buses whipped by in a frenzy. Scattered pedestrians dotted the sidewalks. Was it worth cutting through when she could walk the long way around on brightly lit streets? She chided herself for her sudden fear of the dark. She had pepper spray in her purse. She could see the lights of Congress Street at the far end. Just do it, girl, she prodded herself. When did you become such a wimp?

In the end, her thin leather pumps made the decision for her. Her feet were cold, and her shoes were already pinching. A long walk wasn't enticing.

Thirty feet in, just when the shadows closed up behind her, she heard footsteps. She put her hand in her purse and fished around: lipstick, compact, gum, keys. Shit. The pepper spray was in her other purse. She had switched handbags yesterday because of a court appearance. She stopped but didn't turn. The footsteps stopped.

Her palms were slick. She took two more steps, whirled and turned, holding up her lipstick.

"Leave me the fuck alone. I got pepper spray, asshole." A wild bluff, but it was all she had.

There was no one there.

She watched two cabs blast past on Windsor, their headlights briefly illuminating the top of the street. Had she imagined it? Maybe heard the footsteps from people walking past echoing down the narrow street?

She tried to see into the blackness at the edges of the street, the pools of shadows by the shop fronts, but it was too dark and there were too many doorways and stairwells to be sure she was alone.

She gripped the lipstick tube tighter, turned around, and

started walking again. Her heels clicked loudly on the flagstone pavement. Why didn't she change into her sneakers? Stupid and vain. She must have known on some level that she'd talk herself into a drink. She didn't want to wear sneakers into a wine bar.

After a few steps, she heard it again. She stopped and pretended to fiddle with the strap on her damn high heels. She heard one light, shuffling step, then nothing. It was not her imagination. Someone was behind her.

She took out her phone and dialed Kate again. It rang, then rolled to voicemail. She began talking anyway, hoping the conversation would make this nutjob pause. She carried on a one-way conversation and strained to hear anything in the pauses.

Were they getting closer?

"Hi. Yeah, I should be there in a few minutes. I'm walking down Spring right now. I know, I know. Listen, I'm practically there."

What did they want?

"Just order me something. You choose."

Were they coming faster now?

She passed a narrow passageway that ran between the buildings that fronted the main streets. It was filled with dumpsters, empty boxes, and stray cats picking through the garbage. The alley dead-ended after twenty yards at a chain link fence. No help there.

She felt them getting closer. She stopped and turned again. She had to. The street still appeared empty. She couldn't see anyone. Her hands was aching from gripping the phone and lipstick so tightly.

How long was this goddamn street?

She felt a hand on her ankle, then a second brush her knee. The fear broke over her in a wave. She screamed and lashed out with her other foot. Her shoe came off. Shadows moved. A voice was saying something, but she couldn't hear. Adrenaline made her heart pound. She was reduced to a primitive state with a simple choice: fight or flight. She threw the phone and lipstick blindly and broke into a hobbling run. The heel on her second shoe snapped, and she kicked it off without slowing.

She ran, in stocking feet, clutching her purse like a shield, until she stumbled into the light and activity of Congress Street. A few people gave her surprised looks, then quickly turned away and kept walking, just another moment in the big city.

A cab passed, and she waved it down. The cabbie looked wary as he got a closer look at her, but she already had the door open. She jumped in and gave him her address. He pulled away, and neither of them looked back.

Jaimie managed to get the key in the lock despite her shaking hands and open the door. Lupe was on her before she had the door closed. She threw both deadbolts and moved a small table in front of the door as well. She picked up the cat, hugged her close, happy to have another heartbeat close to hers.

She poured a big glass of wine and took it to the sofa. Some slopped over the side and ran down her arm. She couldn't stop the tiny tremors. She turned the television on for the noise and sipped the wine until she had her nerves more under control. She reheated some leftovers, watched more mindless TV. When her eyes began to droop, she went to the bathroom, showered and climbed into bed.

Despite drinking almost an entire bottle of wine, she snapped awake twice in the middle of the night, sure that someone was in the room with her. Lupe raised her head both times with a questioning expression. She stroked the cat and listened, but heard only traffic from the street and the rattling of water pipes in an apartment upstairs. Both times she got out of bed and checked the bathroom and closets.

The next morning, with sunshine pouring in the windows and scouring away any shadows, she almost felt like herself. She brewed a pot of coffee and ate a bowl of cereal. As she chewed, she thought about the previous night and believed it was her own reaction more than the threat itself that was really bothering her. She had always considered herself a confident person, someone with well-earned armor and a backbone. She had pulled herself up and out of a bad situation and a bad neighborhood. She knew the world, or at least her part in it, and could handle herself. Last night, she lost that. She had panicked. Whatever happened, real or imaginary, had rattled her, pierced right through any armor she thought she had.

———

She felt it right away. Jaimie was a meticulous person and kept things in a meticulous way. With Kate still gone, she had free rein to keep the office the way she liked it. And something wasn't right.

Standing in the doorway, she kept still and let her eyes drift over the open space. Back-to-back work desks, a worn couch, matching coffee table, filing cabinets, mini-fridge, fax/copy combo machine. Nothing jumped out. It had come right up and washed over her when she opened the door, but now it had receded. Maybe she was still spooked and feeling the effects from last night.

She put her bag and coffee down, stepped back, turned off the light, and stood just outside the threshold. She closed her eyes, forced out a deep breath, flipped on the light switch, then opened her eyes. That did it.

Shapes moved against the far wall. She went to her desk.

She always closed down her computer at night by putting it to sleep, clicking on a button that set the screen to black. She looked at the screen now. Colorful shifting patterns of abstract shapes flowed across it and created shadows on the far wall. For her screensaver to be on now, someone had to have been inside and used her computer after she left the office last night.

Did the computer just reboot on its own? It happened sometimes. Was Kate back? The cleaners weren't due for two more days. She was about to walk across the hall and knock on Kate's door when she caught a flash of red. She came all the way around and stood behind her desk. Her high heels from last night sat in a neat pair next to her chair. They were polished and repaired. She looked at the desk. Her cell phone was beside the keyboard next to her tube of lipstick.

A note was written on the pad she kept for phone messages.

'Sorry we missed you last night. See you soon.'

The newspaper printout and the case file for Strong were both gone.

DEDICATION

Logins shrugged his shoulders and tried to get comfortable. The heavy starch on the collar of his polyester dress uniform was irritating his neck. He wanted to rip the thing off and fling it into a corner but, sitting up on the dais, he had to settle for contorting his shoulders every few minutes in an attempt to ease the itch. It wasn't working, and the snug fit only reminded him of the weight he'd put on since getting the sheriff's star. He tried to focus on the speeches, if only for a distraction.

The senator was still talking. He had been at it now for almost fifteen minutes, completely unaware he had lost the audience at least twelve minutes ago. From his rhetoric, you'd think the Heaney brothers were his weekend fishing buddies rather than some small-town cops he had never heard of before a memorial dedication was proposed during campaign season. Every bit of it rang hollow to Logins, and he thought the audience saw right through it as well. Impassioned stump speeches had never been the senator's forte. He had other talents, most not fit for anything other than backroom dealing. Finally, after a last bland platitude, he introduced then yielded the microphone to Tom Sanderson, the former Essex mayor and now a state senator.

Earlier, as Logins had watched the motorcade pull to the curb next to the town square, Logins was surprised to see Senator Harris himself get out of the limo. When he was followed out of the Town Car by a smiling Tom Sanderson, a lot of pieces suddenly started clicking into place, like Hagel's continued presence in town.

There was no doubt that Hagel took the long view of things. Was two years in a relative backwater, political no-man's land like Essex long enough to shape a raw candidate like Sanderson into something more, someone capable of skipping a few rungs on the political ladder from a small-town mayor, to a nobody at the state house all the way to a fresh-faced United States senator from Minnesota? Could he push Sanderson further? It would be a meteoric, almost unheard of, political rise.

Sanderson stood, acknowledged the round of polite applause, smoothed his red and blue striped tie, then stepped to the microphone. He let the clapping subside and thanked Senator Harris for his kind words before launching into his own speech.

The difference between the two men was striking. Hagel's work had paid off. Where Harris seemed stooped and tired, Sanderson's mere smile sent out a ripple of energy that revived the flagging crowd. It wasn't so much what he said, but how. It was a commanding performance. The stock speech expected at such an event rolled off his tongue with an easy and bracing oration that never felt forced or false despite the familiar platitudes. The man was a natural and, with Hagel's help and connections, the sheriff suddenly had no trouble seeing a long and bright political future.

Sanderson, either more acutely aware of his audience or

more averse to lying about the Heaneys' nature, wrapped his speech up quickly. While he and Senator Harris stepped off the dais and moved over to the cloth-draped memorial for the unveiling, Logins thought of another reason Hagel was still lurking and suddenly the constant check-up phone calls made more sense, too.

Logins caught a glimpse of Mike Duffy in the crowd. He hadn't seen Duffy since finding him locked inside the paper's office earlier in the week. Today, he was carrying a notebook and had an old 35mm camera slung around his neck. The *Essex Standard-Times* had missed its second issue since Porter's death, but it looked like Duffy was still acting as a roving reporter, or at least trying. The kid looked frazzled and tired, and something else. Logins watched him watching the two politicians. What was that in his face? Anger? No, that was too strong. Duffy was staring at the entourage with a set jaw that looked ... confrontational, as if he wanted to get them alone in a room and hold his own personal press conference.

The speeches and unveiling complete, the ceremony started breaking up. Duffy must have felt the sheriff's gaze. He looked up and gave him a curt nod. His cell phone must have rung then because he shifted away, pulled it out of his hip pocket, and put it up to his ear. Logins made a mental note to follow up with the kid's parents, see how he was dealing with the shock of finding Porter's body. Friend or foe, stranger or family, dead bodies were never easy. And they liked to hang around in your head. You had to face up to it or it would fester and get under your skin until it started to change you.

I should know, Logins thought.

"This is Duffy," he said answering his cell phone and ducking his head to hear over the murmuring of the crowd.

"Hi, this is Jim McCabe. My son Brian asked me to call you."

In high school, Duffy never had any illusions that he was the most popular kid in class, but he wasn't at the bottom of the social ladder, either. Working on the school paper, he met and mixed with most of the groups in school, and he got along fine with just about everyone. Brian McCabe was more of a jock, basketball and tennis, but he had played sax in the school's jazz band with Duffy. They had bonded over Coltrane and Brubeck and still stayed in touch occasionally after Brian went away to school at Iowa State.

"Right, thanks for calling me back Mr. McCabe—"

"Jim, just call me Jim."

"Okay; thanks for calling me back, Jim. I went to Essex High with Brian. I'm not sure if he mentioned it when you spoke, but I work for the *Essex Standard-Times* now as a reporter."

"Right, he told me. I was sorry to hear about your boss getting killed. That was awful. This town is changing. First, those murders and all that mess two years ago. Now, your boss. This is not the town I grew up in. Don't get me started. Brian said you had some questions for me?"

"Yes, I did. You still work at the Department of Public Works in town, right?"

"Sure. I'll have my thirty in next June at DPW, then its goodbye Minnesota winters and hello Phoenix sunshine."

"I was just wondering if you knew anything about the Orchard View construction."

"That land out on 99 by the Looney place?"

"That's right."

"I know it. They've been trying to build something out there since you and Brian were in diapers. It's always been stop and go. Fits and starts. Most of the farmers ended up selling after the last round of subsidies dried up. Family farms are an endangered species out here."

"Not Looney, though."

"Well, Looney didn't sell, but he was dying like the rest of 'em. He was just five times as stubborn. He hated the whole idea of plowing over that land. I'm sure they bribed, cajoled, and threatened, but no one was ever been able to move him. He's kept both the developers and the town at bay in the courts, even convinced an environmental group to get involved to add more red tape. Something about migrating cranes."

"You guys do any work out there over the years?"

"DPW? Not much beyond the planning stage. The town upgraded the main sewer line out there in anticipation, but we haven't done much else. Until the Looney case gets resolved, everything's on hold. If I remember right, it was going to be a mall with some condos filling out the back of the lot. Not sure why anyone would shop or live way out there."

"You happen to remember the developer's name?"

"Yeah, I actually do. I probably wouldn't remember, but this one had a distinct name. Tuckahoe Development and Construction. You can imagine how my crew got a few jokes out of that one."

Duffy was scribbling notes, trying to keep up with the gregarious Jim McCabe. "They keep re-upping the permits?"

"Last I heard. But I don't keep up with it. Look, if that's it, my lunch break is almost up. I've got to get back."

"Sure thing. Thanks for calling me back."

Duffy hung up. The Orchard View development never came up in any of the published stories from two years ago, but Porter had a lot of notes on it—piles of notes, but no conclusions, at least none he'd written down. Why was that land so important? Duffy was still stuck on the identity of WE in Porter's notes, but if Orchard View was tied up in all of this, then the public paper trail might give him another angle into figuring out this story.

He'd follow the money. Just like Porter taught him.

RIGHT AFTER VI

Alexei left the impaled corpse and walked out of the blood-soaked office. He stood in the entryway foyer. He heard footsteps and doors opening and closing above. The angry one was still searching. He hadn't heard the struggle down on the first floor. Thick carpet and thick walls.

Alexei went up the curving stairs to the second-floor landing. The stairway continued, turned back on itself and rose higher, to an additional floor, but Alexei heard the man searching at the opposite end of this floor.

He started in that direction, keeping close to the wall. The man emerged from a room on the left. He was short and squat, with black hair trimmed down almost to the scalp and a wide, flat nose. His legs bowed out slightly at the knees. Alexei thought he had the look of a wrestler.

His eyes widened momentarily in surprise, then Alexei saw his muscles relax. Animal instincts. He had sized up Alexei's rumpled appearance, his gimpy leg, his graying hair, and considered himself the favorite in this fight.

The man rolled his shoulders and came forward. "I'm gonna rip your arms off and make you choke on 'em."

The man was lost in bloodlust. He should have stopped to consider that Alexei had already killed five of his co-workers. He should have just run down the stairs and fled. Alexei still would have killed him, but he might not have made it as painful.

Alexei could see the butt of a gun at the guy's waist but watched as he pulled a knife instead. He was compounding an already stupid choice.

"Gonna sharpen this baby on your teeth."

He also should have kept his mouth shut.

He moved closer, jabbing and feinting with the knife. Five inches long, serrated, and slightly curved. A showpiece more suited to intimidation than a truly useful weapon.

Alexei watched him and retreated, never taking his eyes off the blade.

Knives had their uses, but Alexei had never favored them for hand-to-hand combat. Too easy to cut yourself or have it turned against you. Easier and safer to use your hands.

But Alexei wasn't stupid. He could take out his own gun and shoot the moron, he was the last guard left, but something about him just pissed Alexei off. Backed up against the stairs now, Alexei pulled his own blade. It was an ugly cousin in comparison to the man's shiny Bowie, but a pro would choose Alexei's two-inch carbon blade any day. The carbon was stronger than steel and the squat blade was sharp enough not to snag on bones or organs. You weren't skinning a deer for your buddies. You were trying to kill a man.

"What are you gonna do with that? Poke me to death?"

That last bit confirmed Alexei's suspicions that the man was an amateur blowhard who had gotten as far as he had on his muscles and bluster. He was a showpiece himself, just like his knife.

Alexei looked at him and smiled.

"What the fuck you smiling at, old man?"

"A dead man."

"That right?" The man lunged forward with a wild swing.

Alexei watched the man's hip shift and anticipated the move. He shuffled forward inside the arc of the blade. The man's wrist hit Alexei's shoulder and the knife just hit air. Alexei brought his own free arm down and pinned the guy's arm and blade against his side. In the same motion, he stabbed forward once, twice, three times to the man's ribs and midsection. The man grunted, more in surprise than pain. He didn't feel it yet, but the fight was over.

Alexei spun out of their embrace, keeping the man's arm locked under his own. The man's elbow was now flexed in the wrong direction. Alexei used his hips and body weight to increase the pressure. The man's face went white and beads of sweat popped on his forehead. The big knife dropped to the floor.

Alexei stepped back further and snapped the elbow with a crunch, then brought his fist and the hilt of the knife around, punching it into the man's windpipe. Any noise was snuffed out. The man's eyes rolled back as he slumped against the wall and died.

Alexei wiped the blood off his knife and slipped it back in his pocket then he bent and picked up the big Bowie knife . He hefted it in his hand. It didn't have bad balance. It was a better instrument than he initially thought. He dropped it back on top of the body. Better than the guard deserved.

Alexei went to the stairs and climbed up one more flight. The stairs ended at a small landing with a heavy oak door adorned with a brass knocker in the shape of a tiger. He smiled. Only three people in the world would likely get that joke.

He tried the knob. It turned in his hand, and he went

inside. He closed and locked the door behind him, taking the key from the inside lock and placing it in his pocket. Once this last bit was done, he planned to get some rest.

The master bedroom took up the entire top floor. Despite its size, the gabled roof sloped low at the edges and gave the room an intimate feel. A large walk-in closet was to the right, along with a tall armoire and a dresser. The bathroom and a sitting area were to the left. He could see the sinks and part of a large tub through the open door. A king-sized bed sat in the middle of the room against the back wall. A large skylight, at least ten feet by ten feet, was set above the bed, giving a clear view of the night sky. A small lamp on the bedside table was turned on. A woman watched him, propped up among a sea of pillows and dark silk sheets. Her hands were in her lap.

"Hello, Alexei."

"Hello, Natalia."

"I'm sorry our last meeting must be like this."

"Yes. Me, too."

"A friendship as long as ours shouldn't end like this."

"Everything ends."

"Always so literal."

Alexei just shrugged. "Pull the sheets back."

She did. No weapons.

"Pillows."

She tossed them off the bed one by one then propped herself against the wooden headboard.

"Nightstand."

She pulled the drawer open then leaned back. There were only two things inside. A gun and a bottle of pills. He picked up the pills. It was in her name, at least what she was calling herself now. He put the bottle on the table and removed the gun. Nothing fancy, just black, small, and lethal. He slid the clip out and put it in his pocket. He put the empty gun next to the pills on the table.

He quickly searched the rest of the room, mostly by feel, he never let his eyes stray from her for long.

"I told them you weren't dead. They never listen to me."

"They listened enough for you to get where you are now."

"Actions and results and, of course, money, got me this far, but I was going no further." She sat up straighter. "These organizations only change so much. Tactics and strategy from a woman? Never."

"Still, an admirable place to end given where we started," Alexei said.

"Yes. I have not shamed the face of my father."

"You never knew your father."

"It does not mean the bastard is not watching."

Alexei moved into the circle of light and stood at the foot of the bed. Natalia was a small woman and virtually disappeared in the large bed. Small and delicate, in appearance at least, with fine cheekbones and porcelain skin that was offset by a mane of black hair. Lying in the bed now, she gave off a sense of 'little girl lost' vulnerability, someone easily underestimated. Alexei knew she'd been making people pay for that mistake for a long time. They had met as children, two orphaned soldiers in Drobhov's ragtag street urchin army.

"I looked for you, you know. I knew if we didn't find a body that one day you would come. We looked, but you hid yourself well."

"There was no shame in hiding. I had to heal."

"Forgive me. I wasn't implying cowardice. I noticed the limp."

"A fall. You were almost free of me."

"I never wanted to be free of you, Alexei. I wanted you to work with me."

"You wanted me to work *for* you."

"It didn't have to be that way."

Alexei paused. "I know that now. You were right about a lot of things. But ..." He shrugged and waved his hand. He sat on the corner of the bed, out of her reach, suddenly very tired. He sank down into the soft mattress, and his greatest desire right then was to keep sinking and forget everything else.

"Drobhov." Natalia finished.

"Yes. An eye for an eye."

"I remember. It's always been your way. Ruthless, dangerous, sometimes foolish, but effective for a certain time and place. But not now. Not anymore. I never understood your attachment to that man. I mean, I understood it on some level, he saved our lives as children, but we paid that debt with interest long ago. Why, Alexei? Why stay? You were never a man for sentiment."

This was true. Sentiment for Alexei was largely an afterthought, something to consider only when it might provide an advantage or expose weakness, but the struggles and bonds of war are just as hard to break as they are to explain. Natalia wasn't with them during those times.

"It goes beyond the beginning. Beyond when we were children. There were times in the Army. Hard times. He stood for me, and I for him. I can't explain it to myself. It just is. Sergei wasn't always that person at the end. Surely, you know that better than most. The loss of his wife was hard. The loss of his child broke him. The bottle was easier. I made a choice to see it through to the end, wherever and whatever it entailed." He paused, rubbing his hand over his face. "Also, sometimes I think it is better to be the man behind the man."

She reached forward and took his arm. He tensed, but she moved no closer. "You can still have that, Alexei. Work with me *now*. Together we can make them listen and, if not, we can *force* them to listen."

It was tempting, so tempting. "I'm sorry. If the situation was different, I would say yes, instantly, but certain lines I cannot cross. You allowed Sergei to die."

"Alexei, please, let the past go. Let Sergei go. It was time. He knew it. I knew it. And somewhere deep down, you know it, too."

He stood. "Maybe. But that was not my choice to make. And it was not yours either. He was not a dog to be put down. I cannot let that go."

She sat back. She had made her case. She would not beg. It was another thing Alexei respected about her.

"Do you still have your pill?" He asked.

"Jesus, no. Do you? I had that thing removed when I left Vladivostok for the last time. But there are always other means." She picked up the orange pill bottle and shook it. Alexei was unable to read the label from where he stood. She unscrewed the top and shook five, then six, pills into her palm.

"They are strong. This will do." She took a deep breath.

"I'm sorry," Alexei said.

"Me, too." She put the pills in her mouth and picked up the glass of water.

Alexei got his arm up just in time. Most of the liquid splashed against his raised forearm. Most, but not all. His face and eyes began to itch and water immediately. His arm burned and the fumes made him choke. He felt his throat tighten. He stumbled backward off the bed.

She'd lulled him with talk and memories until he dropped his guard. He'd almost underestimated her. Almost, but not quite. The bedroom door was the only exit, other than the windows, and it was locked tight. Even if the door had been left wide open, Alexei didn't think Natalia would run. She was smart enough to know this was the best chance she'd get, and she would try to kill him now rather than risk another encounter.

He retreated further, hunched over and wiping at his tearing eyes. He found the knife in his pocket and held it up and ready. He put his back against a corner of the room. He reached out, felt something, a chair, and pulled it in front of him.

He put the knife away now and pulled out the gun. He heard a drawer open and close somewhere to his left. He turned his head but could only see gray shapes and soft shadows. Whatever toxin had been in the glass had bleached the color and most of the sight from his eyes, but he could still just discern shadows. He hoped that might be enough.

"Did you really think I'd lie down and die that easily?"

Her voice was coming from the left. Alexei turned and snapped off a shot.

"I thought you had retained some sense of honor."

"Honor." She laughed. "Honor among thieves. Do you really believe in that? This isn't your precious army anymore, Alexei. Not that I remember much honor from back then. Do you? Do you remember much honor when they came for the sisters? Or burned our villages? Or when they took me for interrogations? I don't. I remember getting raped and stuck with needles and dumped on the street."

Her voice was circling, going right to left. He shot again, anticipating, aiming ahead of her. A small shattering sound.

"I liked that vase."

Alexei held his fire after that. That was her game. Talk to him. Bait him into wasting his bullets while he was half-blind and half-deaf from the shots. But it also meant that she didn't have another gun of her own. Not one in this room. Maybe she thought of her bedroom as a sanctuary, a place she wouldn't spoil with the tools of her trade, a personal oasis amid the blood and testosterone that occupied her waking hours. It didn't sound like the Natalia he knew and grew up with, but she had just finished reminding him that people change.

He didn't want to give her time to fashion a plan, to gain any advantage. He stood and moved out from behind the chair. He sensed movement and felt a hot lance down his side. He turned to his right, but she was already past him and moving away. He put a hand to his ribs and it came back slick. He smiled. She wasn't completely unarmed. Unlike the guy on the second floor, Alexei knew Natalia knew how to use a knife. He wanted no part of that fight.

He retreated back into the corner.

He thought of the skylight. He aimed his gun at the ceiling. The first shot hit plaster. He adjusted his aim. The second shot was on target. Then a third. The shattered glass rained down into the room.

"Clever boy."

Alexei knew he was on the side of the floor with her closet and, more importantly, her shoes. Natalia had been fastidious, a lifelong habit borne out of her time in the orphanage and the sisters' iron fist: leave something out and it would be gone in the morning. She wouldn't leave her clothes strewn around. She was now barefoot and separated from her shoes by a river of sharp glass. Even if she did find something to use on her feet, Alexei would hear her coming now.

The temperature in the room was also dropping. It wasn't more than thirty degrees outside. Alexei pulled his coat close and sat back against the wall.

A stalemate.

CLOSING TIME

Max stood inside the plastic bus stop enclosure and watched the rotating bank clock across the street.

"Five minutes."

"Thank God. This wind is chapping my ass. How do people live in this city? Sure, we have snow and rudeness in Boston, but this place is like living in front of a fan. I hate it."

The late afternoon breeze off the Chicago River was a constant, but Max didn't feel it. He kept his attention focused on the building. Danny smoked down another cigarette and paced inside the tiny waiting area like a dog in a run, anxious and nervous, working up his nut and burning off his nerves.

They'd been standing out here for almost forty-five minutes. Six buses had passed. Max had waved them all on. Given all the people and faces the transit drivers saw every day, every hour, there was little chance anyone would remember the two of them.

This wasn't how he liked to operate. He liked to take his

time, do the legwork. Know the employees, know their families, know their routines. Back at home, he'd spend a month,
maybe six weeks, or more prepping for a job. Here in
Chicago, a city he'd arrived in yesterday morning, he was
going to do a job off a couple of hours of surveillance from a
bus stop. This was how you ended up in jail.

They were in an upscale mixed commercial-residential
neighborhood that, despite newly converted condos, still
favored office buildings. The blue signs tacked to the telephone poles called it New Eastside. He'd picked an anonymous Citibank on a two-way street in the middle of the
narrow block. There was a front and a back entrance. It sat
on the northern edge of Chicago's Loop business district, but
close to a chunk of a residential neighborhood where they
could disappear quickly if it came to that. No direct parking
lot, but enough available street parking. It was the most
promising he'd seen given his constraints.

"C'mon, grab the stuff, let's go."

"Let's do this." Danny stubbed out his cigarette and
grabbed the two duffel bags they'd picked up earlier.

They walked up the opposite side of the street. Through
the large plate glass window, Max saw the manager and two
tellers still left inside. They were chatting and preparing to
close. Another teller had left ten minutes ago. The last
customer had been a Hispanic man dropping off a blue bag of
business deposits at 4:35.

Traffic was picking up on the triple-decker street that cut
through the neighborhood to the south. Columbus Drive to
the north was bumper to bumper, but foot traffic on the
street had slowed considerably in the last half-hour. Max was
sure the street was hopping at midday, but closing in on 5:00,
business done, the sidewalks rolled up and the action moved
elsewhere.

They crossed at a break in traffic and ducked into an alley two doors down from the bank.

"Hand me your backpack," Max said. He placed it on the ground and unzipped it. He peeled off his jacket and dropped it in a heavy-duty trash bag he took from the duffel.

"Gimme your coat."

"Ah man. I love this coat. We gotta ditch 'em?"

"Yeah, c'mon, put it in the bag."

Danny did so, but reluctantly. Back at the cheap airport motel where they'd spent the night, they had changed into matching black jeans, black hooded sweatshirts, and white sneakers that they'd bought at a downtown Macy's the previous day. Danny had made some wisecracks about Max's deteriorating fashion sense, but Max knew that the more unremarkable and alike they looked, the less memorable they'd be individually.

"Here, put this on." Max handed Danny a leather three-quarters length car coat.

"Hey, now this is more like it. Very '70s. French Connection and shit."

Max ignored him. The coats were just another layer of the disguise: functional, easy mobility, and lots of pockets.

"C'mere." Max popped the top on a can of brown shoe polish and used his fingers to rub it over Danny's face. He didn't care if it was perfect. It would cover some of Danny's more egregious cuts and bruises, and the bad makeup job would give the bank employees something to focus on. Better to have them remember brown shoe polish than height, weight, or hair color.

Satisfied, he handed the can to Danny. "Do me." He checked his watch. "Hurry."

When Danny was done, Max pulled two Cubs hats and a pair of dark sunglasses from the bag to complete the disguise. He tossed the trash bag with their coats in the alley's dumpster and covered it with other rotting bags of garbage. He noticed a large Styrofoam coffee cup sitting amongst the bags and picked it up. A nice prop to promote a sense of normalcy.

Guns had been a problem they couldn't solve in a day in an unfamiliar city. If he'd had a few more days, Max probably could have found a couple and risked a buy, but with a day to swing the job and get Danny back to Boston with the money, he had to improvise.

If you could call squirt guns improvising.

They'd filled the insides with sand to add some weight, clipped off the plastic triggers, and spray painted the things a flat black. It was the best they had.

Max was hoping fear and ignorance would keep the bank employees from noticing. For all his chatter, this is where Max needed Danny the most. The job's adrenaline pushed him out on a ledge, and people could feel the crazy coming off him in waves. They didn't want any part of it. They would do whatever he told them.

Danny had insisted on a couple hunting knives from a sporting goods store as backup. Max didn't think it was necessary—if it all went belly up, a knife wasn't going to help —but had agreed, if only to keep Danny happy. He slipped the knife into his pocket, then handed Danny one, plus a package of zip ties.

"You remember?"

"Like riding a bike."

Max took the two toy guns out of the bag and then zipped it up.

"Can't believe we're doing this with squirt guns."

"Just bring it like we're back with the old crew and no one will know the difference. There are only three people to control. We get in, we get 'em on the ground, take the money, and we get out."

"Right." Danny stuffed the fake gun in his waistband and covered it with his sweatshirt. He left his coat unbuttoned.

"Ready?"

"Always, bro. Let's go."

They walked out of the alley and turned toward the bank.

JIMMY OLSEN

"You're kidding."

"Trust me, I'm not."

Kate had spent the remainder of the previous day trying to bluff her way past the online florist's customer service reps to get more information about the graveside deliveries and catching up on two days of lost sleep. She was still drooling into her pillow when Jaimie called. Unable to get any reception at her motel, Kate had stumbled to her car and driven out of town, closer to the interstate, to wrangle a clear enough signal to call back. As Jaimie told her about the photo, Matt Diver, Baker City, the alley, and finally the office break-in, Kate quickly shook off the last vestiges of sleep.

"Jesus, are you all right?"

"I was a bit of a mess last night, but better this morning, at least until I got to the office. I had convinced myself it was all random, just some punks or homeless guys following me. I was rattled, but ready to push past it. Chalk it up to the cost of living in the city. Now, I don't know. It feels," she paused and took a breath, "scarier, but less real somehow. Like I'm a walk-on for a bad cable movie. I'm all mixed up, Kate."

"That's okay. Mixed up is fine. Mixed up is normal. I'm still mixed up and it's been almost two years. It's going to take time." There was a beat of silence before Kate asked, "You have the gun?"

"Yeah, it's right here."

After the Gonzales case had almost killed them both, Kate had bought Jaimie a Taurus 85. Small enough to fit in her purse, this was the first time it had been out of the case in over a year. It had become a running joke between them. It didn't feel like a joke anymore.

"Good. Take it with you when you leave. Keep it on you until this thing is over. Better yet, take some time off. Maybe go see your sister?"

"And deal with my hellion nephews? No way. That's the last thing I want to do. I want to see this thing through. That's the one thing I'm not mixed up about. I didn't like getting pushed around by Smith any more than you did."

"All right." Kate couldn't hold back a small smile, even if Jaimie couldn't see it. That little outburst told her more than anything that Jaimie was going to be okay. "So, you think it was the mysterious Mr. Smith?"

"Had to be, right? Him or his associates, given that they only took the newspaper clippings and our Strong file."

"I agree. And, given my one encounter, he seems like the type to return your shoes like that. A little detail, but a big message, you know?"

"But why? I don't get it. It makes no sense. Why hire us, pay us a good retainer, then try to scare us off and steal the case file?"

"I don't know. I agree it doesn't make a whole lot of sense. I can think of two things. One, something's changed and Mr. Smith doesn't want us working the case anymore."

"Why not just call us and tell us that then? Why go to these lengths?"

"Maybe he wants it to look like a break-in for another reason. Plausible deniability."

"Why leave the coy little note? The more I think about it, the more bizarre that detail seems. What's your second reason?"

"Okay. He wants to find Strong himself and only used us to get a head start."

"That sounds more likely."

"Piggyback our resources and expertise to get a lead."

"Doesn't explain the note, though."

"Might just be his winning personality. He can't help himself. He's a creep."

"But how did he even know we actually had a lead? You hadn't talked to him yet. I hadn't even told *you* about the clipping until right now."

"Only one way I can see, given the timing."

"He's watching us. A bug?"

"Or the computer. We don't exactly have NSA-level security."

"I'll call Miguel and have him check. Meanwhile, I'll get Tom to sweep the office for physical bugs and upgrade the locks. Use some of the asshole's retainer against him."

"Maybe the note is a warning," Kate said, still trying to think it through. "A shot across our bow to shake us up. Provide a reminder that we are vulnerable and well within their reach. Whoever they actually are."

"If Strong turned up dead it would be a big story."

"And we'd have a real good idea where to point the cops. There's a bigger question, too. Why do they want Strong dead? He's already in the frame for everything. What do they stand to gain?"

"Maybe Strong is innocent, and if he does surface eventually he'll blow up the cover story."

"How many of them ever end up being innocent?"

"Not many, but it happens."

"Blech. I hate your optimism. This whole thing is really starting to smell."

"What are we gonna do about it?"

"I hate being used."

"Me, too."

"Good. Two things. First, take care of the computer and the office, maybe fire up the old laptop and grab some Wi-Fi from the neighbors. Then we do what we do best. Find Strong—before Smith. How long will it take you to retrace your steps and recreate the file?"

"Couple hours, tops. Other than the photo and the background materials, most of which you'd already read, there wasn't a whole hell of a lot."

"Right. He might have jumped the gun. He still doesn't have anything except a newer photo, Baker City, and a diner. That will get him close, but if they're not careful and miss their shot, Strong is gone again. I might have another angle, an active link between Tucinni and Strong. Something Smith doesn't have. I need you or Miguel to look into a florist."

Kate recounted what she had found at the cemetery.

"After that, I think it's time to turn the spotlight on our client. See who we're dealing with and why Mr. Smith really wants to find Strong."

———

It was true. The best thing to do was stay busy. Jaimie swiveled her chair to the computer and did a search on Bob's Riverside Diner in Baker City, Oregon. She found a very outdated web page, but it did contain a phone number.

"Bob's Riverside."

"Hi, is Matt working today?"

There was a fraction of hesitation. "No, I'm sorry, he's not."

"Do you expect him in tomorrow?"

"No. He took some time. He had a family emergency. Who's calling, please?"

"Oh, just a friend. Thank you." She hung up.

A family emergency. Everything Jaimie knew about the man said it was unlikely he had a family or, if he did, that he was in touch with them. It had to be a lie. He'd gone to ground. Baker City might not be a dead end, but it was getting colder by the second. Something had spooked Strong, and he'd shed his Matt Diver persona. She tapped her pen on the desk blotter, but couldn't think of anything else she could do from Chicago. Instead, she turned her attention to Miguel.

She picked up her personal mobile—she didn't want a record of this on the business phone lines—and called her cousin.

———

Kate was overdue for a check-in at the sheriff's office. It was a common courtesy for private investigators to check in with local law enforcement when they were in town. It tended to help if their paths crossed later on. Making introductions over a body or from a holding cell tended to be a bad way to start any relationship.

When Kate had first pulled off the interstate into Essex, she'd had other things on her mind. Now that Kate was essentially treading water, she had no reason to put off the chore. It was a part of the job she never looked forward to doing, however. Sometimes the local law got a little possessive and unfriendly about things. It was rare that they welcomed a PI, especially a woman, to poke around in things they usually considered their business. Kate hoped the two-year lapse, even in a big case like the Strong killings, might placate any egos and smooth out her task. But she doubted it.

The low L-shaped cinderblock building that housed the town's emergency services proved easy enough to find without stopping for directions. The lot was empty save for an older navy-blue Sentra with a cat bumper sticker and a newer model brown-on-white SUV with a gold sheriff's star emblazoned on the door. Kate pulled in next to the hatchback.

The heavyset woman behind the reception counter gave her a quick glance and a cool stare. Kate was used to frosty receptions. The bonds of sisterhood rarely crossed over into the workplace, doubly so for strangers or those who crossed weight classes. Kate had two strikes against her before she opened her mouth. Sometimes being an attractive woman helped with her job. Sometimes it didn't.

"That is a really great sweater," Kate said, looking at the stitched feline print stretched across the woman's ample chest.

"Thank you," she sniffed.

"I love cats." Shameless flattery was never a bad place to start.

"Really? Do you have any?"

"Absolutely. Couldn't live without them. I have two. I hate leaving them behind when I'm working, but they are not about to chip in for rent, you know. To be honest, sometimes I think they like the time alone. They're pretty independent."

That might have been laying it on a little thick, Kate thought, but it did the trick. The temperature in the room jumped ten degrees.

"Yes, I know exactly what you mean. Mine are the same way. I think they love a break from their mama once in a while. What type are they?"

"Two from the shelter. Both shorthairs. One is gray. Mr. Smith. The other's a calico mix. Lady Grace. I just love 'em to death."

You always were a natural born storyteller, Katie

"Oh, they sound lovely. I have three waiting for me at home. American tabbies. I have allergies."

"What are their names?"

"Belle, Rex, and Snowshoe." She picked up a picture frame from the desk. "Here."

Kate dutifully made clucking sounds at the cats posed on a flower print sofa.

"Very cute," she said returning the photo. "My name is Kate," she said, extending a hand.

"Lulu. Nice to meet a fellow feline lover. Too many dog people in the world."

"Don't I know it. Listen, I was hoping to get a word with the sheriff for just a moment. Is he in?"

"You're in luck. He's actually in his office. Not the normal state of affairs around here. Small department. He's usually out. Can I ask your business?"

"I'm a private investigator. Just passing through and thought I'd check in and introduce myself."

"Oh," Lulu said. The temperature started cooling, but the woman picked up the phone and hit a button. "Yes, Sheriff, there's a woman out here. Another PI." She raised her eyes at Kate. "What's your last name, honey?"

"Willis."

"A Kate Willis. She'd like a word with you." A pause. "All right." The woman hung up the phone. "Go on back." She pointed to the right and buzzed the wooden gate open. "It's just down that hallway, the last door on the right."

"Thanks, Lulu."

Kate weaved her way through the desks in the open area behind reception to the hallway that led deeper into the building. She passed two empty holding cells on her left before coming to an open door on her right. She knocked on the painted metal frame.

"Come on in."

It was the same man Kate had seen yesterday when she was at the hospital. He was sitting behind an aluminum desk that looked like it should be in a middle school classroom from the '70s, solid, functional, painted a utilitarian beige.

Papers were stacked in neat piles across the front. An older model desktop was off to the right. A phone and small Bose radio were to the left. There was a printer on a stand beside the desk, along with a short stack of criminology textbooks.

Kate could see half a framed photo showing a black dog. She wondered how Lulu felt about having a dog person as a boss. She didn't notice any other personal photos. Black and white historical prints, of what she assumed was Essex Township, dotted the walls with a few lacquer and brass service plaques. The office felt spartan and cold. It also looked clean and efficient. Kate thought Jaimie and the sheriff would get along great.

"Sorry to interrupt."

"Don't be. It's a welcome excuse to stop doing this endless paperwork. My least favorite part of the job. Please," he half rose and indicated a straight back steel chair opposite his desk.

"What is your favorite part of the job?" Kate asked, sitting down and trying to get comfortable in the rigid chair. She meant it as a bit of small talk, but the sheriff looked off and seemed to consider the question carefully.

"I think my favorite part of the job is the kids. Not the 'Don't Do Drugs' speeches, but just driving around and seeing the kids wave and beg for the flashers to be turned on."

"Not catching the bad guys?"

"That's not bad either, but ultimately that's more sad than happy. Most times, I'm just the guy at the end of a series of bad choices. It's usually not the first time we've met. Half the time they're not even bad guys, not really. Just desperate or stupid. So, no thanks. I'll stick with the kids."

He paused and brought his eyes back to hers. They were nice eyes, Kate thought, a dark chestnut brown with flecks of gold, calm and a little sad.

"Enough of all that though. What can I do for you, Ms. Willis?"

"Nothing actually. I'm a private investigator out of Chicago. Like I told Lulu out front, I was just stopping in to let you know I was in town. I have a conceal carry in Illinois, which Minnesota honors, as you no doubt know, and will be here for a day or two."

"Why are you here?"

"I have a client so I can't go into specifics, but I've been hired to look into the Strong case."

The sheriff sat back in his chair and crossed his arms. "You're not the first."

"Didn't think I was. Probably not the second or third, either."

"Nope. We haven't hit triple digits, but we're well beyond two or three. For a time, it was a parade of PIs, bondsmen, skip tracers, bounty hunters, you name it. That mess was two years ago."

"Yes."

"Why now?"

"Client wrote me a check to look into it and here I am. The case is still open, right?"

"Officially yes, the book on the murders will stay open. No statute of limitations there." He picked up a pen off his desk and tapped it lightly on the notebook in front of him. "Is that why you were at the hospital?"

She hesitated. No point in lying. "Yes. I was hoping Mr. Tucinni had regained consciousness."

"Who's your client?"

"Sorry, Sheriff, no can do."

He sighed. "Fine. Thanks for stopping in. I'm not sure what you expect to find, but good luck. And don't harass Stanley Tucinni." He stood.

"Wouldn't dream of it. Anything you'd care to share? You were around back then, right?"

He laughed. "This isn't a two-way street, Ms. Willis. Sure, I was around back then, but just a deputy and, as you mentioned, the murders are still open, so I can't share any details with you."

"Fair enough." She stood and they shook across the desk. "It all ended kind of suddenly, didn't it? I've done the background and it reads like someone ripped out the last twenty pages of the story. Everything just sort of stopped."

"Don't believe everything you read, Ms. Willis." She waited, but he didn't elaborate.

He walked her out to the parking lot.

"You staying in town?"

"At the Parkview."

He raised an eyebrow at that. "You hoping to find that missing agent under the bed?"

"He was staying there?" Kate hadn't known that.

"Yes."

"Makes sense. And I'm sure that was the first place you checked, Sheriff. The Parkview has the best rate around for an entrepreneur like me. Plus, I have an irrational fear of bed-and-breakfast places. Continental breakfast with strangers makes me antsy."

That earned her a smile at least. "Have a good day, Ms. Willis."

By now, Kate was starving. She stopped at the same diner

in town again and filled up on a veggie omelet, buttered toast, and black coffee. After paying the check, she returned to her room and took a shower and brushed her teeth before deciding to head out to the hospital again. It felt like going in circles, unless Tucinni had woken up overnight, but it felt more like action than staring at a fuzzy television and burping up green peppers. She didn't want to bail for Baker City until she knew what Jaimie and Miguel could come up with on the flowers.

The intensive care unit was deserted and as quiet as a library. The only sound above a whisper was the gentle clack of a keyboard from the charge nurses' station.

If the sheriff had put the word out about her, she was likely in for a withering lecture, one she wholly deserved for her deception. She braced herself.

"Any change?" She asked.

The same woman from the previous day just turned and smiled.

"Oh, hi, child. No, no change, but go on down. I'm sure he'll be glad for the company whether he says anything or not."

God, I forgot how much I loved hospital humor. Nurses were the best. Told the most inappropriate jokes.

Kate had found the gallows humor of cops and medical staff an acquired taste. Her father loved drinking with cops and medics. She just smiled and started down the hall.

The whole ward smelled heavily of bleach, soap, floor wax, and flowers. A steady beeping leaked from every doorway, followed sometimes by a whoosh of machine-assisted breathing in its wake.

She found Tucinni in 706, the second door from the end. The room was dark except for a small forty-watt lamp next to the bed. His eyes were closed, and his head was bandaged. One arm was strung up in a cast. The rest of his injuries were hidden below starched sheets and a thin blue blanket. The low light made the bruises and hollows in his face even more lurid and ominous. A monitor clipped to his finger displayed his heart rate on a screen in the corner. An IV bag dripped a clear solution into a blue vein in his left arm.

Kate watched from the doorway for another moment as Tucinni's chest rose and fell. With an effort, she stepped into the room and sat in the vinyl armchair next to the bed.

"Feels all too familiar, huh?" She said, but her father chose to remain quiet for the time being. Neither of them liked hospitals.

He had spent his last month in a similar room waiting for the cancer to really get down to business and eat the rest of him up so he could finally have some peace. She would visit every day and, if he was awake, he would ask her about work, the status of cases or leads, or pending court dates. Toward the end, with the tube down his throat, he couldn't talk, but she kept up the routine. In truth, she didn't know what else to say, and it was better than fixating on his rattling attempts to breathe.

It had been almost five years now. That first year, she didn't think she'd be able to keep the business going. The funeral had been well attended, but drained her savings. Then, the clients and referrals dried up before the grass had started growing on his grave. Slowly, she built a name and reputation of her own. There were still ups and downs, but until these last few lean months, she hadn't woken up at night in a cold panic about declaring bankruptcy on her father's legacy since the winter of that first year. The whole economy was in the toilet now, so she had been cutting herself a little slack on this latest dip.

"Who exactly are you?"

Kate flinched and turned. She was so deep in her own head she hadn't heard anyone approach. He was leaning against the wall, just inside the door, a tall and rangy shadow backlit by the hall lights, all arms and legs with baby fat still filling in and rounding out his cheeks.

"Who are *you*?"

"Mike Duffy."

"Kate Willis."

"You know Stan?"

"Yes. He's my uncle."

"No, he's not."

"Excuse me?"

"He's not your uncle, and you're not his niece. Although Ruby down there does seem to have that same impression."

"What makes you think I'm not his niece?"

"Stan is an only child, lifelong bachelor, and has never mentioned anyone remotely close enough to call a brother or a sister, adopted, taken in, or anything else. Other than his doughnuts, his single lifestyle is probably the one thing he's most famous for in town."

"How do you know all that?"

"He told me. Not now. I did a long profile on him last year. And I don't believe he was lying."

"So, you're a reporter. You look awfully young."

"No law against that, but there is one about misrepresenting yourself to gain access to privileged floors of a hospital. So why don't you start talking and stop avoiding my questions? The nurse is just a call button away. Now, Ruby may look like a sweet, jolly woman, but you should see her when she's mad. I wouldn't want to be on the receiving end of that."

She held up her palms in mock surrender. "Fine. You win. My name really is Kate Willis. I was hoping Mr. Tucinni's status might have changed and I could have a word. I'm a private investigator from Chicago. I'm here about the events that took place in Essex two years ago. You remember that, or were you too busy at the prom?"

Duffy ignored the jab. "I remember. Everyone around here remembers."

"Funny, no one seems to remember when I ask."

"It's not something most people are eager to talk about."

"Touché. So why are you here, young Mr. Duffy?"

"I'm a reporter. This assault on Stan is a big story in this town. I swing by every couple of days to check in and see if there is any change. This time, Ruby tells me no, there's no change, but that Stan's niece was visiting. I found that interesting. Now, why do you want to chat with Stan, Mrs. Willis?"

"It's miss. And I'm here for essentially the same reason you are. Someone put Stan in that bed, and neither the sheriff nor anyone else seems to know who or why they did it."

Duffy pushed off the wall and stood by the end of the bed, first looking down at Tucinni's prone figure, then turning to her. "You think the beating is connected to the events two years ago?"

"Didn't say that, but I'm willing to try to find out."

"And the sheriff isn't?"

"I didn't say that. I actually just spoke to Sheriff Logins. He seems like a nice man who cares about this community, but as young as you appear, even you have to know by now that even the sheriff answers to someone. I happen to think that everything ended pretty suddenly two years ago. The story just trickled out and dried up."

"Like someone wanted a lid on it."

"Maybe."

"So, Stan is Strong's boss at a doughnut shop during the time of Strong's apparent bloody rampage and subsequent disappearance, and you think that somehow ties into this assault on him almost two years later?"

"I know how it sounds, but you asked. Got a better idea?"

Duffy moved from the end of the bed and sat in the room's other chair opposite Kate. She watched something flit across his face, and then disappear.

"I'd still go with thrill kill, loner off the highway, only he didn't finish the job. Got interrupted. Got spooked. But I gotta admit, your theory would make a better story. A lot better. Maybe we should get together, compare notes. I've been around a bit. And, unlike the sheriff, or most folks around here, I'm guessing, I'm willing to talk."

Kate was shaking her head before he finished. She didn't need a teenage reporter slowing her down. "Uh-uh. I don't think so. No offense, you look like a nice kid, but I'll just keep digging on my own."

"You got that much time?"

"If you found it, I'm sure I can find it."

Before Duffy had a chance to respond, Ruby came bustling through the door on her rounds.

"Well, aren't you popular today, Mr. Tucinni."

She looked down at his chart. "Sure is good to see some visitors in here." She turned to them. "He's such a nice man." She wrote a notation, walked over and adjusted the IV, then turned back to them. "You all will have to come back tomorrow. Visiting hours are over for the time being. Time for Mr. Tucinni to get some rest." She shooed both of them out into the hall.

In the bright light of the hallway, he looked even younger than he did inside Stan's room, which made the serious and somber face he wore seem even more out of place. They started walking toward the elevator.

"How about it?"

"What?" Kate said.

"My offer."

"Didn't I just answer that one?"

"I thought I'd let you reconsider. I really think we could help each other. I could still out you to Ruby."

"You could, but now she'll wonder why you didn't come clean earlier. Blackmail is a tricky game."

"You're a stranger in a strange town asking questions about some seriously unpleasant business. How do you think people will react?"

"I'm not hiding anything. I'll tell them I'm a PI and appeal to their sense of goodwill."

"You think that's going to work? You think you'll be the first PI to show up on their doorstep after what happened? C'mon, what do you got to lose? Talk to me."

"My rep, some good publicity of my own."

"I'll make sure you get credit."

"Sorry, that's what they all say."

The elevator arrived and they boarded. An orderly with an empty rolling bed was already inside, and they remained silent on the trip down to the first floor. Kate tried not to look at the depression still sunk into the bed's empty pillow. They exited on the ground floor, and Kate and Duffy continued together toward the main exit.

"Well, if you change your mind, here's my card. Call me anytime."

"Uh huh." Kate took the plain white card with Duffy's name and phone number. She'd never met anyone who looked fourteen but acted like such a nicotine-addicted, whiskey-swilling, 50-year-old beat reporter. She didn't know whether to laugh or cry. So many adults acted like children, and here was a child yearning for middle age.

Outside in the parking lot, suddenly feeling guilty for flat-out rejecting Duffy's offer to collaborate, she asked, "You need a ride anywhere? I could drop you."

"No, I've got my bike."

"Please tell me you mean motorcycle."

"No. My mountain bike. Hey, don't laugh. It's good exercise and saves on gas money. This town's not that big, as I'm sure you will find—"

A car whipped around the end of the last row, moving fast. Too fast. The big engine whined high as the car ate up the empty space between them.

"Watch out!" Kate yelled and shoved Duffy between two parked cars. She dove right after him. She felt the air on her ankles as the car flew past. She heard the tires bite as it braked hard.

Kate knew they couldn't duck and weave for long. She glanced back at the hospital doors but ruled it out. If they made it, a big if, with fifty yards to cover, they could be just as trapped. She doubted the overweight security guard she saw chatting up the triage receptionist would be much help. No, their best asset now was their agility over the big car.

"Follow me." Kate pushed herself up and bolted across the next row as the big car came charging past. It swerved and clipped the end of a parked Toyota. It wasn't as close as the first pass, but the fact that they didn't think twice about cracking the grill of the Pathfinder spoke to their determination.

Kate heard the car brake again at the end of the row, this time followed by a door opening, then slamming shut. She crouched low and heard Duffy breathing heavily beside her. The rest of the parking lot was agonizingly quiet.

"You hear that? The door?" Duffy huffed.

"They're going to try to flush us out. Any idea who they are? What they want?"

"I was going to ask you the same thing."

"Don't know. Given that last try, I think they'd be happy to take us both out."

"We should split up."

Kate realized he was right. She could hear the big car

idling with a low, hungry thrum at the end of the row. She tried to listen for footsteps, but the car's V8 engine drowned it out. It wouldn't be long until someone found them. "Okay. I'll go left, you go right. Make for the woods or grass where it will be tougher on the car. Ready? One ... two ... three!"

They made their breaks, and Kate was surprised when she heard one of them shout, "He's over there! To the right, to the right!" The car's headlights swung over her and were gone.

They were after him? What could he have possibly done that would bring on this kind of heat? When he'd asked a moment ago, she'd almost thought he'd been joking. After what happened to Jaimie back in Chicago, Kate had assumed Mr. Smith had sent his goons to give her a similar message. She turned around and raced back the other way, toward the young reporter, but she knew she would be too late to matter.

———

Duffy knew he'd made a mistake as soon he was clear of the parked cars and back out in the open. He'd cut across two rows of cars into the next section of parking, which was nearly empty. His goal was the high grass berm that ran around the parking lot, shielding the busy suburban hospital from the mostly residential neighborhoods in the surrounding area. He knew those streets and, with the berm slowing or stopping the car, he figured his best shot at losing these guys was over there in the backyards and dead ends.

Only he wasn't going to make it.

The car had cut over a row in pursuit, but then jumped the sidewalk divider and was now roaring up behind him again, framing him in those bright halogen headlights.

Duffy risked a glance over his shoulder and knew it was

useless. He still had thirty yards to go and could feel the car's engine vibrating up his spine.

Duffy swerved right, then left, willing his legs to move faster, but he only lost more of his lead. The big car didn't bite, just kept coming in a straight line like a shark sensing chum in the water.

An ambulance with lights and sirens blaring turned into the ER entrance ramp to Duffy's left followed quickly by a sheriff's white and gold patrol car. Duffy heard the car behind him abruptly ease up. Duffy didn't dare slow, just kept running until he reached the grass berm and climbed up and over. He put his hands on his knees, then sat all the way down, spent. He glanced back and watched the car's passenger catch up and jump in. The car was rolling forward again before the door shut. It shot past Duffy and out of the lot. He could only make out the vague blocky shapes of the men's heads, nothing more.

A minute later, Kate ran over and stood next to him. "Are you okay?"

A cocktail of fear, adrenaline, and exhilaration made his arms and legs shake almost uncontrollably. He rolled over onto his back and took deep breaths, trying to get himself under control. "Any interest in reconsidering my offer?"

RIGHT AFTER VII

Alexei waited. Tears ran down his face. His vision had improved but was still cloudy from whatever chemicals Natalia had splashed in his face. It reminded him of staring out of the cheap but durable Plexiglas the Soviet Army used as windows on its transport trains. Long, rattling journeys across an endlessly blurred and barren landscape, everything outside soft and gray and gauzy.

He wanted to get up and flush his eyes out with water, but he wasn't going to turn his back on her. Not for a second. He sensed she was sitting in the opposite corner, to his left, tucked between the wall and the large armoire. Occasionally, he could hear her moving, a whispering rustle of fabric, a soft exhalation of breath. At one point, he thought he heard her pull a blanket off the bed, but he couldn't be sure. It didn't matter. Morning would change things.

He waited, his ears open and his gun ready.

Another hour passed. Dawn drew closer. He could hear the swallows waking up and calling to each other through the hole in the skylight. Inside, the house remained quiet and still.

His eyes continued to burn, but it was dissipating. His body was flushing it out. He felt a sense of relief. Whatever was in the cup wasn't permanent.

The distant sounds of the morning rush hour had risen up from the commercial strip far below the house when Alexei heard footsteps approaching the bedroom door. A hand tested the knob. Alexei struggled to a standing position, his hip, shoulder, everything stiff and sore. He was careful to keep his body behind the high back chair. There was the sound of a key as it rattled in the lock. The door swung open. Alexei leveled his gun at the brightening square of light and the vague shape of a human form.

"A bit of a mess down there, Ms. Shovanskya." A voice. Thin and reedy, but steady.

"Yes, I'm sure Alexei was thorough." Natalia's voice, tired after the all-night vigil.

"Yes, it looks well thought out. It appears one of the guards let him in."

"A lapse in judgment that he has no doubt rectified."

"Yes, we'll need to find some new personnel."

The voice, now slightly louder and directed in his direction, said, "You're Alexei Yushkin, then? I've heard many things. Why don't you lower the gun? The odds of you hitting me in your current state before I hit you are very low."

Alexei said nothing. He kept the gun steady. His eyesight was not clear, but he was sure he could empty the clip into the doorway before the man could in turn kill him. He wasn't going to die alone.

"I guess Mr. Akunin and his associates should have listened to your warnings a bit more closely, Ms. Shovanskya."

"Yes, but, as you know, it typically takes blood stains or burning piles of cash for those old fools to notice anything. Is there anyone alive?"

"Just Carl, the surveillance guy."

"How did he get by the cameras?"

"Does it matter?"

"No, I guess not. Not now. Like a cockroach, he would have found a way in sooner or later and, like with any pest, you must pursue their extermination with aggression, otherwise, once they are inside, they are impossible to get out."

"It looks like you handled yourself. Not that I had doubts."

"Concentrated liquid pepper spray. Nasty stuff."

The voice turned in his direction again. "Indeed. Very nasty. I'd say Mr. Yushkin is thorough, very thorough, but it's hard to prepare for every eventuality."

There were two quick shots, close together.

No one heard the soft exhale of a last breath over the ringing retort of the gun.

THE BANK JOB

They were too late. The double glass doors fronting the bank were already locked.

"Damn." Max glanced at the clock rotating overhead: 4:57. They weren't late; the bank was early. "Danny, turn around. Move to the right. Watch the street."

"What's wrong?"

"Doors are locked. Now move."

Max didn't want the employees checking them both out through the glass. Looking at one of them across the lobby might look a little odd, but get a look at both of them? No way they'd open the door.

Inside, Max could see the manager leaning against the deposit window chatting with the tellers. Young guy, late twenties, off-the-rack suit, plastic smile. Maybe started off with dreams of being an investment banker, but had washed out and ended up here.

Max held the empty coffee cup, pulled the Cubs cap lower, and turned his chin down into the collar of his jacket. Max knocked on the glass doors and tried to look like a normal harried citizen.

"Sorry. Closed." The manager mouthed back.

Max ignored him and knocked again. "I got deposits. It's not five yet," he shouted back. "Check your clock." Max pointed skyward at the rotating clock.

The man said something to the tellers, who laughed, but then he shrugged and started across the lobby toward the doors. He kept his smile pasted on, but Max could see the annoyance in his eyes.

"Here he comes," Max mumbled.

There was a slight hitch in the guy's step as he approached the door and presumably took a closer look at his prospective customer. Max had his wallet out in one hand and moved the coffee cup up near his lips, shielding most of his face.

"I'll be quick. I promise."

In the end, customer service won out. You never could tell these days. The richest people always ended up dressing the weirdest. It worked to Max's advantage this time.

The manager opened the door and Max pushed him hard in the chest. He stumbled backward on his heels, pinwheeling his arms in an effort to keep from falling on his ass. "Hey!" He shouted.

Max came through the door quickly, stayed on top of him, crowded him, kept tapping him backward to keep him off balance. He dropped the coffee cup and took out his "gun." If the manager noticed anything off, he didn't have the balls to do anything about it.

He heard Danny moving behind him to his left, covering the tellers.

"Hands up. Back away from the windows!" Danny screamed. He hopped over the rail and slid across the counter. Both tellers were younger than the manager and rooted to the spot. "Now! Move! Do it!"

Max watched them. Both took stuttering steps backward and bumped up against the manager's desk and froze.

Danny's psycho routine was great at making people pay attention, but it could easily trip them over into panic.

"Everyone just be cool," Max said in an even tone. "We'll be gone in three minutes. Just keep your cool, listen to us, and everyone walks away without a scratch. Miss, you in the back, in the white blouse, what's your name?"

She was pale, all color drained from her face. Max realized she might faint. Her eyes flitted back and forth between the two of them.

"Hey, look at me." She twitched, but moved her gaze to Max and held it there. He kept his voice slow and steady. "Good. That's good. What's your name?"

"Anna."

"Okay, Anna, why don't you and your friend come out here and join us. Keep your hands up and stay away from the windows or desks."

There were too many variables behind the counter, too many alarms and panic buttons. Better to have everyone out in the open in the customer area.

"Just be cool, Anna, and walk straight out here. You, too." Max motioned to the second teller.

Anna's eyes flicked back to Danny and his gun. Max gave Danny a quick look. Danny lowered his gun and she started walking out. Her co-worker quickly followed.

"Good, real good," Max said when she'd made it. "Right over here, next to your boss. What's your name?" The guy looked like he was thinking about getting tough. "C'mon, no need to be shy."

"Arnold."

"And you," he asked the second teller.

"E-e-emily," she said.

"Okay, Arnold and Anna and Emily. Just be cool and things will work out fine."

"Fine for you," Arnold said.

The adrenaline made Max smile. "Trust me, Arnold, fine for all of us. Just follow your training and let us work. It'll come up aces for everyone. Now, why don't you hand me those keys?" He was slow about it, trying to make a point, but eventually he gave them up. "Thanks, Arnie."

Max walked back over to the front doors, found the right key, and turned the lock.

So far, so good, Max thought. Flying by the seat of our pants, but still flying straight and true.

"Okay, now that it's just the five of us," Max said, coming back across the room. "This isn't your money, right? It's insured. No need to play the hero. The government's got your back. Just relax and you'll all have a nice scary story to tell at the Christmas party. Come on over here, around the corner. Don't want to make you guys into a window display."

Danny secured their wrists and ankles with the zip ties, daisy chaining the ties together for the ankles, and reinforced it all with strips of duct tape from the gym bag.

"Gotta make sure we have a head start on spending this money," Danny said. "Hate to cover up such a pretty mouth, but you can't be yelling yourself hoarse."

He cut a strip using scissors from the desk and pressed it over Anna's mouth. Her eyes widened and her nostrils flared, but she remained still. He did the same to Emily.

"Please, don't put anything over my mouth. I have a cold. I won't be able to breathe," Arnold said.

"You don't sound sick."

"I have allergies."

"Cold or allergies. Which is it?"

"Both. I don't know. I'm nervous. Don't cover my mouth. I'll panic. I won't be able to breathe."

Danny looked at Max.

"No reason to risk it," Max said.

Danny pulled the long hunting knife from the sheath on his belt. Arnold moaned.

"Relax."

Danny took a Bic pen from the nearby desk and popped the ink cartridge out. He then slit a hole in the strip of duct tape he was holding, slapped the tape over the man's mouth, and stuck the pen through the slit.

"There, pretend you're underwater, champ."

Now bound, they dragged everyone into a maintenance closet behind the teller windows.

Max gave the door a thump. "Worst case they find you in the morning." He closed the door.

Max and Danny weaved between the desks in the employee area toward the rear of the bank. They didn't want the vault, no time or inclination to break through that. No need really, either. At the start of each day, a cash cart was stocked from the vault and used to fill up the teller trays and restock the ATM machines, if the branch had one. At the end of the day, the teller trays were emptied in the reverse process.

The cash cart would have plenty. This job was about timing and expedience, not a big score. They needed just enough to save Danny's neck, no more, no less. There was no need to be greedy or get creative. Max was counting on the cart not being locked yet. A branch vault at a big national bank would be on a timer. He was counting on it being one of the last things on the daily task list for the manager. If not, this was all a big risk and a big waste of time.

They came around a corner and found the cart sitting in front of the vault's steel door.

"Holy shit. Look at it all. We got it made!" Danny said.

Max quickly saw that Danny was right. The cart's shelves were covered in lucite and padlocked closed, but both men could see the cash wedged into the space. Each was practically overflowing with cash. Too much cash.

"What gives, bro? No reason for them to have this much cash."

Max studied the cart. "Must be a deposit bank. It's a Friday before a long weekend. The rest of the local branches must have dropped off their excess."

"Oh, snap. We hit the jackpot. Depending on the mix, there's gotta be, what? Half a million here easy."

Max just shrugged. He thought Danny was probably lowballing it. Either way, it met their needs. It was more than enough to get Danny's ass out of the fire. But it would also bring extra heat.

"We don't need it all remember. Let's just fill the backpacks and get out," Max said.

Max unzipped his backpack and took out a variety of tools. They didn't know what they'd find in the back, so Max had purchased a number of different tools based on likely scenarios.

"Try this first," Max said and handed Danny a long-handled screwdriver.

Danny slid it between the lock and the hasp on the first shelf and leaned on the handle. "No go."

Max picked up the hammer then dismissed it. "Here, just cut it."

Bolt cutters were too big and bulky to carry in the backpacks, but a cutting wheel, though it took a bit longer, achieved the same result. The locks on the cash cart were not heavy duty, they weren't meant for long-term protection, and in three minutes Danny had sliced off and opened one side of the cart. It would be more than enough.

They each started grabbing straps of cash and flipping through the bills, quickly, but methodically, looking for dye packs or GPS trackers. Any band of cash that had one they just tossed aside and reached for a new one. They filled their backpacks with clean bundled stacks of twenties, fifties, and hundreds in under two minutes.

They were kneeling and zipping up the bags, preparing to hoist the new weight onto their backs, when there was banging at the front door. They both froze. The front door was out of sight from where they knelt.

"Cops?" Danny asked.

"More likely a late customer hoping to get them to reopen," Max said. Danny nodded and they both waited.

The person banged again, longer and harder this time.

"Oh, Danny boy." The voice was muffled, but recognizable through the doors. "Oh, Danny boy, open up or I'll make trouble."

Max looked over at his brother. Danny was staring at the floor.

Max stood and started walking for the door.

"Mikey, wait. I didn't—" Danny said.

"I know. I made him at the museum. I just thought Frankie would wait for us to finish the job. I should have known this way would give them more leverage," Max said. "Finish filling the bags."

Max walked back through the teller area into the lobby and stopped ten feet from the door. Frankie was standing outside, cell phone in one hand, gun stuck in his waistband. They stared at each other through the glass.

"Long time no see, Sully," Frankie finally said.

"Not long enough."

"Water under an old bridge, my friend."

"Uh huh. Somehow I'm not buying that."

Frankie shrugged. "Believe what you want. It's all in the past. I'm not saying Mr. Carter's not still sore about what you did, but if you came back, showed some respect, were a little contrite, maybe started earning again ..."

"Funny, that's what I thought I was doing now, getting Carter's cash. But here you are interrupting things, putting the whole job at risk. Tripping over your own feet, just like old times, Frankie. So, forgive me if I don't believe you."

"You always did think you were better than the rest of us, Sully. I see turning rat hasn't changed that."

"That's more like it. Now tell me, does Carter want me, or does he want the money my brother stole? How's this gonna play?"

"You can start by opening the door and letting me inside."

"I don't think so."

"I could call the cops, tip 'em off."

"You could, but we're about done here. We'd be gone before they got here."

"I could stay right here. Make sure you stick around."

"That's not the only exit."

"I know. I got some people on the other ones too."

"I don't think so. I remember Little John's problem with flying. No way he's here."

"We're not the only personnel Mr. Carter employs."

"True, but I bet you two goons are the only ones he'd trust with this personal matter off his home turf. No reason to air his laundry with more people than necessary, right? You were alone earlier when I walked by your car at the museum, and I bet you're alone now. No one's making Little John get on a plane. So, I'll ask one more time, how do you see this playing out, Frankie?"

"I could just shoot you." Frankie pulled his gun and leveled it at Max.

Max didn't flinch. "Try again. Bulletproof glass."

"Bullshit."

"See, you never did do your homework. Always preferred the smash and grab. I can't believe you never pulled a serious stretch. That horseshoe must be wedged way up in your small intestines. All the newer banks have to have it for insurance purposes. Let 'er rip. See how that works for you. Just remember to duck."

Frankie hesitated, then lowered his gun, slipped it into his pocket.

"Didn't think this one through all the way, huh?"

"Fuck you, Sully, and fuck your superior attitude. Let me ask you something. How do *you* see this playing out? What are *you* gonna do? Take Danny with you? Babysit him the rest of his life? How did that work out for you last time? Oh, that's right. It didn't. It ended up with your wife and kid in little chunks on your front lawn. You know he's a full-blown addict now? He's putting more up his nose than he's putting on the street. You know how that story goes. He even gave *you* up without much of a fight. Just had to withhold his candy for a bit. The fix trumps everything. Even family. So, go ahead. Take your jabs at me. Your brother's just gonna keep dragging you down. One day I'll walk up behind you and we'll see who's smiling then."

Max let the words wash over him. Nothing he hadn't heard before. Nothing he hadn't thought himself. Nothing he hadn't blamed on Danny before, either. Nothing he hadn't blamed on himself.

Time was ticking. They'd been inside too long. Max started backing up. "Look forward to it, Frankie. Make sure you shower that day so I don't smell you coming." Max gave him a little wave. "Say hello to the boss for me." He turned and almost bumped into Danny.

———

Danny jammed a final bundle into the bag. There was still money on the cart, and it pained him, almost physically, to leave it behind, but he knew Mikey was right. He zipped up the bags and carried them down the hall toward the lobby. He left them out of sight, but ready to grab and go.

He cut through the teller section and checked on the hostages. Everyone was still seated where they'd left them. Arnold was sweating, his chest rising and falling rapidly. A slight whistling came through his Bic breathing tube. Maybe he really did have allergies. Anna looked scared but in better shape. Emily was crying silently into her hands. Danny closed the door and went back to the bags.

He leaned around the corner so he could see the front doors. Sully was standing in the middle of the floor. Frankie was yelling, flecks of spit spraying onto the door, telling Sully one day he'd catch up to him, that one day Danny would drag him down for good. Sully just waved and started backing up.

Just like Mikey, Danny had heard it all before. Sometimes he blamed himself. Mostly, he blamed everyone or everything else in his life. Usually, he'd go out and find someone to punch or find something to stick up his nose until the guilt faded away.

It all rang false now. All his old excuses suddenly felt hollow. They felt like just that: excuses. The years and years of denials crumpled in on themselves, landed at Danny's feet, and lay there demanding an answer. No more sidestepping. No more shifting blame. No more drugs. Danny felt a string, wound tight for so long inside him, snap. His brother had taken the heat for him so many times, and here he was stepping up again. All because of Danny.

He came around the corner and started toward the doors. He grabbed the keys that dangled from Mikey's hand.

Frankie saw him coming and smiled.

"See Sully, someone in your perverted little family has some sense." Frankie pulled his gun back out, a shit-eating grin on his face.

"Danny, wait. I don't—" Max said.

Danny didn't hear the rest. He didn't stop. He picked the right key on the first try and opened the top and bottom locks.

Frankie pulled open the door as the last bolt slid free. "About time you came to your—"

Danny grabbed him by the lapels of his leather coat and pulled. Frankie was bigger, but his momentum was already going forward. He stumbled, then tried to correct his balance by putting a hand out. He didn't see Danny's knife until it was stuck hilt deep in his stomach. Danny pulled the blade up until it snagged on a rib, then let go and staggered back.

Frankie looked at him, looked at the knife, then looked back up at Danny. Blood leaked from the stomach wound onto the handle of the knife then dripped to the floor. He opened his mouth, closed it, then opened it again. Blood misted from his nose. He grabbed the handle of the knife but didn't have the strength to wrench it free. He spat out a thick wad of black blood instead.

"Figures you'd pick the worst moment to grow some onions," he wheezed.

Frankie raised his gun and shot Danny twice, high in the chest.

The bullets spun him around so he was facing Mikey. His jaw dropped open, as if he wanted to say something, but Danny was past speaking. He fell over dead.

Frankie took a step forward, tried to raise his gun at Max, then collapsed on top of Danny.

PIE WITH A SIDE OF SCANDAL

Duffy finished talking and took a pull of Coke through his straw. Kate sat back against the cracked vinyl cushion and tried to fit all the pieces together. After the hospital parking lot, they'd holed up in Kate's motel room, but six hours of bad television and no food had landed them back at her diner. They were sitting in the back. It was late, way past any dinner rush, and there was only one other customer, an older man reading a paperback, sitting at the counter. The adrenaline had worn off from the chase in the hospital parking lot and left Kate shaky and tired. She reached for her mug of coffee. Neither of them could afford to be tired or distracted right now. She doubted whoever was in that car would just give up. Not after the degree of determination they'd already displayed.

"And you're sure about all this?" she asked.

"No, of course not. If I was sure, I'd have already written it up. It would be published. I need sources. I need to reconfirm everything. I need to know who WE is. I need people on the record. If I write what I just told you, I'd have a better chance getting a fiction deal than a front-page headline."

"It's quite a story though, isn't it?"

"Hell yeah, it is. Big enough and twisted enough to get killed over, that's for sure."

She looked at the papers spread out across the diner's table. Organized crime, drugs, bikers, politicians, campaign funds, land deals. No wonder it all blew up. Each on its own was an unstable element. Thrown together it was practically a nuclear bomb.

True or not, and Duffy spun a convincing story, she wondered if Strong might really be innocent. And if it created a seed of doubt in her, she knew any decent lawyer could sell it to a jury. Still, it didn't get her closer to Strong. Understanding him? Maybe. Finding him? No.

She rubbed her eyes and checked the window again. Still and quiet, like you'd picture any quaint small town. Darkness was draped over the rooftops and church spires and cast the streets in shadows. Kate knew a lot of things could hide in those shadows, big city or small town.

She watched Duffy's thumb tap against the side of his glass. His leg was bouncing under the table. The caffeine from the Coke or the rush of telling the story had given him a burst of energy. Kate found herself fighting off a sense of responsibility toward the young reporter. She couldn't just let him go on his merry way. Not yet. If she did, she was certain he'd be roadkill by morning. But getting him through this, or at least to a safer place, was going to slow her down.

Duffy was talking. "This WE is the key. If I can get him or her on record, I think I can convince more people. You come across any WEs on your side of the search?"

She shook her head. "Sorry, nothing comes to mind."

"Can't hurt to ask."

They looked at each other and both realized that yes, sometimes it really could hurt to ask. Or at least to keep asking. Just look at what happened to Porter Gaffigan.

"Poor choice of words," Duffy mumbled.

Kate took another sip of the strong coffee. "The local angle still bothers me. Gimme that part again."

"It won't be strictly local much longer. You know who Senator Harris is, right?"

"Sure, old guy, been in the Senate forever."

"For the moment. He announced that he's retiring next year at the end of his term. The thinking had been that the governor would coast into the vacant seat. He and Harris had been friends for years. But something happened. Whatever it was never came to light. Not yet, at least. They had a falling out. Suddenly the seat was wide open. Around that same time, the senator took a liking to Tom Sanderson."

"Sanderson, the former mayor of Essex."

"The same and now state rep down in the capital. He's only been up there a year or so, but he's caused a stir, been on the news quite a bit. He's got the stump speech down to an art. Lots of showmanship, lacking only substance. It's impressive to watch in a way. It's been a transformation. From small-town nobody to capital city power player. The ugly duckling comes to life."

"Sounds like every politician's dream."

"Exactly. Everyone now seems to believe Sanderson has the inside track on at least the nomination for the seat. The governor will likely give him a fight, but without Harris's backing and his donor lists, it won't mean much."

Kate fingered the small chip in the handle of her coffee mug. "Fascinating story, but what does it have to do with Strong and that bloody weekend two years ago, or with Stan Tucinni in that hospital bed?"

"I'm getting to that. Hold on. You want pie? They have pretty decent pie here."

"No, thanks. I'll stick with coffee."

He slid out of the booth. The nervous shaking leaf that

had climbed into her car an hour earlier was gone. Talking about the story, connecting the dots, had brought Duffy's chain-smoking beat reporter attitude back.

He returned with a thick slice of pecan pie with a dollop of canned whipped cream. He put two forks down. "In case you change your mind."

She let him get two bites down before prodding. "You were saying?"

"Right. How does a retiring senator tie into some meth labs and a bunch of two-year-old stiffs?"

"They were all people, Duffy. Not stiffs. Don't let your cynicism cloud that part. You're not even twenty. You gotta earn that gallows humor, okay? You don't just get to say it because you heard it on TV. You almost joined them tonight, remember?"

The reminder of the close call at the hospital seemed to chasten him a bit and chase his appetite. He pushed the half-eaten pie away. "You're right. Sorry. Point taken. You didn't have to ruin the pie."

Kate picked up her fork. "I did nothing of the kind," she said, taking a bite. It was sweet and good.

"It's all about money."

"That's hardly breaking news," Kate responded.

"Who has it, who wants it, and what they want to do with it. Campaigns are enormously expensive to run and increasingly out of reach for all but the ultra-wealthy. Even state campaigns."

"What about grass-roots campaigning? Getting out the vote? Surely that still works."

"It does. Up to a point. But it all costs. Money to start up. Money to organize. Money to run. Money to get out the vote."

"You can't be seriously saying the senator, a respected and I'm sure well-vetted figure, seeing as how he was the undercard on the big ticket in '88, was financing his campaign through bathtub meth?"

"Of course not. Not directly. I'm sure he's set up some plausible deniability, but Senator Harris didn't come from money. Unlike a lot of his brethren in Washington, his father was a janitor and his mother did laundry."

"I remember the stories."

"And those homespun tales served him well on the campaign trail, but he didn't marry money either or get rich in business. He's been in public service since he was twenty-four."

"And that doesn't fatten the wallet?"

"It can, and Harris is far above the poverty line now, but he doesn't have a personal war chest. He's always been on the hustle. I'm not sure even he knew exactly where the money was coming from, but I'm sure he wouldn't like answering questions about it on *60 Minutes*. Everything is buried under layers of paperwork, smokescreens, false fronts, and dead ends, but if you dig it all up you find a lot of unaccounted for cash in Senator Harris's coffers."

"You got proof of this?"

"Not yet. It's all a lot of conjecture and reams of paperwork that point to a few logical conclusions if you squint hard enough."

"One being that the senator was using his campaign to launder drug money."

"No, I don't think he's that brazen. I'm guessing they would launder it some other way and make sure it came in clean. But what I want to check is how many names and companies on that donor list are real and how many are just strawmen set up to dodge campaign limits. Remember most of this is before super PACs when campaign finance reform at least had some baby teeth. There will be some type of record somewhere."

"So, the profits from the Essex meth went to Harris's campaign?"

"A portion of them, a few rungs down the ladder and washed through some shell companies and donated by straw-men, but yes, that's my guess."

"In exchange for what?"

"Favors, money, influence. Take your pick."

"Who do you think is behind the drugs?"

"I don't know. Not the bikers, ultimately, I don't think. They're usually just distribution. Maybe the cartels, but it's a long way up here from the border. Could be a gang or a more structured organization."

"The mob, you mean?"

Duffy shrugged. "I don't know enough about that world so I can't say. Call it what you want, but I think an organization like that would get more use out of Senator Harris than a biker gang. Do you know about the Orchard View development project?"

"No. Should I?"

"Probably not. It was, or still is, I guess, a development project out in the northwestern part of Essex. They were going to buy up and consolidate a bunch of family farms and turn it into a shopping center with some condos. It's been in court forever. One of the farmers is holding out. But guess who is a significant donor to Harris?"

"Orchard View."

"And guess whose employees are also big fans of Senator Harris?"

"Orchard View."

"Technically Tuckahoe Development Corp., but right again. But do you want to know the most surprising thing?"

"More surprising than the rest of this story?"

"Tuckahoe Development doesn't exist except for their lawyer. They have a physical address in Wyoming and, if you plug that into Google Earth, it's a random ranch house at the end of a cul-de-sac. And, if you do an incorporation search on that same Wyoming address, you come back with over five hundred other companies using that as their address."

"A shell for the shells."

"Exactly. Very murky legal waters."

"Perfect for laundering some money, but things went bad in Essex?"

"A body falling out of the sky isn't exactly good for keeping a low profile. I doubt Essex was their only operation. Meth isn't exactly a cutting-edge drug. It's more about volume. Essex was probably just a spoke on the wheel. But, yes, something went very wrong. New partners? New middlemen? Who knows? Something was the flashpoint."

"And Harris's people, and whoever is ultimately behind Orchard View, used Strong as the fall guy to make it easily disappear."

"Easy enough to do for a powerful person like the Senator. Call in some markers. Strong was a newcomer. He'd lived here less than a year, ends up having a blank history. He was an easy bogeyman to hang the whole thing on and make sure no one took a closer look. Turn over one shell, find another."

"And they got away with it."

"Seems that way, at least until Porter started asking questions. The town cops were in on it somehow and they just got a memorial dedicated to them. Senator Harris gave a speech. You know who else gave a speech?"

"Who?"

"Sanderson. The incident two years ago might have just brought Sanderson to Harris's attention."

"Quid pro quo? Help us smother this and we'll see what we can do for you?

"As mayor of our little burg, he certainly showed little upward ambition. Talk about lemonade from lemons."

"But why? Why would Harris, a man about to leave the Senate with accolades and respect and a nice legacy from Congress, do it?"

"Besides the money? You'll have to ask him, but it's funny you mention '88. To get so close to the summit, yet get turned back? I wonder how that feels. I wonder what it might do to a man."

"Okay. For argument's sake, say I buy all that. Politicians are strange animals to begin with and God knows prolonged exposure to power has a way of warping people. But why come after Tucinni? Or you?"

"Loose ends. Tuccini is a means to Strong, I think. Strong is the wild card. No one knows what he saw or what he could say if he ever surfaces. Me? Same reason Porter got killed, I suppose. Someone's getting nervous. They know someone is looking under rocks, trying to connect all those dots. They can't be sure what Porter told me." Duffy pulled the pie back to his side of the table. "There's some big announcement, a press conference, down in the capital next week. Everyone assumes that Harris will be giving his endorsement to Sanderson, officially anointing him his chosen one. I don't think they'd like any other stories out there that might cast him in a bad light, even from a piddling paper like the *Essex Standard-Times*. It would be coming from Sanderson's hometown and might carry some weight. It would almost surely get some coverage on the Internet. Maybe it gets some momentum. Nothing drums up interest like a scandal. All of sudden you have a firestorm no one wants to deal with and your reputation, your protégé, and your legacy are going down in flames."

She leaned back in the booth and tried to think it through. It was a compelling story, still all conjecture, a silk web spun by a rookie journalist, easily shredded by any decent lawyer or media consultant to sound like a crackpot conspiracy. Still ... She flipped through the stack of transcribed notes Duffy had pulled from his backpack. She stopped and moved back a few pages. Something had tugged at her.

Zamora. The name C. Zamora was written in the right margin with the notation "H&R?" underneath.

"Why is Zamora in here?"

"You know him?"

"Not personally, but he was a reporter at one of the Chicago dailies. How did he pop up in Gaffigan's research?"

Duffy turned the notes around so he could see what she had her finger on.

"Right, the potential hit-and-run guy. I don't know what Porter was after there. Zamora wrote a feature piece on Essex. He later ends up dead. Gaffigan just had that note in the margin just like you see there. I copied and translated the notes the same way. Wait." He took the folder and flipped to the back, handed her two stapled sheets.

She looked at them. Photocopies of the original accident report from the CPD. Porter must have kept some friends in the department despite his move out here. She read it through and confirmed pretty much what Daniels had told her earlier. Zamora was jogging near the lake on a road without sidewalk access. There was an ample shoulder, but the report noted the warm weather and heavy fog that morning. What had Gaffigan seen? What made him go after this report?

She read it again.

"Is this all of it?"

"I think so." He pointed to the numbers "1 of 2" in the corner. "Two sheets total. Why?"

"Skid marks."

"Skid marks?"

"There's no mention of skid marks. Even assuming the

driver hadn't seen Zamora, after he hit him a natural reaction would be to hit the brakes."

"Right. Unless he didn't know he'd hit something."

"Maybe, but doubtful you could hit a full-grown man and not know it."

"So, then what?"

"Unless it wasn't an accident."

"You think he was targeted."

"You think there would have been skid marks in the hospital parking lot?"

Kate rubbed her thumb over the divot in the mug. Were they reaching? Zamora writes a profile on the Essex County case that barely hints at scandal and then ends up dead. Tragic coincidence? Things like that happen every day, all over the world. Or maybe he was pushing for more than he wrote. Maybe there were more stories in the pipeline. She made a mental note to call Daniels back and see what the paper did with old employee notes and story files.

"Maybe you're right. Maybe they, whoever they are, are intent on this cover-up. Maybe they thought they'd already done that last time. But they got complacent. Or sloppy. Left a couple loose ends. First Zamora, then Gaffigan comes sniffing around. Now you. Maybe it shook them up. Right on the cusp of this transfer of power it's all threatening to float back to the surface. It could take down the anointed golden boy and cut off the fat contracts and powerful influence they've enjoyed. They decide to go scorched earth. Lay waste to everything and anything that could come back on them."

"And that includes Strong?"

"Yes. And you." She thought of Jaimie's story. "And me."

It hadn't been her skills or reputation that led Smith to her. It had been her expendability. She felt the anger start to burn at the back of her neck.

"And definitely Strong. If what you have here is true, you

destroy anyone and anything that you aren't one hundred percent sure won't come back and bite you in the ass. And how do you find a fugitive who's eluded the police and the FBI for two years?"

"How?"

"You don't. You make the fugitive come to you."

RIGHT NOW

Alexei waited a moment, then dropped the gun on the chair and went into the bathroom. He splashed cold water in his eyes for almost five minutes until the colors and angles started to seep back in. He wiped his face dry on a hand towel and glanced around. His vision was now like looking at a child's runny watercolor, but still better than before. The itching, incessant burning had stopped. He went back into the bedroom.

"I take it you received my note, then," Alexei said.

"Yes, it was very generous, and I accept your terms."

"Good."

"You did mention one additional condition."

"Yes." Alexei took a folded and wrinkled piece of paper from his pants pocket. "I need you to help me find this man."

———

They looked for Max Strong for a year and had come up empty. They pushed, they intimidated, they cajoled, they spread money around, but still had nothing. It was a stone-cold trail and a big, wide open world. The man knew how to cover his tracks.

Today, they sat in the big house's first-floor office. Rooms for Alexei were just waystations. He had little interest in a room's décor beyond its barest function. He had largely left Natalia's house untouched. He did ask Smith to find a couple new rugs to replace the ones with bloodstains.

"Perhaps he's dead," Smith said. "He could be lying in some potter's field as a John Doe. Anonymous."

"I do not believe that. He's a fighter. He didn't survive that night only to get clipped crossing the street or choke on a hamburger. He's out there somewhere."

Alexei had met Smith one time before, reaching out about Natalia. It was at a summit meeting one of the bosses had held up in Riverfront Park. A lot of posturing, a lot of talk, a lot of nothing accomplished. Drobhov and Alexei had been on the fringes, new and nominal players, but Alexei noticed Smith. Natalia stuck out like a blonde in China in the roomful of men, and Smith was always at her elbow. Just like in the Army, equals sought out equals. Alexei made a point of finding him and briefly introducing himself during one of the lulls in the endless talking. Alexei liked the calm, strict efficiency of the man. It was obvious, even at a distance, that the man was in control of himself and the situation. Alexei thought he would have made an excellent staff sergeant in the Army. And perhaps an ally in the future. He'd been right.

"We could keep grinding it down and find him eventually, but I think we're going to need help if you want to find Strong sooner rather than later."

"Who?"

"We have a lot of resources, but we need to be able to point them somewhere. We need a pro to give us a lead. Someone who tracks down people for a living. Someone who will see something we missed."

"You have someone in mind?"

"Yes."

"You realize that if he succeeds there may be reper-cussions."

"Her."

"What?"

"It's a woman."

Alexei rubbed at the scar on his leg. "Doesn't change anything."

"Of course not."

"Okay. Do it."

Alexei had been happy to leave Smith nominally in charge. It made sense from a business and a personnel perspective. The presence of Smith kept the existing operations running with just a few speedbumps after Alexei took over. Alexei knew he had no patience or apti-tude for directing things from behind a desk. Leave that all to Smith. Alexei was better in the field, reading and reacting to situations. He knew, and, more importantly, he believed Smith knew, who was in charge if push came to shove.

"There may be another way, an alternative," Smith said.

"What's that?"

"We apply pressure. Make him come to us."

"Flush him out, you mean?" Alexei's fingers traced the raised welt of jagged flesh through his pants. "You just told me the trail was cold. No family, no friends. No past, appar-ently, either. His girlfriend is dead. His roommate is dead. Even his landlady is dead. Who's the hook?"

"No man is an island. He may have lived in Essex for only a short time, but he must have had acquaintances, if not friends."

"But to flush him out, to make him angry enough or fool-hardy enough to break cover, it has to be someone he cares about. I don't see a person like that in his life. Not someone we know about or can get our hands on."

"The doughnut maker."

Alexei paused and thought about it. It could work. He sensed that, despite being a hard man who had pushed him to an inch of his own life, Strong had a streak of compassion in him, a weakness. "Okay. Let's apply the pressure. Burn it from both ends."

Smith stood up and smoothed the crease in his pants. "I'll get on it right away."

"Better send two. On the second thing. That old bird is tougher than he looks."

———

Another month had passed, and they were back, sitting in the office. Alexei flexed and unflexed his fingers on the top of his cane. His inability to bounce fully back from the mill injuries had worn his patience down to a nub. The only things that filled his mind were pain and thoughts of killing Max Strong.

"I can't take another empty report."

"Matt Diver."

Smith pulled the printout from the file folder and handed it across to Alexei. It was a photo cropped from a newspaper story.

"She found him?"

"Take a look. What do you think?"

Alexei stared at the photo. He had never actually seen Strong in person. He'd seen all the news reports after, of course, but in Essex two years ago, he'd only been a voice, then a shadow from the bottom of that pit.

He looked at the man wearing the checked workpants and T-shirt in the photo. Was this the man who had lived in his head all this time? Occupied his thoughts? Been the reason for crawling through that tunnel?

What did he see?

Nothing.

He was an ordinary man, a cook, a laborer, looking uncomfortable having his picture taken. Thinner, shorter hair, and not as tall as Alexei had pictured in his mind, but so ordinary, so banal and almost forgettable, that Alexei wanted to tear the picture up and demand Smith find someone else. Someone better, tougher, more worthy of the hate and pain Alexei felt throbbing through the scars in his shoulder and leg. More worthy of the revenge he had in mind.

He almost told Smith all this before he noticed the eyes. It would be hard to hide those eyes. Alexei could finally see the true man in those eyes. The man who had beat him, almost killed him, and sent him sprawling to the bottom of that mill. Those were the eyes of a worthy opponent.

"It's him." He let the photo drop to the desk. "Where did she find him?"

"Small dot of a town in Oregon."

"How?"

"Not totally sure. Not all of it was written down in the file. Does it matter?" He motioned toward the paper. "You see the results."

"Yes, she's good." After all their own fruitless searches, she had found him quickly. He could always appreciate the work of a pro. "It was the right call to go with a pro."

Smith just nodded.

"Do we know if Strong knows about Tucinni?"

"I called the diner mentioned in that story. They say he's gone. Family emergency."

"So, he knows."

"Yes, I think so."

"Good."

"What's next?"

"You'll take care of the PI?"

"Yes."

"Then I'm going to Essex myself."

Alexei leaned on the cane and stood up. There was no other reason to stay here. Smith would keep things running here. He'd finally found Strong. He would close this unexpected chapter of his life, then he would figure out what to do next.

"There's one more thing you should know," Smith said.

"Tell me."

"Natalia knew she had hit a glass ceiling in the organization. That she would rise no higher."

"Yes, she told me that no one was really happy to have her at the table."

"Yes, that was certainly true. It is a group of men where egos often get in the way of good sense. They gave her the sex trade because that's all they could ever imagine a woman understanding. She laughed at them as she sharpened her knives. She didn't care if her mere presence at the table galled most of the other pahkans. She was determined to move higher. She was cultivating her own assets, preparing a nest egg if someone ever made a move against her."

"She wasn't passing them up?"

"Not all of them. She kept some for herself."

Alexei nodded. The organization was always trying to compromise those in power. It was how they insulated themselves. Even as the organization fragmented in recent years, the practice would have continued. The simplest way was through prostitutes and blackmail. It was a racket as old as the Bible.

"So, what's the problem?" He asked.

"It's interesting how the world works. Here is where our two stories may intersect." Alexei fought to keep any sign of irritation from his face. He'd grown accustomed, but no less irritated, to Smith's sometimes roundabout way of talking. "Have you heard of a man named Donald Harris?"

"The politician."

"Yes. He's a congressman in Washington. Powerful, been there forever. Has control over a few key committees. Represents Minnesota. He was one of the ones Natalia didn't pass along. He was hers. Her biggest chip. It's actually been a nice quid pro quo. He's provided some contracts and favorable land deals; we've provided some votes and some money."

"So, we continue the relationship."

"There's the rub. He happens to be retiring. That won't affect his power too much. He'll still have plenty of influence for a while. Congressman Harris has selected the former mayor of Essex as his handpicked successor."

"I don't see how this affects us? Just keep Harris in your pocket, compromise the former mayor, God knows that shouldn't be hard, and do what you think is best."

"Agreed. And Sanderson, the former mayor, is already taken care of. Normally, that would be the best course of action; however, there have been some reporters poking around into the mayor's background now that he's about to go high profile. They are asking some uncomfortable questions about some of the mayor's more murky relationships, which include us and our employers. They also seem very keen on figuring out what happened that night in Essex."

"Anything that could come back on us?"

"We are protected to a degree. There are a lot of layers between us. If they untangled the chain as far up as Drobhov, they would find him dead, the same with Natalia, but if the ship starts going down, I am concerned our partners could look to save their own necks."

"And offer up ours?"

"Or make enough noise that the bosses see it as a nuisance that would best be served by us disappearing."

"I see. And Harris and his people are not capable of cleaning up their own mess? They picked Sanderson. Didn't they do any background?"

"They tried. It had the opposite effect. It seems to have stirred things up more than anything else. So far, two reporters that were getting too close were handled, but they think another one picked up the story."

"If the reporter goes public?"

"Depends on how much he knows. That's not really clear at the moment."

"You're in contact with someone down there?"

"Yes, I've already told them to back off until they hear from us."

"Will they listen?"

"I think they're nervous. Very nervous. Harris does not want his legacy and any vestige of power he can keep flushed down the toilet like this. They do not want the story to come out. Even a hint of it."

"Give me a name and an address."

BORROWED TIME

Max looked down at the bodies and couldn't decide whether Danny had done him a final favor or ended up screwing him one last time. He was sure Frankie's shots would attract some attention, quiet side street or not. He needed to get out. Now.

He pushed Frankie's body to the side so he could see Danny and used his thumbs to close his brother's eyes. Then, he grabbed the wallets off both men. It wasn't much, but anything to slow down the investigation.

He grabbed the two black money bags. The bodies should tie up the cops for a bit, maybe get them thinking the job went sour and both perps killed each other over the split. The employees in the closet might add to the confusion before they helped.

No time to hit the security system. There were likely offsite backups, anyway, so it was a waste of time. The tapes would set the cops straight, but he'd take any head start he could get. Every extra minute was an extra mile down the road.

He went out the open front door and down the sidewalk

toward where they'd parked a car, around the corner, out of sight of the bank's windows, then stopped. He recognized the car. Frankie's rented sedan sat in a tow zone right in front of him. Max weighed his decision.

While Max had been shopping for their clothes and tools, Danny had boosted an Accord from the Amtrak station parking lot. He'd picked Max up, then they drove around until they found another Accord, same make, model, and similar color, in a downtown garage. They'd swapped the plates. They now had a stolen car with clean plates. It gave them some cover until the driver returned to the train station or the guy in the garage noticed the plate swap.

Now, he stood in front of the Buick LaCrosse that Frankie had likely rented from O'Hare. A discreet rental agency sticker was stuck to the windshield. Was it rented in his own name? Probably not. Was it safer than driving the stolen Accord even with somewhat safe plates? Maybe. Probably. The rental papers were on the seat. He'd be extra careful. If he was pulled over, he could probably spin a story. He looked back at the bank. The outside camera was angled toward the door and directly in front, where the armored car would sit. It didn't cover the Buick.

He peeked in the window. The keys were in the ignition. That clinched it.

He opened the back passenger door and put the bags in. He could hear a siren coming down Columbus from the north. Behind the wheel, he took off his hat and glasses, then pulled away from the curb.

He passed two lit-up cop cars three blocks out from the bank. He pulled to the side and watched them blast past. They didn't give him a second glance. Their jaws were set, their eyes locked forward. Max made a right at the corner. Ever since he'd started pulling jobs, he'd always mapped getaway routes with right turns. Easy to remember, and you never got stopped in traffic for too long. It always surprised him how many jobs went south over simple things.

He made two more rights, then merged onto the triple-decker expressway. Traffic was heavy but moving. He took the small pack of baby wipes from his hip pocket and scrubbed the shoe polish from his face. He felt the tension easing on his neck as he melted into the evening commute. Danny was dead and he'd have to deal with that at some point, but right now the immediate danger was in his rearview mirror. Two miles later, he switched over to the interstate and headed west.

News of the robbery didn't hit the radio until Max was twenty miles from the Iowa border. He switched the radio off. There weren't enough details to matter.

Max drove Frankie's rental car west into Iowa, then turned north toward Minnesota. It would have been faster to head directly north into Wisconsin, but he was willing to sacrifice the distance for the safer, less expected route. He'd followed the rental agency map he'd found in the glovebox for an hour until he ran out of map. Now, he was now going by feel, doing his best to go north by northwest on the smaller roads, avoiding the main arteries, sticking to regional free-ways and commercial strips. He didn't think there would be roadblocks, but why take the chance. You controlled what you could.

He stopped once, after three hours, at a rest area next to a thin, brackish river north of Route 80 in Iowa. The small cinderblock building, picnic benches, and scenic overlook were deserted. Max couldn't blame anyone. Calling the view over a small gulch and trickling stream scenic was generous in the best light.

He spent five minutes in the men's room scrubbing the remaining brown shoe polish off his face and hands, then bought two candy bars and a soda from dusty vending machines. He didn't hold out much hope for the taste, but he was only interested in the sugar and caffeine. Before getting back on the road, he dumped the Cubs hat, sunglasses, and leather coat into separate trash bins. He didn't have any other clothes, so he was stuck with the black jeans, black sweat-shirt, and shiny white sneakers for now. He scuffed the shoes up some on the parking lot before getting back in the car.

Four hours later, he spotted the familiar octagon-shaped tower and landing lights of the regional airport an hour south of Essex. He slowed and took the exit.

The airport was just big enough to accommodate regional jets, two national car rental outfits, and a long-term parking lot. He spent the last half-hour toying with the idea of returning the car to the rental agency just to throw another wrench into the investigation, but decided not to risk it in case any witnesses had caught the plate and the car had been flagged. He followed the signs to the long-term lot, took a ticket, and left the car in a space in the last row. He wiped down the interior as best he could, left the keys in the ignition and the doors unlocked. He took the two duffel bags of money and walked back to the cab stand outside Arrivals.

No cabs in sight. He went inside the terminal building and found a gift shop. The black-on-black outfit was making him feel conspicuous, a bit too memorable. He trusted his gut. He bought a maroon and yellow Minnesota U sweatshirt and changed in the men's room.

He went back outside and sat on the curb. Soon enough, an old green and cream Checker cab pulled to the curb. It had likely been picking up passengers since the early '70s, but it still looked in good shape. He would have preferred an anonymous Yellow cab, but beggars can't be choosers. He climbed in.

"You know Essex, off route 202?"

"Bit of a hike, this time of night, isn't it? Gotta be at least an hour from here."

"I'll pay both ways."

The man shrugged. "Put up half now and you got a deal."

Max handed him two hundreds, then put his head back against the cracked vinyl.

Ten seconds later, Max felt a finger jabbing into his shoulder. Max snapped awake with his hands up, ready to swing.

"Whoa, buddy. Easy."

Max blinked, then relaxed. "Sorry."

"You were out like a light. Couldn't rouse you."

They were pulled to the shoulder on a dark two-lane road. No streetlights, trees on either side. No identifying markers.

"Where are we?"

"Just off the highway. On 202." The driver jabbed a finger over his shoulder. Max turned in his seat and saw the off-ramp and headlights going past on the interstate.

Max rubbed at his eyes. "Okay, keep on going straight here a couple miles. I'll let you know."

The driver nodded and pulled them back out onto the asphalt. Max put his head back but didn't sleep. Two days ago, he wasn't sure he would ever get this far. But here he was, and now he needed a plan. One advantage of being a fugitive with few friends was that it didn't take long to run through his options.

"Just leave me here."

The cabbie rolled to a stop at a four-way intersection with a blinking yellow to handle the occasional traffic. An old, abandoned Getty station with a tow yard and rusting rotary-style pumps sat on one corner. A fenced-in scrap metal salvage yard was to the gas station's right. A rectangular metal diner shaped like a railroad was on the opposite corner. A neon pink CLOSED sign glowed in the window. A couple meager streetlights flickered overhead.

Altogether, it didn't look like a welcoming place to slow down, let alone get out.

"Here? You sure, buddy?"

"Yeah, here's good. Just pull into the lot there."

"If you're short on cash, I don't mind driving a bit more off the clock, get you where you need to go."

"I appreciate it, but here's good. My cousin runs the salvage yard there. He's coming by to pick me up. Just caught an earlier flight in."

The cabbie didn't push it. He was getting his money either way. He pulled a U-turn and stopped in front of the padlocked fence. Max paid, gave him a good tip, then stepped back with the bags as the cabbie drove off. He didn't want the driver to see where he was headed. He watched the red tail-lights flare once, then disappear around a bend toward the highway. He stood and waited, letting the cool air wake him up. No other cars passed. Max started walking.

———

Emma Looney answered the door with a shotgun.

Max stood a few feet back from the door, making sure he was squarely in the porch's floodlight. He kept his hands open and down at his sides. He'd left the bags in the brush up by the mailbox. No need to get Emma involved in that part of things.

"Frank said you'd come back one day. We used to argue about it. Not sure I ever believed him, but here you are. That man was usually right."

"I was sorry to hear about his passing, Emma."

"Me, too."

"Frank was a good man. He always treated me square."

"Frank always tried to see through to the good in people. Can't deny him that."

"No, no one could. He gave me a ride that day. Gave me some money for a bus ticket. He didn't have to do that."

"No. Some days, I wish he hadn't. I think it was that money killed him in the end more than the cancer."

"Money? The bus fare?" Max was confused.

Emma just looked at him for a good long time. Max stared right back.

"After you were gone, he used to talk about you quite a bit, you know. Always said you had an honest face. Probably couldn't play poker for shit. Frank took some pride in reading people that way. That was how he hired on any help when we needed it. Stare 'em square in the face. Size 'em up. Decide on the spot. Never did have any trouble with our farm hands over the years."

She stepped outside onto the porch, letting the door swing shut. She kept the gun on her hip, but pointed it up and away from Max.

"You really don't know, do you?"

"I don't think so, but I think I'm finally beginning to get an idea."

Emma shook her head. "Maybe someday you'll tell me what really happened that night. I never believed what the papers or the television programs said about you. Frank used to get worked up about it. Everyone wanting to make you out to be some kinda bogeyman, the second coming of Charlie Manson."

"What did you think?"

She sniffed. "I leaned more toward Frank's side, but I kept telling him you weren't some white-winged angel, either."

"Sounds like you had it about right."

She came off the porch and walked past him. "Follow me."

She led him away from the house, down the worn dirt path to the barn. Max could see, even in the pitch-black of the country night, that the farm had started going fallow without Frank's care. The barn's paint was chipped and fading. The weeds and underbrush were pushing further into the rectangular fields. The tractor sat still and was covered with a weathered tarp. This working farm was disappearing, and nature was creeping back up to reclaim its turf.

Emma unlocked the padlock using a small key she took from her pocket, and they stepped through the inset door below the block and tackle of the hay hoist. She threw some switches inside the doorway, and four of the big overhead lights buzzed to life. It was enough to see by, but it stayed dim.

"After Frank passed, my son Paul sold most of the usable equipment and livestock at auction. We tried to sell the whole farm with the provision it stayed a working farm, but couldn't find any takers."

"Developers?"

"Oh, sure. We had them lined up to the cities, but I wasn't going to trample over Frank's memory like that. They're going to have to wait until I've joined Frank before they get their money-grubbing hands on our land." She moved deeper into the barn, out of the light. Max followed. "Maybe I was wrong. Maybe that money didn't dig his grave. That's not fair to put on you. The cancer was coming either way, and the cash did help tie those lawyers in fits." She gave a dry laugh. "It was nice to have the shoe on the other foot for a bit. Money can't buy happiness, but it can make life a lot easier."

She led him down the big central aisle. The animals were gone, but the smell of hay, musk, and manure still lingered. The odors had leached into the bones of the barn and would probably never leave until it was bulldozed under.

Emma stopped in front of the last stall. A truck was parked, nose out, covered up with a worn canvas tarp. She turned and faced him.

"I wouldn't let Paul sell the truck. No one was likely to care about the title on a farm truck or make a connection to that night, but it just didn't feel right. Like selling the farm. And you know something? Frank never said anything, one way or another. Believe it or not, he never even told me about the money. I found it on my own. Let him know in my own way that I knew. We never spoke about it out loud. That was Frank's way, too."

"Stevie hid it in the truck," Max said shaking his head.

He'd thought about the briefcase off and on over the past two years. He knew it had never turned up, at least not in a place the papers heard about. In all those daydreams, Max had never thought about Walter Langdon's old truck. It was almost dismally comic that he had been driving around all night with it in the back and never knew it, then just giving it all away for the price of a bus ticket.

"Stevie Pinker?" Emma said.

"Yeah," Max said. "It's a long story." He pulled the tarp off. Langdon's old Chevy sat there looking about the same as the day Max handed the keys over to Frank. He glanced in the passenger window. Someone had swept out the floorboards, but otherwise it looked untouched. The broken ashtray still hung loose and open next to the gear shift.

"Frank didn't drive it much, but he kept it tuned. I'd hear him turn it over a few times a year. Once or twice, he'd drive it up and down 202 late at night."

"Where's the money? In the back?"

"Yes. In that compartment in the bed. It wasn't like we could put it in the bank. In the end, we just left it where it was."

Max walked around the side of the truck and opened the storage box bolted to the back of the cab. The metal brief-case sat inside. It looked remarkably ordinary for all the damage it caused. He pulled it out. The locks had been jimmied open, and the lid was held fast now by two small vice clips.

"Before you count it, I'll tell you we used a bit of it now and again for expenses and whatnot. And the lawyers, like I said. Mostly the lawyers."

Max was shaking his head. "Far as I'm concerned, you can have it. Sounds like you're putting it to good use. I have an idea whose money it is and doubt he'll ever come this way looking for it. Believe it or not, I just came by to ask about borrowing the truck for a couple days." Max laughed with little joy. "I had no idea about the money."

NICKEL AND DIME

The sheriff sat in his office with Porter's autopsy file open in front of him. He was staring at it without really seeing it. He didn't have to read it to know what it said. The man was dead. Shot twice, once in the eye and once in the chest. There would be a proper medical term listed somewhere in the report, but it netted out the same: dead. The sheriff had spent the past hour trying to decide what he was going to do about it.

He finally closed the file and put it aside. Porter was dead, and the work he was supposed to be doing was still undone. A bark of laughter echoed down the hallway, Lulu gossiping with her sister on the phone. He stood and pressed his hands into his lower back before walking over and shutting the door. It helped, but not much. That woman just had one of those voices that carried, even through steel and concrete.

He returned to his chair, but not his work. Instead, he turned on the small television set sitting on one of the bookshelves. He typically used it to catch the news or maybe a Twins game if he was staying late, catching up on paperwork, which was most nights. Even the Twins were a welcome distraction from the forms. No one ever told you just how much of a cop's life was paperwork. Even a small rural outpost like Essex produced a brutal unending ream of forms, minutiae, and whiteout. Scattered about his desk were haphazard piles of fugitive posters, Homeland security memos, concealed carry permit applications, the county court schedule, accident reports, even announcements from the National Park Service on increased bear activity in Minnesota parks. All of it requiring his attention in some way.

He flipped through the channels. No game tonight, just a weeknight movie, a romantic comedy. Logins recognized the lead actress but hadn't seen the film. He flipped over to a station with regional news and resigned himself to the paperwork. He left the television on to compete with Lulu's voice. It wasn't much of a contest.

Over the next hour, he worked his way through the weekly logs and timesheets, signing and dating each one, then moved along to the accident and incident reports and other memos that needed his attention. By the time he'd cleared his inbox tray, the credits were rolling on the movie and the announcer was teasing the upcoming ten o'clock news. Logins bumped the edges of the paper into a neat stack, then put the sheaf of reports in the outbox for Lulu to collect.

He sighed and picked up the folder with next year's budget requests. Above and beyond the usual forms, this was by far the worst part of being sheriff. The town council preached public safety, then nickel-and-dimed every request from the department. He had to scratch and claw for every holster or uniform shirt, never mind larger expenditures the department truly needed, like training courses, more computers, or more officers.

This fiscal year would be particularly useless as the council was still smarting from having to pay for upgrades and repairs after the shooting spree two years ago. Insurance covered the building damage and replacement communications console, but not the upgrades to radios and other comms so everyone could actually use the new console. Logins knew they would hold that outlay against him for three or four more years. He flipped through the stapled sheets. The department could use a new cruiser, but even with the detailed cost/benefit analysis that Logins drew up showing the maintenance and fuel efficiency savings of a new cruiser paying for itself within five years, he had little doubt it would receive a rubber stamp denial.

He dropped it back on his desk when a story on the news caught his attention.

"... a brazen robbery at a bank in downtown Chicago this evening at the height of the rush hour commute. No customers or employees were seriously injured in the robbery."

It was a generic wire report that had been picked up and probably only used to fill some time. The sensationalistic nature of the story didn't hurt either. A grainy still from the surveillance camera popped up onscreen and showed two men with ball caps pulled low and black coats, but not much else. The tape was going to be next to useless if that's the best they had. The voiceover continued as the scene shifted from the still to exterior shots of the bank. "Two suspects, however, are dead, but police believe one or more are still at large and should be considered armed and dangerous. Neither the police nor the bank is saying how much money, if any, was stolen. More on this story as it develops. From New Eastside, I'm Maria Vanopolis for Channel 7."

A story on the president's foreign trip came on next, and Logins used the remote to lower the volume. He wondered if the thieves had gotten any money. Or enough to make a difference. A successful bank robbery in a major metro area was an increasing rarity. Banks had upgraded their security and technology in the last decade or so, especially in cities, and police were better equipped to lock down and track suspects. It just wasn't that easy. They hadn't had a bank or armored car robbery in Essex or even the larger county since he'd been on the job.

Another of Lulu's laughs bounced down the corridor and under his door. Way out of his jurisdiction. He had plenty of his own problems. He picked up the budget requests again, determined to make one more pass before calling it a night.

A LIGHT IN THE WINDOW

Back at the dark intersection near the scrapyard where the cab had dropped him earlier, he let the old truck idle at the four-way and sat with his wrists propped on the Chevy's steering wheel. He had a vehicle, but now where should he go? A motel seemed too risky. Stan's place was empty, but the well-kept houses on that street sat shoulder to shoulder, and he didn't want to risk the neighbors dialing up the sheriff if they noticed any activity. He had briefly considered asking Emma if he could sleep in the barn, but could already see the effect his visit was having on her in the pinch of her mouth and her stooping shoulders.

He needed sleep. Should he drive a few towns over? Maybe stop near the interchange north of St. Paul? He knew there were a couple big truck stops and cheap motels in that area. A one-night stay, in late, out early, was the norm and wouldn't raise any eyebrows. He weighed his fading stamina against the safer, more anonymous hotels an extra fifty miles would get him. He decided he'd sleep better if he put in the extra miles.

He put the truck in gear just as a car crested the hill and

went through the intersection, going east to west. The car's extra-bright halogen lights swept through the truck's cab and briefly cast everything in a harsh bluish-white light before the car disappeared down the road and back into the trees. Max shut his eyes and let the hotspots dancing across his vision fade. When he reopened them, he found himself staring at his key ring hanging from the truck's ignition, and he knew where he could go.

In those first weeks after the bloody events in Essex, when Max was hopscotching across small towns and back roads, he kept mostly to himself. He headed south, determined to put as many miles between himself and Essex as possible. South also meant a warmer climate and less need for shelter and extra gear.

He got into a routine. Walk when he could, hitch if he had to, and when his funds dipped low enough that he started worrying about his next meal, head to the closest metro area and pick up some day labor jobs, digging swimming pools outside New Orleans, landscaping in Fort Worth, roofing in Phoenix, irrigation ditches in Flagstaff. Always cash jobs, never staying more than a week before moving on.

When he wasn't on a job, he would sometimes go days or weeks without speaking a word to anyone until he became too cold or too hungry to keep up his nomadic, bivouac ways. Only then would he risk a hot meal at a roadside diner or a cheap bed at a truck stop or campsite.

He was in a trucker bar outside of Reno, eating a cheeseburger, when he saw the promo on the television mounted over the bar for the news magazine show doing a story on Essex. His picture flashed on the screen. His prison file photo. It was not a great resemblance, given how he'd worked and lived the past three months, but the food still caught in his throat. The bar was mostly deserted in the middle of the afternoon, anyone in there was paying more attention to their glass than the television, but it felt like everyone was drilling holes in the back of his head. He dropped some money on the bar and left.

The next two weeks were the worst part. He was skittish and jumpy. He rarely slept for longer than an hour or two at a stretch. He lived off water and jerky. His nerves stretched tight, he would bypass towns and spend long stretches walking alone, as far from roads as he could get.

A month after the story aired, he risked a visit into town and stopped at a coffee shop in a town just over the Washington border. They had a couple of old computers for rent in the back. He bought a large coffee and some time on one of the old desktops. He was ready to bolt the entire time, but the woman behind the counter barely glanced up from her paperback as she made his change. He logged on and found, to his surprise, that the story had dried up. Completely. There was no follow-up. Either the world had moved on or someone wanted the story to disappear and serious pressure was being applied to make it all go away. He'd even been taken off the Most Wanted list.

He searched through the Minnesota papers and then moved on to the Chicago ones, but could find no mention of himself or any subsequent search for a missing ATF agent. He checked the ATF list of agents killed in action. No mention of Michaels. Could he have survived? No, Max didn't think that was possible. Then what? Even if Michaels was working off the reservation, on his own, the ATF would still need to know where he was. Unless he was deeper in the shit than he let on and the agency was happy to let him just disappear, too. Farfetched, maybe, but possible. Sweep the whole stinking mess under the rug and hope nobody noticed the smell.

With his remaining computer time, he had created a new anonymous email account and sent a short cryptic message to

Stan before closing the browser and logging off. Checking that the attendant was still engrossed in her book, he used his shirt sleeve to wipe down the keyboard and chair. Despite what he'd just read, or more accurately not read, paranoia still stuck to him. He knew it probably would for a long time.

————

He sat in the parking lot and looked up at the light that was on in the second-floor window. He knew it was the office that doubled as a guest room with a pullout sofa. Had the place been sold? He thought back to the emails with Stan. No, he didn't think so. Stan would have mentioned it. He had been gentle, almost protective, when it came to talking about Sheila, but he would have said something if the place had finally cleared probate and been sold. It had been almost a month and a half since he lasted received an email from Stan, but after almost two years in legal red tape, he couldn't see the court suddenly getting its act together and resolving the title in six weeks.

A car pulled into the lot, and Max slid lower in his seat even as the car turned and drove off to the other half of the lot facing away from Sheila's condo. It was creeping up on 11 p.m. and the cluster of condos, built when both the economy and Essex were looking at a brighter future, was quiet. That was only the second set of headlights Max had seen since he pulled in an hour ago. Not even a dog walker had passed in front of the windshield. But there was that light in the window. He decided he wasn't ever going to figure it out by sitting in the cab, and if he waited any later, he'd look even more suspicious slinking around in the shrubs. He opened the door, got out, and pressed it closed again with a quiet click.

He followed the sidewalk around to Sheila's building, then up the small brick path that led to her door. He mimed pressing the doorbell, stepped back, and waited. He didn't know who might be watching. The outside overhead light was on, but Max remembered those were controlled by the building, not the individual units. Sheila had been peeved about it, tsked under her breath about the wastefulness. He pretended to hit the doorbell again. After a brief pause, he stepped off the stoop and looked into the window to the right of the door.

Even without any lights on and the blinds half closed, he knew it was Sheila's furniture. Two overstuffed leather chairs and a matching couch fronted a large antique armoire that housed the television and stereo. The court had not settled the title dispute, which meant the condo was still in Sheila's name and the key he had would still open the door. The only question left then was who was inside?

He looked up again at the light. A security precaution? A lamp on a timer to make it appear that the place was occupied? The light changed. A shadow moved across the wall. Someone was in there.

Max used the key from his ring and eased the door open. He heard a car out on the road but didn't turn his head. He wouldn't rush it. Finally, with the door open just wide enough, he slipped inside. The alarm code, gone from his head since he left, popped back into his mind like a muscle memory, only he didn't need it. The console glowed green and unarmed. He didn't bother looking around downstairs, especially in the kitchen. No reason to revisit those memories. He turned left and went up the carpeted stairs to the second floor.

The light from the guest room at the end of the hallway was the only light. The door to the master bedroom was closed. The only other room was a bathroom halfway along the corridor. Max stepped off the top stair and made his way toward the light.

A step past the bathroom, he knew he'd made a mistake. He felt the presence behind him half a second before he felt the gun barrel on his neck.

"Wrong house, buddy."

"Wait, I ..."

He didn't get any further before his head exploded and split in half with a sickening crack that ran down his spine and into his heels. He went to one knee and tried to turn and face his attacker, but the other man was quick and stayed on him. Two more blows to the head with the butt of the gun and Max felt his legs go to jelly.

FROM CHICAGO

Hagel looked out his door at the dark rows of empty cubicles while he held the phone to his ear. Most people had left hours ago; even the cleaning crew had come and gone.

He cut the voice off. "Jesus, I don't care what he said. Who's ultimately paying you, huh? ... That's right. I am. That means I'm the boss. That means I decide. So, get it done and don't call me back until you do."

Hagel tossed the phone back on his desk, where it skittered through a pile of papers and ended up resting against his laptop. God, he was tired. All-nighters used to be a matter of routine. He was getting soft. Or old. He leaned back and rubbed his eyes.

He tried to remember back to previous campaigns. Did he feel this tired all the time? Had they all been this tough? All the two- and four-year cycles blurred together. He remembered the late nights, there were always late nights, but not this overwhelming bone-deep fatigue. Did he really have the energy to do this again? The willpower? This Senate run was just the first step. The plan was to go higher. Much higher.

The only light on in his office was a small green accountant's lamp that had once belonged to his father. It would probably qualify as an antique now. What does that say about me, he thought. The small lamp was probably the only light on in the whole building, which is why he'd gone ahead and just made the call from his office.

He swiveled his chair around and changed his view so that he was looking out the small porthole window that cast his office in milky light even on the brightest of days. Now, it was an opaque and oily black. His own vague, distorted reflection stared back. He had come so close with Harris, only to be undone by the man's own vanity. It still sent a flicker of anger through him that made him grind his teeth. If the man had only listened, they could have rolled right into the oval office.

Now, near the end of his career, he had a second chance, a long shot sure, but it was there with Sanderson. The man was raw, no doubt, but he had the awww shucks small-town appeal and was a magician with the stump speech. He only lacked the seasoning. Hagel could help with that, but it would take time. Six years at least, maybe eight. Time and money. Christ, a lot of money. Campaigns today were ninety percent cash, ten percent talent. Sanderson had more than enough talent. For God's sake, half the people in Washington could barely hold a coherent conversation, they were just empty suits, but they had the smile, the families, or the connections to get the cash.

None of it would matter if he couldn't get through the next couple days.

He needed to sleep. He'd call it a night and be back again before anyone else tomorrow. He spun his chair back around and then almost tipped it over in surprise at seeing the dark shadow blocking the doorway. How long had he been standing there? He hadn't heard the guy approach. How had he slipped past the guard in the lobby?

"Jesus, you startled me." He tried to bury his surprise. "Who are you? What do you want?"

"I'm from Chicago."

A bloom of fear wormed through Hagel's gut.

"Chicago, sure. We're not supposed to talk for another week. And not in person."

"Things have changed. I was told you knew that."

"Yes, they called. I knew the people changed, but I assumed the arrangements with us wouldn't be affected."

"You were told to back off."

"Well, I'm not really sure you understand the whole situation. It shouldn't have any impact on you or on our arrangement. We're just trying to get some things cleaned up on our—"

The man moved out of the doorway. He walked with a noticeable limp and carried a cane. As he stepped closer to the desk and into the lamp's small pool of light, the sight of him choked off further words. The man had a nasty scar running from his eyebrow to his upper lip. He was older, with streaks of gray slicing through his black hair. He wore an expensive overcoat on top of a tailored suit and, during the day, would not have looked out of place standing in Hagel's office, save for the scar and the coiled intensity that radiated from him. It was that sense of barely tamped-down violence that made every muscle in Hagel's body want to run.

"Don't tell me about my plans, Mr. Hagel. You have no idea what my plans are."

"Of course, I didn't mean to—"

The man's hand twitched toward his pocket and Hagel stopped.

"The only thing you need to do is tell me one thing. Where are those men you were just speaking to on the phone headed?"

"I don't know. I don't. That's the truth. They're in a car, following this reporter."

"The young Mr. Duffy?"

"How did—"

"Never assume we don't know what you're doing, Mr. Hagel."

"Right. Okay. I only wanted—"

"Call them back and find out exactly where they are."

THREE MEANS LESS FOR ME AND YOU

Both men were starting to get irritated. Their chosen field was not one known for subtlety. First, Jenkins had called and told them to keep the woman and kid in sight, but no more than that for now. No problemo. They were getting paid. They'd picked up the tail at the woman's motel.

Then, sitting in a diner parking lot watching the kid eating pie, someone *else* called, claimed his name was Hagel. He told them to forget Jenkins, he held the purse strings, and to follow through with the original job. Neither of the two men liked the fact that another person knew certain details. It left them more exposed.

They called Jenkins. He had some choice words about Hagel, but confirmed he controlled the money. It was irritating, but they were freelancers, ready to aim and fire for the right price. Together, they agreed they would finish the job.

Now, as they followed the woman down a dark country road, Hagel called again.

"Where are you?"

The driver looked around at the dark featureless land-scape. "I have no idea."

"Okay, fine," Hagel said. "Pull over and stop, then retrace your steps for me. This town is the size of a postage stamp. It shouldn't be hard to figure out."

It wasn't.

"You're out on 515 by the lake. Stay put, someone will be joining you shortly."

———

"What did he say?"

"Said to wait here. Someone is coming out to meet us."

"Meet us?"

"That's what he said."

"What does that mean?"

"I don't know. That's all he said before he hung up."

"Meet us and work with us or meet us and give us more intel or ... meet us and what?"

"How many times I gotta tell you? I don't know. He just said wait."

"I don't like it."

The driver was quiet a moment. He wasn't the contempla-tive type, which is why he was generally regarded as very good at what he did. After a moment, he said, "Me neither."

"Any way you look at it three is trouble."

"Three means less for me and you."

"Exactly."

"What do you want to do?"

"Finish the job. The original job. We got a job. We finish it, we get paid. That's how it works."

"Fine by me."

"Good, let's go then."

"The woman and kid are gone."

"Just drive. We'll find them. Not a lot of places to hide out here."

LIKE A HORROR MOVIE

They had just left the diner. She was just beginning to relax and think that getting Duffy home was the right decision when she spotted the headlights again as she turned off Main onto Cypress.

Watch your backside, hon. Two cars in the city, during rush hour, I might understand, but in the dead of night in podunk Minnesota?

"All right, Dad. I see 'em." Kate mumbled.

"What's that?" Duffy asked from the passenger seat.

"Nothing."

Ever since Smith had snuck up behind her like it was amateur hour, Kate had become hyperaware of being tailed. She was determined not to let it happen again. She'd pulled over four times on her drive to Essex. She knew she was nearing the border of being careful and stamping her passport with full-blown paranoia, but tonight's hit-and-run attempt at the hospital hadn't helped.

A hundred yards down Cypress, she watched the headlights follow her around the corner. A car behind her on Main Street? Sure. On a residential street like Cypress? Less likely.

How had they found them again so easily? The town was

small, but not that small. She felt the skin on her neck pucker and the muscles in her shoulders tighten. They must have picked them up at the motel. She'd told the sheriff herself. How many places were there to stay in this town? They must have been watching them inside the diner the whole time.

Get a grip, she willed. You don't even know if it's them. Could just be a coincidence.

Sure. Big car, boxy headlights, creeping behind you. What do I always say about coincidences, hon?

She didn't want to alarm Duffy or put his parents in danger, or anyone else living on this street for that matter. He'd be safest with her for the moment. She needed to string this out, think of a plan.

"Hey, Duffy."

"Yeah?"

"Did you know Sheila Jackson?"

"Strong's girlfriend? No, not really. I recognized her picture when it was in the paper. You know, someone you'd see around town. She was attractive, someone who'd stand out a bit in a town like this."

"Do you know where she lived?"

"Sure, the new condos that overlook Lake Meade."

"Could you show me?"

"Now?"

"Why not? You got something better to do?"

"Sleep."

"Overrated."

Duffy shrugged. "All right. Take a left here. Go around the block and back up to Main."

Kate followed his directions. The headlights followed behind them like rats in the same maze.

"Left here."

She turned and passed Stan's doughnut shop and

continued west. The headlights disappeared. She let out a breath she didn't know she'd been holding.

Duffy directed her a couple miles outside town onto a narrow road that was flanked by a large fallow field that stretched off into the darkness on one side and a construction site on the other. Earth movers and other large yellow equipment sat idle in the dark. A set of headlights reappeared behind them. The same ones? Kate couldn't tell from this distance. She slowed.

"It's just up ahead, on the left, past the construction," Duffy said.

Kate was still trying to think through the best course of action when the headlights behind her blinked out and went dark. She braked the car to a halt in the middle of the road. No other cars were visible in either direction.

"What's going on?"

She waited. Ten seconds. Twenty.

"Kate?"

Almost a minute now. Nothing.

"Kate?"

The big shadow of a tractor-trailer appeared coming from the other direction. She took her foot off the brake and steered the car back into the right lane.

"Thought someone was following us."

Duffy turned in his seat. "I don't see anyone."

"Me neither. Guess I'm a little paranoid given how the day has gone so far."

They came to the entrance to the development, marked by a carved wooden sign and some low shrubs.

"This one?"

"Yeah, that's it. I think she was toward the back a bit. Fifty-seven? Something like that. I'm not sure. You don't wanna go inside, do you? I'm not sure who's living there now."

Kate followed the small painted signposts and pulled into

the lot that served condos forty-five through sixty-five. She kept her eyes on the rearview mirror. Still nothing.

"No one, according to the court documents."

"Whaddaya mean?"

"I mean it's stuck in probate."

"Then who is that guy going in the front door?"

"Where?"

"Look. Right there. On the stoop."

Duffy pointed, and Kate saw a man in black pants and a maroon sweatshirt opening the door to number fifty-seven and pushing inside.

"You sure it's fifty-seven?"

"No."

She parked the car at the end of the row. "Jaimie just checked the court records earlier this week when she was putting together the case file." She took out her phone and scrolled through her email until she found the right one. "It's fifty-seven." She opened the door and started to climb out.

"Where are you going?" Duffy asked.

"I'm following him."

"Why?"

"Because it's what I do."

"Your job is to follow strangers into houses? Like a stupid horror movie chick?"

Kate rolled her eyes. "Yes, exactly like that. Except I also have this." She held up her gun. "And he didn't look like the bogeyman."

"The truly creepy monsters never do."

"I'm just going to knock on the door and ask some questions."

"At eleven at night?"

"No law against that. Besides, we know he's awake. Look, just stay here and keep your eyes open."

"What do I do if I see something?"

"Gimme your phone."

He handed it over and she plugged her number in. "Call me."

"You got a gun for me?"

"What do you need a gun for?"

"If those guys come back."

She shook her head. "Just call me or text me 911 and I'll come running with the gun. Worst case, I left the keys. Take off."

"I don't have a license," he said, but she was already gone, leaving Duffy to slouch down in the passenger seat.

———

She did plan on knocking, but, as she came up the steps, she saw the door was open a crack. Kate slipped inside and listened. She kept the gun down at her side but nudged the safety off. She felt the familiar wave of adrenaline and nausea crash through her body. The hallway in front of her was dark. She went forward and stood in the kitchen, then moved through the living room, checked the bathroom. The whole first floor was dark and empty. She went back to the front door. She glanced out the front window and could just see the top of Duffy's head in the car.

She could see lights up on the second floor. She climbed slowly. The stairs were carpeted, and she kept her footfalls light. She paused halfway up and watched shadows move against the wall at the top. Everything was quiet until the sound of tape ripping from a roll punctuated the stillness like a clap of thunder. She raised her Bobcat out in front of her and took the last four steps.

The rooms on either side of the hallway were dark. One looked like a bathroom—she could make out the round edge of a toilet—the other larger, a bedroom maybe. The light came from the room at the far end. A pair of booted feet, pointing up, was visible in the doorway. The legs and torso disappeared into the room.

The harsh sticky sound of tape again, and then a man moved into view at the end of the hall. He was on his knees, his back to Kate. He picked up the boots and started wrapping the ankles in silver tape. She made her decision and moved quickly down the hall while the sound of the tape covered her approach.

He started to turn at the last moment, his shoulders twisting, his head coming around, an instinct telling him he was not alone. He was quick. He shifted his weight back, tried to stand while reaching back for something, but Kate was on him. She lowered her shoulder and caught him flush in the chest. He fell backward and clipped his head on the side of a dresser. Kate kept going with the charge and rolled back onto her feet, gun raised and ready, but he was out. She watched for a minute, but he wasn't faking. She saw a smear of blood on the dresser's wood. She moved closer and touched his wrist to check for a pulse. He was alive. She picked up the duct tape and used it to bind him just like he had done to the other man. She picked up the Glock from the floor just inside the door. She frisked him for another weapon but found none.

She stepped back. Now what?

"Now what?"

She spun around. "Jesus, Duffy. You don't sneak up on someone holding two guns."

"Sorry, my bad." He backed up into the hallway. "I'm new at this."

"Well, Christ, unless you want that on your tombstone, try to remember that life rule next time. Why are you inside?"

He looked sheepish. "Always had a nervous bladder."

She could only shake her head. "Nice try. More like afraid you were going to miss out on the story."

He shrugged and tried changing the subject. "What's going on here? You take out both these guys? You're badass."

"I can't take credit for that one." She looked down at the guy for the first time and paused at his face. Something there. Something familiar. "He was already like that."

"You want me to call the police?"

"Not yet. I walked into the middle of something. God knows what this guy was planning. Plus, what would we tell them *we* were doing here?"

"Good question. What *are* we doing here?"

"Look, like I said, this is what I do. I poke things with sticks and see what happens. I want to know what's going on before we call the sheriff. Go back downstairs and lock the front door. Check the windows and back door, too, while you're at it."

She thought he would have more questions, but he just turned and disappeared. She was thankful for that. She sat on the bed. He had a point. What were they doing here? She expected to talk to the guy they saw enter, try to get a look at any papers or possessions still in the house for a clue. She didn't expect to find another guy in here and walk in on an assault or something worse. She pulled out her phone and opened her email program, then scrolled back until she found the right email. She opened the attachment.

Duffy came back. "All set."

"Good. Help me get them off the floor." She slipped her phone back in her pocket. "We'll put one on the bed and the other on that chair. Then we'll see what we've got."

The guy with the boots, the one Kate hadn't tackled, groaned and opened his eyes after they managed to get him on the bed. He squinted against the light, then shut his eyes again.

"Duffy why don't you turn off the light in here. Leave the one in the bathroom on. Both these guys are gonna have splitting headaches when they wake up."

Kate sat on the antique trunk at the end of the bed and looked at the man. Duffy returned and leaned against the door jamb.

"Better?" Kate asked.

The man on the bed didn't say anything, but opened his eyes and kept them open.

"I'll take that as a yes, Mr. Strong."

Kate saw a small flinch at the corner of his eyes, but nothing else, so quick that she might have imagined it.

"My name is Matt Diver, not Max St—" He stopped.

Kate raised an eyebrow. "Matt. Max. Call yourself anything you like. My name is Kate Sanders. I'm a PI. I was hired to find you. I didn't think it would be like this, but I've learned it rarely goes the way I anticipate. This here is Duffy. He works for the local paper. He's got some interesting ideas you might like to hear, but we'll get to that. First, who's your friend?"

"No idea. He clubbed me before I had a chance to ask. Who hired you?"

"Can't answer that one."

"Was it Alexei?"

Kate paused. That was a new name.

"No, not Alexei then. Not directly. You seem smart. Smart enough to find me at least, so you're probably smart enough not to work for that psychopath. He must have sent someone else."

"I don't know any Alexei. I was hired by Sheila Jackson's estate."

"Bullshit. She had no family. No one close."

"She had a brother."

They all turned and looked at the guy slumped in the

Queen Anne chair in the corner. He kept his eyes closed, but continued. "Half-brother, anyway."

"Kyle?" Max asked.

The man opened his eyes then. "She talk about me?"

"Not often, but sometimes. You were serving over in Afghanistan. She worried. She hadn't heard from you in a while."

"Yeah, I was never good about staying in touch."

Max turned his attention back to the woman sitting at the end of the bed. "Now that we got the introductions straightened out, why don't you tell us how you came to work for the Russian mafia?"

The Russian mafia. Jesus, Kate, what have you got yourself mixed up in?

Kate sighed. "I knew I should have trusted my gut. This thing had a bad smell from the start."

She recapped her meeting with Mr. Smith and their case to date, then she had Duffy tell his story. That one took longer. Throughout, Strong kept quiet and watched them with his pale grey eyes.

"Jesus," Strong said when Duffy had finished. "I knew something hinky was going on, but I didn't know it went that far. I thought Heaney just had a mean streak. I didn't think he had any kind of ambition beyond holding onto his meager fiefdom in this town."

"Why'd you run?" Kate asked.

"Like Duffy said, I was the logical fall guy. I could see that. I have a history. More than you were probably able to dig up. Even if I surrendered, I was looking at some time in custody while it was sorted. Jail would have been complicated and probably life-threatening. And, maybe it never would get sorted. If what you said is true, there would have been plenty of reasons for them to just railroad me into a cell and throw away the key. I was willing to take my chances on the road."

There was silence, but no objections as his explanation sunk in.

"I could use some water," Kyle said.

"Good idea. Duffy, why don't you head down to the kitchen and get these guys something," Kate said. "I'll see if I can find some aspirin."

"Sure." Duffy pushed off the wall he'd been leaning against and headed for the door. As he passed the bedroom window, it exploded in a shower of glass and splinters.

"Down!" Max shouted. "Everyone on the floor." He rolled off the bed. Kyle slid off the chair and landed next to him.

"Someone kill the light."

Kate crawled over to the bathroom reached up an arm and hit the light switch.

There were no more shots. Everything was quiet.

"Kid, are you all right?"

"I think so. Just some cuts. Not the first time someone's tried to kill me today."

"Take a deep breath."

"Okay. And?"

"Still feel okay? No leaks anywhere?"

"I'm good."

"Who's shooting at us, Strong?" Kate asked.

"I thought you would know. I just got to town tonight. No one knows I'm here. You told me someone took a run at the kid earlier tonight. Best guess, it's the same crew. Or Alexei has someone else sniffing around and, now that you found me, you've become expendable right along with me."

She thought of the headlights. "The latter doesn't wash. No one knows I found you."

"So, it's the kid. His theories must be making someone really itchy."

There was a sharp bang, then a crack of wood splintering from downstairs.

"Listen, if his story is true or close enough to send some hitters after him and his boss, then I'm not the crazy killer everyone's made me out to be, right?"

"Maybe."

"Yes, maybe, or no. I can guarantee we're all on the same side for this one. If you'll cut us loose, maybe together we can figure something out before whoever is outside gets inside and gets serious. We can always go back to our tea party later."

Kate knew if it was the same two psychos from the hospital, she didn't stand a chance without some help. She was trapped on the top floor of an unfamiliar house with a teenager and two duct-taped strangers.

Another crash, followed by the sound of breaking glass.

"That's the door. What's it gonna be?"

Kate took the Leatherman tool off her belt and cut Strong and Kyle loose. She handed the Glock to Strong, who passed it over to Kyle.

"I'm better with my hands."

Kyle checked the slide, dropped the short magazine out, then popped it back in and nodded.

"All right. Kid, crawl over and get in the bathroom. Lock the door and open the window. Only jump as a last resort."

He didn't wait for an answer and turned back to the other two. "I'll go down the hall. Hide in that first room. You two stay here with the kid."

He looked around the room.

"Kyle, here, help me with this."

They moved the long bureau a few feet away from the wall and lined it up with the door. "You can get some cover behind this." He knocked on it. "Cherry. Hard as steel. Sheila didn't go for that cheap particle board crap."

A SILENT GUN

Alexei drove up and down CR 515 twice before he decided that he was in the right spot and that Hagel's men were not. It didn't surprise him. The third time he drove past the condo entrance, the familiarity washed over him. It was the owl. It was hard to forget a three-foot bronze and metal sculpture. This is where he'd killed the woman two years ago.

He decided he'd try the group of condos first. He'd only passed two other turnoffs within three miles, one a state park and the other a large office park. Neither was likely at this time of night. It was a good bet everyone was somewhere behind the owl.

He took the turn and almost rear-ended them. The car was pulled to the curb near the second cluster of condos. One guy was leaning against the driver's side door, smoking. He felt the man's eyes on him as he passed. Alexei didn't see a second guy. He drove past once without slowing and reached the cul-de-sac at the end, turned around, and considered his options.

He took his bag from the footwell and took out his PSS.

An old KGB friend had given him one of the silent pistols as a gift. He rarely used it as it wasn't overly accurate beyond fifteen meters, but it was very quiet, just the sounds of the metal components rubbing against each other as the bullets fired. No need to rely on a bulky suppressor.

He drove back the way he came and braked opposite the first man.

"Excuse me." He tried his best flat American accent. "Could you help me out? I'm a little lost. I'm looking for 157. Is that this way?"

The guy looked over, said nothing, just gave him a dead-eyed glance, then swiveled his head back toward the woods. Alexei remembered from his last trip that this second cluster of condos were the mid-priced ones. They had some token privacy with a ring of old trees that hadn't been clear-cut to make way for the development. The top tier, at the end of the road by the turnaround, had the big lake views. The lowest rung was closest to the road, back by the entrance.

"Nothing? You a dumb mute? Listen, you don't know, you don't know, just say so. No reason to be an asshole."

The guy's mouth twitched, but he kept his eyes on the woods. He looked amused. He probably was not used to anyone giving him lip. He dragged hard on his cigarette, then dropped it before crushing it under his heel. He pushed off the car door and came toward Alexei.

The gun took too long to clear the window. The man was quick. He had terrible people instincts, but good reactions. The first shot grazed his ear as he ducked and dodged left. Alexei compensated and aimed again. The second shot was high, but more on target. The man took a shambling step, them slumped back onto the curb.

Alexei left him there, drove forward, and parked his car in the low-priced lot near the road and walked back. The kill shot had hit the man in the neck and left a lot of blood on the grass and sidewalk. Let someone puzzle that out tomorrow. Alexei rolled him over and stripped off his coat. He wrapped it around the man's head and upper body then opened the car's trunk and wrestled him inside. With his leg, it took longer than he wanted, but no cars passed and no one shouted or asked what the hell he was doing throwing a body into a trunk. Sometimes he could understand why so many people loved suburbia.

Moving a dead body is awkward and never easy. By the time he closed the trunk, he was out of breath and sweating. He massaged his throbbing leg. He hated every reminder of this weakness in himself. He took out the metal pill box and dry swallowed one, paused, then took another and let it dissolve under his tongue. The itching bugs behind his eyes went back to sleep. He knew the fuzzy relief from the pain would follow shortly. He limped off toward the woods to find the second man.

The remaining trees were old and tall, but the aesthetically pleasing landscaping had thinned out any undergrowth and low branches so that Alexei could see through the strip to the other side. A small worn track, maybe made by the residents or dog walkers, ran through the center. He stayed in the trees but followed the general direction of the path.

Alexei was scanning the edge of the woods and the grassy clearing beyond when he heard the first shot. Small caliber, not too loud, but loud enough in this drowsy town. Someone would call it in. He traced the echo backward. Abutting the condos was a tall wooden fence with a gate and storage shed in the middle. Inside the fence, smaller fences subdivided the condo backyards and patios into individual plots.

The dead man's partner was standing next to the communal storage shed and firing at the upper story of the condo directly to the left of the shed. He'd shot out one window. Someone was definitely calling the authorities now.

As Alexei watched, the light flicked off. Now it was just an opaque black mirror. What had the man hoped to accomplish? Alexei was beginning to revise his opinion of these guys as professionals.

The man left his spot. Alexei followed. The guy never looked back. The man went over one of the small fences, then up to the condo's back door. Alexei watched and waited as the guy tried the knob. Locked. He tried his shoulder, then kicked at it before he gave up and broke the glass square nearest the knob with the butt of his gun.

Alexei agreed that the female PI was a loose end who needed to be dealt with at some point, but Alexei didn't have any real beef with this kid reporter. It was likely in Alexei's best interest, certainly the organization's, if the whole story behind the Essex mess remained buried and they were able to retain a degree of leverage over Harris and Sanderson, but if it came out, so be it. It wouldn't affect Alexei. He had little interest in politics or the privileges it could garner. He understood its purpose, sure, but he was more black-and-white in his worldview and, right now, he only cared about these people insofar as they could help him find Max Strong. That burned far brighter in his self-interest than blackmail.

He needed them alive. He had to move on this guy before he botched things completely.

Before his injury, Alexei would have taken the guy outside, done it quickly and efficiently, but in his current state, even with the pills sanding down the worst of the pain, he figured inside would provide more cover even if it introduced more variables. He limped across the grass, maneuvered over the fence and up to the open door.

He paused just inside the threshold to listen, and the layout came back to him as the living room and kitchen resolved in front of him. He could hear the guy's slow, careful steps moving away down the hallway toward the front door.

The stairs were near the front door. If everyone was upstairs, no need to get them involved. It was cleaner to do it down here.

He started to move in that direction to line up a shot when he heard a voice that stopped him cold.

AN AVERAGE GUY

Max took a slow breath and caught the fading scent of the dried jasmine Sheila liked to keep in a small bowl near the guest bed. He didn't let his mind go there, snapped it shut, and focused on the stairs. He pressed himself against the wall and waited until he heard the familiar squeaking creak of the second step and knew someone was coming up.

"We called the sheriff's office," Max lied. "They should be here soon. Let the kid be."

A bullet punched into the ceiling of the guest room and set his ears ringing. Plaster rained down on Max's head. Answer enough.

He crouched down. The guy was armed, so he needed to get in close. He would spring out low and hard, aim for the guy's knees, neutralize the gun. Get him off balance and take the fight to the ground. Kate had said there were two at the hospital. Max had to hope they both weren't coming up the stairs at once. If they were, this was a suicide run. He had to hope that one of them would think twice before shooting at his partner.

Over his ringing ears, he could now make out the sound of a siren in the distance. Too far to help, but getting closer. The shots or the broken window must have woken a neighbor. One problem at a time. If he didn't time this right, he wasn't going to need to worry about the sheriff.

He tried to control the adrenaline and focus on the stairs.

All his senses wanted to dial in on the approaching sirens.

His mind was screaming at him to run.

The jasmine tickled his nose.

Beads of sweat ran down his scalp on to his neck.

He heard something, hard to pin down what, and then a muffled thump like a sack of groceries dropped on a table.

Had the guy tripped and fallen in the dark?

Max edged closer to the door. He listened. The hallway was silent. He laid on his stomach and risked a quick, low peek around the doorway. A dark shape on the stairs. Prone. Motionless. The siren wailed closer. Through the guest room window, he could see more lights coming on in neighboring units. He couldn't wait any longer. He crawled out on his belly, arms and legs tensed to spring.

The guy was slumped against the banister halfway up. Two tight shots in the back had likely punctured his heart. What the hell? Shot by his own guy?

Max crept the rest of the way downstairs and stood in the front hall. He could see the back door ajar, a pane of glass shattered near the knob. He went through the kitchen and living room, making a circuit. Empty.

He called back up the stairs. "All clear. Come on out. Bring the kid, we gotta move."

After a moment, Kyle appeared at the top of the stairs, Glock raised and ready. He took in Max and the guy on the stairs and lowered the gun.

"What happened?"

"No idea. I found him like this."

Kyle knelt and looked at the wounds. "Three shots?"

"Yes. The first one was from him and aimed at me. It's in the ceiling up there. I didn't hear anything else for the other two."

"Suppressor."

"Maybe. It was hard to hear after that first shot."

"Kate said there were two. His partner?"

"Who else? But why?"

They both stared back down at the guy, but he wasn't offering any answers. He was just an average guy. Medium build, trending toward skinny, sandy brown hair. Even dead, he didn't make much of an impact. A perfect disguise.

Max searched the guy quickly, careful not to step in the blood, but didn't come up with anything other than a pack of Extra spearmint gum and the Browning Hi-Power handgun he'd dropped. He left the gum but took the handgun.

"I can't be here when those sirens show up."

NIGHT MOVES

Alexei slowed, then pulled off into an abandoned lot with a crumbling square foundation so far gone he couldn't tell what it had once been. No roof. No door. A flagpole and a rusty stanchion for a sign stood out front. A garage or a gas station maybe. The leeward side offered cover from oncoming traffic. That was his only requirement. He tucked the car in tight against the remaining wall and turned off the engine.

After shooting the second man, he'd backtracked to his car, let the first sheriff car blast past, then pulled out and drove south, away from Essex, until he found this fossil of a building. Now, he waited.

Ten minutes later, longer than he expected, headlights lit up the cracked asphalt and litter of the lot. He watched a black or dark green Acura go past and continue up the road. It didn't slow or change speed as it passed. He watched the low-riding taillights recede on the long straightaway and, as they blinked out of sight, he keyed the ignition and began to follow.

He knew they would all be on edge and he kept well back,

sometimes letting them slip out of sight. On the interstate, looping back around toward Essex, Alexei used the few other cars on the road as cover and closed the gap. They took the first exit for Essex, the one that put them a mile or two short of the town center. He drifted further back and coasted down the ramp. At the bottom, he checked in either direction. No cars visible. He took in the immediate surroundings. A couple fast food restaurants, a gas station, a five-and-dime department store, and a motel to catch the few truckers or desperate families that happened to pull off. A vacancy sign glowed pink in the dark.

He parked the car in the five-and-dime lot and walked across the street to the motel. There were a couple cars scattered in front of motel doorways along with one piggyback tractor-trailer spread over a whole row of spaces, the cab either too small or cramped to allow the driver to sleep inside. None of the cars was the Acura he'd followed. He walked around back and found it squeezed in next to the dumpster and the motel's laundry room.

He walked back across the street to wait. He was good at waiting.

HOTEL, MOTEL

Duffy didn't know if it was the diner food, seeing the dead body on the stairs, or the nerves of being attacked again, but his stomach was in serious turmoil. He couldn't take it anymore. He slipped his feet out from under the sheet and onto the thin motel rug. He'd taken off his shoes but left the rest of his clothes on. Kate was snoring softly on the other bed. The two men were in the next room. Max Strong was in the next room. It was still hard to wrap his mind around. He grabbed his wallet off the nightstand and went out the door, flipping the security latch so it blocked the door from closing completely.

Duffy had spotted a soda machine outside the office on their way in. His mother always used to give him a pop when he complained of stomachaches as a child. He hoped it would be a good antidote now. He had called her from the motel earlier and felt bad about lying to her, but he knew she would worry less if she thought he'd decided to visit some friends up at Elmira for a couple days.

Halfway down the hall, someone had discarded two convenience store pizza boxes, likely bought and reheated at

Murray's across the street. Duffy passed the stacked boxes in the hall. He stopped. Everything was quiet save for the rattle of the ice machine and the red glow of the soda machine by the office. Was it the pizza? He looked back at the boxes. Tombstone. Not his favorite, and a creepy omen given how his day was going. He reached down and picked up one of the boxes and turned it over. Nothing. Whatever had made him stop was gone. He put the box down and kept going. Then stopped again. The penny dropped. He saw Porter's apartment. The broken dishes in the kitchen, the shredded sofa cushions, and the discarded movie posters. He smiled. He knew who the WE in Porter's notes was.

He fed a dollar into the machine and studied his choices before punching the button for a Schweppes ginger ale. He leaned his head against the machine. He hoped the can would settle his stomach. The machine burped up his pop. He turned to walk back to the room and almost bumped into the guy. Duffy gave a little gasp of surprise and dropped the can.

"Sorry, you startled me. I didn't—"

The man's flat eyes instantly told Duffy this wasn't a chance encounter. He turned to run, but the man was already reaching for him. He felt a hot pain in his shoulder that spread upward to his neck.

———

Kate woke up to traffic noise and a shaft of sunlight cutting across her eyes. She burrowed under the sheets at the touch of a light breeze and threw her arm over her head to block the light and get back to sleep. Then she sat up.

Last night came back to her in a flash. Why was she feeling a breeze? She glanced around the drab motel room. The room's door was propped open. She looked to her left. Duffy's bed was empty. The bathroom door was open and dark. He was gone. She grabbed her watch off the table. Five minutes after five. They'd been asleep for almost four hours.

The adjoining door was closed. Neither Max nor Kyle had wanted to go on record for an additional room, so they popped the cheap lock on the connecting room door for the extra beds. She went through now. Max sat up immediately at the sound. Kyle was propped against the headboard, gun raised.

"Whoa. It's me." Kyle let the gun drop back to the bed.

"Is Duffy in here?" She asked, even though their expressions told her he was not.

Max was already moving toward the door. He brushed past her, did a quick circuit of her room, and came back. "How long?"

"I'm not sure. I crashed pretty hard. Could have been any time after we turned the lights off."

"We slept for what? Four hours? Figure you would have woken up or registered movement for the first twenty minutes, half-hour. You didn't hear anything?"

"Nothing."

"Me neither. Kyle?"

He shook his head.

"You think he went home?" Max asked.

"Doubt it. Kid was pretty freaked out last night. I heard him call his mom and tell her he was staying over with some friends."

"I agree. I didn't get the sense he was going to bolt, either. Okay, I've been up for twenty minutes and didn't hear anything, so we were in deep sleep or he was really careful. No reason to think he was sneaking around. So, he's been gone for at least three, maybe three and a half hours at the outside. Maybe less, but not more. His wallet and shoes are gone, but his notebook and keys are still on the table."

Max moved to the window above the old metal

AC/heating unit. It fronted the balcony and had a view of the street. He gently pushed a corner of the curtain aside and looked. After a minute, he dropped his hand and the curtain fell back in place.

"Nothing looks out of place. No cars idling. No one obviously waiting."

Kyle was tying his shoes.

"Meet me downstairs in five. Less if you can do it. We gotta find that kid. And Kate, don't leave those notes in your room."

"You think someone took him? With me sleeping in the same room? After trying to run him down earlier, why not just shoot us both?"

"Don't know. I only know that he's gone."

"He could have just gone down the street for breakfast."

"You think he's the type to do that?'

"No. Not after last night. Like I said, he talked a good game, but he was scared."

"He wasn't the only one." Max headed for the bathroom. "Five minutes."

Kate desperately wanted a hot shower but had to settle for scrubbing her hands and face with lukewarm water and gargling some tap water before throwing Duffy's notes and her few belongings in her bag and heading out.

She found Kyle waiting by the car holding a can of soda.

"Found this next to the machine. On the ground."

"And? You think the kid went for a soda?"

Kyle tossed the can to Max, approaching behind her.

"Might explain why he left the room," Max said. "He just thought he was running down the hall." He turned it over in his hands. "Warm. Been sitting out there for awhile." He fingered the scuffed dent on the bottom. "Dropped, too. Anything else?"

Kyle shook his head. "No blood."

"Where are we going?" Kate asked as they piled into her car.

"If we figure three hours, he's got at least a hundred and sixty-mile head start. Maybe more if he took some chances, but I doubt he would risk being pulled over with the kid in the car."

"That's a lot of ground to cover." Kate pulled out a map and unfolded it. "A lot of ground."

There was a shortcut, Max thought. "Either of you have a cell phone? No, check that. Wait here."

Max jumped out of the car and jogged to the payphone that sat under the rotting eaves of the motel office next to an empty and rusting cigarette machine. Max expected the phone to be out of order but got a clear tone when he picked up the receiver. Small miracles. He pulled the dog-eared card from his wallet. He couldn't tell you why he kept it, only that he couldn't throw it away. Like a piece of gum on the bottom of your shoe or a bad penny, it just kept finding its way back into his wallet.

He plugged four quarters into the phone and dialed the first number. The one that he'd used last time. A mechanical recording told him the number was not in service. He tried the second number. It rang three times before someone picked up. Max waited on the other end. He could hear the other person breathing down the line.

Finally, the voice said, "You're a tough man to get a hold of, Mr. Strong."

They'd only had the briefest of exchanges in the past, but the voice was unmistakable.

"I tend to like it that way. You have the kid?"

"Yes."

"What do you want?"

"1241 Evergreen Terrace, Chicago," Max said as he got back in the car. "You know it?" He asked Kate.

"I know of it. It's outside the city proper. Big homes. Let's just say no one cuts their own lawn in that zip code. Why?"

"I called Mr. Smith's boss."

"Alexei."

"The very same."

"You have his number?"

"Part of that long story. He has the kid."

"Duffy is just bait, right? A means to an end, like Stan. This guy just wants you."

Max winced, but couldn't deny it. "I think Duffy has a legitimate story. No, I know he does. It could hurt Alexei or his organization. But, yes, he primarily wants me, although don't think he'll stop there. The man is a class five tornado. He'll kill anything or anyone that gets in his way."

"Like my sister," Kyle said.

"Yes, like Sheila. And Stevie. And Mrs. Langdon. And Porter Gaffigan. And probably a score of others we don't know about. I thought I killed him once already, but he's a hard man to put down and, if you miss, he'll chase you to the bottom of the world to settle up."

"Then let's put him under for good this time."

Kate shook her head. "Jesus Christ. You guys are talking about killing this guy. Executing him."

"No, I'm talking about trying to make us all safe. You don't have to get involved in this, Kate. This was never about you. You were just another pawn he ultimately used. If you can get us to Chicago, we'll take care of the rest."

"I'm already involved, remember? Pawns are always the first ones to go." She thought of Jaimie and the alley and just kept shaking her head. "Let's get to Chicago. Get the kid first."

EYE OPENER

Miguel Alvarez rarely woke up before noon, so when he opened his eyes the man with the gun had been waiting for almost two hours.

He didn't appear all that happy.

Miguel Alvarez wasn't particularly happy about the situation, either.

"Mr. Smith."

"You don't seem particularly surprised."

"No."

"Not particularly scared either."

"Not the first time I've seen that end of a gun. How'd you find me?"

"You're not as good as you think you are."

"I doubt that."

"I'm sitting here, aren't I?"

"Just means you have someone better than me. Did you bring any breakfast, or do you just like watching people sleep?"

"You can learn a lot about someone by seeing how they sleep. Who put you on to me?"

"I don't know his name—"

Smith shot him in the arm. It was a .22, and the small pop probably wouldn't be heard outside the apartment.

Alvarez yelped, maybe in surprise, maybe in pain, and then clamped a hand over the wound. Blood began to seep through his fingers.

"I already know it was your cousin Jaimie. I just wanted to see if you'd lie."

The kid's jaw bulged, but he kept his mouth shut and gripped his arm tighter.

"You call her yet and give her this?" Smith indicated the folder he'd found on the desk.

Miguel shook his head.

"Good." Smith took a T-shirt from the floor. "Here, tie that off above the wound. I don't need you passing out yet."

Miguel managed to wrap the T-shirt around his upper arm and pull it tight with his teeth.

Smith took a piece of thick stationery from his pocket, unfolded it, and dropped it on the bed.

Miguel glanced down at the list of neatly printed addresses.

"I'd like you to do something for me, Mr. Alvarez. Two things, actually."

TIGHTER THAN A HOOKER'S WALLET

God, his leg ached. Driving always made it worse. He fingered the brass knob on top of his cane. Where was Smith? He should have been back by now. Alexei had no idea what do with this kid. He was just the chum to attract the bigger fish. He knew it was short-sighted, but hearing Strong's voice again in that condo had narrowed his vision down to one myopic goal: kill him. Get retribution for Drobhov and get revenge for his crippled leg. Never mind that he had killed this man's girlfriend or driven him out of his life to become a fugitive. Those were happen-stance, casualties of war, collateral damage. If you were in the game, it was a chance you took.

Without Smith's guidance, Alexei fell back on his training. The boy was a prisoner of war, no more, no less. Alexei knew what to do with POWs.

"Get up."

The boy looked up at him with tear-streaked cheeks, then stood on swaying legs.

"Go. To the left. Open that door."

He poked the boy in the back with his cane and kept his

gun hand out of reach, but tense and ready. He doubted the boy would try anything, but he hadn't slept in almost thirty hours and wasn't taking chances.

"Down."

The stairs disappeared into the dark and the boy hesitated. He wasn't the first. Alexei flipped the light switch to the left and the fluorescent bulbs flickered to life down below.

He prodded with the cane again. "Move."

Cobwebs hung in lazy strands from the pipes running overhead. To the right was a storage area filled with boxes and old housewares from previous owners. To the left was a pool table covered by a green tarp. Lawn chairs and dusty cardboard boxes were piled around it. Straight ahead was a small wooden door that led to the house's wine cellar.

"Open that door there." The wine cellar was built by one of the bosses long before Natasha, maybe during America's strange courtship with Prohibition. He knew she hadn't drunk alcohol and now, with Alexei's taste only for vodka, the dusty bottles stocked inside were wasted on him, too.

The twenty-by-twenty room was dark, dank, and smelled of cork and wet stone. There were no windows, just a couple bare bulbs for light. The fieldstone walls were at least eighteen inches thick. He pushed the kid inside and locked the door. He put a shoulder to the solid oak planks and was confident the simple lock was enough to keep a scared teenager captive for at least a couple hours.

After maneuvering back up to the top of the stairs, he flipped the light switch off. There was nothing more powerful than darkness to keep a prisoner docile.

He stood in the kitchen, still catching his breath from climbing the stairs. He pulled the little case from his pocket, weighed it on his hand, then put it back. He hooked a chair with his cane and dragged it over. He sat down and let himself relax for a moment. He let his chin fall to his chest, almost begged his mind to let him sleep, but knew it was no use. The icepick-like pain in his leg kept him awake with a brutal, throbbing efficiency. He pulled the case back out and let the last pill dissolve on his tongue.

———

Strong stood at the window and watched Kyle moving back toward the house. He didn't know how good the surveillance cameras were, but he had to admit that Kyle wasn't making it easy. The man could disappear in plain sight. He'd slip between shrubs and small trees and not disturb the branches. He used the shadows and the glare of the sun to melt into the landscape. More than once, Strong was staring at one spot and he'd see Kyle appear ten feet away. It was unnerving.

Two minutes later, he heard Kyle's light tread coming up the stairs and figured he'd only heard that sound because Kyle was being polite.

"Where'd you learn those tricks?" Max asked when he came into the room.

"Army. Force Recon." He offered nothing more.

"What do you think?"

"That place is locked up tighter than a hooker's wallet. Multiple cameras. Motion sensor lights. That electrified fence is sunk down at least a foot, probably three. Surrounding area is clear of debris."

"Would going after dark help?"

"No."

"Any suggestions?"

"In our time frame? Think of something else."

"Kate, any ideas?"

She was sitting on the bed. It was designed like a race car and was obviously a little boy's room. They had chosen a house two down from the address Alexei had provided. It offered a clear view to the west side of 1241 Evergreen. A pile of wet newspapers on the porch had tipped them off that the house may be vacant. They parked their car at the bottom of the hill in a strip mall a couple miles away and walked back up separately. The locks and security system on this house were antiquated compared to the fortified fort down the street. They were through the back door in less than a minute. Kate proved to be very good at locks.

"None, sorry. Storming the fort isn't exactly my specialty." She stood up and stretched. "I'm going to check in with Jaimie." She started out of the room.

"Something coming," Kyle said. He was leaning against the wall by the opposite window near a beanbag chair and a poster of Bears linebacker Brian Urlacher. "It's lit up."

Max moved next to him.

"You think someone saw us come in?" Kate asked.

"And waited two hours to call the police?"

"Maybe. Might just be a drive-by to check on things."

"They don't wait two hours to do a courtesy call in this neighborhood."

"False alarm. Yellow lights. Looks like a utility truck."

Max glanced at the digital clock next to the bed. "Electricity still running."

"Gas company." Kyle moved back and Max took a closer look.

"CS&G truck. Hold up," Max said.

"What?" Kate asked, still standing in the doorway.

"There's more than one. There's three or four. Cop car coming up the hill now, too."

"We gotta get out of here," Kate replied.

"And go where?" Max stepped back from the window and sat down on the bed.

"Somewhere the cops aren't. You're a fugitive, remember?

And if I'm found with you, I've got a boatload of awkward questions to answer."

"If they were coming for me, Kate, they wouldn't come in four utility trucks and one cop car. We sit tight until we know more. Can you go down there and find out what's going on?"

"And how do I do that?" she asked.

"Just go down and ask. The era of small-town beat cops is long over. No one knows who lives here. Four utility trucks and a cop car show up on your street and any normal person would be curious. More than curious. Probably worried."

"Why me?"

"I can't go and, between you and Kyle, you look a bit more innocent."

Kate just shook her head. "I'll try to take that as a compliment." She disappeared out the door.

Kyle was back by the window. "Second cop car now."

Max was silent. He sat on the bed. There was nothing he could do but wait until he had more information.

"Door to door." A pause. "Only one person has answered so far."

"You don't get to afford houses like this by staying home."

"Kate's up."

Max got up and stood side by side with Kyle. They were careful to stay far enough back from the window so that they wouldn't be seen. He watched Kate walk down the curving brick path that fronted the house and stop by the cop car that idled at the curb. She leaned down and put her arms on the window.

"Nice."

"She's good."

At one point, Kate threw her arm back, indicating the house. Both men took an instinctive step backward. A few seconds later, Kate turned, waved, and retraced her steps back up the brick path. A moment later, she was standing in the doorway.

"Gas leak. Big one. They're evacuating everyone as a precaution."

"For how long?"

"He didn't know exactly. They're telling people forty-eight to seventy-two hours."

"So, he's gotta move him," Kyle said.

"More than likely."

"I gotta get back out there. I told the cop I was housesitting and was just going back in for my bag."

"Okay, we'll go through the woods. Meet us down by the car."

They both watched again from the window as Kate left, carrying a black duffel bag she had taken from a downstairs closet. She waved to the cop, who smiled and said something in return, then she disappeared behind the tall box hedge that grew along the property line.

"He's going to think we did this."

"Yes, but we didn't."

"It can't be a coincidence."

"If it's someone else, then who?"

Kyle shrugged. "I'm new to this, but it's going to make him angry."

"Pretty sure he's already there."

They waited for the cop cars to move further down the street.

"Out the back?"

"Always my preference."

VARIABLES

Kate was leaning against the driver's side door of the Acura, tapping her phone against her leg, when Max and Kyle walked up. Max was sweating and covered in burrs. Kyle looked like he'd just spent the last two hours sitting on a couch, maybe watching a ball game.

"What took you guys so long?"

"There's not exactly a path through those woods," Max said. He brushed a scrap of leaf from his hair. "What's got you all amped up?"

"I know where he's gonna take him."

"Really? How?"

"I'll tell you on the way. Get in."

A thick atlas was open and stuck between the two front seats. A brown bag sat in the passenger footwell.

"Water and snacks," Kate said. "Help yourself."

Max took a bottled water, then another, and passed one back to Kyle.

Max picked up the atlas. It was folded open to a page showing the northern reaches of Michigan. "How far we going?"

"Looks like about four hundred miles by the map."

"That's a long way. You're sure about this?"

She held out her smartphone. Max felt dumb. Go to prison for a few years and technology whips by in the fast lane. So far, Max found he got along just fine without one, but sometimes not taking the time to catch up made him feel like a Luddite.

"Go ahead, it won't bite," Kate said. He took the phone. "Hit the green button there."

Max found himself looking at a list of addresses. There were five of them. One of them was the street they'd just left.

Kate tapped both her thumbs against the wheel and kept talking as she drove. "Remember the incident with Jaimie I told you about?"

"Some guy gave her a scare in an alley."

"Right, well, it shook both of us. Truth be told, Smith gave me a hinky feeling the first time I met him, but," she shrugged her shoulders, glanced out the side window, "I needed the money. After that incident, we decided to find out a little more about our client. It took some time and some serious digging, but we uncovered a few things. Jaimie just called and sent that over."

"A property list."

"Smith's properties, or ones with ties to him through corporations he's involved with or shell companies he's set up."

"Therefore, also Alexei's properties. Or ones he has access to, at least."

"Bingo."

"So, if Alexei needs a bolt hole to regroup, you're thinking he goes for one of these. But why this one up in the peninsula?"

"I checked the other ones while I was waiting. One is a restaurant. Two are apartments in the city. The fourth is the house we just saw get evacuated. The fifth is the one upstate, practically Canada. Which would you choose?"

Max ran through the options. The restaurant was out. Too public. He wouldn't want the unpredictability of the city apartments, either. Too many people around, too many witnesses. A curious neighborhood, a chatty doorman, thin walls, too many other things to think about. Kate was right, the more isolated the better. That fortress of a house was the best option, but this isolated address was a close second. It promised the most control and the most insulation from outside factors. Max thought there was one other reason, too. It was the place where he could take his time once he had Max and killed the others. Alexei was arrogant enough not to see any other outcome.

"Are you sure this is the complete list? What if there is someplace else? What if there's some blind partnerships set up as owners on some plot of land somewhere?"

"Then we're screwed. But Jaimie's good. I think this is the list, but I'm willing to listen to other ideas." No one had anything better. "I gotta trust her, but there is something else."

"What?"

"I had Jaimie run some checks on the address. The electricity is on."

"Do we know if anyone else lives up there?"

"No, you don't understand. It was just turned on. Thirty minutes ago."

A CABIN IN THE WOODS

Alexei cut the tape on the kid's ankles and half-pulled, half-pushed him out of the trunk with his good arm. The kid groaned, stumbled, and fell on to his knees in the dirt. It had been a long, painful drive for both of them.

Eight hours of hard driving had made the bones and muscles in Alexei's leg saw against each other like pieces of jagged metal. The cloudy softness from the pills was long gone. He leaned hard on his cane to take the pressure off for a moment, then prodded the kid with the end of the cane to get him moving. The kid took a few steps to find his legs but seemed steady enough by the time they reached the house. Alexei was lucky the kid was still in no shape to take advantage of his own weakness. If he made a run for it, there was no way Alexei could catch him. Then again, where would he run to up here?

The door was open like Smith said it would be and Alexei quickly stashed the kid in an upstairs closet, re-taping his legs, and wedging a desk chair under the handle to keep it secure. He limped back downstairs to the kitchen and dug through the liquor cabinet until he came up with a quarter full bottle of strawberry Stoli. He thought it must be someone's idea of a joke, but he wasn't drinking now to enjoy it. He found a juice glass in a cabinet, rinsed out the dust, then poured as much of the bottle into the glass as he could fit. He swallowed the first half quickly, standing by the sink. As the artificially sweet burn moved down his body and into his legs, he felt the knot of pain in his hip untwist just a bit.

Damn Strong for making him so weak, he thought. Damn him for making him feel this way. He took a slow sip and tried not to taste it. The thought that his revenge was close did more to ease his pain than the alcohol ever would.

He knew he needed to look over the house and outside terrain to prepare, but all he could think about was getting off his feet and easing the aching pressure on his leg. He had time. After Strong found the house on Evergreen empty and the street cordoned off, he would have to call again and that would start the clock.

He checked his phone. A signal, a very weak one, but still no calls. Alexei figured he could afford a few hours of rest. He picked up the bottle, limped across the room, and fell into a chair opposite the fireplace. He put his keys and wallet on the sideboard and made himself as comfortable as he could.

He'd never been to the cabin before, only heard about it from Smith. Built by one of the first Italian bosses and handed down through the years, first more Italians, later the Russians. It was originally a small waystation for whiskey runners to take cover or swap rides. It wasn't much to look at, but that was the point, at least back then. Smith told him the basement was dug double deep and twice the width of the house to store barrels of blended Canadian malt coming across the border. Since the Volstead Act had been repealed, the cabin was mainly used for hunting and rustic liaisons. The basement was empty. Most of the time.

The house had been renovated a couple times. The result was comfortable, but still far from lavish. The ground floor was one large open room with exposed beams and hardwood floors. The kitchen was set in the back right corner, with a large pine dining table separating the prep area from the living room centered around the fireplace. Stairs bisected the room and led to the second floor, with three small bedrooms and a bathroom.

Alexei left the lights off and watched out the back window as darkness fell. The stars were bright white spots against the night sky, as if someone had used a pin to pierce a black curtain. It was so much brighter than the city. The reptile part of his brain told him that tactically the bright starlight would be good. He'd see them and their shadows coming. Alexei eased back into the lumpy chair. Alexei liked the modesty of the place, the simplicity, and the stillness. Once this was over, he decided he'd make a point of coming up here more often.

He dug in his suit coat pocket and came up with the pill case. He'd refilled it before they left Chicago. He sipped his drink as he flicked the top open and closed, open and closed. At the start, after the doc had announced the infection was gone and he was on his feet and out of bed, he'd thought it was just a matter of time, that the pain would gradually lessen to a small point, then one day disappear. That didn't happen. The pain didn't budge. It was a part of him now. It lived inside him, a constant debilitating weakness that only the pills could shrink. He gave up the charade with himself and crushed one between his teeth and chased it with a swallow of strawberry vodka. The pills were a part of him, too. He dropped the case next to his wallet, put his head back against the chair cushion, and waited.

He knew he should get up and go outside. That would be the smart play, unexpected. Find some blind or nook in the trees. Lure them in, then snap the trap closed. But he was so tired and he had time. Strong hadn't even called yet. He pulled his phone out and checked the signal again. Weak still, but steady. The call would go through.

He felt hands pressing him down into the chair's cushions. His eyelids like bricks. So tired. Something wasn't right. He knew the pills. He knew the slow creeping softness. The pleasant fuzziness that pushed the pain into the background. This wasn't right. This was a black train. He tried to pull the case out but dropped it. He pushed back against the overwhelming drowsiness with all he had and managed to stand up. Some air, he needed fresh air. He took one step toward the door, caught his foot on the corner of the end table, and crashed to the floor.

TUNNEL OF TREES

They made good time all the way up through the town of New Hope. After that, they had to slow down as the freeway dead-ended and gave way to single-lane state and county roads. Any maps Kate was able to bring up on her phone were spotty, only showing the larger state roads, not the smaller, meandering, sometimes unpaved local roads. The atlas, only covering the surrounding metro area, was long past being useful.

They pulled into a gas station as the freeway dwindled down to single pot-holed lanes in either direction. With its free-standing rotary pumps, it looked more like a museum piece than a working station, but a sign that was flipped to open hung in the doorway. Max went inside while Kate navigated the rustic dials and hoses of the pump. He found three rows of clean, well-stocked shelves with a drink cooler running along the back wall. A weathered old man in a faded embroidered western shirt and bolo tie sat behind the register listening to an AM station playing gospel music. Max carried three bottles of water and a package of jerky to the counter.

The old man looked like he'd manned this post since long before the roads were paved and the gas pumps necessary and would be here long after it all finally returned to dust. He eyed the merchandise before punching the keys of the cash register with knobby fingers. The big receipt wheel rattled and spun.

"Five seventy-six."

Max handed him a ten. "You live around here?"

"Close enough."

"You know the area north of New Hope?"

"I know some fishing spots. A deer blind or two. What do you have in mind?"

"Looking for a house, 66 Cummings?"

The old man looked out and watched Kate wrestle with the pump. "You visiting?"

"Meeting up with an old friend."

"Don't know that particular house, but Cummings runs across 54 a few miles past the Baptist church with no steeple up yonder." He ripped the receipt off and sketched a quick map on the back.

"Thanks."

The man squinted out at the lowering sun. "If you don't know where you're going, I suggest waiting 'til tomorrow. Finding places up here ain't easy, even when you got a key and a deed. You never been there before? Forget it. You get turned around. You get lost, you end up with a cold night in the woods. Or worse." He dipped his head at the newspaper rack to the left of the register.

Max scanned a front-page that had a story of a hunter attacked while bow hunting for deer.

"It's cub season. A mama sow will do anything for her cubs."

"Thanks. I'll take it under advisement."

"Do that and I'll see you on the way out. Think I'm just a crazy old coot?" He just shrugged and went back to his music.

On the narrow roads, darkness came on fast like a rolling wave and washed away their sense of direction. Max feared the old man was going to be prophetic, but after three false starts they found State Road 54, marked only by a rusted metal sign nailed into the trunk of a gnarled oak. They might have missed it completely and driven by if someone hadn't tagged the sign with bright red Class of '09 graffiti.

They followed SR 54 until they found the steeple-less church, the left side of its roof caved in, then made a left to stay on the old man's receipt map. Cummings Road, if they were even on it, was an unpaved dirt strip that narrowed in the first half mile until it was barely a single car length wide. The bushes and trees edged closer as if anxious for a look at any visitors.

For a half-hour, they moved slowly deeper into the dark woods looking for driveways or property markers, trying to avoid any hole that might snap an axle. The cones of light from the headlights were swallowed up in the tunnel of trees. Kate inched the car along. It was tedious work.

"Wait. We passed it." Max said.

"What? Where?"

"Look at that tree there. To the left. There are numbers nailed to the trunk. Seventy-six. You said sixty-six, right? We must have missed it in the dark."

"Christ. You're right. It couldn't have been far. We passed that rusty mailbox for sixty-five ten minutes ago."

"Let's leave the car and walk. It will be quieter, and we're less likely to miss the turnoff again."

Walking back from the other direction, it was easy to see how they'd missed it the first time. The dirt driveway made a sharp left turn almost immediately. Coming from the south, the drive looked almost like a solid wall of trees with just a shallow depression carved out. It was almost an optical illusion. If you knew where to look, it was obvious; if not, you'd pass right by.

"Hidden in plain sight," Kate said.

"I'll go first," Max said. "Let's space it out a bit so we're not easy marks if someone is waiting in these trees."

Kate's eyes danced around in the dark. A natural city girl, Max could sense she was a bit out of her depth. Kyle just nodded. Max looked back at Kate. "You want to get the car turned around? Wait up here?"

She shook her head, seemed to steel herself. "No. I'm in. Let's get on with it."

"I'll go first, then Kate. Kyle, watch our backs."

They started down the path, keeping close to the sides of the driveway and the cover of the trees. After forty yards, they doubled back, then again. The drive was a series of looping S-curves. Max stopped by a large boulder at the end of the last turn. He could see a square cabin in a roughly circular clearing. The cabin was dark, but a car was parked in front. If Alexei wasn't there already, then someone else was inside holding down the fort until he arrived. He suspected it was Alexei; despite Kate's quick work, they had too much time to overcome.

"Jesus, would it have killed them to make this driveway a straight shot?" Kate whispered, coming up behind Max.

"It's by design. To screen the house, as well as slow down any potential threat. It's a great choke point for an ambush."

"Speaking of," Kyle murmured, appearing at Max's elbow.

"Right. A straightforward approach isn't ideal, but I'm not sure what else we can do." He gestured toward the house. "Someone is in there or nearby. These woods are thick, and I'm afraid I'll blunder around in there worse than out here in the open."

Kyle peered around the boulder for a moment. "You work out the approach. I'll use the woods and flank you."

"Not a bad idea. The fact that there are three of us might still give us some element of surprise."

"Give me five minutes."

Kyle took a step into the woods. Another step and he was gone.

"Creepy," Kate said.

Max could only nod. "Let's take it slow."

They left the driveway and worked their way along the edge of the woods. It took twenty minutes of slow work to make it to a point opposite the corner of the house, more than enough time for Kyle to get set. Max looked across the front of the house and down the one side he could see toward the back, but nothing had changed. No movement. No light. If the car hadn't been parked out front, he'd say it was abandoned.

He turned to Kate. "If things go sideways, just start shooting over my head and give me a chance, then get back to the car and take off. I'll meet you at that motor lodge across from that gas station. If I'm not there by morning, get back to Chicago and—"

"It's not going to come to that."

Max thought there was a very real possibility of it coming to that, but stopped himself from arguing further. Kate getting out alive, preferably with Duffy, and back to Chicago might be the best he could hope for in a second confrontation with Alexei, even with Kyle watching his back.

He still had the gun he'd taken off the dead man on the stairs in Sheila's apartment. He pulled out the Browning HP now He pulled the slide back to check that there was one in the chamber then double-checked that the safety was engaged before pulling back the hammer and slipping it back into his belt.

"I'll be back with the kid in a few."

They had agreed on the southwest corner of the cabin as an approach because it kept the small amount of moonlight at his back and had the least amount of windows. The western side had a high casement window toward the back, then a gap before the two up, two down window pattern picked up again along the southern face. They had pegged it as the bathroom, and both agreed it gave him the best chance not to be noticed. It was logical, but it didn't make crawling away from the tree line any easier.

He took the last fifty yards on his knees, toes, and elbows and tried to stay as low as possible. He kept his chin in the grass and resisted the temptation to look up. As long as clods of dirt weren't exploding around his head, he figured he was doing okay.

After ten agonizing minutes that felt like ten hours, his left hand reached forward and scraped against the puckered cement foundation. He stood up with his back against the house and brushed off the grass and dirt. Looking back the way he'd come, he saw the tree where he'd started, but not Kate. He didn't bother to even check for Kyle.

He pulled the gun back out, crept around the corner and approached the first window. He risked a quick turkey peek. He let the image replay in his mind. With no lights it was difficult to see. It was more of a sense of the space than any details. Open floor plan. Kitchen. Long table with bench seats. Only shadows on the far side. He pressed his back against the cabin's rough exterior again and listened, braced for a shot or shout that would tell him he'd been seen. Nothing. No movement or reaction from inside. He waited a final beat, then moved on.

After the initial window, there was a plain pine door that was stained to match the wood siding, no peek-through windows on either side that might allow a view inside. There

was no knocker, no doorbell, no other adornments, just a
door with a gold-plated knob that looked to be roughly in line
with its matching counterpart in front of the house. He
moved past the door to the last set of windows.

He risked another look. This side of the cabin was a long
living room. On the far end, there were two couches forming
an L-shape around a flat-screen TV mounted on the wall.
Closest to the window were comfortable-looking loveseats
and chairs grouped around a stone fireplace.

In the middle of the room was a body, facedown and
unmoving.

Max looked twice to be sure in the dim light. He couldn't
tell if it was Alexei, or if he was alive or dead.

He backtracked to the door and turned the knob. Locked.
He kept low and went around to the front. This door was
unlocked. He slipped inside. The place smelled stale and
musty.

Max left the door open in case he needed a quick retreat
and moved to the left, into the living room, and cleared the
sofas with his gun up. It was Alexei. He kept his finger tensed
on the trigger as he stared down at the body. He watched the
man's back rise and fall. He was alive. A bead of sweat rolled
down Max's scalp. He flexed his other hand and tried to
control the adrenaline flooding his system. Six pounds of
trigger pressure and Alexei would be dead. It would be over.

Or would it?

He picked up a pillow from the couch and threw it toward
the prone body. It hit Alexei in the legs but caused no reaction. He moved closer. He needed information. He needed to
know how far his name had spread. If this was just a personal
beef between him and Alexei, it could end here and he could
walk away. If his name was marked within the organization, if
this vendetta had more backing from people up the chain of

command, he could take a dangerous enemy off the board, but it wouldn't be over.

Max knelt down and searched him. A suit pocket held a gun and he took a knife from around his ankle. He tossed both on the sofa, out of reach. He stepped back and looked at the man who had ruined two of his chances at a clean life.

He thought of Sheila.

He raised the gun.

Lowered it.

Raised it again.

There was a loose flap of skin near Alexei's forehead, right at the hairline. The blood had clotted and matted his black and silver hair. His face looked haggard and tired. Rings of gray were etched deep under his eyes and loose, wrinkled skin hung off his jowls. Even without the red smear of a scalp wound, Max could see that something wasn't right with him. This wasn't the same man that had come for him at the mill.

He looked at the table next to one of the reclining chairs near the fireplace. A wallet, keys, and a small metal case sat next to a vodka bottle with just a sliver of clear liquid remaining in the bottom. A cane leaned against the wall. He stuck his own gun in his waistband and picked up the little case, flipped it open. Pills. Small, white, and unmarked.

A muffled thump came from above. Duffy. The shock of finding Alexei on the floor had pushed the kid from his mind. He put the case down.

"Hey kid, it's Max. If you can hear me, make some noise."

Another thump, this one louder. He walked into the kitchen.

"Keep going," Max called again.

It didn't take long to find him stuffed in a second-floor closet. He was sweaty, dirty, and dehydrated. Max hauled him out and cut the ties on his hands and legs. Duffy stumbled and struggled to stay upright on his cramped legs as Max guided him to a desk chair in the corner.

"Thanks," he croaked in a cracked and whispery voice.

In the brighter light of the bedroom, Max could see Duffy had a line of grease across his temple, likely from riding in a trunk, and an angry-looking knot on the back of his head, but otherwise looked okay. He was young. He'd survive.

"Think you can make it down the stairs?"

"In a minute maybe." He rubbed at his knees and calves. "Let me just get some feeling back."

"Take your time."

Max went across the short hall into the bathroom. It was once probably called a water closet, made up of just a walled-in corner with a toilet and a washbasin. Max rinsed out the plastic cup next to the sink and filled it with water. He walked back and handed Duffy the cup. He drank it quickly, spilling some down his chin.

"More, please."

Max refilled the cup. After the second cup was gone, drunk slowly this time, Duffy stood, steadier on his feet now.

He took a deep, shuddering breath. "Let's get the hell out of here."

Back down on the first floor, they found Kyle, face and clothes creased with dark mud, standing over Alexei's prone body.

"This him?"

Max nodded. "That's the guy."

"You?"

"Nope. Found him like that."

"What now?"

"Not sure. I want to get some information out of him. If this is just him on a bender for me, then we can have it out and be done. After Sheila, I helped clip his boss. We were supposed to have a pass, but if that was fumbled and he's recruited more people, or the organization changed their mind, then I need to know what's coming."

Kyle just nodded. "I'm in this only for Sheila. This guy kills my sister, he's gotta be held accountable. Anything to tie him to Sheila other than your word?"

It was the longest he'd heard Kyle talk.

"Probably not. Nothing he couldn't beat with a good lawyer. Not unless we find a better witness than me or someone to corroborate."

Kyle just shook his head and paced the short distance between the sofa and the fireplace.

Max watched him. Kyle's lips moved as he walked, but no sound came out. His hand gripped and re-gripped his gun, almost a mirror of the actions he'd done himself ten minutes earlier. He waited for Kyle to come to a decision. He had a right to choose as much as Max did. If he wanted to take Alexei out back and sandbag him in the river, Max wouldn't stand in the way. Despite everything Alexei had done, Max knew it wasn't in him to pull the trigger on an unconscious man. Self-defense, yes, he'd proved that. In the grip of white-hot anger, yes, he wasn't proud, but he'd proved that, too, during his life. More than once.

"I might be able to help," Duffy said.

The two men looked at him.

"Duffy, I don't think you want—"

He waved Max off. "Not that. But I think I might have someone to corroborate. Or at least help build a better case against him." He nodded at Alexei. "Maybe not for Sheila, but racketeering or something to tack on to my kidnapping. Pile on some more years so he never breathes free air again."

"Like what?"

"Remember I told you about Porter's notes?"

"Sure."

"Well, one of the primary sources was someone Porter called WE."

"You told us it was a dead end. You don't know who it is. Neither do any of us."

"I think it might be the sheriff. The new one. Logins. The WE initials in the notes. I think it stands for Wyatt Earp. It was a frozen pizza box, of all things, that jarred it loose. Tombstone. Porter loved Westerns. Had old one-sheets from the classics hung up in his apartment. And it fits with Porter's sense of humor. The sheriff is one of the few people who could pull all those threads together. We all agree the investigation got muzzled at some point. Maybe that didn't sit well with Logins. Maybe he started feeding it to Porter in hopes that it would all come out."

The back door opened. Max and Kyle both spun around, guns up.

"Whoa! Whoa! Stand down." Kate stood in the doorway, hands raised, breathing hard. "There's a car coming."

WAITING FOR THE GAFF

Alexei's senses came back slowly, like big overhead halogen lights cracking on in an airplane hangar. In the absence of everything else, long-instilled training took over. He didn't move. He kept his breathing slow and shallow. He let sound, then sight, then sensation leach back in. He gathered intel. There were voices, more than one, and heavy footfalls vibrating the floorboards. His head felt fuzzy. Everything was too loud and jumbled, like listening to the radio through heavy static. Words criss-crossing from English to Russian and back again. A sudden surge of nausea rolled up from his stomach into his throat. He swallowed it down.

He concentrated on the voices. They were talking about someone. At least two voices. One of the voices was familiar. It took a moment, but the dulled synapses fired. Strong. His bad leg seemed to throb in concert with his thoughts. Then a third voice. The kid. His plan had worked. Strong was in the room. He just wasn't in any shape to see it through to the end.

It wasn't in his character to be passive. He knew there was

always a tactical advantage in surprise. The heavy static in his head had cleared, but he guessed his range of motion and reactions would be limited and dull. The question was how much? He had no idea and no way to find out without tipping his hand. He could feel the loose snap on his ankle sheath. Whoever had frisked him had done a thorough job. He had to hope the element of surprise would compensate for his lack of weapons and other physical weaknesses. A long shot, but his only shot.

He measured the footsteps coming closer, then away, then back. The conversation in the room had stalled. They were all deep in their own thoughts and hadn't noticed any change in the man bound on the floor. Alexei pictured the layout of the room. Measured the footsteps. He needed to get one guy on the ground fast and get a weapon or leverage or both. He tensed his shoulders and knees to roll toward the approaching footsteps. Away. Away. A turn and coming back. Wait for it. Two more steps. Wait.

A voice. Female, coming from behind him, at the back of the house. He was putting everything he had into timing the steps and missed what she said. Whatever it was caused a swift and immediate reaction. They were gone. Alexei didn't have to open his eyes to know. He could feel the emptiness and sudden stillness of the house. He was alone.

He opened his eyes and rolled over, or tried to. His body reacted badly. His legs were full of paralyzing pins and needles and as useless as bags of sand. Any attack he mustered would have been laughable. He would have looked like a fish flopping helplessly on the deck, just waiting for the gaff.

That voice likely saved him from an ignominious end.

He grabbed the arms of one of the cushioned chairs and pulled himself to his feet as bright light flooded the cabin walls. Headlights. Alexei listened to the deep rumble of a V8 pull to a stop in front of the cabin. Four car doors opened and slammed in the night.

Smith walked in the front door, followed by three large men in black suits. Alexei vaguely recognized their faces. They didn't matter. He looked at Smith. "There are four of them. Two men, the kid, and a woman. Probably the PI."

He didn't notice the gun until Smith had it up and pointed at him. It looked comically large and incongruous in Smith's manicured hand.

He never heard the shot.

WOKE

They were in the trees, making their way back to the road, when they heard the sound. It creased the night and rebounded off the surrounding hills so that it sounded like it came from everywhere at once. They all stopped and hunched instinctively.

"Was that—" Duffy asked.

"Gunshot," Max replied. He looked at Kyle. He saw the same look he knew was being reflected in his own eyes. Leaving Alexei alive had been a mistake. Back in the woods, with a familiar itch between his shoulder blades, Max knew he couldn't start over again.

It had to end here.

He turned to Kate. "Looks like most of these places are summer homes. I didn't see any lights the whole trip in. Can you take Duffy and hole up in one of them until this thing is over?"

She nodded. "What are you going to do?"

"Make sure it's over."

They crept back the way they came, Max following in Kyle's footsteps, trying to mimic the man's silent movements through the thick brush. Moving carefully, it took ten minutes to make it back to the clearing that surrounded the cabin. Kyle waved Max up next to him. He mimed something Max didn't understand. He pointed.

It took a moment for the shades of darkness to resolve into shapes, but he spotted the two slumped forms against the more impregnable black of the wooded backdrop. They were sprawled side by side halfway between the house and the backyard that sloped down to the river. Another dark shape limped away from them and went around the far side of the house.

"Looks like he woke up."

Max nodded. "How do you want to do this?"

Before Kyle could answer, another gunshot punched the air, the muzzle flash lighting up the front yard like a signal flare.

Kyle was already moving.

EXECUTION

The sound was like a bomb going off inside his still cloudy head. His vision doubled, and vertigo made him stumble back and press himself into the solid rigidity of the chair.

The bullet passed by his ear and thunked into the bookcase behind him, caught and held by the thick pulp of the stacked pages. A wasted shot, Alexei thought.

That was Smith's first mistake.

Alexei shut his eyes as the room rolled and pitched. He counted to ten. The room was still wobbling when he opened them again. Whatever he'd taken was still working its way through his system.

Smith had lowered his gun and let it hang by his leg. "How are those horse tranquilizers? Strong enough?"

"You've been holding out on me, Smith. Those are much better than the Oxy."

They really were, Alexei thought. The nausea and dizziness were fading now. He felt ... nothing? No pain. His constant companion for the last year had become so chronic, even with fistfuls of painkillers, that Alexei almost felt naked now without it. But it was truly gone, at least for the moment, and the next few minutes were all that mattered. His limbs felt puffy and slow, but, for the first time since the fall, his leg wasn't throbbing, itching, and begging him for relief.

Alexei's lips turned up in an imitation of a smile. Smith should have shot him on sight if he was going to make a play, but the man was a talker, more a politician than a soldier.

That was his second mistake.

"Honestly, I didn't figure you'd notice," Smith said. "You've been pouring those pills down your throat for so long, I was afraid you might have built up some immunity. As it is, they should have dropped you for at least eight hours."

"We all have our vices. Mine are pills. Yours are those boys you meet on Thursday afternoons. At least I have an excuse."

Smith's neck flushed deep red, but he kept his composure. He turned to the two men on his right. "Frisk him, then take him outside and kill him. Leave him in the woods for the animals." He turned back to Alexei. "You'll be bone and gristle in less than a week."

"If you hadn't noticed, I'm not much more than that now."

"I've noticed. And I'm not the only one. It's one of the reasons I'm here."

Two of the men stepped across the room. One of them handed his gun to the other and came forward to frisk Alexei. Strong, or someone in his group, had already taken his gun and knife, so there was nothing for them to find. If they had any thoughts about the empty holster or ankle sheath, they didn't voice them.

The man stepped back and took his gun back. Alexei noticed both of their handguns had suppressors attached. Alexei had no respect for those. If you needed silence, you moved in close and used a knife or, better yet, your hands. Suppressors were a lazy shortcut. Even worse, they were an unreliable shortcut. They screwed up your aim, overheated the barrel, and were prone to jamming up the gun. Besides, who was going to hear the shots way out here? Were they worried about the deer snitching? They were too conditioned to working in the city.

He filed this away and then turned his attention back to Smith. "Why else are you here, besides the concern for my little addiction?"

"Do you ever wonder how exactly I got this far, Alexei? I mean, look at me. Really look at me. Any of these three could break my neck without breaking a sweat. I'm sure you, even in such a decrepit condition, could kill me as well."

"I always figured you were holding something, enough of a something to give you the leverage to keep that skinny neck in the clear."

"Not a bad thought. One I've had myself from time to time, but blackmail is very difficult to pull off in the long term. No, it's much simpler than that. I take the time to think."

"You're a higher-order primate than the rest of us knuckle draggers?"

"Sounds unbelievable, doesn't it? But it's that simple, and it's true. While you're popping those pills or making yourself crazy about this guy who set you up and humiliated you, or while these lunks are pumping iron or oiling their guns, I'm thinking. I'm planning. I'm creating opportunity. I'm making you look incompetent and dangerous, a loose cannon who might blow up in everyone's face. I whisper things. Emphasize certain things. I create a gas leak. I leave a trail of crumbs that brings everyone here. Then, when I offer a solution, it's with everyone's blessing, even their gratitude. No one likes dealing with difficult employees."

Alexei nodded and tried to look sufficiently cowed by the speech. "You have a point. I was always better in the smoke of battle than I was at theories or classroom stuff. Give me the man who can get the job done. Not the one who simply talks about getting it done. That's why I stuck with Drobhov until the end. He was better at seeing around corners. I was better at actually going around them. We were an effective team."

"Until he started seeing answers in the bottom of cups."

"Like my leg, he had his reasons. I don't begrudge him any peace he found in the bottle."

"I know about Drobhov's wife and child, but, see, that's the problem. The key to longevity in our line of work is not losing focus despite the temptation or the vices. Drugs, women, booze. Even tragedy. All distractions. You need the patience and the discipline to see the long view. It's never about the guns, or the bullets or the blood. All of those things are simply the byproducts of the plan."

They stared at each other from across the room. Alexei was talked out. The management lesson now over, so was Smith. He just didn't know it yet.

"You two take him outside and finish it. You, get the car. I want to get back to civilization."

As his executioners approached, Alexei tried to stand and took a limping, stumbling step forward. He looked at the younger of the two thick necks. "Could you hand me my cane?" He pointed to the polished mahogany stick leaning against the chair. "It's that, or you two have to carry me out. Even with these horse tranqs, my leg is a mess. At least let me walk to my own funeral."

The man lifted the light, amber-colored cane and looked at Smith. Smith had handled the cane many times over the past two years and knew it would be about as effective as a maestro's baton against these guys. Smith nodded, and the man held out the cane to Alexei.

That was Smith's third mistake.

Smith was right about the cane. It wouldn't be very effective as a weapon. Not without pressing the small indentation disguised as a knot near the top and releasing the three-inch stiletto blade from the bottom.

Even dulled by industrial narcotics, Alexei was no physical match for the two men. Bodies pumped and primed in the gym, they could probably bench press Alexei with one arm, but he was equally positive that they had no business being in a fight with him.

Outside, playing up his limp as they crossed the backyard, he flicked the blade out in one stride, pretended to stumble the next, and fell to one knee. The man on the right, the closer one, reached instinctively forward to support him. Alexei used those instincts against him and stabbed up and back into the fleshy part of the man's throat. The blade punctured the man's voice box and sliced through his esophagus. There was no sound except an off-key whistling as the wounded man tried to breathe. Alexei dropped the cane and pivoted around his body, using it as a shield.

The second man reacted better than the first and squeezed off two shots in rapid succession. One bullet hit his partner's chest. The second missed high and sailed into the woods. The whistling gurgled to a stop.

Alexei grabbed the dead man's hand, which was still locked uselessly around the trigger guard, and fit his own hand over it. He fired two quick shots. The second man fell like a puppet whose strings had been cut. He was missing an eye and half of his left cheek. The whole incident was over in less than five seconds and, thanks to those suppressors, with little more sound than the breeze rustling through the treetop canopy.

Alexei retrieved his cane and wiped the blood from the blade with the dead man's tie. He took one of the guns as well and started walking back toward the cabin. He unscrewed the silencer and dropped it in the grass. No reason to hide his intent now.

He walked around to the front of the cabin and found the third thick neck smoking a cigarette while leaning against the door of a Caddy. The man's back was turned as he stared up the driveway. It figured that a guy like Smith wouldn't let his guards smoke inside. Alexei paused and leaned his cane against the side of the house, then shot the man in the head before continuing on toward the front door. He took some small measure of satisfaction in listening to the echoing boom of the shot as it bounced off the surrounding bowl of trees.

Smith was even more stupid than his thick necks. Rather than take a defensive position in the house or, better yet, run like hell out the back, he opened the front door and stood framed in the light.

"What was—"

Alexei took his time and allowed himself a small measure of satisfaction.

"Sometimes it's all about the execution, Smith."

Alexei squeezed the trigger just as two bullets pinged off the hood of the Caddy to his right. He flinched which threw off his aim. He watched in frustration as the doorframe cracked and splintered next to Smith's head. He fired again and thought he might have caught Smith as the man finally woke up from his stupor and dove back inside. A moment later, the door kicked close.

Alexei dropped to one knee, then slid closer to the Caddy for cover. He started to peek over the hood to try to spot his attacker, but another bullet shattered the car's sideview mirror, inches from his head, and he dropped back behind the front tire. Who the hell was shooting at him? Had Smith been smarter than he thought and brought more guys? Maybe in another car and left them up the road as backup? No, Alexei couldn't see it. Smith was too confident in his own plans. It had to be Strong and his people.

He'd heard three in the room at the time, four if you included the boy, but maybe more outside. He couldn't be sure. And he couldn't stick around. If there were more, and they were serious, Alexei was a sitting duck out here. He needed to get out and regroup. It burned his gut to be this close to the man who caused him daily agony and be able to do nothing about it, but walking into a string of bullets wasn't his idea of a noble end. You clawed and fought and, if necessary, retreated until you could come back and attack with double the ferocity.

He leaned out and tried to grab the dead guy. Bullets sent up clods of earth around him. He fired two shots back just to keep them honest. It took three lunges before he could drag the guy safely behind the big car. He went through the dead man's pockets and got lucky. He found a set of keys in the pants pocket. He pulled open the passenger side door and slid across the seats. Staying low, he started the car and made a tight U-turn in the grass and weeds that made up the front yard. He paused and let the lights illuminate the tree line but didn't see anyone. The shooting had stopped. He pointed the car up the driveway and hit the gas.

As he turned out onto the narrow hardpan road that led back toward New Hope, the car tilted violently and exploded in a shower of glass and crumpling metal. Alexei's head snapped sideways and pinballed off the driver's window. He stared back at the bright red spot of blood in the cracked safety glass and watched it narrow down to a single pinpoint as he blacked out.

FOOD CHAIN

Head to head, the big muscle and metal of the Caddy would have been no match for Kate's Acura. The little low-slung coupe would have crumpled or glanced off the bumper like a fly off the windshield, but, from the side, it could at least slow down the bigger car. Max aimed for the driver's side door, for maximum impact to Alexei, but misjudged the speed of both cars and ended up colliding with the back passenger side and most of the rear panel.

The impact blew out the Acura's airbags, which punched Max's head sideways into the car's support beam between the front and rear seats. The impact caught him behind the ear and left him dazed and suddenly drowsy in the talcum powder infused air. He let his head drop against the slowly deflating bag and coughed as he inhaled more powder, but he was now too sleepy to care.

He woke to someone pulling at his arms. He opened his eyes and saw only white. The airbag. He turned his head to the side and was poleaxed with a driving pain like railroad spikes being driven into his pupils.

"Bet that stings," Kyle said.

Max raised his hand and lightly touched the swelling knot behind his ear.

"More than you'd believe."

The door was stuck and wouldn't open far enough for Max to slide through, so Kyle helped him shimmy through the broken window. He couldn't have blacked out for long. The now deflated airbags hung from the dash like cast-off ghosts, but the engine still ticked and hissed as it cooled.

Max glanced at the other car. His misjudgment might have worked out for the best. The rear impact had twisted the car sideways into a neat bowtie around the trunk of a massive oak that stood sentry at the end of the driveway. The back was crushed inward from the impact with the Acura, while the engine block in the front was pushed up and out over the hood by the thick, gnarled tree trunk.

The car was also empty.

"Where is he?" Max couldn't let all this be for nothing.

"Not sure." Kyle pointed across the road into the deeper woods that hadn't yet been squared off into neat lots and hunting lodges. Max could see ferns and low shrubs trampled into the dirt. "Shouldn't be hard to track."

"No? This guy is ex-Soviet Army. A stone-cold killer. A goddamn predator. It's pitch-black out here and—God, what is that smell?"

It was strong and pungent and coated the inside of his nose like primer paint. Now that he noticed it, he couldn't not. It filled all his senses.

"See how the engine is buckled and exposed there?"

"Yeah."

"Door is caved in like yours. He likely climbed out through the windshield and put his hand or arm on the radiator as he climbed out. That smell is burnt flesh. We'll find him. You can't hide from that smell."

Max took two steps toward the road to give chase, then had to stop and put his head between his knees as the trees began to sway like wet noodles. He felt his stomach shift, then he threw up the water and jerky he'd eaten on the drive up.

"Concussion."

Max nodded. He wiped his mouth. He felt a little better. Kyle handed him a bottle of water. He took a few tentative sips and handed it back.

"You good?"

"Good enough."

Kyle took the lead. They stepped across the road and into the woods.

———

Alexei stopped and leaned against a tree to catch his breath. Something crashed through the underbrush to his left. A spooked deer probably, he thought. He looked back the way he'd come but saw only darkness. He glanced down at his hand. Even in the dark, he could see it was red and blistering, a throbbing mess that promised a future filled with more pain. Whatever pain the tranquilizers had dammed up, touching that engine had blown it apart. His leg and hand now throbbed in concert.

He'd lost the bodyguard's gun and his cane in the crash and hadn't wasted time looking for them. His only thought had been to get out of the car, a sure death trap, and get away. Retreat and regroup. Find some shelter.

Now, he thought he might have overestimated his opponents. Pinned down next to the Caddy, it had felt like a coordinated attack, but maybe it was a last gasp instead. Maybe running had been a rash decision. The car had offered some bit of protection. Doubling back to the house would have been smarter, but in the moment the pain and shock had twisted his thoughts, overrode his training. Now, he was caught out in the open in unfamiliar territory.

He tried to use a branch to support his aching leg, but it felt awkward and he tossed it away. Then, he changed his mind and picked it up again, if only to carry it. He felt better with a weapon in his hand even if it was only a yard of wood.

He continued deeper into the woods. He still heard nothing behind him. Had Strong and his friends given up pursuit? Could he stop and rest until morning? It was cold, but he'd survived far worse. Branches snapped and cracked in front of him. He crouched and scanned the darkness for any movement. Had they gotten ahead of him? Tried to outflank him? It was hard to think through the throbbing pain. He strained to listen and noticed how quiet it suddenly was underneath his ragged breathing.

He knew that quiet.

It was the empty spaces between concussive artillery bursts.

It was the gathering of breath before an attack.

A noise, behind him now.

He turned, and liquid yellow eyes flashed once in the moonlight before coming at him.

Alexei set his feet to meet death head-on.

One swing and the branch was wrenched from his grasp. In a detached way, he noticed his arm was still holding the branch. It was now just ten yards away.

He felt the hot, rank breath of the big animal on his face.

He watched the next blow arc toward his head.

He tried not to die screaming.

———

"You hear that?"

"Yes."

"What *was* it?"

Kyle shrugged and kept moving.

"Didn't sound human."

Ten minutes later, Kyle stopped and knelt. He pulled a small Maglite from his belt, turned it on.

Max had to blink and look twice to recognize that he was looking at a shoe. It looked wrong, soaked with all that blood. A horror movie prop, with the white stump of bone and bloody mass of tendons still on it.

Kyle moved forward into a small grouping of tall pines. Max followed, and felt a sudden jolt of primal fear on his neck. They were being watched. By something.

They found three more pieces. Later, it would be the ear that Max saw most often when he closed his eyes. Neatly sliced and bloodless, laying on a bed of burnt orange pine needles. It looked like it had been dropped deliberately. Like a warning.

EPILOGUE

The phone next to the mechanical bed rang in the middle of the night, but Smith was awake. He winced as he reached over, but picked it up on the second ring. He listened a moment to the quiet breathing, then said, "Hello, Matt."

"I'm leaving that name behind."

"Is that what you do?"

"It's what I do now."

"A lonely life."

"I'll manage."

"It took you a long time to call. I was thinking I had maybe trusted too much in Ms. Sanders's detective skills."

"She found you in two days. I wanted to put a little more distance between us."

"I understand, but let me say personally that I have no intention of trying to track you down."

"You were expecting my call?"

"Yes. I had the distinct impression that you were tired of loose ends trailing along behind you. Tough to start over when the past keeps sniffing at your heels like a stray dog."

"We both know he was a bit more than a stray dog."

"True. But he wasn't the only one I was thinking of."

Max paused. Did Smith know his full history, or was he just guessing?

Smith continued. "Let me say again, I have no interest in continuing our friend's passion for revenge. It's not good business. Plus, you saved my life in a way, and did me an extraordinary favor on top of it."

"What about Duffy?"

"The wunderkind reporter? What about him? His story cleared some of the mud off your name, and it looks like it might end a few political careers, but my employers will be fine. I harbor no ill will toward Duffy, either."

"You're a forgiving man."

"Please don't mistake my pragmatism for forgiveness."

"You set him up. You tried to set us up."

"I only had Mr. Alvarez supply some signposts. I nudged things in certain directions. What happened, happened. It's over. It's done. Yes?"

"Yes."

"Are you interested in a job? I could use a man with your ... particular skill set."

"I'm not looking for a new boss."

There was a pause. "Maybe another time then."

There was nothing to say after that. Max hung up and walked back to the car. Kyle looked at him as he dropped back into the driver's seat. Max was getting better at reading what passed for conversation with Kyle.

"He said he's not looking for us."

Kyle looked over at him.

"I believe him. He's a son of a bitch, but mostly bloodless. He prefers profits to war." He turned the engine over but didn't put it in gear. "He did offer us a job."

Kyle raised an eyebrow at that.

"I turned him down."

"What now?"

Max looked out the windshield at the cars racing by on the freeway. He let his mind drift to Danny.

"You ever been to Boston?"

Kyle shook his head.

"I was thinking of heading back home. Couple people I need to see. I could use someone watching my back."

Kyle shrugged. Max took that as a yes, dropped the gearshift into drive, and pointed the car east. Smith was right. He was tired of his past chasing him down. It was time to settle up.

Get more free books, crime fiction news and other exclusive material.

I'm a crime fiction fan. I love reading it. I love writing it. And I love connecting with other fans about it. Talking with readers is one of the best things about writing.

Once a month I email newsletters with crime fiction news, what I've been reading, special offers, and other bits of news on me and my writing. There might also be the occasional story or picture about my dog, Dashiell Hammett.

If you sign up for the mailing list I'll send you some free stuff:

1. A copy of the Max Strong prequel novella SLEEPING DOGS.
2. A copy of the short story collection OCTOBER DAYS, which includes the award-nominated short HOW TO BUY A SHOVEL.

You can get both books, **for free**, by signing up at mikedonohuebooks.com/starterlibrary/

Did you enjoy this book? You can make a big difference.

Reviews are the *most* powerful tools that I have as an indie author to bring attention to my books. Honest reviews of my books help bring them to the attention of other readers.

If you've enjoyed this book, I would be very grateful if you could spend a few minutes leaving a review on the book's Amazon page. It can be as short as you like.

Each review really makes a difference.

Thank you very much.

ABOUT THE AUTHOR

Mike Donohue lives with his wife and family outside Boston. He doesn't think reading during meals is particularly rude. Quite the opposite.

You can find him online at mikedonohuebooks.com.

Printed in Great Britain
by Amazon